A FEAST
FOR
STARVING
STONE

A FEAST FOR STARVING STONE

BETH CATO

47NORTH

Text copyright © 2024 by Beth Cato
All rights reserved.

Published by 47North, Seattle

www.apub.com

Amazon, the Amazon logo, and 47North are trademarks of Amazon.com, Inc., or its affiliates.

ISBN-13: 9781662510311 (paperback)
ISBN-13: 9781662510304 (digital)

Cover design by Philip Pascuzzo

Cover images: © Dolucan, © Nik Lebowski, © anuwat meereewee, © seamartini, © rdegrie / Getty; © Imagine CG Images / Shutterstock

Printed in the United States of America

For Nicholas. Always be your authentic, awesome, autistic self. The world is yours.

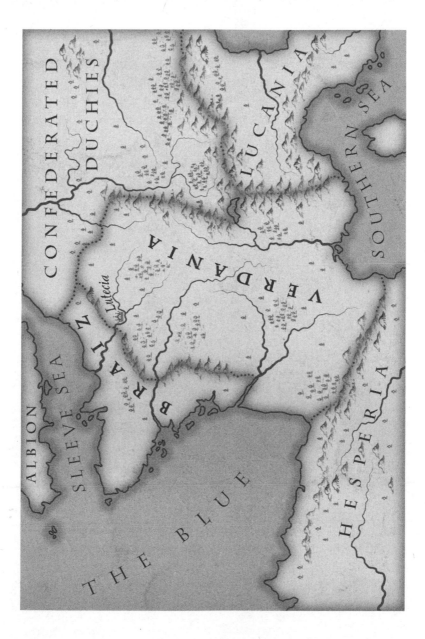

MAGIC AND THE FIVE GODS

The Five Gods have graced people with dominion over land and sea, and designated that which we may eat and be empowered by. Magical powers are imbued through food alone. To scorn what the Five have granted us is to be a guest insulting the host.

Rare family lines are blessed through their tongues with the ability to sense and understand food in ways that no others can. In Verdania, these people are called Chefs, trained from their youngest years to master cuisine through their heightened perception. Chefs take ingredients derived of divinely blessed flora and fauna and call upon the Gods to awaken the magical potential in the foods they prepare. In this, they serve the Gods and Gods-ordained rulers.

Among Chefs, a select few have empathetic talents; they can perceive food as others would taste it and customize dishes to their preferences, whether they work with ingredients common or magical. They can maximize flavor and magic to a degree beyond that of other Chefs and talented cooks.

Gyst, God of the Unseen and Unknown ✕

Overseer of fermentation, yeast, molds, even infections—things that often begin as or remain invisible or strangely small yet are powerful. Gyst feeds on secrets. Caves, cellars, and bakers' kitchens are his favored domains, as are any places shadowed and private, where privy details may be whispered for Gyst's ever-listening ears.

Hester, God of Hearth and Home 🔥

Hester is the warmth and coziness of home—but also an entity of crackling rage. After all, the same hearth fire that cooks meat to make it edible and delicious can also raze the building to the ground. Hester is fabled to have traversed Verdania with such regularity that her heavy tread created its ponds and lakes. Though Hester is worshipped the world over, Verdanians regard her as their home-born God and plead for her favor by throwing their choicest foods to the flames.

Lait, God of Milk and New Life 🐄

Loving and beloved matron of new mothers and infants, human and otherwise. Spring is her season, care and compassion her emphases. Around the world, Lait's Houses care for orphaned and abandoned children, and Lait blesses those who donate food, especially milk and cheese, to help those in need at her Houses and to the temple-kitchens known as pentads.

Melissa, God of All That Is Sweet 🐝

Sugar beets, honey, ripe fruits, and even a loved one's kisses are under Melissa's regard. Nobles enjoy confectionary delights that melt upon the tongue or marvel at sculpted sugar extraordinaires, but even the humblest of denizens can enjoy the harvest of the hive or hearken to the peals of so-named Melissa's bells, which celebrate special occasions in any town of considerable size.

Selland, God of Salt 🔨

A God fluid in nature, equally of the salty ocean and the briny wetland and the high-mountain cave crusted with crystalline deposits. Blustery coastal storms embody his might, as does the single pinch of salt that awakens the incredible flavors within a dish. The God of Salt asks for no offerings. No, Selland takes what Selland wants and is fickle with his favor, even to the seafaring people who hold him closest to their hearts.

We follow two women. One is more than four decades in age, silver joined with the black of her hair. She hides her innate skills as she labors as a common cook. The other is sixteen years old, a princess who adores horses and her coastal kingdom.

The elder is Adamantine Garland, a Chef from Verdania with a tongue touched by the Five Gods. She can empathetically taste any food she is near and is adept at using magical ingredients called epicurea. As a Chef, she is royal property of Verdania—or was, until she deserted sixteen years ago. Back then, a spat between the countries of Verdania and Braiz resulted in the dissolution of marriages between all citizens of both places, forcing a split between Ada and Braizian musketeer Erwan Corre. She refused to serve the country that severed her beloved family. Ada's prolonged success in hiding comes to an end when mysterious assassins show up at her door, forcing her on the run with her ailing paternal grandmother.

Meanwhile, unbeknownst to Ada, the newborn daughter she sent away with Erwan has been raised not as his but as a princess of Braiz. Solenn is ignorant of her actual parentage as she ventures to Verdania to wed the heir, one Prince Rupert. This union is intended to repair the long rift between the countries just as their northern neighbor, the isle of Albion, acts with renewed aggression.

At a presentation event prior to her nuptials, Solenn's inherited Chef abilities awaken, warning her of a poisoning attempt on her fiancé's life. She spills the tainted wine, saving him. Afterward, she speaks in privacy with her beloved guardian, Captain Erwan Corre, and discovers that he is in truth her biological father. Together, Solenn and Erwan work to uncover the poisoner within the palace, but their efforts result in failure. Not only does Prince Rupert die in agony, but he does so by a rare Braizian epicurea, his demise orchestrated so that Solenn will take the blame. She escapes royal imprisonment with the aid of a new friend, Aveyron Silvacane, who reveals he can shape-change into a horse—and that he, and others like him, are actually epicurea. One of the Five Gods, Hester of Hearth and Home, has cursed Aveyron and his fellow "kin" from the magical realm of Arcady to become prey for humans.

After getting her grandmother away to safety, Ada attempts to track down her assailants, but her efforts lead her to her own estranged mother's black-market epicurea business. There she finds the assassins were sent after her on behalf of an old enemy, Mallory Valmont, recently released from what should have been a fatal prison sentence. Almost two decades before, Ada had spearheaded the effort to hold him accountable as both a murderer and cannibal. Valmont was widely regarded as a hero for his battlefield prowess, but the source of his might was a sordid epicurea, rupic. He had his enemies cursed into becoming magicked stone, which he then ground down to ingest and empower himself.

Ada finds that Valmont's frail body is now sustained by a strange and powerful epicurea akin to rupic: powdered stone that carries the magical signature of Hester herself. Ada covertly steals the divine powder. Upon finding his medicine missing, a bereft Valmont goes on a murderous rampage within the house before hurrying away to acquire more.

Before Ada can follow, she encounters people who radiate strangely to her Chef senses. They are led by Comte Brillat Silvacane, Aveyron's father. She's baffled and horrified to recognize that these humanlike beings are actually epicurea; he is likewise appalled to be in the presence of a Chef, a person who has, in ignorance, butchered his magical relations. Even so, they come to an uneasy alliance to pursue Valmont and stop his sacrilege.

As they travel into the wilderness, they encounter Erwan and his musketeer band, who have continued to track Prince Rupert's true murderer. The various plots are snarled together: the prince was slain by an agent of Albion, with Solenn implicated to destroy the alliance between Verdania and Braiz, while Valmont has been supplying Albion with vast amounts of epicurea that will undoubtedly aid their forces in the forthcoming war.

Accompanied by Aveyron, Solenn travels to Arcady, the realm of magical beings. There, she draws upon her diplomacy skills to ally with the ruler, an ancient dragon named Queen Abonde. All magic is more powerful in Arcady, and that includes the essence of the Gods. Solenn is manipulated by the God of Unknowns, Gyst, who roots himself within her body. She discovers that Gyst is her maternal ancestor and the reason for the especially strong Chef skills she shares with Adamantine. Gyst begins to control Solenn at his whim, and she desperately seeks the means to regain her autonomy.

Through Queen Abonde, Solenn learns of Adamantine's quest. She and Aveyron go to aid their parents, and it is good that they do, as Mallory Valmont and Hester have formed a powerful alliance. Since breaking the world to alter its magic, Hester has been frozen in isolation, with only fleeting connections with the outside world. The God is despondent, suicidal. She will not stop Valmont from eating of her stone body and assuming her place as God. Gyst, however, does not agree with this plan, and controls Solenn to engage the fire-wielding Valmont/Hester in battle. Solenn struggles to free herself, realizing in the course of her internal fight that she is imbued with her own divinity. She could kill Gyst and assume his godhood—but would end her human body in the process.

Solenn surprises Gyst by seizing full control of herself, tapping her divinity to kill Valmont with the aid of Ada and her companions. She then does the one thing she can to stop Gyst from reasserting dominion over her body—she severs her own tongue, thus removing the direct conduit to the Gods. Gyst is successfully evicted, and with Valmont dead, Hester is again locked within her immobile statue.

Ada, Erwan, and Solenn take in a brief reunion before they must go their separate ways.

Wounded Solenn, along with Aveyron, flees to Braiz and the limited sanctuary it can offer as the continent verges on war; Erwan, with Comte Silvacane, returns to the capital of Verdania to continue the political fight on Solenn's behalf; meanwhile, Ada travels to retrieve her grandmother, vowing to reunite with Solenn and Erwan in Braiz. She prays that her family will at long last be together, but with two of the Five Gods now resentful of her and Solenn, Ada's appeals for divine aid may bring contrary results . . .

CHAPTER ONE

SOLENN

People place much emphasis on how Chefs are profoundly blessed by the Five Gods, but truly, anyone who can taste food, who can be strengthened by the harvest offered by our wonderful world, who can enjoy the company of loved ones during a shared repast, is likewise blessed.

—August Chef Gurvan of the city of Nont in Braiz

Princess Solenn of Braiz was but sixteen years of age, but as a student of diplomacy, she understood the delicacy of corresponding with foreign leaders. Her responsibilities carried even more gravitas as she was the only human ambassador to ever exist between the world of people and the parallel magical realm of Arcady, whose residents were understandably hateful toward the humans who slaughtered and consumed them. Another complication: the target of her missive was a queen thousands of years old, who also happened to be one of the few dragons still in existence.

A groan of frustration escaped Solenn's throat. She again set her pen in its rest and reached for a glass of water. She took small sips and angled her head to guide the liquid back to her throat. August Chef Gurvan had told her to be patient with her progress, but it was hard. Everything felt harder these days, though to anyone looking at her, she appeared the same as when she had traveled to Verdania a month ago, albeit much thinner. No one could readily see the scars and burn welts hidden by her clothes or the emptiness in her mouth where her tongue once lay.

She returned to her pen. This letter had to be finished and sent tonight. She composed it as an inquiry about the welfare of the queen's agent Comte Brillat Silvacane, but her foremost concern was for his traveling partner, Captain Erwan Corre. Three weeks had passed since she and Erwan had parted ways, a moment heightened by fresh pain and tears. Brillat had accompanied Erwan and a contingent of Braizian musketeers as they returned to the Verdanian capital of Lutecia to settle myriad legal and diplomatic affairs.

No word had come from them or of them since.

The lack of official news from Verdania was not a complete surprise, as both countries had expelled ambassadors and issued terms that could only be described as vitriolic, but not even traveling merchants had come with specific reports. What they had said of the general state of affairs, however, didn't bode well. Tension had risen to a fierce simmer in Verdania. There'd been riots. Conscription calls. Word of rebellion—people wanting to fully eschew the rule of King Caristo, now that his heir was dead. Facts were few, rumors virulent.

Before things further escalated within Braiz's southern neighbor, Solenn needed Erwan home. She needed her father.

A soft knock shuddered through the door. Solenn stoppered her ink and rose to answer. This had to be important. She'd given express orders not to disturb her.

"Princess." Her musketeer attendant Jean bowed in greeting. His silver-embroidered blue cassock draped to knee level. A rapier was affixed to his side by a baldric, two pistols at his belt. Security wasn't lax around her, not even in the comfort of her childhood home. "Word comes from the Corre château. A new Chef has arrived. You are invited to sup there tonight. Your mother is already visiting the estate this evening." Her father was away in the Braizian capital of Nont, attending to preparations for the imminent war with both Verdania and Albion.

This message was coded in a way that denied the full context to even her most trusted musketeers. The new Chef could only be Adamantine Garland. The woman who had birthed her. Her arrival meant one less worry, one less future missive. Solenn gestured with pinched fingers to the nearby rolling sea. Selland be thanked.

Then she considered the rest of his words, and her ire rose. "My mother is already there?" When they'd spoken at breakfast, Mamm's plans hadn't included the Corre château.

Jean hesitated, likely requiring a moment to decipher her speech. Without a tongue, Solenn had difficulty pronouncing many letters and syllables, and had to focus her efforts on the sounds arising from her throat. Most people in her home château didn't know she could speak at all. Self-conscious and often frustrated, she practiced her speech with a select few.

"She departed a few hours ago," Jean said, an apology in his tone.

Solenn couldn't be angry at him. She had asked not to be disturbed—but she also knew Mamm had likely taken advantage of this to slip away and meet with Adamantine first.

She loved her parents. They loved her. She still couldn't help feeling angry, however, that Prince Morvan and Princess Katell had lied about the circumstances of her birth for the entirety of her life. There was no shame that Solenn was adopted—not even Braizian court, with its snobberies and rivalries, regarded such a thing negatively. But her parents had known that Solenn had the potential to become a Chef with a tongue blessed by the Five Gods. They hadn't prepared her for that possibility, nor had they permitted Erwan to do so.

Her ignorance had carried dangerous consequences, not only for her body but for the world.

Using the pencil tethered to her slim leather-bound table book, she wrote on the first page. *Thank you. We'll leave immediately.* As much as she wanted a prolonged visit with both Adamantine and the Corres, she had to come back here tonight to finish her letter and prepare for tomorrow. She'd already resolved to travel to Nont and meet with her grandparents for the first time since her return to Braiz. Her duties as ambassador could wait no more.

"Will you take Maiwenn or Aveyron, dimezell?" Jean asked. "Dimezell" was equivalent to "mademoiselle" in Verdanian, but overall, Braizian was far less formal with dialogue. Honorifics weren't constant here.

"Aveyron." She still worked in time to ride her beloved Maiwenn most days, but this trip needed to include her friend, who also acted as an intermediary with the kin.

Jean bowed. "He'll be readied, dimezell. I'll inform the lieutenant." Lieutenant Talia was acting as her lead guardian in Erwan's absence. Solenn had known Talia since childhood, and Jean for some five years. She trusted both with her life.

Solenn locked up her letter to dry, though she had little worry about its theft. Nothing about it would make sense to people beyond Adamantine and Erwan. Humanity had no comprehension that the ingredients from which they derived magic originated from intelligent beings with their own parallel civilization. The very name of the realm of Arcady was known only to her.

Solenn quickly changed into a riding habit in the bright blue of a precious sunny Braizian day. It was undeniably in the mode of the Verdanian capital of Lutecia—they set the fashion trends for the continent—but atop her head she still wore a low coiffe, the lace headdress worn by Braizian women. To that she added a few more pins in anticipation of wind. A hooded wool cloak came next, as rain visited Braiz more often than the sun.

In the courtyard she met both Jean and Talia. Alongside their fully tacked horses stood Aveyron. The juvenile Camarga stallion had a white-gray coat that tapered to dark gray at the hooves, muzzle, and ears. He wore a saddle with a breastplate but no bridle. His keen eyes studied her as she approached.

"Adamantine arrived," Solenn whispered to him. "Let's be sure to stop and talk on the way back. I'll tell you everything." An ear flicked in acknowledgment.

"I have the satchel, in case it's needed," Jean murmured. It held clothes to fit a lanky young man.

With permission relayed by Queen Abonde, Talia and Jean had been brought into confidence regarding Aveyron's nature—and only that—so that they could better support and protect him and, by extension, Solenn.

They rode out at a brisk pace. Laden clouds swayed low, gusts carrying the harsh tang of salt even with the water still out of sight just to the north.

The north, where Albion lay a mere day's sailing away. Albion, a more imminent danger than Verdania, the very reason Verdania had been provoked to war. Braizian spies had relayed word that warships were congregating at Albion's southern ports. Corvettes and single-deck frigates with Albionish colors had been spotted scouting the Braizian coast. Meanwhile, many trade vessels hadn't arrived at Nont and other ports. Everything indicated that Albion was abandoning their recent subterfuge to engage in outright aggression.

Solenn had borne the responsibility of preventing war. She may as well have been tasked with using her pinkie to quell an avalanche.

Jean led the way up the slope's worn path, and then suddenly, the wide panorama of the Sleeve Sea sprawled before them. Dark skies loomed over an ocean turbulent and near-black as the day's light faded. Experience among these waves made Braizian sailors the best in all the continent—that, and their inherent reverence and reliance upon Selland, the God of Salt.

"I don't see any krakens or ships today," Talia said, the wind softening her words. A spyglass was usually required to observe the flail of tentacles far out in the water. The lack of ships wasn't strange, either, not with much of Braiz's fleet obliterated, and yet . . . and yet . . . Solenn frowned. She had a profound sense that there *should* be ships today.

How? Why? She squinted toward the north. Virga hazed the liminal zone between the clouds and the sea. Albion couldn't be seen from this vantage point, but she knew it was there, like a sheathed knife tucked beneath clothes, honed and ready to cleave flesh.

The wind whirled around her, and with it came Selland's powerful presence. It sent a cold chill traveling up her fingers to rest warm and secure within her chest. Often, the God's attention came as a comfort, but now she felt increasing unease.

Jean glanced back. The wind bobbed the long white feather in his three-cornered, cocked hat. "Princess?" he asked. As far as she knew, he had no innate sense of Selland, nor did Talia. Few people did, but Erwan was among them. Aveyron, being both inhuman and magical, made clear his awareness of the divine with his antsy footwork and pivoting ears. He acted like he sensed a predator, and he did. Selland may have been said to be father of the ocean and Braiz itself, but he was also chaotic and violent. The wave that tickled at toes could also drown.

Solenn motioned the need to stop. She dismounted and walked closer to the cliff's edge. She had detected nothing magical since she had severed her tongue to break the control of Gyst, the God of Unknowns—and what she sensed now felt *bigger*. She was eerily reminded of when she had teetered on the verge of godhood, aware of Gyst's myriad unknowns in dank cellars and grape skins and garderobes. *Something* was near, like a voice with words she couldn't comprehend.

"Do you see something?" called Talia, caution in her voice. Solenn's musketeers would be worried about her proximity to the edge, especially in this wind, but she experienced no fear of falling or exposure to lightning. The approaching storm held no electricity. She perceived that, as sure as an empathetic Chef knew flavor.

Solenn gazed down the rocky slope to the thin beach. Where the waves met the shore, the water was gray and white with darker blotches of blue. Bobbing bits of blue. There were five, ten—too many to count. They cluttered the rocks, with more floating in on the coming waves.

Her heart turned cold and heavy in her chest. "Talia! Jean!" she yelled, the words tearing at her throat.

Her musketeers rode up behind her. With an inarticulate noise, she pointed to the water.

"Princess—" began Jean, rising in his stirrups to gaze downward. "By all the salt in the sea. No."

"Oh, Selland," breathed Talia.

"Jean, come to the beach with me," Solenn said, struggling to be heard over the wind. "Talia—"

"I'll ride for the Corres' to raise the alarm." Their château was closest, and Talia and her horse had won more races than Solenn could recall.

Solenn looked to Aveyron as Jean dismounted his chestnut, leaving the two horses together. Aveyron gave her an encouraging nod, unspoken intensity in his gaze.

Talia set off at a gallop while Solenn and Jean picked their way down to the beach. They carefully worked around boulders larger than they were, pebbles and hard mud underfoot. Wind-born mist made the ground slicker as they neared the sand, which was only thirty feet in width at the current tide. More rocks formed a jagged, sporadic wall within the water. The wind rose again, colder, penetrating layers of cloth. Solenn slogged through the sand until water toyed at her boots, beckoning her to follow its pull to the depth of Selland's embrace. Jean trudged another five feet to where the nearest body bobbed, caught between two hulking rocks. The wind whipped his cassock back, the snap of cloth audible even against the ocean. He grabbed the corpse, heaving it toward the beach. A wave provided a gentle shove to help as water eddied around the ankles of his jackboots.

Both Verdania and Braiz used blue as their primary color, though in different shades. Water-drenched cloth of both countries looked similarly near-black at a distance. A person had to stand close to tell the uniforms apart, to take in the distinct lace at the cuffs and at the neckline.

This sailor was of Braiz, but then, she'd known that even from above. She'd known it in her soul.

Dozens already cluttered the beach. More were floating in. Unwilling to speak or even try, Solenn pinched her fingers in gratitude to Selland. He was bringing Braiz's sailors home.

War was no longer imminent to Braizian shores. It had arrived.

CHAPTER TWO

SOLENN

As the faces of the Gods are unknown and inexplicable, we know the Five by their symbols. In the case of Selland, that means a salt rake, a tool often used for harvesting granules. Such devices consist of long handles with crossbars at the base that can be flat or teethed.

—Excerpt from *Manual for Tour Chefs*

Solenn and Jean couldn't drag all the bodies onto the sand. There were too many, more floating in by the minute. The accounting of the dead wasn't a task for them alone.

They climbed up the cliff again. No one yet approached from the Corre château. They galloped back toward her home on the outskirts of Malo. Even if Solenn had been readily able to speak, she had no desire to do so. This was a time when the gravity of grief caused words to sink downward into stillness, like an anchor into a bay.

Darkness had fallen, and people were completing the last of the day's chores or gathering on stoops throughout the village. "Sailors were brought home!" Jean cried as they galloped past. Their quick approach to the château brought soldiers and musketeers running to meet them at the gate.

"Selland has returned sailors to us," yelled Jean, standing in his stirrups within the bailey. Cries rang out all around. "Princess Solenn found them. Lieutenant Talia has already ridden for the Corre demesne. Ready wagons—we need the strongest among—"

"Do any live?" shouted a woman. Solenn knew her to have three children in the navy.

"How many bodies?" yelled another man.

Jean shook his head. "We saw none alive yet, and the numbers—a ship's been lost, for certain."

More cries, more wails. People scrambled to gather supplies and more help.

As Solenn swung from the saddle, bells began to ring from the pentad steeple: Melissa's deepest, more mournful bells. She'd last heard them in Lutecia, when they had announced the death of her fiancé, Prince Rupert. Though the tone was the same, the bells felt different here. Rupert's death had been horrible and personal, as her newly awakened empathetic tongue had cursed her to experience his agonizing decline even in advance of his own suffering. But the deaths of these sailors were multitudinous and, in a way, even more personal and horrible.

These sailors had likely died because of the war Solenn had failed to prevent.

Reverberations rang dully through her bones, to her soul.

Her marriage to Rupert was supposed to strengthen the bond between Verdania and Braiz, unifying the continental neighbors against ambitious Albion. But Albion had sabotaged everything with detailed care. Solenn's lady-in-waiting, Madame Brumal, had been a secret agent. She'd made at least one other attempt at killing Rupert before she'd succeeded, and did so with a Braizian epicurea to make certain Solenn would be blamed. Solenn eventually escaped imprisonment on the palace grounds with Aveyron's aid, which led her to the realm of Arcady, and Gyst—and Gyst—

No, this night was difficult enough. She wouldn't, couldn't, dwell on the God of Unknowns and what he'd done to her.

Solenn would be expected to stay in Malo, where she could be warm and dry, but she had to return to the beach. Sand from this coastline had traveled with her in a box to Lutecia. The grit between her fingers had been more precious than any jewel.

She was going back—and Mamm and Tad weren't here to order otherwise.

"I hope you don't mind getting wet in the coming storm," she said to Aveyron. He replied with an incredulous snort. She swung herself astride again and rode to wait near the gate. When Jean approached on horseback, he opened his mouth as if to say something, then gave her a tiny nod. She took that not as permission but as understanding.

Rain began to fall in a sudden, wavering sheet as they rode through the village, twenty riders behind them. More riders and people on foot emerged to join the party. A thin figure on a dapple gray steed trotted up beside Solenn. The wind caused the figure's deep hood to flare back, revealing a clean-shaven, careworn face she knew well. August Chef Gurvan.

"Princess." Gurvan had the kind of deep, resonant voice that indicated he could not only speak well but sing. "I came to Malo to do rites for an old sailor. Now this news—and I heard that you were the one who found these sailors. Is that true?"

She nodded.

"Well, well. One never knows what the waves will bring." The old idiom sounded flippant when spoken by others, but Gurvan said it with thoughtfulness and care.

Despite being lashed by a head-on wind, they rode fast. Solenn was glad to have Gurvan's quiet presence at her side. He understood the limits of her speech. He understood her. He was the August Chef who'd named her before Selland at her first half-year, on a beach close to Malo. He'd immersed her in the sea and then held her aloft to meet the kiss of the wind. Most babies cried after their dunking, as she knew from witnessing many ceremonies herself, but she'd been told that she laughed with sheer delight.

The rites for the dead of Braiz involved water too. Though every person the world over understood that at death they'd be escorted by Gyst to know the resolutions of their mysteries, people of different places called upon different Gods to bring final peace for the vacant corpse and surviving family.

It was said that, in the cold of the far north, bodies were left out to ice over through the winter, and that only when the ground thawed were they buried with an appeal to Lait to inspire new growth in the turned earth. In nearby Verdania, bodies were buried within the five-day week of death, with all Five Gods appealed to; the incineration of a body was offensive there, as only the best of foods should be sent to Hester through her fire, not corpses.

In Braiz, the dead were returned to the sea. These sailors, however, weren't ready for that final step. Selland had brought them home so that their names could first be known among the living. With that done, they'd then join the God of Salt in the black fathoms below.

The group dismounted along the cliff. People from the Corre château had already arrived. Leaving Aveyron with the other horses, Solenn took her time working her way down the now-slippery slope. Jean stayed an arm's length away, Gurvan on her other side.

"August Chef. Princess." Talia had to yell to be heard over the surf and wind as she greeted them on the beach.

"Oh, mercy of the Five," Gurvan said. "There are so many."

Amid the frothing water, the bodies were like apples floating in a barrel. They couldn't have been more tightly packed.

Rain mingled with tears on Solenn's cheeks. These sailors needed to be accounted for, but these conditions now made the beach dangerous for the living.

Selland. Solenn called to him in her mind, as she had previously conversed with Gyst. *Please calm your waters and wind for a time. Let us mark these sailors' names, cast salt upon their lips, then weigh them down to know your depths.* She pinched her fingers toward the dark heavens.

The rain stopped. The wind lessened.

Solenn was jolted at the suddenness of the weather's shift; nor was she alone in that. The people around her exclaimed, their voices clearer even as the thrash of the waves remained loud. Solenn felt eyes upon her, and found Gurvan studying her with a peculiar expression upon his face. She hadn't told him anything of her recent interactions with the divine, but as he was the most skilled Chef in Braiz, perhaps he perceived something about her.

"Selland shows us mercy," Gurvan said, projecting his voice. "Let's work fast." No one needed a reminder that Selland was a fluid God. They may have five minutes, they may have five hours, but however long this respite lasted, it was a blessing.

The strongest of the group ventured into the waves and began to drag waterlogged bodies high onto the beach. Solenn tugged on Gurvan's sleeve, gesturing around. After a second, he took her meaning. "No, I had no Chef accompany me today. My usual assistant is ill."

Solenn pulled her table book from the beeswax-treated pouch at her waist and folded back the hard cover.

"You would—" Gurvan looked startled. "You're not a Chef, to be my official inscriber." She *was* a born Chef, but he didn't know that. "I can write, but . . ." The process would be slow.

Solenn gripped her pencil, her brow furrowed. She was ready. Talia stood close by, holding an oil lamp.

Gurvan glanced to the sea, then above. "You found the sailors. Yes. It is right that you are involved. Let's begin."

She had seen drowned people before, but the bloated, blued bodies would never cease to be disturbing. Murmurs around her agreed that the sailors hadn't been in the water for more than a half day. Each body was faced upward to be recognized—had they a face.

"Marie-Jeanne Jégou. From Cambear," he said, reading the thumbnail-size steel the sailor had been given upon enlistment. The alloy emblem had likely been formed in the bloomery furnaces of Nont, lost in the conflagration last year. "Blessed be Selland, for bringing you home."

The August Chef turned the tag to the other side, to the etched emblem of Selland, a long-handled salt rake with rows of teeth along the base crossbar. He stroked the image with his thumb, then pulled the necklace over the dead woman's head.

There were no obvious injuries to her body. That wasn't true of the next sailor. An arm and part of the man's torso were gone.

A cannonball had done this.

"Jakez Bosser, of Nont," said Gurvan.

Solenn knew the grotesque sight would stain her memory worse than blood in any cloth, but she looked upon him nevertheless. He was one of her people. She recorded his name, his home, the nature of his injuries. She memorized his face, the ocean-altered stench of his viscera. He couldn't have been much older than her. He didn't look as though he'd shaved yet.

"That's from grapeshot," Talia murmured as they moved to the next body. The man's legs were riddled with holes, the calves broken into zigzags that ended in stumps. Grapeshot consisted of smaller-caliber rounds packed into a canvas bag that dissolved when the carronade fired. The result, a spray of bullets that was devastating when used upon land or sea.

"I know this man," said Gurvan. "He served on the *Tanguy* out of Bressa." He blinked fast. "I conducted his wedding."

Solenn included that information. The ship's name would need to be relayed to Nont by fast horses. The war council must know which vessel had been lost.

Gurvan swayed, his face sagging with grief. The chains stacked around the fleshy curve of his hand chimed together. "The loss of the fleet at Nont. It plays so well into our enemies' hands now," he murmured, shuffling to the next body.

Solenn felt as if the world had gone especially still. He was right. The timing of the tragedy was terribly convenient to Albion's aims. They needed Braiz neutralized so that it could be trampled over on the way to vast, valuable Verdania. The fire last year had obliterated much of Braiz's capital, along with its naval superiority. Three sailors of the Braizian warship *Everett* had been identified as the arsonists. They had been tried, convicted, and were now imprisoned.

What if the disaster had in fact been caused by agents of Albion?

She'd heard her parents, Erwan, and her grandparents mutter more than once about Lord Whitney of Albion. His clever battlefield ploys had almost crushed the united forces of Verdania and Braiz sixteen years ago. He enjoyed intricate strategies. He seemed capable of such foresight.

Braiz had to start thinking ahead in such a way if they were to survive, but for now, all Solenn could see was a row of dark bodies by lamplight. The roar of nearby waves obscured the sound of her pencil as it moved across page after page, countless sorrows chronicled in few words.

CHAPTER THREE

ADA

When preparing salt cod, it is vital to pay attention when the fish is at last placed in water to cook. When the liquid begins to tremble with heat, the fish must be drawn to the side of the pot so that it can poach without boiling. In this way, the fish cooks without becoming mush and none of its nutritive elements are lost.

—Excerpt from *Manual for Tour Chefs*

The process of *waiting* could contain diverse amounts of agony. There was the impatience that came of hunger paired with the scent of food that was nearly done, the anxious energy of anticipating private time with a husband after weeks of separation during military deployments, or prolonged minutes spent with an ear tilted to hear the bells that signaled the end of an especially frustrating day of work.

Ada's impatience to see Solenn again, however, was teaching her a new kind of torment.

"You believe the salt cod will be palatable for Princess Solenn?" asked Vicomtesse Gwenael Corre, leaning forward on her thighs. She wore what could only be described as traditional Braizian garb, a brightly dyed red surcoat over a lace-edged shift. Worry curved her brows. Her pale-blue eyes had been inherited by Erwan—and by Solenn in turn—but neither Gwenael nor her husband was aware of their blood connection to the princess they clearly adored. The vicomte was currently away to oversee fortifications at a holding farther west.

"From what I can imagine, yes, but I've had no direct experience with people who've endured the loss of their tongues." Ada's Braizian sounded cumbrous after almost two decades of disuse. "I'll need to speak with Princess Solenn as soon as possible to find out her personal preferences."

At that bland statement, Ada again cast her eyes on the closed door to her right, willing it to open and admit her daughter to the parlor. To her compassionate former mother-in-law, she was certain she came across as merely anxious to help a young woman who had suffered a recent grievous injury and had difficulty eating ever since. No one here knew—they could never know—that Erwan had brought Solenn to Braiz sixteen years ago, when she was days old, with the intention that she be raised in this very household. That's what Ada had planned when she said her farewells. Instead, Erwan had found the prince and princess mourning the loss of their own newborn. Solenn had then been quietly adopted, becoming a princess.

"I'm just glad you haven't been subject to such a punishment yourself after all of your years living as a rogue," Gwenael said, tears in her eyes.

In Verdania, there was no greater punishment than for a Chef to lose their tongue. If she were fool enough to return there and be captured after sixteen years as a deserter and so-called rogue Chef . . . Well. Things would not be pleasant for her. Good thing she had no plan to be a ninnyhammer.

"I'm grateful that my grandmother and I have avoided such a punishment as well." Ada reflexively motioned gratitude to the Five Gods with a flared hand.

Gwenael nodded. "Yes. You're both here and free. All we need now is for Selland to bring Erwan and his troops homeward." The words were optimistic, but Ada recognized anxiety in her warbling tone.

From the time Ada had entered the château hours before, she had repeatedly heard mention of Erwan's delayed return. No one had dared voice their fear that he was dead, Ada included. Saying the words gave them shape. Possibility.

Ada had been separated from her husband for sixteen years, ever since their marriage—like all marriages between Verdanians and Braizians—had been nullified by King Caristo. She had never stopped loving Erwan, nor he her. Now that she knew they might possibly have a future together, she intended to cling to that hope like cat hair to satin.

"Katell did tell you that your employment here doesn't bind you to daily labor, didn't she?" asked Gwenael.

Ada bobbed her head in a show of respect as Solenn's mother was named. "She did, yes." Though that had proved to be a small part of their private conversation. Much of it had focused on Solenn. Katell had apologized for the dangers that Solenn's royal upbringing had brought upon her, but also expressed fierce love and pride for her daughter. Really, Ada couldn't have hoped for a better adoptive mother for her child.

Gwenael pressed on. "All we ask is that you communicate with our cooks whenever you wish to labor in the kitchen. Beyond that, your time is your own. We say that to all the rogue Chefs who come through here."

Until Ada had arrived, she hadn't been aware that her former in-laws were part of her same effort to help Verdanian Chefs desert their country and the continent entire, lest they be extradited to Verdania again. She still couldn't disclose her role as one of the first links in that chain, as doing so might endanger her friend Petry and other contacts still in the south.

"You are something of a special case, however," Gwenael added, her lined face creasing more deeply as she smiled.

Ada had met Erwan's parents only twice before, about two decades ago, but her initial impressions remained true. She loved them both. Now, knowing how they cared for Solenn, that was even more true.

The door opened. Ada turned, sucking in a breath. Had Solenn arrived? A Braizian musketeer entered and bowed, plumed hat to his chest. As he rose, she caught his grieved expression. Had something happened to Solenn? An accident, an attack—

"Vicomtesse. Selland has brought sailors home," said the musketeer.

Gwenael rose. "Where were they found? How many?"

Ada stood as well, her heart pounding. A ship had been lost. The cause could be weather or error, but her thoughts went foremost to Albion. Had the intermittent war between the continent and isle fully flared anew?

"Lieutenant Talia reports that the beach where they were discovered is slightly closer to us than to Malo. As to the numbers, light is fading, but she estimates a full warship was lost."

"Sailors will wash ashore everywhere along our coast," Gwenael murmured. "We must deploy scouts. Has someone informed Katell?" Solenn's mother had said she was going to work on correspondence prior to dinner.

"Yes, even as I was sent to you."

"If Talia is here—where is Princess Solenn?" asked Gwenael, moving toward the door.

Ada listened with extra care.

"She was the person who found the sailors. Talia left her with Jean at the beach."

Of all the people, *Solenn* had found the dead sailors? Considering their recent encounters with the divine, Ada couldn't dismiss this discovery as coincidence.

"I'll coordinate our people here," said Gwenael. "I trust that many are already assembling to depart?"

"Of course, and more will come as word spreads," he said.

"Prepare a mount for me as well," said Ada.

"Ada!" Gwenael's loving familiarity came through in her shocked tone. "You've already ridden much of the day. You—"

"Your kitchen will know what to do in this particular situation. I do not, but at the beach, I might lend my strength to the recovery." And if Solenn was there, Ada would bask in her nearness. "There is my grandmother, however—"

"You left her with Mari, did you not?" asked Gwenael.

"Yes, but Grand-mère will be up and about soon, and I don't want to burden a girl we just—"

"Mari will take care of her," Gwenael said with finality. Ada didn't want to argue over the matter and distract her hostess from more important concerns, so she let the matter go. Mari had looked to be around eleven years of age, but there'd been a quiet competency about the child that inspired immense trust in her from the start.

Ada followed Gwenael as she strode away, taking crisp command of both people and supplies. She noted that Erwan's mother moved slower these days, a pronounced limp in her gait, but then, she had to be near seventy. Ancient for a woman who had been a musketeer in her youth, alternatively parleying and fighting with their country's neighbors to the north and south alongside her husband.

How many generations had lived and died through these near-constant wars between Verdania and the isle of Albion over the centuries? How many more would suffer yet in these next weeks and months? Must this cycle continue to spin around like a wheel?

Ada assisted in loading blankets, potent apple brandy lambig, and other supplies onto a wagon, noting with longing as a first group departed. Minutes later her own turn came. She accompanied several wagons into a wavering rain. As the sound of crashing waves grew louder and the downpour suddenly ceased, Ada recognized harsh prickles upon her tongue. This storm hadn't paused; it was being checked by divine power. Selland's might felt strange here near his ocean node. There was a vibrancy to it, an underlying taste of grief like tears upon her tongue. The God *mourned*. Ada pinched her fingers in respect as she dismounted, joining others who stood near the cliff. Waves thrashed below, the water only visible in scattered glimmers of lamplight. She had to lean forward to see the narrow beach. Moving lights revealed dark lumps upon the pale sand. There were easily fifty bodies laid out, with more being dragged to the shore as she watched.

Leather creaked beside her. The musketeer who'd delivered the dire news had joined her to stare downward. He was too young to have participated in the combined Verdanian-Braizian Thirty-Fifth Division in the last war, but his features were familiar. She'd probably served with his kin.

"Is their ship known?" Ada asked, gesturing to the dead with a tilt of her head.

"The *Tanguy.*" He paused, taking in a rattling breath. "And the *Elby.*"

Ada jolted. "Two? Were they first-rank?"

"Yes, two. They were paired. But no, we have few first-rank ships left after last year. These were only two-deckers." Beneath his narrow mustache, his smile was brittle.

Only. A two-decker ship hosted six hundred sailors and marines. If all hands were lost, that meant well over a thousand dead. If three-deckers had been destroyed, that number would've been much higher.

"Is there evidence of battle?"

"Indisputable proof, I'm told," he said, tone dull. She wondered if he'd yet seen bodies riddled with grapeshot, and hoped not. She would spare everyone that sight if she could.

"You said Princess Solenn discovered the sailors. Is she still here?"

The way he stared at her made her worry that the query had been too bold. Erwan had warned Ada that she would need to keep a discreet distance from Solenn or people might notice not only their physical similarities but their mutual affection. "She's down there right now. She rode to Malo for aid, and then returned." He pointed to the beach. No one was recognizable from above, and yet, if Ada concentrated to delve through the divine fog, she perceived epicurea below.

She hadn't sensed the stuff in weeks, not since the turbulent days when she'd learned disturbing new truths about the magicked ingredients she'd been privileged to wield her entire life. Verdanian Guild teachings emphasized that epicurea, and the magical powers it bestowed upon people, had been provided to Chefs by the benevolent Gods. That was somewhat true. God Hester had been the one to make that designation, blessing humans but cursing an entire civilization of living, thinking creatures to be ruthlessly utilized for their parts and potential. Throughout her life, Ada had used epicurea as an ingredient—as a main dish, or to season meat, or to mix with flour, or as a vessel to age wine—and felt the Gods' attention as she called upon them to awaken the inherent potential of the food she prepared. She'd been assured that she was divinely blessed, an expert in her field, and she had believed that.

So much of what she understood had been a lie.

The variety of curatives that Ada now sensed were the sort carried by a pentad-based Chef. It would only be right for such a person to come here from Malo and conduct rites.

"You're the new Chef come from Verdania, I gather?" the musketeer continued.

"Yes." Good, he had created justification for her question about Solenn.

"You'll be cooking for her. I'm glad. She's starving, these days."

Katell had implied that Solenn had lost weight, but his frank observation made the situation sound more dire. Ada felt a fidgety need to speak with Solenn this very instant and figure out how best to aid in her daughter's recovery, but there were more pressing concerns of life and death.

"Do you know how I might help, here and now?" Ada asked.

The musketeer looked between the water and the increasing crowd along the cliff. "I told myself that I'd assist by bringing the injured back to the château, but now . . ." Despair occupied the space of words left unsaid. "They need no more helpers on the beach, as there's little room there. So I don't know what to do. I don't know."

Ada left him there, anchored by his grief and indecision. She started toward the wagons but noticed a hide of pale gray that stood out among the gathered horses. While most of the others had been picketed to the grass, the young Camarga lacked any restraint. His head was aloft, watching her approach. Magicked beings were apparently like empathetic Chefs in that they could perceive other magic in their vicinity.

"Aveyron," Ada said softly. He huffed in greeting. "Forgive my impatience, but how is Solenn?" At his snort, she realized her error and sighed. "Right. My apologies again. I should keep to yes and no questions when you're in this form. Then answer this: Is she truly starving these days?"

He blinked at her as if in surprise, then nodded.

"Is it . . . no, everything I want to ask is too complicated, and she'd be the one with the answers. I know Erwan hasn't returned. You've had no word from him or your father?"

Aveyron's head lowered, shaking.

"Are you worried?" Ada asked, even more softly.

His nod was immediate. Ada had spent little time with the dapper Comte Brillat Silvacane, but held him in the highest respect. Aveyron's concern increased her own.

"I wonder what more we can—"

She stopped, whirling around to stare at the laden sky. Something was up there. Something like epicurea.

Behind her, Aveyron stomped a foreleg. She glanced back to take in his flattened ears and bared teeth, his own gaze upward.

"It's not alive, is it?" she asked. "By the potency it must be something . . . processed . . . by a Chef." There was no kind way to phrase

how magicked beings could be skinned, butchered, or otherwise rendered piecemeal.

He nodded.

Whatever was above them seemed invisible against the low clouds
and darkness, or was invisible because magic endowed such power. She
didn't like that thought, as the only ingredient she'd encountered that
bestowed such an ability was the cat magic that she had discovered
herself and kept secret.

Most disturbing of all, Ada couldn't identify what she had
detected. For all her criticisms of Verdania's Chef Guild, their training was thorough. She could identify the breadth of the country's
mundane and magical ingredients—and many imports as well—by
simply being near them. The last time she'd been stumped by a new
discovery, the item had been the ground-down powder of the God
Hester. It had radiated Hester's innate heat, minerality, and might.
This . . . this *thing* above her, its presence fainter by the second as it
moved inland to Braiz, had no recognizable connection to the divine.
No brine of Selland, no sweetness of Melissa, no herbal tang or milk-
iness of Lait. Definitely nothing of Hester and Gyst. But whatever
it was radiated incredible power for her and Aveyron to recognize it
even as it faded away.

The thing was traveling south across the thin country of Braiz.
Verdania lay on the other side.

It seemed to come from the north. From Albion.

"Do you know what that was?" she whispered, leery as other people
approached the horses.

Aveyron's ears twitched, his mood uneasy, neither nodding nor
shaking his head.

"You have suspicions?" she asked.

His nod was subtle, but clear.

"We must talk later," she whispered, moving onward before they
could be overheard.

At the wagons, her hands found busywork as she helped to unfold and cut old sailcloth to shroud the dead for their final trip to Selland's embrace. Her mind stayed occupied as she continued to ruminate on what she'd sensed, her gaze often traveling toward the cliffs in hope of a long-awaited glance of Solenn or to the skies in dread of another mystery.

CHAPTER FOUR

SOLENN

To make potage de santé, first make a broth of capon, a castrated young rooster. To this add potent herbs to specific effect, such as chicory to soothe the stomach or bittersweet cardoon for overall vigor. Do not include other ingredients such as mushrooms or additional herbs. The power of this restorative soup is found in its simplicity.

—Excerpt from *Book for Cooks to Excel as Do Chefs*

No one present on the beach could deny the intercession of the God of Salt. The storm checked its fury for the exact amount of time required for Solenn to record the information of each dead sailor who'd washed ashore that night. As her pencil finished its last letter, the wind returned with a howl, threatening to rip the pages from their tacket binding. She had just tucked the book within the security of the pouch when the heavens released the great weight of their tears. Several people floundered to the sand beneath the heavy downpour. Solenn stayed upright only because of the strength of Talia's grip.

Jean's support kept August Chef Gurvan's spindly form moored tall as he faced the water to bow. "Our gratitude for your patience as we worked," he called. Solenn felt warm prickles of Selland's attention. He seemed so strangely *present* these days. Before she went to Verdania, she might have gone months without sensing him nearby. Though she knew he was a God of mighty fluctuations, she still took comfort in his oversight. Perhaps he might offer a counterbalance to Gyst, who also likely monitored her but with an intent of vengeful mischief. "These sailors' bodies are ready to know your depths."

Gurvan faced the people nearest to him. "We all must go up the cliff, with care. We'll station watchers among the boulders there. In this weather, there's no worry about birds or other scavengers getting to the dead. Selland will keep them or take them, as he wills."

"As he wills," everyone echoed. Solenn mouthed the words.

The trip up the slope was slow and challenging, every step treacherous. Even with the aid of her musketeers, Solenn made it to the top assured of future bruises, but at least she'd avoided banging her face or breaking anything. Others weren't so fortunate, including Jean. A cut wept pink down his cheek, the rain washing the blood away. Hoods and hats offered no protection against such force. Selland wept, she thought, but he also raged.

At least one God favored Braiz, but Selland alone couldn't save them. They needed more divine and magical allies. To think, she'd been worried about how she'd establish an alliance between Braiz and the Coterie of Arcady in the six-month time limit she'd been granted. She now needed to figure out how to do it in days.

As Solenn mounted Aveyron, she heard the muffled jingle of tack as another horse drew close. She jolted in surprise as she recognized Adamantine—or Ada, as she was usually called. Her birth mother. In the shock of her discovery on the beach, Solenn had totally forgotten the important reason she'd ridden for the Corre château. How long had Adamantine been here, and she hadn't even known?

"Princess Solenn." Adamantine bowed over the cantle. Rain coursed down her face. Solenn suspected the droplets were masking tears, as both tears and rain streamed down her own cheeks. Oh, by Selland, but she was relieved to see this woman again. She'd met her birth mother only once before, and that had been during a battle. That near-death struggle, and its excruciating aftermath, hadn't given them an opportunity to do more than sop up blood and strategize. Really, Solenn yearned to just stare at Adamantine for a while and recognize the ways in which they were alike.

"We briefly met recently," Ada continued. "I am a rogue Verdanian Chef by the name of Adamantine Garland. Some among your staff may know me or have heard of me from when I was married to Captain Erwan Corre. Our marriage was dissolved with diplomatic relations at the end of the last war."

Solenn greeted her with a nod and a wave of her arm. She knew Ada's introduction was a necessary act for Talia, Jean, and others close by. Some of them would know that Erwan and Ada had been briefly reunited around the time that Solenn lost her tongue, but how and when they had all come together had been left vague in her recounting.

They began the wet slog toward the Corre château.

"I'm aware of your current condition," Ada said to Solenn in what could only be described as heavily stilted Braizian, "and I've been tasked with arranging meals at the Corre château that might be to your liking, then perhaps cooking sometimes at your home in Malo. The cooks are already preparing salt cod for tonight. Is that acceptable?"

Solenn hesitated a moment. She was still considering what she'd recently learned about meat harvesting, both mundane and epicurean, but she also knew that for now, she needed to take in whatever food she could. Salt cod sounded more palatable than many dishes too. Flavor wasn't her biggest concern, though her sense of it had been greatly diminished. It was the actual eating *process*, something no one else seemed to accept no matter how many times she'd written about it. She had no tongue with which to maneuver food and spittle. Morsels became stuck in and between her teeth constantly. So many times, she'd felt a crumb on her lips and strained her stub of a tongue as if to swipe it away. She couldn't.

Even more, the way in which she now ingested foods gave the God of Unknowns another avenue by which to attack her. Gurvan had warned her that he'd known a Verdanian rogue Chef who'd received the ultimate punishment—the loss of his Gods-touched tongue—and sought refuge in Braiz. He'd died because food or fluid had gone the wrong way and into his lungs, causing pneumonia. Every time Solenn gagged on something, she remembered that peril.

She thought of it again as she gave Ada a tiny smile and a nod.

The old fortress loomed ahead. Ada frowned as she seemed to consider what to say. "I won't deny that I'm ignorant about what you're enduring right now, but I want to remedy that. With your permission—and that of Vicomtesse Corre and your mother—I'd like to be close enough that I can perceive your experience and find means to improve upon it."

Whether Ada's acute perception arose from her experience as a Chef or from maternal intuition, Solenn could only be grateful. She readily nodded, gesturing to Talia.

"We'll relay Princess Solenn's approval," said Talia. They rode within the bailey, which was unusually loud and crowded at this hour.

"My thanks." Ada gesticulated to both Talia and Jean, then again bowed to Solenn. "I look forward to conferring with you again later, Princess." With a final tiny nod to acknowledge Aveyron, she rode onward to where the commoners tended their horses beneath an overhang.

Solenn stared after her. Their public reunion had to be performed as if they were largely strangers, she knew, but she felt a pang of sadness all the same.

"So that's the infamous Chef-wife he was forced to part from," Jean whispered to Talia. There was no need for Solenn to inquire about the

Beth Cato

"he" in question. They spoke of Erwan. "I never saw her when we had Madame Brumal and the Albionish pinned down at Rozny."

"I did," Talia said simply. "The captain must've invited her here, which is good. What happened to them wasn't right."

Solenn had known Erwan's loving presence most every day of her life, but she was reminded that he'd had a life before her existence that she knew little about. She pinched her fingers to Selland, a quiet plea that her birth parents be reunited again soon.

The grooms had plenty of other horses to tend to; she took care of Aveyron, dissuading offers of help. "Adamantine's right. We all must talk later," she whispered to him, to which he agreed. She settled him into a stall, and as she exited the stable, she encountered August Chef Gurvan.

"I must continue onward to Nont now." Surprise must have shown in her eyes, as he softly smiled. "Yes, even with the weather as it is. I don't mind. Better for this storm to strike now than an hour ago. Word of what happened will be reaching Nont soon. The pentad will be busy as people come to grieve." At times like this, pentads did what they could to nourish people's bodies, with the hope that such care would also nourish the soul. The nearby small pentad in Malo would also be cooking large quantities of potage de santé by now and mixing bread dough to rise for tomorrow and the coming days.

Solenn pulled out her tablet, turning to a fresh page. *The list of the lost will be copied tonight.* Vicomtesse Corre would delegate the task within the household. Multiple copies would be deployed across the realm in the coming days. Pentads attended to the sorry work of notifying the bereaved.

"Thank you again for your contributions tonight. Selland holds you in clear regard, and I understand what an onerous task that can be," he said softly. Even as an empathetic Chef within Braiz, he had to be careful about how he addressed the negative aspects of the Gods' touch.

Solenn's attention went to Talia, who stood nearby, staring into space. The lieutenant had been deeply shaken after recognizing several

30

sailors from Malo among the dead. Solenn waved to Talia to draw her eye, then began to write.

Take a fresh horse and ride with Gurvan to Malo to notify the families of the bereaved. Jean is with me.

"But, Princess—"

Most of the other villagers who came to the beach will be working through the night. Everyone in Malo must be awake with worry right now. Breaking the news will be a terrible responsibility for you, but

She stopped writing midsentence as Talia began to speak. Her expression had shifted from grief stricken to resolute. "I can do it. Otherwise, August Chef Gurvan will be swarmed as he rides through town, and he must press onward to Nont."

"Indeed, I must," Gurvan said. "Thank you for taking on this sad duty, Lieutenant." He flared his fingers to bless her.

Minutes later, as Solenn passed through a corridor with Jean, Mamm swept upon her, as cold as the wind outside.

"You went back to the beach *after* returning to Malo? Why?" Mamm examined her up and down as if for injuries.

As Solenn wrote, her hand shook with anger. How could her mother question her as if she were a child? Under other circumstances, Solenn would be a married woman by now! *Cold and rain are normal.*

"Normal enough weather for here, yes, but you—" Mamm stopped herself, seeming to recognize the scene she was causing. "You're well enough?"

I'm fine. Excuse me, I'll go change now. She continued walking with rigid strides.

Nothing had changed within the small room she'd always known as her home away from home, but she'd changed. *That's* what perturbed Mamm—and Tad. He'd been spending most of his time in Nont since she'd returned, and that wasn't merely because of his work on the war council. He looked at her as if she were a broken thing he didn't know how to fix, and now he needn't look at her at all.

She didn't like to see the scars on her body, but she wouldn't pretend they weren't there. She didn't like the emptiness in her mouth, but it was hers. She wasn't *weaker* after all she'd gone through, but she was *different*. Yes, she tired more quickly—in large part because she wasn't eating and drinking as much as she should—but she still retained her wits. She just might need the occasional nap to fully exercise them.

She was well aware of the whispers that shadowed her through the hallways. The pity. Even the domestics had mused that Solenn was now useless because, without a tongue, she was considered unmarriageable and best not seen in public at all. Braiz wasn't like Verdania, where obstreperous Chefs were punished with the severance of their prized organ, but stigma around that loss likely existed the world over. Everyone knew that Chefs were closest to the Gods because of the divinity of their tongues, and the lack of that important bit of their body—to be born as such or to endure damage through accident or illness—was judged as a physical signifier that they were furthest from the blessing of the Five Gods.

Solenn had to guffaw at that. The opposite was true for her, for anyone. Nothing about the Gods was so simple.

She went to the traditional Braizian chestnut box bed against the wall and opened the bench seat to pull forth a change of clothes. Her hands trembled as she switched attire, the recently tailored garments now strangely loose on her body.

She would like to say that she didn't care about the gossip, but that would be a lie. She cared. She wanted to prove the doubters wrong. Her worth wasn't bound to her tongue or her womb. She was Braiz's ambassador to the Coterie. She knew that truth, even if few others did.

She would carry that confidence when she spoke with her grandparents on the morrow.

A knock at the door signaled the arrival of a maid bringing refreshment for the wait until supper. Solenn set the small platter of bread, butter, and honey upon a table near a hearth fire that burned fiercely until she took her seat. The flames seemed to withdraw beneath the largest log and stay there.

"You're watching me that closely, Hester? You'd deny me warmth after everything this night has wrought?" Solenn asked, voice a bare rasp. Hester had caused fires to act in such a way multiple times in recent weeks. "I suppose that's just as well. We need to talk." She took a sip of the pomace-derived piquette, which was much lighter in alcohol than wine and did a better job of clearing her throat than water. Jean must have requested it on her behalf.

"I'm angry, Hester." She hoped that the God could understand her speech, as she scarcely could herself. "I know you understand rage. You're stuck in your statue form. I'm here, being treated like a *child*. I'm not angry at you, though. Even though you burned me. Even though you would have let Mallory Valmont kill me." Solenn ripped apart the bread hunk with both hands. It had come from one of the twelve-pound loaves the kitchen here made every few days, and by its stiffness, this one was a few days old. Ripping apart something solid and strong felt good.

She used a nubby knife to lacquer butter across a knuckle-size piece. Her stomach growled. She was hungry. She was always hungry these days, but it took so frustratingly long to eat. "Here. I know you understand hunger without satiation too."

She thrust the buttered bread into the flames. The fire seized the offering. Rather than spread honey on the remaining bread, Solenn dipped her spoon into the crock. She used her upper lip to empty the spoon into her mouth. Adamantine could've probably told her where in Braiz the hive had originated and what flowers the bees had gathered the nectar from, but Solenn's remaining stub recognized the honey as sweet and delicious. That's what really mattered. Even more, it soothed her throat and placed something in her stomach.

She tore off a small piece of bread and chewed it, using her finger to prod the lumps within her mouth. She didn't need to be self-conscious in front of the fire. Hester finished her portion, the char blending in with the ashes, so Solenn gave her the rest of the loaf. The flames lapped it up without hesitation.

Aveyron had explained to her that the Gods began as human and became something more thousands of years ago. Hester, as God of Hearth and Home, loved humans best, and grew angry for their sakes as they endured assaults by the kin. She had nursed her anger for years, hoarding the power she gained from offerings and prayers. How Hester became a statue was unclear. What *was* evident was that she became an incredible repository of might, and used that to tear apart the kin and the world. Her attack had left her frozen in place for the thousands of years since.

Gyst and his sibling Gods had herded Solenn, Aveyron, and their parents to interfere with Hester's interaction with Mallory Valmont. Gyst hadn't wanted his sister-God to effectively die by suicide, but neither had he any idea how Hester could be saved from her current stasis. He wanted to leave her where she was, in a prison of her own making. Better for her to linger in abject misery than release the chaotic, embittered Valmont upon the world.

"I know with certainty that the God of Unknowns doesn't know as much as he thinks he does," Solenn said. "*I'll* find means to help you speak again, Hester. I made a vow to you. My family keeps its vows." She spoke of her blood and beloved family together.

She wanted to do more than help Hester to speak. She wanted to make another ally.

Solenn finished her piquette and honey. Thus fortified and restless, she exited her room to find Jean in wait. "Princess. Are we going to the dining room?"

Not yet. You go ahead and break your fast. As her sole personal attendant present, he'd be required to stay vigilant while she attended supper. When he looked skeptical, she wrote on: *I am surrounded by soldiers and musketeers who know me. I'll be safe.* As if to illustrate her point, three soldiers passed by, genuflecting.

She pointed in the direction of the kitchen, doing her best scowl. Jean sighed. "Fine, I'll take my meal now."

Solenn continued to the courtyard by herself. She needed to include whatever recent news she could gather in her letter to Queen Abonde.

The rain had ceased again, the night colder. Several dozen people faced an elder musketeer, who stood partway up the stairs to a guard tower. "And at three, our next group dispatches. You know who you are, yes." People throughout the crowd raised hands. "Our morning shift—" More hands reached toward the clouds. "Very good. The rest of you, please, get rest. Tomorrow brings more work and sorrow. Selland preserve us all." Voices jumbled as people began to split off into groups.

Ugh, she'd had terrible timing, but perhaps she could still overhear something of use. Solenn hopped off the stairs and into the shadows before anyone could chastise her to go back inside.

About ten feet away, beneath the dry overhang of the roof, she spied a short, round figure, a woman with brown skin in a pale, brightly clean cook's frock. Despite the late hour, the woman gazed about with curiosity. Beside her was Mari; she seemed to have grown since Solenn had seen her last, but she was the same as ever, her lace-capped blonde head bowed as she crocheted lace. She needed no light. Her fingers knew what to do.

Solenn knew what to do as well. She had never before met this woman, but she recognized and loved her. Smiling, she approached her great-grandmother to at long last make her acquaintance.

CHAPTER FIVE

SOLENN

With Selland's aid, one may preserve butter for long periods. Prepare a brine with enough salt to float an egg, and into that place the butter in hand-size lumps. It will keep, sweet and fresh. Is it not amazing how Selland can do so much with so little?

—Excerpt from *Book for Cooks to Excel as Do Chefs*

The old woman straightened as she watched Solenn approach. Mari glanced up, then dipped in a curtsy, as appropriate when wearing a skirt. "Princess Solenn," she said in stilted but clear Verdanian for the benefit of her companion. Solenn was glad they'd been paired. Mari had demonstrated gentleness and patience last year, when she had taken care of a beloved baker here who had become fragile after losing her children and grandchildren in the Nont disaster.

"Ah, *you* are Princess Solenn! I've been looking for you." The old woman reached for Solenn's hand, and Solenn was so surprised that she let herself be grasped. "Come along." She pulled her up the stairs and into the château.

Solenn wanted to ask where they were going, but there were too many people about for her to speak comfortably—nor was the woman likely to understand her inarticulate, accented Verdanian. The old woman moved at a steady hustle, giving Solenn no opportunity to pull out her table book.

With her free hand, she tapped Mari on the shoulder. The girl glanced over. Solenn shrugged, one-armed, making questions clear in her face.

"I don't know where she wants to go," Mari said in Braizian, most of her focus again on the lace she was making even as she walked. She crocheted almost every waking moment of her day. "We've spent most of the past while in the cellar. She talked to herself a lot, assessing the bottles, barrels, and foods. I ended up sitting on the stairs as she wandered. She has a *lot* of energy for a woman of her age." Admiration warmed her tone.

As they passed beneath lit lamps, Solenn used the opportunities to appraise her great-grandmother. Her skin was darker than Solenn's, a warm chestnut. She remembered that Erwan had said her maternal line hailed from an isle in the Southern Sea that had passed through various rulers over time. The brief time Verdania had held it, they'd brought the resident Chefs back to the continent. Solenn wondered whether this woman knew of stories told by her own parents or grandparents about their place of origin. She yearned to know more about that side of her family. Erwan's line felt dull in contrast—Braizian all the way back, only becoming landholders in the vicomte's time through his profound service to the Crown. The whole family was as pale as cream, eyes usually blue, their noses bold and smiles bolder.

Her great-grandmother hummed a merry song to herself. Solenn didn't recognize the tune, though it seemed danceable.

They stopped at the cellar door.

"Why are we back here?" Mari asked in Verdanian, for which Solenn was grateful.

"We need to go down there," Madame Garland replied. Solenn wished that she knew what to even call her, but the Verdanian address felt acceptable.

Mari opened the wooden door. The hinge emitted a moist creak. The smell of dankness and earth arose through the opening.

The smells of Gyst.

Coldness trickled along her spine as Solenn remembered Gyst controlling her body. She had yelled within her own mind to be allowed to speak, to move, unable to do so much as brush an irritating strand of hair from her cheek. The God of Unknowns had been confident of knowing all, that he understood Solenn's needs better than she did. He considered his domination to be kindness, generosity, even as she felt shackled and bound within her own familiar flesh. Powerless. Helpless.

Solenn's breaths came fast. Terrified as she was, she willed her legs— *she willed her legs*—to keep up with her great-grandmother.

Sporadic candles remained lit along the stairwell. People had likely been going in and out through the evening to fetch supplies. Madame Garland's fingers were calloused and strong as she guided Solenn down to stand upon the hardened clay floor. The surface underfoot was called toadmud and formed the base of most Braizian houses beyond the major cities. The mix of sand, clay, and ash looked pale gray in the dim light.

"See! Here we are." Madame Garland sounded triumphant. "I brought her."

Wait, what? Solenn looked to Mari, who was so startled that she glanced up from her lace.

"Who are you—" Mari began to ask.

"Really?" Madame Garland's head tilted to the side. "I suppose." She jerked on Solenn's arm, hard, sending her toward the toadmud face-first. Solenn caught herself on her hands and knees, the impact jarring through her bones. She pivoted around, onto her back. Madame Garland stood there with a frown, her head still tilted.

"He wants me to welcome you to his domain," Madame Garland said. "He recommended that you grovel."

Oh, no. No, no, no.

Her heart thundering, Solenn hated that her first instinct was to freeze in terror like a deer or rabbit, as if stillness would mean she hadn't been seen. There was no hiding here, however, not in Gyst's moldering domain. Not anywhere. He was a God—and yet, she also could've become a God. Tears squeezed from her eyes as fierce desperation shattered her immobility.

She would not be manipulated by Gyst again, nor would she permit her great-grandmother to suffer anything similar.

"Mari, find Chef Adamantine Garland," Solenn said. Mari must have understood some of her words, as she immediately scampered upstairs. The door clanked, the sound echoing as she fled.

"Gyst. Stop whispering in her ear," Solenn said. That had to be what was going on. The God couldn't directly manipulate Madame Garland as he had used Solenn—for reasons Solenn couldn't comprehend, her body had been especially accessible to his control—but he was obviously giving suggestions to a vulnerable woman.

The only positive that Solenn could glean was that Gyst was weak in the human world. Even in this place of his power—surrounded by products in various stages of fermentation, distillation, and mold—he would be able to manifest his voice for only a limited time.

"When a God is present, they must be regarded with respect," Madame Garland said in a chastising tone. "You would do well to refer to him as 'Most August Gyst.' I learned that in my first year of training!"

Gyst had harped on Solenn about his idea of "proper respect" when he was in control of her movement too. "Respect must be earned," she retorted, but the woman's blank look said she didn't understand. And yet after a moment, Madame Garland nodded.

"Respect must be earned," she echoed. "Yes, that is true among people, for certain. But the Gods do much for us. We can't take that for granted, even though everything we know of as food existed before they did. They make it all *better*."

Gyst was good at his work with his millions upon millions of unknowns, yes, but he was also an insufferable boor.

"Let's go upstairs," Solenn said, standing and gently gripping Madame Garland's arm. She gestured upward to make her intent clear.

Scowling, the older woman shook off Solenn's hold. "No. Even if he's being petulant—yes, you are—it is rare for a God to speak. We can't simply *leave*."

They could, but Solenn couldn't drag her up the stairs, nor would she leave her great-grandmother here alone.

Madame Garland's head tilted again, angled toward the darkness from which Gyst must have been speaking. As scared as Solenn was, she took incredible comfort in that she couldn't hear him or see a trace of his misty form. The sacrifice of her tongue had been sufficient.

"Most August Gyst is disappointed in you. He says . . . you need allies right now, don't you? What washed ashore tonight will happen again and again, until what remains of your fleet is gone. When your armies march to confront the might of Verdania, don't expect better. You could've worked with him to hold back marsh-foot, disease, and rampant infection, he says. Instead . . . oh dear. Most August One, truly? That seems terribly petty. Instead of making those awful things more awful, why don't you help lovely bread to rise all the better?"

Solenn gawked, needing a second to realize her great-grandmother was berating Gyst about his priorities.

The old woman continued: "Or bless the contents of wine bottles so that they last longer than six months?"

The verve of Madame Garland struck Solenn as an even bolder proof of their familial tie than their similar skin tones and defiant jawlines.

"Gyst," Solenn said to the darkness. "You didn't want to be allied with me. You wanted to *rule* me." She spoke Verdanian so that Madame Garland might understand.

"Hmm." Madame Garland made a thoughtful sound. "He's reminding us that he's a God. Well, of course you are—anyone can see *that*." Solenn was taken aback once again by the old woman's assumption that everyone could see Gyst, then understood that this was another sign of the inconsistencies in her great-grandmother's mind. "He says he knows various unknowns, and he can—"

"You don't know all unknowns, Gyst." Solenn knew that as a fact. She'd dipped into Gyst's well of divinity. She'd experienced his same vision for a smattering of minutes. "You see many things people cannot, yes, but it was very clear to me that *I* remain a mystery to you. You may see a lot, but you don't *listen*."

Solenn knew that when Gyst had possessed her, he had relished in experiencing the world through a human body. Seeing colors as does a person. Feeling textures through her fingertips. Experiencing pain— burns, cuts, the scrapes of rocks. He obviously hadn't cared that she felt the pain too. His selfishness was as profound as his power.

Feet pounded down the wooden steps. Ada charged into sight, her expression belying ferocity. "Grand-mère, are you—" Her gaze focused on darkness feet away from her grandmother. "Gyst." Ada could apparently see him. He was expending incredible amounts of power to make this show of force. Her gaze shifted to Solenn with worry. "Are you hurt?"

"He's threatening me. Threatening Braiz." Her throat struggled to make the words sound as they should.

"Such a mighty God to behave in such a petty way," Ada spit.

"I was telling him much the same," said Madame Garland. "He really should focus more on bread, cheese, and wine. The good things in life. Why *anyone* would make gangrene *worse* when they could enjoy melted cheese on fresh bread with a nice white wine, I don't—"

"I tried to get her to leave," Solenn said to Ada.

"I don't think the two of us together could pull her away." She gestured to Selland, Melissa, and Lait in sequence, urgency in the motions.

"Maybe if we—oh." A smile split Ada's face as she stared deeper amid the shelves. She lunged into the darkness.

A small popping sound echoed somewhere beyond sight, followed by the distinct slosh of liquid. This gained Madame Garland's attention as well.

"Oh! Is that—"

Ada stepped into the stronger light near the stairs. She held a wine bottle. Bubbles crowned the top and cascaded down the side, wreathing her fingers in bubbles. "Gyst isn't the only God with us right now. Grand-mère, what do I have here?"

"A sweet wine from Rance, aged—my goodness, over ten years. Usually wines that sweet and potent are exported to Ruthenia—they do like them more than Verdanians, which is one good thing I can say about their tastes," Madame Garland said as an aside to Solenn or Gyst, or perhaps them both. "Bottled wines don't usually last longer than a few months unless a Chef is monitoring closely. I noticed this one when I was walking around and even told Melissa she had done her work well . . . and Gyst, too, of course." The Gods often partnered in such ways.

"It's open now." Ada held it up. Bubbles plopped onto the floor. "We need to drink it, and for something this special, we need proper cups. Can you show us where we can find some, Princess?"

Solenn was awed. Ada was *brilliant*. "Of course, Chef. But how did you . . . ?"

"Most August Melissa visited long enough to cause the bottle to burst. She and my grandmother have always had a close relationship. She was looking out for her." Adamantine motioned a bee's path as a show of gratitude to the God, only for her posture to shift a moment later. She scowled into the darkness, making it clear to whom she now spoke. "My grandmother has always been devoted to you, too, and you know it. Don't drag her into your tragic opera, August Gyst." She gripped her grandmother by the upper arm. "Let's go before we lose all of the fizz."

"*That* would be the true tragedy," Madame Garland said, climbing upward without hesitation.

At the top, Ada glanced back. "Oh, Five. That was a despicable act." Solenn tilted her head questioningly. Ada continued in a bare whisper, "He's deployed much of his available power, I think, but what he has left he's using to destroy things down there. He's ruining cheese that shouldn't have spoiled for weeks. Several wine barrels and bottles just exploded too. He's doing what Melissa did on a broader scale, and out of sheer maliciousness." Outrage shook her voice. The faint noise of dribbling fluid acted as perturbing punctuation.

Solenn looked to Madame Garland with worry, but she was happily murmuring to herself about sweet wines.

A small, pale figure stood beneath a lamp at the top of the stairs. Mari clutched a saltcellar with both hands, her expression grim.

"What—" Ada started to ask.

"It was Gyst, wasn't it?" she blurted. "Your grandmother kept acting like she was speaking with him earlier, but I thought it was just Chef-talk, but he was *truly* there, wasn't he?" she continued, breathless. "So I grabbed salt to help us keep him away, because nothing preserves like Selland's blessed salt. He saves food, memories, everything!"

Tears warmed Solenn's eyes. She pinched her fingers, appealing to Selland to bless this sweet, thoughtful girl.

"Clever move, to fetch salt," said Ada. Her tone indicated that she had some experience dealing with children. "You're right—that *was* Gyst, and he was being rude. Melissa stepped in to help us, so we don't need the salt now. Can you put that back and get us a cup to share? My thanks!" she called after Mari as the girl dashed away.

Mari had actually left behind her lace in order to help Madame Garland. Solenn wondered if Ada grasped how truly extraordinary that was.

Mari returned almost immediately. They retreated to a storage room just off the hallway, where Madame Garland took a long drink of fizzing wine, followed by a blissful sigh. Ada partook next. Solenn shook her head to decline before being asked; the bubbles would be too unruly in her mouth. As for Mari, she was again working her lace. She'd brought in a lit candle as well and set it upon the central worktable.

"Mari," Ada quietly said in Braizian as Madame Garland finished off the bottle, "I think my grandmother will return to our room now. I'm going to ask for guards to be placed near the cellar and . . ." Her brow furrowed. "I don't think Gyst will be able to manifest like that again anytime soon—but then, I hadn't considered he'd make such a move tonight." She blinked back tears, but her flushed skin and furrowed brow showed more anger than sadness.

"Why would Gyst do that at all?" Mari asked.

"People think being a Chef is all blessings, but it's hard to work with both the Gods and people. The Gods *are* like people, really. Just more powerful," Ada said in a frank way that surprised Solenn, but Mari seemed to readily accept an answer suffused with truth. "Grand-mère? Are you ready for rest now?"

Grand-mère had a smile of supreme satisfaction. "Yes, I think so. Such a drink might keep some people awake all night with a racing heart, Princess," she said, regarding Solenn, "but not me. I'm unique."

"Yes, you are, Grand-mère," Ada said, walking her to the door. She shut it again as soon as her grandmother and Mari were outside. She allowed her weariness to show on her face. "I hate placing the burden of her care on a child, but I think Mari handled that better than most adults."

Solenn had her table book out in an instant. The sheet she wrote upon would be thrown into the first lit hearth she found. *Did you see Melissa in the cellar as well?*

"No. I've never seen or heard her, only witnessed her actions. A few weeks ago, her bees also herded a horse my way when I needed one most urgently."

Could she become more involved?

"You mean, as involved in our lives as Hester and Gyst? I don't know. That's her choice. What I said about the Gods being people—you know how true that is. Some people, seeing a neighbor in need, will open up their household, offer up the entirety of their pantry and whatever clothes they have. Another neighbor may bring a single meal. That meal is still a blessing to appreciate." Spoken like a true Chef. "I should've considered that Gyst would try something like this. His attention on us has been obvious. I'm guessing you've endured the same."

She didn't want to tell Ada that several of her cuts had developed brief infections after the battle. That would only make her upset. *Mostly I've found fires to be reluctant.*

"Neither God can be trusted," Adamantine said with obvious grief.

Now was definitely not the time for Solenn to bring up her renewed vow to help Hester.

"I need to clean the cellar," continued Ada. "That mess is mine. I also need to ascertain if anything intact has turned toxic."

Solenn sucked in a small breath. That loss of food was her fault, happening just as her people engaged in war. Every bit of food in that cellar could be essential to the survival of this household in the coming months.

Ada looked her up and down. "You're sure you're not harmed?"

Solenn glanced down. Some dirt from the floor had smeared her suit, but it'd brush off easily. She shrugged.

"Very well," Ada said. "I'd best go. Your meal will be done soon. I've now been given full permission to oversee you as you dine as well. You'll probably notice me lurking about." Her smile expressed soft yearning. With a dip of her head, she exited.

Ada wasn't simply kind and considerate of Solenn's needs; she was also thoughtful of the staff. At the same time, she was brusque and pragmatic, her tone with the Gods often personal, verging on belligerent. She'd had a hard life, and it showed.

Solenn found her somewhat intimidating, but also *dazzling*. She better understood why Erwan still spoke of Ada with such reverence and love.

Solenn put away her table book and lingered a moment before picking up the candle. She expected the light to spitefully gutter out within its pool of wax. Instead, it remained consistently bright.

What did that mean? She remained leery on the walk back to her chamber. The candle remained her bright companion the entire way.

∽

Solenn knew she was being watched as she ate, but she was most perturbed by Mamm's near-constant oversight, the teary plea in her eyes that asked, *Why aren't you eating more?* Never mind that such scrutiny was exactly why she *couldn't* eat more. Prodding a finger around in her mouth in front of everyone was something she hadn't attempted since age three, but oh, she wanted to. A piece of carrot was stuck in her back molars. She could've excused herself from the table, and yet, she wanted to be present. She wanted to hear the somber talk about the war and, even more, be surrounded by the people she loved. She'd missed Vicomtesse Corre with ferocity. That woman had taught her how to keep her seat while on a jumping horse, and always made sure Solenn was sneaked her own jar of caramel on Melissa's high days because she knew the girl loved to eat it straight with a spoon. Their deep fondness for each other now made even more sense since Solenn knew this was her grandmother. She hoped that the vicomte and vicomtesse could know the truth of their connection someday, but Erwan needed to be part of that decision.

She caught another glimpse of Ada at the entrance to the dining room, this time as she spoke with Jean. Her birth mother had come and gone like a squirrel from a hole, her furrowed-brow analysis amusing in contrast to Mamm's hawkish glare. This time, however, Jean stepped forward to stand at Vicomtesse Corre's back as he awaited a pause in the conversation.

"I beg your pardon, Vicomtesse, Princesses." Jean gestured behind him. "Chef Garland brings forth an idea that may aid Solenn as she dines."

Ada literally dragged out her concept: an old dressing screen, one that Solenn had hidden behind as a young child down in the cellar. As Ada carried the paneled stand over to where Solenn sat, she could see the object had been cleaned, the wood still dewy from hasty wax.

"My apologies for the interruption," Ada said, leaning the screen against the wall so that she could bow, "but as I was granted permission to do so if I—"

Vicomtesse Corre gasped. "Oh! A screen to shield Solenn from view as she eats? Of course. Whyever did none of us think of that?"

"Vicomtesse, sometimes it's easier to believe that when someone returns, everything will be as it was," Ada said in her soft, husky way. Solenn glanced at Mamm to see her expression was thoughtful. "The idea occurred to me only because of an experience I had during the war. I once supervised a supper for a visiting general. He'd been badly burned in a munitions explosion. The muscles in his face were taut. He had to chew with his mouth open and wouldn't do so in front of other people, but socializing over meals was essential in his daily duties. The solution, provided by his faithful sous-lieutenant, was to seat the general with everyone else but shield him from direct view with a screen. He actually traveled with several fold-out screens to use whenever he ate. Princess Solenn, if I may?"

At Solenn's nod, Ada unfolded the three-paneled screen to surround her chair on the side nearest the entrance. Through the painted paper, she could see Mamm's silhouette two seats away, and only glimpsed Vicomtesse Corre's shoulder as she leaned back in her chair.

"Will this help?" Ada whispered from within the privacy of the screen. She stood mere inches away, her body still fragrant of horse and dampness.

Solenn nodded, emotion thickening her already-strained throat. So much love in Ada's subtle gesture. "Thank you," she mouthed.

"You're welcome, Princess," Ada said softly, then spoke louder. "I'll now leave you to your—"

Yells and loud clatter rang from elsewhere in the house. Everyone at the table lurched to stand, Solenn included. Her head and shoulders emerged above the screen. Beside her, Ada reached beneath her cook's smock to withdraw a knife while the musketeers near the door gripped their rapiers.

"It's Yanik!" cried Jean from the doorway. Musketeers stepped back to let through a staggering man in brown and green road-spattered clothes. Even knowing this was Yanik, Solenn didn't recognize him for a moment. Stringy yellow hair draped to his shoulders, a bushy beard foreign on his face.

He'd been in her retinue to Verdania. He'd stayed behind to assist Erwan.

Yanik dropped to one knee, head bowed. "Princess Katell. Princess Solenn." His voice broke as he said her name. He'd wept over her condition when he beheld her at Rozny. Tears filled her eyes to see him now, haggard but home. "Vicomtesse. I come bearing news from our enemy, Verdania."

Choice wording, that. Knowing him, and how he practiced his songwriting as he rode, he'd spent hours deliberating what to say at this very moment.

"We will witness your telling," said Mamm. A formal response.

Yanik raised his head to regard everyone at the table, his eyes widening as he seemed to recognize Ada. Pain deepened in his features. "I grieve to inform you that Captain Corre and my peers are being held captive in Verdania, to be tried in the stead of the missing Princess Solenn. By the abuse in our treatment, by the blatant bias in their judgment, I say with certainty that their lives are to be forfeit, if they are not already."

At that, he bowed his head again and wept.

CHAPTER SIX

ADA

People often praise Chefs for their mastery of flavors and cooking, but let us not forget that part of our expertise draws from our knowledge of batterie de cuisine, our arsenal of cookware. Many cooks appreciate copper pots but must rely upon their eye to know when the interior must be re-tinned, lest diners be poisoned. Chefs, especially those blessed with empathy, perceive the grim repercussions of hot copper in contact with food. For this reason, young tour-Chefs will review pots in the villages and towns that they pass through and should take note if cooks brag about the greening powers of a pan. The resultant gherkins may indeed be a beautiful, vivid green but endow great woe when eaten!

—Excerpt from *Manual for Tour Chefs*

Ada remembered Yanik from twenty years prior, when he was a bright teenager acting as aide-de-camp for Erwan in the Thirty-Fifth Division. He wrote terrible poetry, she recalled, and did so with such enthusiasm that it was impossible to do anything other than encourage him.

He didn't need encouragement to express himself now as, with slow deliberation, he explained the Braizians' poor reception in Lutecia and how the musketeers had come to be in such a dire situation. At the palace, Captain Erwan had presented evidence regarding Princess Solenn's innocence, including the person of Madame Brumal, who with tear-filled eyes asserted her own guiltlessness. Court regarded the accusations against Comtesse Alarie with all seriousness. The paperwork and epicurea in her château made it clear that she'd been involved in the black market epicurea trade, thus leading to her imprisonment within the palace itself.

Ada schooled her reaction to this news, just as she had whenever she'd heard any public mutterings about her mother.

Comtesse Esme Alarie. The widowed bourgeois bride had busied herself over the past two decades in her illicit enterprise, likely the largest in all the realm. She had never so committed herself as a mother. Ada had been a secret daughter, born before Maman had wed her comte. Ada now kept her own secrets in turn; she had asked that Erwan foster a lie to Maman that she had died in the battle around Hester's feet, where her kidnapped mother had stayed bound in a pit through the worst of the fighting.

"Captain Erwan was questioned day after day about our so-called plot against Verdania," said Yanik. The weary man had been provided a chair and sat, as had his audience. Solenn's screen had been moved aside as well. "They refused to consider that Albion had orchestrated the scheme, not us. For once, they deemed us intelligent." His wry comment acknowledged the popular Verdanian idea that Braizians were simpletons. "The investigators wanted to know where Solenn was now and how she had escaped the tower at all, though we found out that the palace had put forth news that she'd been recaptured. Thank Selland we already knew that to be a lie, or we would've torn the place apart brick by brick." His smile for Solenn was gap-toothed and fond.

Solenn, who had been taking in his testimony with a furrowed black brow, smiled back with equal endearment. With a pang, Ada realized she'd probably grown up with the musketeers in her party, likely engaging with them much more than she had her own royal relations.

Ada wiped away tears, with no shame for her reaction. Erwan was in imminent peril. Solenn was grieving. Her mother . . . well, Maman was getting what she deserved, but that was still a cause for sadness and anger.

"We couldn't leave the palace. It wasn't safe to do so, not with sentiments against Braiz as they were," Yanik continued. "The mood of the city worsened overall going into the next week as refugees began to arrive. This news came from Comte Brillat Silvacane, our indispensable support and mediator. A strange kind of civil war has erupted in the Verdanian countryside, an outright rebellion in the name of Merle Archambeau."

Exclamations erupted around the table. "Riots and unrest we knew about, but *Merle Archambeau?*" asked Katell. "King Caristo's long-imprisoned cousin?"

"The same." Yanik paused to sip the musca wine that had been served alongside the salt cod. Ada perceived the welcome relief brought by the smooth liquid, its flavor reminiscent of seashells and green apple. The minimal effervescence would make it easier for Solenn to drink, too, and Ada saw that she'd had half her glass. Though she was overwhelmed by many dark emotions, Ada took in that sight with a measure of satisfaction.

"Merle Archambeau was stripped of his titles years ago," murmured Gwenael. "That was supposed to make him impotent as a figurehead for such rebellions."

"It didn't," Yanik said with bluntness. "Instead, he's being celebrated because he *is* title-less . . . as if he's one of the people."

Ada guffawed. She knew she wasn't supposed to speak—she shouldn't even still be seated in this company, but Katell herself had gestured her to stay beside Solenn. "'One of the people.' The man hasn't left a thirty-bedroom estate in some twenty years. I doubt he's ever had a livre in his pocket. I don't trust most gossip that emerges from court, with reason," she said, meeting the eyes of those around her. "But Merle Archambeau was cosseted as a child and has been treated even more so as an adult. A spoiled lapdog in the city, at least, will look out windows to watch what happens on the avenue. Merle has no concept of the outside world at all."

"That matches what our spies have related as well," confirmed Katell.

"Why is this civil war especially 'strange'?" asked Gwenael. Her fingers clenched a napkin.

"Because it feels doomed to fail from the start, Vicomtesse," said Yanik. "These rebels call themselves 'the Blessed' and wear red tabards to symbolize Hester's fire. Small, armed groups are targeting cities and ports, attacking soldiers and sailors, posting notices everywhere that call for Merle Archambeau to rule and Caristo be slain. On my way here, as I rested in a barn with refugees one night, I heard stories about how the Blessed are stealing and distributing royal epicurean stores. They aren't hoarding these ingredients for use in battle, though, but using them frivolously. There's no overall sense of discipline or strategy, and yet, they're disrupting the country in most every way."

In Verdania, all the realm's epicurea was supposed to be the property of King Caristo and, through him, the military. The army's massive ingredient stores focused on enhancing fighting prowess and survival. Ada was disturbed to think of that arsenal in the hands of ignorant civilians.

"A distraction." Solenn's slowly enunciated words startled the table. "Verdanian forces are still largely disbanded for winter. Their military commanders had come to Lutecia for the wedding festivities. The loss of epicurea leaves any gathered soldiers more vulnerable. The timing of what's happening isn't an accident."

Ada couldn't help a grim nod. Her daughter knew of what she spoke.

"Albion," spit Gwenael.

"Lord Whitney in particular," said Katell, her mouth a hard line. "That man needs to die."

"Oh, Princess." Tears trailed down Yanik's cheeks as he gazed at Solenn. "To hear your voice means so much."

"I lost my tongue, not my throat." She chastised him in a raspy yet gentle tone, the words requiring a moment to decipher. "But please, continue."

"Of course, though it especially grieves me to relate the next part of my tale to you." Yanik inhaled deeply to compose himself. "Sympathetic figures within the palace warned us that we were to be Caristo's prime game pieces. The blame for the current chaos, to his thinking, could only be placed upon the murderer of his son and the murderess's representatives."

Solenn's eyes squeezed shut, her head bowed. Ada yearned to wrap an arm around her for comfort, and was relieved when Katell reached across the table to grip Solenn's hand.

Gwenael leaned back, her expression of twisted agony. When no one spoke up, Yanik softly continued. "Comte Silvacane found means for one of our number to escape our current mild confinement within the palace. I was selected." He stared downward.

Erwan, honorable as he was, would never leave his musketeers behind, not even knowing Ada and Solenn were in need of him here.

"You were the right choice," Princess Katell said, her voice soft.

There was a long pause. "It is kind of you to say so, Princess, but . . ."

"Your wife had twins last year and is due again soon," Gwenael said in a crisp tone that tolerated no debate. "Your children should know their father."

"How many days ago did you depart?" Ada asked. A fluid plan began to form in her mind.

"A week, as I was given—"

"A Camarga. There's no other way you could've made the trip so quickly," Ada finished for him, her plan solidifying like water to ice. "This horse came courtesy of Comte Silvacane?"

"Yes." Yanik looked surprised—and weary. He smothered a yawn against his fist.

"We owe this Comte Silvacane an immense debt," murmured Gwenael.

"I wouldn't be alive without his aid," said Solenn, which caused the others in the room to gaze at each other, pensive. Ada could only guess at the amended version of events that Solenn had offered to explain her escape and the loss of her tongue, and it seemed that the Silvacanes had been a necessary omission until now.

"We will honor him if given the opportunity," said Gwenael, "but for now, dear Yanik, you require food and—"

Ada stood in eagerness, then bowed as an apology. "I'd love to cook for him, Vicomtesse."

Gwenael's small smile showed no offense was taken. She had to know that Ada's motivations weren't purely altruistic. "Yanik? Would you like to refresh yourself and dine before continuing to your family in Malo?"

"Yes, Itron. I doubt I could make that short journey otherwise . . . not unless I was thrown in the back of a wagon, and I *would* like to return with some small measure of pride."

Ada needed a moment to translate the unfamiliar Braizian word: "Itron." A high term of respect for a lady, a word that went beyond noble titles. Braizians she'd served with during the war had referred to Hester, Lait, and Melissa as "Itron" during moments of intense need or gratitude.

Vicomtesse Gwenael stood, everyone else doing the same in her wake. When Yanik teetered on his feet, Jean and another musketeer flanked him to hold him up. "Very well. I don't think I need to request that your peers aid you, Yanik, as I already know they will, just as the Chef here will cook whatever meal you most desire."

"Will a 'musketeer's breakfast' still meet your liking?" Ada asked.

Yanik's exhausted smile seemed to wobble. "You remembered! Yes, thank you, Chef-Lieutenant Corre." He didn't catch his error in calling her by her old rank and name as he hobbled away with help, nor did anyone correct him. The words pierced her, both familiar and strange.

Ada made her own respectful exit from the dining room, but not before replacing the screen around Solenn. The cod had gone cold, but she knew Solenn was still hungry.

As Ada hurried to the basement kitchen, her heart pounded as if it would escape her chest and race onward to Verdania. Erwan had been alive five days ago. A mere week. By the Gods, she could only pray he still lived and breathed. After so many years apart, she'd only recently been reunited with him for a single day, and much of that had been occupied by a hard ride, culminating in battle. He'd wanted to court her again. Erwan *couldn't* be dead now, he couldn't, and not by the order of that chancre of a man, King Caristo. It was his fault they'd been forced apart.

For so many years, she'd been embittered by the separation from her husband and child. She'd dared to let hope bloom. She couldn't lose that brightness now.

Few cooks remained in the kitchen as they completed their labors. When Ada explained her purpose—and that she would complete the cleanup in their stead—the area was readily ceded to her control. Her hands shook as she began to work, but within a minute, she had regained her equilibrium. Nothing calmed her like the rhythm and ritual of cooking.

A standard Braizian breakfast consisted of buckwheat crêpes with fillings to preference, but Yanik and many other musketeers had favored something heartier yet still simple. Her first priority was to find the long-handled tool called a salamander, which she set so that its pentagonal end rested over the fireplace coals. That fire continued to burn steadily. Perhaps Hester's attention was elsewhere.

Ada brought a long, serrated knife through a day-old bread loaf. The crust crackled as the blade came through, crumbs shattering across the table. She topped three thick slices with thin cuts of local cheese aged some two months, its texture firm yet pliable. She knew without sampling that it tasted of fresh cream and the earliest grasses of the new year, with a hint of salt from the nearby sea. By experience, she also knew the yellow cheese would melt beautifully.

She tucked the prepared slices in a still-hot oven, then pulled sausage from the pantry. The pork intestine–cased saucisson sec had been made last fall. The white mold that coated the outside was a welcome sign of Gyst's blessing. The interior consisted of pork with only a touch of beef, the coarsely ground mix including chopped chestnuts, diced dried apples, and a cheese similar to abree. She sliced the entire length of sausage into fat coins, then checked the oven. The bread had crisped golden on the bottom. She set it on a platter and grabbed the glowing-hot salamander tool. Standing back, she held the heated end over the melted cheese to create a mottled brown top, just as she could use the same tool for a crème brûlée.

She had just poured perry into two wooden cups when Yanik came down the stairs. His steps were more assured now; movement had done him good, as had time with his comrades. He now wore a musketeer's cassock, his hat in his hands, his clean face creased in a weary smile at the sight of her.

"The captain expressed great hope that you'd be in Braiz by now," he said, taking a seat across from her at the table, his hat set on the neighboring chair.

Her heart physically ached. Oh, Five. Erwan had been talking about her. He wanted to be here with her. The confirmation hurt worse than any stubbed toe she'd ever experienced.

"I only arrived today," Ada said.

"Much seems to have arrived today. I was just told of the sailors on the nearby beach." Tears glistened in his eyes. "You escape war, thinking to return to the peace of home, only to find there's no refuge."

"I relate to your words more than you even realize. Now eat. I can perceive your drool as you stare at that cheese."

He reached for a slice of bread as she did the same. She hadn't eaten since sometime that morning, and she knew she needed her energy for the days ahead.

"Where do you expect that your comrades will be imprisoned by now?" Ada asked. She wouldn't give voice to worse possibilities.

She sensed the cider meeting his tongue, refreshing in its chill, its alcohol potent and sharp enough to clear more of his fatigue. Ada took her own drink, delighting in the sweetness. Her grandmother would approve.

"I thought the tower was most likely. Princess Solenn escaped from there, after all. Caristo would relish in us wallowing in the same place. Captain Corre, however, believed it'd be the bastille."

Ada grimaced. "The palace loves to boast that the tower is secure— though your princess proved that wrong—but the bastille there truly is the nastier of the two." The rock-walled dungeon lay beneath the very barracks of the palace guards. At any time, a third of the guard was likely to be sleeping or idling in the building—which she knew because she'd regarded the whole facility with morbid fascination when she'd berthed there a few times in her youth.

She took another bite of bread, the cheese stretching as she pulled it away. "The bastille will be problematic," she mused to herself. "Multiple doors, thick walls, hundreds of guards . . ."

"You're planning a rescue operation, then." Yanik didn't sound the slightest bit surprised.

"Spring is usually a pleasant time to visit Lutecia, anyway. There'll be some nice spring goat cheeses available in the market."

"Mm-hmm. For that very reason, Captain Corre bid me to tell you that you're not to be daft and make any effort to liberate him on your own. 'Go to your old friends,' he said."

A light laugh escaped her. This day had been terrible in so many ways, but by the Five, it felt wonderful to still be understood by the man she'd never ceased to love. "I suppose I'm somewhat predictable." She drained the rest of her cup.

His expression sobered. "I'd join you, if I were allowed, but I've already been ordered to stay in Malo. The captain knows you, and my superiors here also know me." His tone turned bitter.

"Yanik, some other people will tell you, with good intentions, that you're blessed to be the one who returned. They're not wrong, and yet you can simultaneously be blessed and cursed at once. That guilt will be a heavy burden to bear, so please, let others help you lighten it."

He wiped bread crumbs from his lips as he ruefully shook his head. "You were always honest about such feelings. Thank you for that. And for the food."

"Anytime," she said fervently. "Now go and do your utmost to enjoy your wife and children."

"I will." Yanik donned his hat as he moved toward the door. "I'll pray for you, Chef-Lieutenant. If anyone can return our captain and comrades home, it'll be you." He spoke with a faith that she didn't deserve, but could only acknowledge with a nod.

She finished cleaning the kitchen and, after a last draught of perry, exited the kitchen. The clouds had cleared to create the kind of brisk, star-bright night that Braizians described as salt-tossed, as if Selland had flung a handful of salt into the dark bowl above.

Ada remembered when Erwan had first described the stars as such to her. They'd been working together as officers for a few weeks, their relationship cordial. Their love hadn't been the instantaneous passion depicted by operas—not like the famed Maria and Draco, catching each other's eyes across a ballroom and bursting into song like springtime birds. Oh, Ada had noted the new Braizian officer assigned to their joint international effort was good-looking, with wavy black hair and cornflower eyes, but she was focused on her work, not a tumble or a deeper relationship.

She considered Erwan in a new way as they labored together one night. Again, this wasn't the stuff of an opera—the real drama had occurred in previous days, when an Albionish incursion had broken a levee, flooding a Ricardian village. She and Erwan attended to dull but necessary paperwork by lamplight. Their notes detailed a tragedy, and their sporadic conversation was lighter by necessity. She had known little of Erwan up until that point, and couldn't remember the specifics now, only that she realized she liked and respected this person. By the way he looked at her, she believed he reciprocated the feeling.

He'd pointed out the stars when they stepped outside to stretch their legs. It'd been a brisk spring night, much like this one. "In Braiz, we call this a 'salt-tossed sky,'" he'd said.

"I perceive that to be an adequate amount of seasoning," she'd quipped. It was a lousy joke about Chef skills, but he'd chuckled all the same.

"That's good. I'd trust Selland to get that right." A wistful expression came over his face as he gazed upward. "The stars look a bit different from this far northeast, but they are still recognizable. That means that home is not far away."

She'd shrugged and said something to the effect that she'd been raised in Lutecia, but after years as a tour-Chef in training, she had no specific home.

"I recommend finding one someday," he'd said in a light tone.

Weeks later, snuggled close to him beneath the stars, she'd realized she had finally found a home with him. When they were together, the world felt right.

Ada wanted that rightness again.

She had no doubt that her decision to leave for Verdania to save Erwan was the correct one, but she knew a sense of abiding sadness. She treasured any time she could be with Solenn, but she selfishly wanted more. At least her grandmother would be in good care here.

She crossed the grounds to the barn to confer with the other late arrival this night.

Once inside the low-roofed, broad structure, she spotted a white equine head peering over a half door. A moment later, a thinner, near-identical head lifted to appraise her as well. Ada resisted the urge to bow in greeting to the two companions in the stall.

"Aveyron Silvacane, good to see you again," she murmured to the younger, grayer of the two, and then faced the other. "Comte Brillat Silvacane. Thank you for seeing Yanik safely back to Braiz. I'm honored to make your acquaintance again."

CHAPTER SEVEN

SOLENN

Piquette is a drink made of the pomace left over when wine grapes are pressed. Pomace includes seeds, grape skins, stems, and bits of fruit, to which water and a sweetener such as honey are added, then allowed to ferment. Similarly, cider piquette is made of apple pomace. Such a thing is often concocted by farmhands with the sludge that'd otherwise be fed to animals. Piquette is much lighter in terms of flavor and alcohol, and therefore a refreshing, safer beverage for children as well as adults wishing to avoid inebriation.

—Excerpt from *Book for Cooks to Excel as Do Chefs*

Erwan had recently told Solenn, repeatedly and with deep fondness, that she and Ada were alike in many regards. Even so, Solenn was surprised to find Ada already speaking with the two Camargas in the barn.

"Brillat?" she asked as she rushed forward, as she hadn't yet encountered him in his horse form. At the larger horse's nod, she released a glad cry. When Yanik had said he'd returned on a Camarga, she'd desperately hoped that his mount had been Brillat. Smiling, Ada stepped aside to grant Solenn space at the stall door. Solenn bowed her head against Brillat's, forehead to forehead, then pulled back. He released a gentle huff. She then stroked down Aveyron's muzzle. She could only imagine his profound relief.

"We all must talk," she rasped, then pulled out her table book. She turned to Jean, who respectfully lurked five feet away. *Please inform my mother that I'll return to Malo now.* She then tapped Ada on the forearm and wrote to her. *Will you ride out with us a short distance?*

"Of course, Princess," she murmured.

Are you adequately recovered to be ridden? Solenn wrote to Brillat. Aveyron had told her that Camargas retained their literacy in equine form, though the way they viewed colors changed significantly.

Brillat bobbed his head.

"Princess, should I . . . add more articles of clothing to the satchel?" Jean asked softly, to which she nodded. "I'll gather what we need and alert your mother of our departure." He left.

Eschewing the aid of grooms, Solenn and Ada saddled the Camargas and Jean's horse. He returned, but not alone. With him was Princess Katell, her own guards trailing behind. Mamm's face carried grimness that made Solenn feel a swell of anger and dread. Mamm was going to tell her that she shouldn't go forward with her planned trip to Nont but stay cosseted in Malo. Solenn would not, could not, do that. She and her mother were about to squabble, and oh, she hated squabbling, and certainly didn't want to do so now, when their lives were in such tenuous—

"Solenn, when do you expect to return?" Mamm asked.

Though Solenn held her table book ready, she sufficed with a slow shake of her head. She'd had to tell Mamm and Tad many half-truths in recent weeks, and she was sick of the deceit.

"I see." Mamm took a deep breath. Here would come the denial. "I want you to promise to write me, often as you can."

Solenn gaped for a moment, then hastily wrote. *Of course.*

"Your father tries to post a letter to me most every day we're apart, but I understand . . . if you can't keep the same schedule." She looked past Solenn to where Ada waited with the Camargas. "You're going to ride for Erwan, aren't you?"

Ada took a few steps closer. "I'll speak with Vicomtesse Corre about my departure momentarily, but yes."

Solenn sucked in a small breath. She had hoped that Adamantine would say as much, but the declaration grieved her. They'd had so little time together.

"Good. She'll be glad you're doing so. You're not . . . intending to travel together?" Mamm looked between Solenn and Ada, frailty in her soft voice.

Solenn knew this was a question that she must answer, not Adamantine. *Our paths take us apart.*

Mamm nodded. "I understand." Strangely enough, at that moment, Solenn believed she did—and that Mamm somehow comprehended that Solenn's journey led not to Nont, but somewhere beyond. "You'll both be in my prayers." Her hug snared Solenn, wrapping around her back and clinging tight. They rocked in place for a moment, fear and desperation pressing on them, drawing them closer together. Mamm had held her much like this when Solenn had departed for Verdania a month before, but there was more urgency to it now. A deeper sense that this moment might never come again. And yet, they had to pull apart. They had to murmur their farewells. They had to share final glances across the courtyard.

Her eyes blinded by tears as they rode away, Solenn was relieved to let Aveyron lead them into the nearby hills. They picked their way along a slope thick with broom, stopping in a flat area with few shrubs.

"Princess." Jean tossed her the satchel. Caught off-guard at the increased weight, she almost dropped it. "I hope the sabots fit. Dare I ask . . . is Comte Brillat Silvacane present?" He nervously considered the newer Camarga.

There was a moment of stillness. She knew that Brillat was aware that Queen Abonde had permitted two of Solenn's attendants to be aware of the Camargas' secret, but even so, it was an awkward subject to broach aloud after thousands of years of secrecy. Finally, Brillat bobbed his head, mane tossing.

Jean released a long exhalation, as if still in disbelief about what he was going to say. "I must thank you now for your aid to my comrades. If ever you both are in need of anything, please, do inform myself or Lieutenant Talia." He bowed from his place on horseback, then rode a short distance away.

Solenn and Ada dismounted and removed the saddles from Brillat and Aveyron. Aveyron took the satchel strap in his teeth, and then he and his father trotted for the scant cover of nearby brush.

Solenn faced away. "They have no qualms about nudity but act out of respect for me, though I *have* seen male bodies before." She spoke Verdanian. For the sake of subterfuge, they'd brought no lantern. Her voice, strained as it was, would have to suffice.

Ada hesitated in a way that indicated she needed time to understand what Solenn had said. "I've seen thousands," she said in a rueful way. "Privacy is nonexistent in the army. I notice you're speaking Verdanian. They don't know Braizian?"

"They don't," she said.

"That makes sense, considering where they hail from."

"By the way, supper was delicious," Solenn said, yearning to address the topic while she could. "But I'm especially grateful that you introduced the screen."

"My mentors always said that being a Chef meant more than reliance on my blessed tongue," Ada said, looking away as if shy. "It's about how best to enjoy food. Perceiving what people need beyond their preferred flavors."

Solenn considered that statement. "On the topic of perception, I couldn't sense Gyst at all during that confrontation earlier, nor did he make an effort to control me. Removing my tongue seems to have worked to prevent his efforts, but I still perceive when Selland is near."

"Erwan always could, too, though he hasn't a drop of Chef's acumen," Ada mused. "Your entire self is Gods-touched, Solenn, and as you already know, that's both blessing and curse. Flex those blessings like a muscle to compensate for the less-pleasant aspects."

Flex those blessings like a muscle. She liked that idea.

The two Silvacane men joined them. Both were tall and thin, their silver hair loose to their shoulders. By starlight, their skin was even paler than that of ginger Braizians. Their loose clothes were hemp, and Brillat's trousers reached only to midcalf. He had an expression of tolerant discomfort as he walked in his unfamiliar wooden shoes.

Solenn was keenly aware of the late hour and the early start required in the morn. Therefore, once greetings were made, she asked Ada to tell them of Gyst's attack in the cellar. That done, Solenn then explained her plans from here. "I'm going to Nont tomorrow to petition my grandparents on behalf of an alliance between Braiz and the kin, and to state that I must leave the country."

Ada frowned. "You're still restricted in what you can reveal to them, aren't you?"

"Yes. But I can't let that stop me. I'll say what I'm permitted."

"They won't want you to leave," Ada added gently. "Not even with a full battalion."

"I know." Solenn really didn't need the reminders of the impossibility of her position. She had to try nevertheless.

"I assume you've been engaging in diplomatic correspondence with . . . others beyond the veil?" asked Ada. Solenn knew Adamantine was aware that the place existed but not its name or who held power there.

"I've been sending and intercepting missives on Solenn's behalf, but the process is slow," said Aveyron.

Solenn could tolerate the slowness if she were making progress with Queen Abonde, but the leader of the Coterie had refused to loosen her restrictions in any way. As the queen couldn't risk walking the human world, Solenn would need to go to her—somehow—and make an emphatic appeal.

"Your priority must be that Braiz cease use of epicurea," Brillat said. "No alliance can move forward until that's accomplished."

Solenn bristled. As if she weren't aware of that necessary, frustrating stipulation.

Ada burst out a bitter laugh. "To ask *that* as war begins assures that Braiz will fail. They don't utilize ingredients as aggressively as Verdania and Albion, but they still rely on magicked soldiers and healing agents."

"Our kin won't ally themselves with humans who empower themselves by our corpses," Brillat said plainly.

Solenn addressed Ada. "My greatest predicament is that I can't explain to my grandparents why humans must cease to use magic." She wasn't even permitted to state that epicurea was derived from civilized beings.

"You'd face a terrible challenge even if you *could* describe why," Ada murmured.

Aveyron swept his arm to indicate their group. "We truly set the example that should be used as we proceed. Change can happen. Who among the kin would have ever thought we'd ally with a Chef, and an empathetic one at that? Or that she'd willingly eschew epicurea once she knew the truth of its origins?"

"If we could start small . . . ," Solenn murmured. She pressed her hands together, looking to the salt-crystal stars, breathing in the mustiness of wet grass. She thought of the sailors bobbing among the rocks and who among the kin they would have trusted with their welfare. "Krakens."

"I beg your pardon?" said Brillat.

She wasn't sure if he couldn't understand her speech or if her tangent had confused him, or both. "Krakens," she repeated. "Braizian sailors hold deep reverence for krakens as Selland's mightiest children in the Sleeve Sea. They do not attack or eat kraken, not even if they're starving. That would be sacrilege." Truth was, among sailors, cannibalism would be more acceptable than eating kraken. People were people; krakens were part of the divine. Albion, though it was an island largely reliant on the sea, didn't agree, and had ruthlessly hunted krakens in recent years. But then, to them, anything magical was fair game for exploitation.

"Comtesse Esme Alarie had kraken steaks in her stores," Ada said quietly. "It's not a popular dish in Verdania. I can only imagine her kraken-derived ingredients were destined for Albion."

"They were," said Brillat. He would know, having read the full manifests.

"If more people understood they could trust a living magical ally, they wouldn't need to rely on epicurea," said Solenn. "There will always be exceptions to that, of course. People who crave personal power. People like Lord Whitney."

She thought again of the Port of Nont disaster and wondered if Lord Whitney had conspired to cause that as well. It was another matter to investigate when she was in the city on the morrow.

"Speaking of Lord Whitney and his machinations," said Adamantine. "Earlier tonight, I was with Aveyron when some kind of potent epicurea flew overhead, going southward. When I say 'potent,' I don't simply mean a Chef enhanced its power. Hester is the only thing I've encountered that was mightier."

Solenn's breath caught as she met Aveyron's eye. Queen Abonde was the only entity she'd met who was remotely similar to the presence of the Gods. Could this be . . . was Albion using dragon ingredients in their attack on the continent?

Brillat and Aveyron looked decidedly uncomfortable. Solenn knew from previous experience that they weren't permitted to speak of Queen Abonde's existence.

Adamantine studied them with pursed lips. "Aveyron, you recognized what it was, didn't you?"

"I can't know anything with certainty," he said.

She rolled her eyes in exasperation. "We can't stay here all night. You—"

"Don't ask what they can't answer," said Solenn. She really wanted confirmation of this horrible shift in war tactics as well. "You already suspect what this was. Ask about *that* alone."

"You *are* your father's child. A natural mediator." Ada's fond expression flashed with grief as she addressed the Silvacanes. "Very well. In Chef's lore, there's one flying creature regarded as the best of all: dragons. One hasn't been reliably sighted in Verdania in something like three hundred years. Could Albion be utilizing dragon in their attack?"

Aveyron and Brillat shared a grim look before Brillat answered. "It's possible. Dragons are nearly extinct in most of the world, but there are known to be enclaves in Caldia." Caldia: the northern highlands of the same isle as Albion, said to be remote and beautiful. The denizens there had warred with Albion for centuries but remained under strict rule.

"Why are dragons considered the best of all epicurea?" asked Solenn. The tales she knew focused on their beauty and ferocity.

Brillat sighed. "Because, to their grief, most every single body part of a dragon is imbued with crackling magical might, especially within the scope of war. Considering the size of their bodies—as large as multi-story Lutecian buildings—their potential to empower soldiers is beyond compare."

"They are the chickens of the magical world," Ada muttered. When Brillat recoiled with blatant offense, she hastily continued, "Because every single part of them can be used. Nothing in a chicken goes to waste."

Aveyron guffawed. "The parallel rings true, awful as it is," he said. Brillat humphed, his look of irritation fading.

"I suppose that's one more thing I should be wary of as I cross Verdania," Ada said, her gaze flicking to the heavens.

"How early are we leaving?" Brillat asked Adamantine.

Her eyebrows rose. "I hadn't presumed to ask you to endure that hard journey again."

He stiffened, his posture noble in his poor clothes. "I'm a Camarga. I'm built for endurance. It would take you over a week to make the trip with a string of mundane horses. You need steady speed. Besides, if I were to presume anything, it would be that I am also counted as among Erwan Corre's friends. He is an unusual man, kind and thoughtful. I will not see him ill used by Verdania."

But Erwan may already be dead, Ada's risky venture in vain. *Everything* they were doing may well be in vain. Maybe the Gods were carrying them on a doomed course, like the dead sailors bobbing to the beach.

Solenn's fists clenched. No. She must maintain hope. She was alive. She had chosen to stay alive—she had rejected death and divinity to be present here now. This fight wasn't yet done, not for her or Adamantine, and not for Erwan.

"I'll stay with Solenn, of course," said Aveyron. She shot him a grateful smile.

Ada deliberated for a moment. "Before, I picked up on some hints that you can relay messages by cats. Can we communicate with each other by those means from afar?"

"Do you see cats here?" Brillat spread out his arms. "No? All cats carry inherent power—they are required to divide their time between worlds, as must we all—but few carry sufficient amounts to act as escorts or couriers. Fewer still would willingly do so."

"Cats will be cats." Ada gave her head a rueful shake.

Solenn took Ada's hand. "Be careful. Erwan wouldn't want you to sacrifice yourself to save him. I don't want you to do that either."

"Noted." Ada squeezed her hand. Her fingers felt incredibly strong. "I love you, Solenn. I always have. I'm fiercely proud of you. Trust in your intuition."

Trust in her own intuition. Faith in herself. Wise words, when the Gods had proved themselves fickle.

CHAPTER EIGHT

SOLENN

When Braizian farmers kill their pig for next year's salt pork, some brine from the previous year is always added. "Salt remembers," they like to say. The old brine will teach the new its duties. Bakers carry on bread dough in much the same way. In their case, they say, "The unknowns know what to do." Similarly, among people, we elders teach the younger. And so life lessons carry on. And so we try to survive.

—August Chef Gurvan of the city of Nont
in Braiz

Solenn had always found Nont to be a beautiful city. Now, even in partial ruins, she found it to be more so.

Its buildings were arranged in tiers along a steep granite slope, her grandparents' sprawling royal château as the spired crown. From that high vantage point, on a clear day, a watcher with a spyglass could make out the faint white chalk cliffs of Albion. Farther down, where the city stretched out like the base of a soup bowl, the land remained mostly empty where the shore met the water. Much of the blackened earth and debris were gone, blank brown in their place. Out in the bay, some initial work was underway to rebuild the long fingers of the piers that had burned. She'd heard estimates that it'd take five years to complete the rebuilding of the naval facilities.

Five years. Would Braiz even exist as an autonomous country at that point, or would it be a colony of Albion?

No. Nont was tenacious, as was the rest of Braiz. She would fight to make certain her kingdom remained free.

They rode through the city to the Grand Pentad, the largest kitchen-temple in Braiz. It followed the standard interlocking pentagon format of all pentads, but bigger, taller, its roof peaked high like an antiquated coiffe. The gray stone walls wore smoke damage with pride. Half the blue-green slate roof was new, as portions had burned in the conflagration.

Solenn was here not for worship, but for a respectful conference. As part of that, Jean's saddlebag carried a massive bread boule made fresh in Malo that morning.

Lunch had obviously just been served for those in need, the scent of cooked pork lingering in the air. Talia spoke with an acolyte, who set off to find August Chef Gurvan. Solenn trod softly through the echoing nave. Painted blue skies and clouds covered the ceiling high above. She had most frequently attended the small pentad in Malo on Sellandsdays, but she'd always appreciated the beauty and scale of this place, where she came for high holidays and family events.

Gurvan joined her as she stood before the broad hearth of Hester's chamber. The flames steadily burned.

"Good to see you again, Princess," he said, chipper despite a certain lack of sleep. He wore a stained smock over his formal regalia in Braizian blue. "How can I be of assistance today?"

She motioned to Jean, who passed her his laden hemp bag. He then joined Talia at the entrance to ensure Solenn had privacy. Most penitents would be visiting Selland's room.

I must discuss matters with you in confidence. After Gurvan vowed to do so, Solenn continued writing. *I request that you act as a mediator between myself and Hester. I need to gain greater understanding of her.*

His craggy face looked thoughtful. "You wrote to me with several questions about the Gods during your convalescence as well." He'd tended to her during her first week back in Malo. "How can I help?"

As you've witnessed, I have a close connection with Selland. How can I encourage a greater bond with Hester, beyond feeding her? Solenn hefted the bag. She could smell the bread, and he likely could as well.

"Food is a good way to work your way into anyone's heart, but as for Hester . . . she is all about the meaning of home. You should understand you're in her home too." Seeing her blank expression, he smiled and continued. "Much emphasis is placed on Braiz being Selland's and Verdania being Hester's, but those are truly near-modern political divides. In the time when Hester walked the continent, kingdoms didn't exist as they do now. There were hundreds of petty tribes trying to survive. Hester traversed what is now Braiz with great regularity."

That's why Hester ponds are found here. The small bodies of water were most commonly found in the hills. Old tales said Hester caused them by pacing Verdania's land, but Solenn now knew her massive stone feet likely made the imprints in Braiz as well.

"Exactly. So in truth, Hester is our native-born God as much as she is Verdania's. Would you like me to present that bread to her?" he asked. She handed him the bag, and they both knelt on the woven rug before the fire. His calloused hands stroked the crispy rind.

Can you tell me what you sense of her as you make the offering?

"Of course, Princess." He closed his eyes, then tossed in the bread. Flames leaped to accept the gift. Gurvan opened his eyes as he sat back on his haunches. "Much is made of Hester's rage in our current stories, but old literature portrays her in a more complicated manner. As an empathetic Chef, I've often detected wordless yearning from her. Right now I knew a wave of . . . sadness and hope . . . together. Do you understand why that is?"

Solenn nodded but made no effort to elaborate, instead asking, *What makes Hester happy, other than food?*

He reared back in surprise. "Well! That's something I've never before been asked. People come here to thank Hester for making *them* happy, for fostering a cozy home. But as to what pleases her . . . there may be some disagreement on this among my comrades, but I think she's the God most outwardly like us. Hester doesn't hide her frustration—or her joy. She's the least stoic. If she's like many expressive people I've known, then acknowledgment means much. She wants validation. Love."

To think, a God who craved such attention had been largely deprived for thousands of years. Hours or days of solitary confinement could drive a person to absolute despair. Hester's prison of her own making had been so much worse.

"I have been asked before, many times, about what makes *Selland* happy," Gurvan continued. "I don't have an easy answer for that either. Unlike the other Gods, he doesn't ask for offerings. He simply . . . is. That's very difficult for people to accept. We naturally want definitive answers. Nothing about Selland is definitive."

Solenn hadn't intended to ask about Selland, but she was glad for this insightful tangent. *He's a fluid God.*

"Yes. There's an ebb and flow to all he does. In our earliest canon, Selland is a woman, the mother of the ocean in partnership with Lait. Only a millennium ago did the language shift toward the masculine. Who knows? Maybe in a hundred years, a future August Chef will somehow be informed that Selland prefers another address." He shrugged. "We'll be fluid as he bids us."

Solenn liked that Selland had a past connection with the feminine. It made her feel closer to him; maybe that helped him to understand her, too, whereas Gyst had never made an effort. In many ways, Gyst came across as the worst kind of man, steeped in his own arrogance and righteousness.

She pushed herself to stand, Gurvan joining her. *Thank you for your time today.*

He splayed five fingers against his heart. "I hope I was able to help not only you but Hester. I should revisit some books I haven't read in decades and contemplate her nature more. I thank you for that." After bowing to the fire and to Solenn in turn, he walked away.

Solenn remained in place to tear her current page from her table book, adding it to the fire. The sheet instantly blackened and curled to ashes.

She rejoined Talia and Jean. She'd already scheduled a meeting with her grandparents later in the afternoon. That meant they had time for another important stop first.

The royal prison was halfway up the slope between the Grand Pentad and the château. She had never been inside before, and regarded the impregnable-looking granite exterior with impatience as Talia and Jean addressed the matter of her admission at the gate. The gendarmes, and the chief who soon emerged, were in denial that Princess Solenn herself would want to visit such a horrid place. Despite their rapiers and badges, Talia's and Jean's very credentials were called into question, as they weren't in uniform. They'd done their utmost to blend in with the crowds, Camarga aside. The matter was finally resolved when several musketeers stationed in the facility, drawn by the drama, testified to their identities and that of Solenn.

While this got Solenn within the bailey, her progress remained obstructed.

"Oh, Princess, you cannot go to the prisoners' cells. They are set deep, very deep!" protested the chief. Despite the brisk air, the man sweated profusely. She wondered what he was hiding but had to admit to herself that after the previous night's events, entering a domain favored by Gyst didn't appeal to her.

Have the Everett sailors brought to me in an upstairs room. Not like this was an ideal place either. Despite its oppressive stonework, the whole building was imbued with a level of dankness that implied mold and rot, and the officials she'd met thus far seemed gangrenous of the soul to match.

The man dripped sweat. "I confess, two of the sailors are quite ill. The third man, however—"

"Bring him," snapped Lieutenant Talia in her most commanding voice, which was quite fearsome after four decades of soldiering plus numerous children and grandchildren.

Do you believe that the sailors are actually ill? she wrote to Jean and Talia as they waited in a small interior room. They both understood what she truly wanted to know.

"Being kept in such deprivation does lead to illness and shortened lives," Talia said. "And yet . . ."

"These sailors are hated more than taxes these days," mused Jean. "They wouldn't be treated well." An understatement, quite likely. These sailors were convicted of starting the fire that had obliterated the fleet, killing thousands of people and harming far more. The guards here would have lost homes and families. No, no, the sailors wouldn't be treated well at all, which made Solenn's visit all the more important.

"This place reeks of despair like a summertime cesspool," muttered Talia, gazing around with blatant disgust. "It should be razed by Graecian fire. We need to treat prisoners better than this. We're not *Verdania.*"

Graecian fire was the stuff of legend, a concocted weapon of war that burned hotter than normal fire, even doing so atop water. "I feel like I need to bathe after even standing here," said Jean, tugging at his tunic.

Solenn agreed with their sentiments.

After an annoyingly long wait, the naval cartographer Aotrou Corentin shuffled in under escort, his hands and ankles bound by hemp rope. He was a walking skeleton, his skin pale as bone. He probably hadn't seen the sun in half a year. He gazed upon her, his eyes bulging in a gaunt face lined by a shaggy yellow beard. Moisture beaded his hair and darkened his shirt; he'd evidently been hastily cleaned.

Bring a chair for him. She wrote with anger that threatened to break her thick pencil. The chamber had but one chair, brought for her use.

The guard balked. "A chair can be a weapon, Princess. We can hold him up—"

"We will speak with him in privacy," said Jean, a hand on his rapier. "A chair, now, or the Princess will gladly give hers to him." Solenn promptly nodded.

A moment later, a guard returned with a wooden chair. The gendarmes departed. Corentin collapsed into the seat. Talia shuffled to stand at his side, letting him lean on her. Sympathy and anger curved her brow; Solenn had told her companions about her reasons for this interview, but the abuse committed against this man should've been considered grievous even if he were guilty.

Corentin showed no flicker of reaction as Princess Solenn was introduced to him. His fatigued condition would make it all the more difficult for him to understand her speech, Solenn realized. She turned to a fresh page in the table book.

As she wrote, Talia read the words aloud. "Do you remember the night of the fire?"

"Better than my own name. Better than any other event in my life." He spoke in a bare, broken whisper. "I've relived that night a thousand times as I try to understand what happened. I don't remember setting a fire. I'd been drinking with shipmates. We were on shore leave after weeks at sea, traveling between Rochy and Nont. Storms made the way feel especially long."

Solenn nodded encouragement. She'd only ridden once to Rochy, Braiz's farthest south and west port against the Blue, but as a child the rainy journey had felt incredibly long to her as well.

"What do you last remember before the fire?" Talia asked.

He stared into the wall, blankness in his eyes. "I laughed at some joke. Then everything was black. I opened my eyes. I was on the cobbles. It was hard to think, but I knew I wasn't drunk. I don't get drunk." He said this with conviction. "There's no fun in being sick. I did that once, and that was enough." That matched his testimony in her notes. "My friends were nearby. I tried to rouse them. I couldn't. I became aware of nearby bells. Yells. Screams. There were crackles—a mighty fire." He looked down, a hand pressed to his face.

"What happened then?" Jean asked with gentleness from his post near the door.

"Port gendarmes rushed upon me. 'You did it, you did it,' they said. 'What did I do?' I asked them. I was confused. 'The fire,' they said, but that didn't help me to understand. I still don't understand." His voice faded.

The people who witnessed your fire-setting were never identified, correct?

"The prosecutors had ten statements from gendarmes who said that people had pointed to us, saying they saw us do it, but the actual witnesses are known only to Gyst." During the trial, the assumption had been laid forth that the witnesses had likely died in the fire. That now felt too convenient to Solenn.

How can I help?

That question caused his gaze to rise and finally meet Talia's eyes, then hers. "I want to see my children and wife again. And the sea. I miss the sea." The words emerged, limp, his voice as dry as high sand dunes. He sounded as though he hadn't had water in hours.

Solenn requested refreshment for herself but had none of it. Talia helped Corentin drink as Solenn stepped into the hallway with Jean.

What royal rights do I have here?

He sighed. "None, truly. They could have denied letting you speak with him at all, but were too shocked by your arrival to do so. The very nature of the sailors' imprisonment is ordained by your grandfather's pen."

That meant that they couldn't be moved to other rooms, but perhaps other elements of their care were still within her purview.

The chief awaited her down the hallway, nervous curiosity upon his rounded face. His expression went slack as she spoke with slow deliberation.

"Corentin said nothing about his life and treatment here, but his condition raises concerns. I would like to review the logs for his meals and water."

Such logs were required and were easy to check off without doing anything at all, but when the chief sputtered about backlogs and ill jailors, she knew the staff here hadn't even made that effort.

She kept her gaze cool. "I'll bring your lax recordkeeping to the attention of the king and queen this very afternoon. I'll also request an investigator be sent here to check on the prisoners' cells, food stores, and treatment." She knew the very woman to request for this duty too: the sailors' lawyer, whom Solenn hadn't met but knew to be their stalwart defender. The chief blinked for a moment, evidently needing time to interpret her speech, then spouted denials and apologies. She turned away in undisguised disgust.

Solenn and her musketeers exited, the man groveling in her wake. "We'll get to the château with perfect timing," said Jean, checking his pocket watch as they reclaimed their horses.

Solenn rested a hand against Aveyron's neck, bowing her head next to him. "Albion caused the fire and set up the *Everett's* sailors to take the blame," she whispered to him. "I'm certain of this, even though there's no evidence."

Not here in Nont, anyway. Any proof would be across the Sleeve Sea, likely in Lord Whitney's bureau. That was a thought to revisit later.

⌒

"Mamm-gozh, Tad," Solenn said as she bowed before her grandmother and father within the private parlor. Her grandfather, she'd been told, had to attend meetings elsewhere, and she took no offense in that. With war preparations underway, she was grateful to even have this audience.

Mamm-gozh wore traditional garb in fine fabric, her spring blouse embroidered with appropriately in-season flowers. Her layered silk skirts ended at midcalf, showing stockings and gleaming black sabots. Her white coiffe extended a stiff three inches atop her head, broad lace tendrils dangling to her shoulders. Tad's garb, like Solenn's own, reflected contemporary influences from Verdania with a buttoned justaucorps and trousers, but included Braizian lace and embroidery.

"Oh, Solenn." Mamm-gozh stood and held out her arms. Solenn embraced her plump form, her table book pressing against her hipbone awkwardly. Her grandmother's body had always reminded her of stacked pillows, warm and ready to burrow into on a sad day. She smelled of rose water. As Solenn pulled back, she had to study her face closely. Mamm-gozh's wrinkles showed in all their glory; she hadn't ingested rose fairies recently. Good.

Tad stood and clasped her hands. His smile was tight. When he gazed upon her, it was with considerable worry. And guilt.

In her convalescent days right after her return, she'd tried to assure him that what had befallen her in Verdania wasn't his fault, but she could tell the written words had failed as a balm.

Solenn could have claimed a chair now, joining them in an informal circle at the hearth, but instead she backed to the rug again to face them. Tad observed her position with an arched eyebrow. Solenn had just established a serious tone for this conversation.

"I must speak to you on important matters," Solenn said. "As my voice wears out fast, I have asked Mouskeder Talia ar Malo to provide assistance with my first point." She hated delegating, but she also understood her own limitations, and didn't want to fully rely on her table book. Talia advanced from where the other musketeers lurked near the doors, dropping to one knee before the queen and prince. She rose after they gestured her up.

"I am of the belief that Albion is behind the fire that devastated Nont last year," Solenn said. They took in this statement with thoughtful expressions.

Solenn had outlined her argument for Talia. Hands at her back in parade rest, the lieutenant recalled with precision Solenn's observations on the vastness of Albion's plot, their obvious advance preparations for the current war, and relevant details from the conflagration and recent testimony.

"Do you, good musketeer, agree with the princess's assessment?" Tad asked in his frank way. Like his father, the king, he always welcomed the thoughts of those presumed beneath him. Solenn could never imagine King Caristo doing such a thing.

"I do, Majesty," said Talia.

"The sailors remain convicted based on witness testimony, insubstantial as it is," said Tad. "We cannot free them. They would be massacred in the streets. Their families already live within the protection of their local pentads."

"We could use sailors of their experience aboard ships right now too," said Mamm-gozh, sighing. "But shipmates must trust each other."

"We'd need evidence as heavy as the City-Eaten-by-the-Sea to release them, and for them to be truly free and safe in public," said Tad. "But that said, we can attend to the matter of their treatment."

"Thank you." Solenn motioned to Talia, who bowed as she retreated. Solenn had saved her voice to represent herself as she made her next statements. "Now to address the most vital reason for my visit. I need to take my leave of Braiz to engage in a diplomatic effort for the sake of the realm. I cannot reveal where I'm going or whom I am speaking with, but I will not be meeting with Albion or Verdania. Nor am I presenting myself for marriage."

"This . . . diplomatic endeavor. Does this connect with what you have left unsaid about what happened to you as you fled Verdania?" asked Tad, even more worry lining his face.

"Yes."

Her grandmother and father shared glances. She wondered at their private speculations regarding her escape, how Ada had come to be involved, and why she had truly resorted to severing her own tongue.

"What do you bring forth in these negotiations?" Tad asked. He and Mamm usually handled international diplomacy on behalf of Braiz. Solenn had learned everything from her parents and called upon those early lessons now as she spoke slowly to think through each word.

"I'm not offering anything on Braiz's behalf now. It is too early. Right now, I need to listen to the other party."

Her grandmother's hands rested upon the roundness of her belly, which was emphasized by her high-waisted skirt. "I'm concerned for your well-being, and that of Braiz. We love you. You could be kidnapped or killed, or the other side could use you to manipulate us. Verdania and Albion have already attempted to use you in such ways and would do so again if given the opportunity."

"Where *could* you possibly be going, if not those countries?" asked Tad. By his hard tone, Solenn could already tell he wasn't likely to be persuaded. "The Confederated Duchies are closest to us, but still over a week away from Nont. Lucania and Hesperia—you would spend weeks in transit, and that alone is dangerous."

Solenn didn't hide her gestured appeal to Selland. "I wish I could say more. There's danger in this mission, of course, but I trust the party with which I'm meeting. They have the honor of Braizians."

Tad shook his head. "We almost lost you, Solenn. I cannot approve of this . . . mysterious effort." He gestured Gyst's X.

If only he knew the sordid enjoyment that Gyst was surely experiencing at this moment. She could imagine how he would crow in her head: *See? If you had* my *help, you would've succeeded!*

But he was only present in her mind through her imagination. Her mind and body were hers. Her success—or failure—would be her own. She took strength in that.

"But I wasn't lost. I'm here," she said.

Tears glistened in his eyes. "Your outward injuries have barely healed at this point. You must stay safe, Solenn."

"Safe?" Her voice rose. "Over a thousand of our sailors likely died this past day. I personally looked a hundred of the dead in the face—had they a face at all. War comes at us from every side. Any safety here is temporary."

Mamm-gozh shifted in her seat. "I agree."

Solenn checked a gasp of relief.

"None of us is truly safe," the older woman said, "not here, not now. We had word this morning that Albion's soldiers are coming ashore in the east, as they have in so many past wars, but this time everything about them feels different. They want to crush us and move onward. You, Solenn, have already outwitted them recently. They won't have liked that one bit."

"And that's exactly why she must be where we can guard her. We should have fifty musketeers around her, not two!" declared Tad, his cheeks flushing.

Fifty? She wouldn't be able to go anywhere or do anything!

Mamm-gozh sighed. "That's my first inclination as well. That's why I asked after her well-being first." She shifted to address Solenn directly. "You're right. You're alive and home now because of the choices you made on your own. You've shown good judgment. We need to respect that."

"Has she?" Tad's tone was unusually harsh. "We don't know what happened. There are gaps and mysteries in her story, though not near as many as in this endeavor she proposes."

At that, a full argument broke out between her father and grandmother. Her family didn't normally raise their voices in such a manner, but then, their tempers were likely frayed after being awake half the night awaiting updates on the lost ships.

So many more vessels would be lost if she didn't get to Arcady to palaver with Queen Abonde.

Solenn approached the fireplace. Did this drama amuse Hester the way it must delight Gyst? That possibility made her angry. Solenn wanted cooperation between people, Gods, and the Coterie. Why did everyone insist on making everything as difficult as possible?

She grabbed the fireplace poker and ash shovel and clanged them together. The argument stopped.

"I can't yell over you," Solenn said simply. At the far side of the room, one of the musketeers emitted a soft snort. "Please give me leave to make this effort. Otherwise, we may be doomed, and you know that.

You know how our fleet compares to Albion's. You know how our army compares to Verdania's. If things continue as they are now, we will lose."

"You can't say that, Solenn," said Tad. "You are speaking of Braiz!"

She bowed as a show of respect but continued, softly, "I love Braiz too much to lie."

Her father rubbed his clean-shaven face, his cheeks flushed with emotion, and he offered no counterpoint. He suddenly stiffened in his seat, gazing past her. Solenn turned to see that another musketeer had entered.

The woman bowed as she stepped forward. "Prince Morvan, Queen Privela. The admirals have assembled. King Myles requests your attendance."

"Very well," said Tad. "Inform him that we'll be there within the quarter hour." Beside him, Mamm-gozh nodded, her lips tightly pursed. "Solenn, stay tonight in Nont. Unless some other matter arises, tomorrow we'll return to Malo together."

That was that. The issue was declared done. She'd return to Malo to be cosseted there until Albion overwhelmed the coast and continued inland. Mamm-gozh was likely right too—Albion wasn't setting up for siege warfare. They were going to push hard through Braiz.

The messenger departed with a bow. Mamm-gozh rustled past, her lack of farewell implying to Solenn that they'd speak more later, likely at dinner.

Tad approached Solenn, his expression sorrowful. She shook her head, unwilling to waste more precious words on him. She whirled around and left, Talia and Jean falling into step beside her.

"Princess, where do we go now?" Jean asked softly.

Where indeed?

"Dimezell." One of her grandmother's musketeers beckoned, whispering, "If you would follow me?" With a quick look around, she followed. Down a hallway she went, Talia and Jean alert at her heels. They were led inside an archival room rich with fragrant paper and ink. The door closed behind her.

Mamm-gozh and three of her other attendants awaited inside. Her cheeks were flushed and her breaths fast. She'd evidently hurried here.

Solenn dropped to a knee, head bowed. "Majesty." Dare she hope . . . ?

"Rise, Solenn," Mamm-gozh said briskly. "I know you felt you needed to make your request formally, but really, sometimes it's best to avoid such channels. You're young, though. Of course your first instinct is to do things *properly*." When Solenn opened her mouth to argue, her grandmother shook her head. "Oh, I understand that you couldn't simply *go*. You know your musketeers would be punished for dereliction of duty. Nor would you want us to worry excessively—or to scatter our forces in search of you." Solenn nodded. Mamm-gozh gestured to the musketeer who had guided Solenn. "Assemble travel supplies suitable for a young woman, with quick discretion." He hurried away.

"Mamm-gozh, what are you—"

"Mouskeder Talia ar Malo. Mouskeder Jean ar Malo," Mamm-gozh said, ignoring Solenn but for a wink. "I require you to attend me."

Queen Privela was claiming Talia and Jean as her own, superseding Solenn's authority.

The two musketeers bowed. "As Your Majesty wishes," they said in unison.

"You are to wait in this room for the next hour, after which time you'll serve me."

They bowed in concession. Talia wouldn't look at Solenn. Jean appeared outright aggrieved, his lips a tight line. She wished she could explain more to them, but their ignorance was necessary. They'd be questioned. It was risky enough that they knew about the double nature of the Silvacanes.

"Permit me a minute." Solenn wrote a quick letter to Tad, offering no apology but that her absence would worry him. She folded the letter and pressed it into Talia's hand. Solenn turned to her grandmother, not ready to say farewell just yet. *I know you have little time to spare, but would you like to see my Camarga? His name is Aveyron.*

As she suspected, Mamm-gozh's expression lit up at the very suggestion. "Of course!"

Accompanied by her grandmother and her other musketeers, Solenn left her usual company behind. She kept her table book in her hands.

Why? she scribbled, angling her table book to show Mamm-gozh alone as they left the room. Their pace was leisurely, nothing alarming about their movements, though Solenn had to keep nodding as people in the busy corridor greeted her.

"You're right," Mamm-gozh said in a low voice after they'd walked for a minute. "If Braiz doesn't form a new alliance or alter its strategy, we will . . ." She stopped speaking, obviously upset. "I do not like these mysteries around you, though. They stink of Gyst." She wrinkled her nose. She had always been sensitive to odors, favoring her rose water. "When you return, and you *will* return, you will speak truthfully with me. If you can," she added, no doubt understanding that Solenn would be forthright if allowed.

Solenn nodded. They traveled down the stairs. As they paused for soldiers to pass, she wrote, *I have an important request of you. Stop using rose fairies.*

"Stop—" In surprise, Mamm-gozh had started to read aloud. "Whyever would you ask such a thing?" Her grandmother used no other epicurea unless she was severely ill.

Solenn shook her head, frustrated, then mouthed, "Please."

"Well!" Mamm-gozh sounded a bit huffy. "Such an act of vanity is hardly appropriate amid war, so this is no great sacrifice on my part. Very well. I will not indulge in them again, but you *will* explain this request to me at some point."

Solenn nodded in relief. She'd brought yet one more person in accordance with Queen Abonde's demand—only a few hundred thousand more to go. *You don't need them anyway.* At that, her grandmother humphed, but sounded pleased. Truly, she was a handsome woman. She didn't need the fake prettiness that the eaten fairies could bestow upon her for the span of a party.

Upon their entry to the stable, grooms gathered, ready to lend aid. Mamm-gozh asked them to saddle Solenn's Camarga while she stood at his bare head.

"He has excellent points," Mamm-gozh said. "He makes me yearn for the Camarga I had when I was a girl. Margotton came and went across twenty years of my life. I never knew when I might go to the stable or field to find her gone, or for her to have returned. I miss her. I always will." Aveyron listened with perked ears.

Solenn had been raised on Mamm-gozh's tales—another reason she'd pleaded for a Camarga of her own as a child, only to be reminded repeatedly that such horses couldn't be bought. Now she understood that Margotton had likely left to cross the veil, reunite with family, and live in human form for a time. Oh, how Solenn wished she could reveal the truth to her grandmother and ease the heartbreak that lingered still.

Maybe on her return she could do so. Maybe.

As the grooms departed, her grandmother's other musketeer returned. Solenn accepted the laden pack with a smile even as Aveyron laid back his ears, stomping a foreleg upon the straw-covered earth.

After a moment to think, Solenn understood his reaction. Epicurea had been packed for her. That was fine—they'd return the remains to Arcady, where they belonged. She grabbed the additional bag with his clothes, which Jean had left hanging nearby, and fastened both to the back of the saddle.

Mamm-gozh took in their interaction with a wistful expression. "You take good care of her," she said to Aveyron. Mamm-gozh turned her imperious gaze to Solenn. "Represent us well. May Selland fill your sail and season your days."

Solenn pinched her fingers as a returned blessing and then mounted up. Aveyron needed no guidance. No one had been told to stop her at the gate; no one anticipated that she'd leave against her family's blessing. Or, rather, most of her family's blessing.

Outside the château, Aveyron sped his walk downhill, traffic thick in the afternoon. Only after they were through the city gates did he rise to a canter, soon leaving behind the city, the ocean, the road. The wind pushed at Solenn's back as if to nudge them faster, faster. Tears of cold and sorrow filled her eyes and dried in trails down her cheeks.

She was profoundly grateful for her grandmother's support, but leaving like this would only make her job more challenging upon her return. As an ambassador, she needed to work *with* her full family as she negotiated between parties.

When she returned to Braiz, would her parents and grandfather listen to her at all, or would she be locked away for her safekeeping like the poor sailors of the *Everett*?

CHAPTER NINE

SOLENN

To make fish chowder, take a variety of freshwater fish, eel being the most essential. Be certain to have at least two bottles of dry white wine or cider for the broth, and more for serving.

—Excerpt from *Book for Cooks to Excel as Do Chefs*

Solenn and Aveyron rode for hours. After a while, Aveyron finally slowed, ears perked, staring west toward hills furred with broom and gorse. His nostrils uplifted, testing the air.

"What is it?" she asked in a bare whisper.

He curved his head to almost touch her knee, then jerked away, repeatedly, pointing to the ground. "You want me to dismount?" At his nod, she did so, then stripped off his saddle. She faced away while he changed form, and by the time he was done, she had unfastened the bags.

"I'll take the pants and shoes for now," he said. She passed them behind her and then looked in the new bag packed on her behalf to check on the food. She found raisins, hazelnuts, walnuts, and a cut from a large boule. Not foods she could easily ingest these days, though they were otherwise good for travel. At least she didn't need to be self-conscious when dining with Aveyron.

"Are we close to the dolmen?" she asked. The old stone remnants of the Hester-blasted city of Ys acted as doorways for nonfeline kin to cross the veil.

"We're almost there, but we need to go that way first. I sense something strange," he said, pointing. "I'll carry the saddle if you take the bags."

They passed through a forest and up along a rocky, brush-heavy slope. He motioned her to move slower. She suddenly wished she had a better weapon at hand than the eating knife at her belt.

They rounded boulders to find a human-size mound wrapped in beeswax-treated cloth. "This isn't the source of the scent," he said. After a quick glance around to confirm no one was hiding close by, he kicked the bundle. Metal rattled beneath. He lifted up one side while she hoisted up the other, revealing a stack of muskets, powder horns, and bags of shot. Near her feet, hemp bags with food stores were sealed in tins—hardtack like that used by sailors, the biscuits cut with scalloped edges like flowers. She'd never seen them shaped like that before. The tins had no words, only etched numbers.

Aveyron tapped her on the arm, motioning her to come. He audibly sniffed the air. Leaving the supplies uncovered, their saddle and bags on the ground, she followed him farther along the ridge. He began to breathe hard, as if he'd been running. Since he faced away from her, it took her a moment to realize that he was mightily fighting the urge to be sick.

"I can't." He finally gasped and turned away, retching.

Before them, she caught a glimpse of another covered lump, but as she walked closer, she found it to be as long as a wagon. Dew had collected in dips along the top, but there was no accumulation of dirt or leaves. This hadn't been here long.

Unlike Aveyron, she smelled nothing. That meant he perceived epicurea. The dead of his kin.

He looked impossibly pale as he rejoined her, and together they folded back the tarpaulin.

Beneath it was a structure made of incredibly long beams of wood with expanses of translucent skin secured to the spans. It put her in mind of a folding travel tent, except there were leather straps and fasteners. Was it a harness of some sort? She found it difficult to picture the object in use, dismantled as it was.

She tugged on a beam, lifting it up. The lightness! She felt like she'd just hoisted a large feather. A feather. The nature of the beams, how they fit together—they reminded her of the mounted skeleton of a bird in her grandfather's library.

"This is a wing. Or wings," she said. What she had taken for wooden poles were bones, magically light. She stroked one. It was smooth, polished, not coarse in the typical way of dried bone. "Remains of a great rare bird? Or . . ." She gasped in horror. "Is this what you and Adamantine sensed flying overhead?"

"Maybe," he said hoarsely. "But with certainty, this is made from what was once a dragon."

The bones, the skin . . . the remains were massive. This, paired with the supplies . . .

"Albion has invaded us on dragon wings."

Someone had flown here. Maybe more than one person, and they'd hauled goods to supply themselves and other agents. The invaders could be in Nont even now, meeting with spies, gathering intelligence, committing sabotage.

"We need to get away from this foul thing," Aveyron said, his voice burbling.

"Can we destroy the wings?"

"Dragons are almost impervious to fire. The bones are strong, but they can break, so the old tales say."

"Can I try—or will Queen Abonde—"

"The greatest offense is for the dead to be further abused, but I can't . . ."

Solenn gestured for him to go back to the supply stash.

She placed her right foot midway along a bone and then, with both hands at the tip, bent it back. The amount of flexibility was incredible—she had the horrible thought that dragon bones would make fantastic long bows—but when the pole had almost bent back double, it finally snapped. The explosion caused her to fall on her backside. She stood, brushing off bone shards with a shudder, then returned to the long bone to break it again, and again. She repeated her attacks on the other wing.

She later found Aveyron digging through the supplies, packing away additional foods for them both. His coloration had improved. "I'll need to eat and drink once we're farther from here."

"Of course. Should we take a gun as proof of what we found?"

"No, let's take this instead." He held up a powder horn. Albionish words were etched into the tusk ivory.

"We can't leave the rest as it is, or it could be utilized. We need to get the powder wet." She paused, considering the distance to a stream, but thought of something else with a vicious grin. "Aveyron, you haven't relieved yourself since we departed. Do you think you might . . . ?"

He laughed weakly. "You're asking me to urinate on the ammunition?" He paused. "That's not a bad idea."

Aveyron attended to the matter, and Solenn deduced that it would be fine to leave the goods exposed to the weather. By the clouds overhead, rain would likely arrive by nightfall.

Only after traveling away and upwind did the pair stop to eat. Thus fortified, they continued another hour to reach the dolmen. The old stones towered in a perfectly circular grove, evening birdsong pleasant. Aveyron reverted to human form and garbed himself.

"Will crossing the veil make me feel sick as it did before?" she asked. She pulled their packs into her lap after she sat on the ground.

"I don't know," he said. "You're the first person to make this trip, with or without a Gods-touched tongue."

The first person in all the world. That still struck Solenn as strange. Why her? Why was she such a focus of divine and magical interest?

She nodded to confirm that she was ready. His fingers stroked the air, as if playing a harp she couldn't see, and then reality dropped from beneath her.

 ࿋

Solenn promptly discovered the answer to her question. The loss of her ability to perceive magic *did* lessen the disorientation and nausea that came with traveling across the veil, but dizziness still kept her grounded for a moment. Full night was underway in Arcady, a dark span of sky above. On this visit, she wasn't greeted with a halberd at her neck as she had been last time. Instead, elaborately armored otter guards stood back about five feet, their halberds in one hand, their empty clawed fists against their chests in respect.

"Ambassador Solenn ar Braiz." The human-size speaker had thick black whiskers that drooped like a mustache, and to her surprise, they spoke Braizian with a river country accent.

And they'd called her "ambassador," not "princess." Despite the worries of the day, she knew an exhilarated tingle. Here, she *did* have respect, and it was respect of her own making.

"Hail, my neighbor," she reciprocated in Braizian. She mimicked their salute, minus the claws. "Were you told to expect us?" At her side, Aveyron groaned, shaking his head to acclimate himself.

"We've been alert at this station in case you were to come. We're to provide you with sustenance and anything else you may need."

What a different welcome this was indeed. "Aveyron?" She switched to Verdanian. "You've done the greater labor today. How long would you like to rest?"

"I need only liquid refreshment and an opportunity to share information."

"My pardon, monsieur." The otter shifted their language as well. "Your kind wouldn't have need of our northern tongue, I suppose."

"No, but I can speak passable Lucanian in marketplaces, as I doubt you can." The otter emitted a soft bray that Solenn interpreted as a laugh. "We bring dire news, of which I'll alert you first."

Aveyron told them of the dismembered dragon as he removed the unicorn tisane that had been packed for Solenn, handing it to a guard for appropriate commemoration. The otters, alarmed by news of the found wings, escorted them inside their station for further conference.

The sturdy cottage was like many found in western Braiz. A hearth fire released pleasant warmth, a fragrant fish chowder in a pot. The familiar clay toadmud floor made her smile. A heavy wooden cupboard rested against a wall, a long table with mismatched chairs in the intervening space. Just as she would expect in a human home like this in Braiz, a doorless cupboard held several bagpipes and oboes. Through an open door to the next room, she caught a glimpse of a double-height box bed of dark wood; the whole barracks would be lined with more such beds. The only thing that wasn't western Braizian was the fish; past Malo, people did not eat much fish because of the harshness of the water. The people there favored pork instead.

She found these similarities and differences to be fascinating. Upon becoming an ambassador to Arcady, one of her earliest questions had been in regard to the dietary habits of the realm's diverse beings; she knew from her parents' work that many negotiations involved social meals, and she needed to avoid offense. As Aveyron had explained it, kin did not eat kin—magic apparently tasted vile to likewise magical beings—and they generally maintained the habits of their "cursed" forms. That meant Camargas, in their human bodies, could and would eat meat and cheese but preferred grains and vegetables. Carnivores still enjoyed meat but, as in the case of these gigantic otters, prepared full meals rather than indulging in raw repast.

"By what name should we call you, good otter?" Solenn asked.

"Captain Emt, a boar of seven years," he said. He pulled a scroll from a cubby, unfurling it on the table to reveal a watercolor map of

Braiz and the borderlands. "The gate you used is here." Emt tapped a long claw.

Aveyron described their route, indicating a rough area in which to find the now-broken dragon wings.

Emt pulled back, whiskers swaying as he shook his head, his tone grave. "A Caldian dragon. Such a loss. We'll deploy scouts throughout the vicinity. There are likely more such wings to be found." She wouldn't have thought an otter could look grieved, but he did, as if aged twenty years in an instant. She had the sudden sense that he'd seen far too much death in his life.

"I hate that you're probably right," Solenn said.

Emt's armor, a cuirass woven of tight braids of red and blue cloth, creaked slightly as he moved around the table. "Some wings may already be unusable. The skies can be as unfriendly as the sea, as our bird friends can attest. The weapons stash you described implies that this is no mere exploratory mission. They're in Braiz to wage war."

"Are there no scouts currently in the vicinity?" she asked.

"Most of the kin in Braiz in this season cannot come to Arcady," Captain Emt said in a gently correcting tone. "They're bound."

"Oh. Of course." Solenn felt bad that her thoughts had focused so much on how kin were abused as epicurea when the greater problem was that Hester had cursed all kin to live six months of the year among people. Some beings had to serve this time in long blocks; others, like cats, could apparently do hours here and there. No matter how their time was served, most had to do so while largely stripped of their magical abilities and other inherent attributes and skills. In the case of these otters, that apparently included a major shift in size and the loss of humanlike speech. "Pardon my ignorance."

"Ignorance in search of enlightenment has no need of apology," said Emt, his words coming across like a common saying. "Excuse me." He walked to the entrance to confer with another otter.

"He seems to understand my speech more readily than many people," she said to Aveyron, her words a bare rasp.

"Remember that not all kin vocalize speech, and many that do have mouths that differ in construction from those of humans. What you may think of as lisps or disordered speech are common here, not unusual or noteworthy."

If only humans could be so accepting, Solenn thought bittersweetly just as Captain Emt returned. "Our scouts are leaving, including a bird carrying word to Queen Abonde. Now, how may we restore you for your journey?"

Aveyron drank water, while Solenn accepted a hot tisane that included honey. Minutes later, Aveyron changed form, and they resumed their journey. Before long, the incredible trees and spires of the magical city came into view. Creatures and beings of all manner paused to consider Solenn as she passed. The blatant animosity that had previously greeted her was absent, but neither was her arrival one of warm fanfare. Most regarded her with curiosity and ambivalence, which she thought was fair.

At the palace, the pair were soon called in to see the queen.

The royal meadow looked different now, as the tall trees that ringed the open expanse were bushy with spring foliage. This time Solenn knew there'd be watchers beneath that canopy, representatives of the kin.

Queen Abonde waited in the middle of the field. Her diaphanous white robes rippled in a slight breeze, her angled gold eyes set in a face halfway between human and serpentine.

As Solenn approached and dropped to a knee, she realized the greatest change of all: she couldn't sense the queen. The suffocating magical miasma around her was gone.

"Queen Abonde," she and Aveyron said together, heads down.

"Raise your eyes to mine, Aveyron Silvacane de Camarga and Ambassador Solenn ar Braiz." Abonde adjusted her accent between the two names. "Sit or stand, whatever brings you comfort after your long day."

An odd allowance from royalty, but a welcome one. Solenn and Aveyron both sat in the moist grass. She tucked up her knees, while Aveyron crossed his.

"Majesty, my voice has reached its limits," Solenn said, best as she could. "I will rely most often on writing. I hope this is acceptable." Abonde dipped her head in acquiescence. "Your intermediary, Aveyron Silvacane, has agreed to summarize recent events to speed our conversation."

"Majesty." He dipped his head. "Did a courier deliver news of what we found in the Braizian hills?"

"Yes." Queen Abonde paced, her long sleeves drifting. Beside Solenn, Aveyron suddenly quivered as if he were being buffeted by a violent wind. Solenn remembered well how Abonde's moods reverberated through her potent presence. The dragon was surely ready to burst with rage and grief. "I would hear a full description from you, Monsieur Silvacane."

Aveyron laid out the facts in concise format. Abonde asked a few curt questions. When Aveyron was done, she paced more.

"I may be the last of my kind in this region of the world," Queen Abonde said softly. "You must comprehend, Ambassador, how personal this war is for me and many others of the Coterie. You should also be aware that the length of the wing bones that Aveyron has described indicates a mature adult, as old or older than me. The epicurea derived from their massive body can empower thousands of soldiers." *Thousands.* Even worse than Solenn had feared. "But if this epicurea came into the hands of Braizians, they would use it as well, would they not?" She sounded not angry but sad. Despairing.

Solenn thought a moment before she wrote. *They would, because they don't know better. Nor have I been permitted to educate them.*

Queen Abonde snarled. Solenn understood from watching and learning from her parents that negotiations with an emotional party often didn't go well, but this discussion couldn't be delayed. Too many lives were at risk, kin and human alike.

With an appeal to Selland, Solenn continued. *Braiz is already vulnerable as war begins. If they cease using epicurea now, that only makes their failure more certain. An alliance means that all parties involved are contributing. We need to be unified in our vulnerability and grow together from there.*

There was a long moment of dread quiet. "As if we kin are not already vulnerable."

"We are weak on our own. We'll be stronger together," Solenn said, struggling to project her voice. She returned to paper. *The Coterie needs to present itself as a better option than epicurea.*

"You are asking for us to make ourselves known?" Incredulity rang in Queen Abonde's tone.

Solenn's heart pounded in anxiety, her fingers quivering as she wrote. *Hiding hasn't worked, Your Majesty. We can anticipate what will happen if things continue as they are. Braiz will fall. Verdania will fall. The continent will be plundered by Albion.*

"If we reveal ourselves, humans will hunt us all the more."

Aveyron spoke up. "Some would, yes. There'll always be sadistic individuals who seek such sport. I confess my own personal fear: if the truth of the kin is exposed to humans, the true magical nature of Camargas might also be revealed. I also know, however, that my kind will not stay safe even if, as Solenn says, things continue as they are. Both Albion and Verdania regard Camargas as horses of prestige. They would break us and utilize us in their war. And once Albion conquers Verdania, they will pursue their ambitions across the continent." He said this in a chillingly matter-of-fact way.

He was right. Albion would rule the world, if given the chance. If empowered by epicurea.

Gyst feeds on secrets. Stop feeding him. Secrecy hasn't saved the kin of Albion. The Coterie can be spared similar mass extinctions if we rally together now. On that subject, I have a proposal. She paused to think through each word. *The Braizian military cannot wean itself from epicurea all at once, but select units can.*

"Go on."

Oh, how Solenn wished she could read more emotion on the queen's inscrutable face. She continued.

When I first met you, I mentioned that our navy could partner with krakens. I believe this more strongly now. Our sailors hold krakens holy unto Selland. They do not attack them, nor do krakens attack our sailors. Our ships already carry limited epicurea, mostly curatives. If a ship is devoid of such cargo, will a kraken partner with them?

"I cannot speak for krakens in this regard," said Queen Abonde. Not a surprise, considering the nature of her rule.

I would like to confer with them, then. She wrote the words with confidence, even as her heart raced. Her, addressing the most adulated magical beings of Braiz. Something about that struck her as even more audacious than conversing with Selland.

She didn't expect the queen to laugh.

"You would negotiate with krakens?" Abonde said. "Truly? I can't help but wonder at your arrogance."

Solenn felt a prickle of anger. *There's a difference between arrogance and desperation.*

Queen Abonde's smile was thin. "Yet there can also be much overlap between the two. You've scarcely dealt with land-based kin and you'd go right to the mightiest of the sea?"

Aveyron cast Solenn a worried look. She took a few deep breaths to gather her wits. She couldn't afford to lose her temper with the dragon queen.

You're the mightiest among land-based kin, aren't you? Solenn wrote, presenting the words with the most gracious smile she could muster.

"I am." Queen Abonde had no need for modesty. "But you are scarcely more than a human child. As your people say, 'Don't wade where there's a riptide.' I now must declare this audience at its end." She gestured with an upwardly cupped hand. Aveyron scrambled to his feet, so Solenn did the same. "I have many other pressing issues to address, as you must understand. Your previous cottage has been modified in wait of your return. Take your rest there, Ambassador, and allow your voice time to recover." With that, she nodded, and in an instant was gone.

"But . . . ," Solenn whispered into the emptiness.

"Solenn, she's right. You need to rest. We both do." Aveyron gave her arm a gentle tug, drawing her table book toward its pouch.

She wouldn't deny that she needed to rest, but they had so much more to discuss. Nothing had really *happened*. Queen Abonde had actually laughed at her idea of carrying forth an alliance with krakens. She'd *laughed*.

Tears in her eyes, Solenn gestured to Selland, as if he might somehow preserve her people against her continued failures.

CHAPTER TEN

SOLENN

Lambig is what the Braizians call apple cider brandy. The distilled beverage is potent, with finer examples often described as imbued with an aroma that evokes spices and verdant woods. In more remote areas of the country, locals use lambig as a treatment for illness. Enough of such a drink, certainly, could make a person believe in their own wellness for a time.

—Excerpt from *Manual for Tour Chefs*

Solenn felt something tickle her face and lurched upright, her gasp echoing in the confined space of the box bed.

Gyst. His cowl. He was—no, he wasn't. It was the lace fringe of the quilt.

She collapsed again with a soft moan. Her heart rampaged in her chest. There'd be no getting to sleep again, not anytime soon. From now on, probably anything that softly brushed her face would trigger her memories of Gyst and what he'd done.

She slid open the box bed door and swung out her legs to step on a sheepskin rug. The cottage provided by the Coterie had indeed been modified in her absence. The furniture inside had been changed from what might be termed generically Lutecian to an interior that was profoundly Braizian. That meant an enclosed box bed sized to fit her and heavy cupboards made of traditional cedar and of Braizian design, all of them old and used in a way that made them feel comfortable. The blankets, towels, utensils . . . all were obviously from Braiz. An entirely new room had been added too—a private space for Aveyron.

Sunlight shone through the window. Sunlight? How late was it? She pulled on a thicker dressing gown and entered the common room. She drank water poured from a full jug upon the table. She'd now been in Arcady for two days and used that time to rest, write vague letters of assurance to her family, attempt conversations with neighbors of all species, and read what few books about the Coterie that Aveyron had been able to find in Braizian and Verdanian. Even so, her ignorance felt like a stain she couldn't wash out. Nor did she know what course to take from here.

Adamantine had to be well into Verdania by now. Solenn needed to do her part so that when Erwan came home, it would be to a place intact and safe.

And Erwan would come home. He must.

The front door kicked open. Aveyron entered, his arms full of wood. By the jagged ends of the branches, all of it looked to be salvaged. "You're up," he said with a smile on his face. He released the wood into the hearth-side rack. "How are you feeling?"

Solenn rubbed a hand against her chest. Her heart was still beating too fast. "My quilt brushed my face. I awakened, thinking it was Gyst." Her words were audible but still hoarse.

"Oh, Solenn." Aveyron's face crumpled.

"I'm fine. I know I'm in control of my own body." She waved her arms around to prove it.

"Your voice is better today. That's good."

She shrugged. A stronger voice might be helpful if she knew some new tack that might convince Queen Abonde to actually negotiate.

"You cannot give in to despair, Solenn. Look at where you are." Aveyron spread out his arms. Shreds of bark fell from his sleeves. "You're a human in Arcady. You earned a role as ambassador."

"True. My job hasn't been canceled, but the alliance has yet to do anything. Has any word come from Braiz?"

"Nothing since last night." He'd arranged for bird couriers to deliver updates. The most recent had verified that the broken dragon wings, and two more such structures, had been found. More Albionish troops had landed in the east, and warships had been briefly sighted off Nont.

She stood, pacing before a fire that remained placid. Hester had ceased her persnickety ways after Solenn's harsh talk with her in Malo. Dare Solenn hope she had at least achieved a neutral relationship with *that* God?

Solenn paused to stroke the carved lintel above the hearth. She hadn't looked at it closely yet. The five-inch-tall beam spanned some four feet, the entire surface intricately carved with krakens, seals, dormice, pine martens, red deer, and more beings of land and sea. The work looked new, too, nothing like the furniture.

"This wasn't here when we first came to the cottage. Who made this?" she asked, her gaze going upward. The design continued up over the stones as well, carved vines and small birds extending all the way to the ceiling.

Aveyron moved to stand next to her. "That looks like the work of my friend Lyria. She carved the horse statue that I gave to you as a wedding gift."

"That statue! Oh, how I loved that thing." Solenn had never seen such craftsmanship before. That was one of the few belongings she regretted having left behind in Lutecia.

"She's a dryad, a living tree. I haven't spoken with her since our return, but she was part of our contingent in Verdania. She helped to bring home our dead while we engaged with Hester. This work is the kind of thing that she would do as a quiet show of gratitude."

Solenn stroked the granite. The gray sheen of this particular stone reminded her of Hester's statue. "How can she work so beautifully with stone *and* wood?"

"Trees grow from stone. They know its heft and cleavages and how to work with it, work through it."

She looked to the fire again, her thoughts returning to the offerings of bread and words she'd provided to Hester in the Grand Pentad.

Stone. Carvings. Offerings. Fire.

Solenn whirled around. "Aveyron, do we need to stay in Arcady?"

He blinked. "You want to go across the veil? It would be a long trek back to Braiz."

"No, I want to travel to Verdania. Do we need permission?"

"We haven't been forbidden from leaving," he said slowly, thoughtfully, "but I should leave word of our intentions with court."

"This trip won't take long, if all goes well."

Aveyron pursed his lips. "Dare I ask where we're going and why?"

"I think," Solenn said, regarding the fire, "that we need to pay Hester a visit."

CHAPTER ELEVEN

ADA

When the meat has cooked to tenderness, add the eggs, grated cheese, parsley, marjoram, mint, and vinegar, stirring constantly until incorporated. This will result in a meat soup that will warm the gut as if you've swallowed Hester's very fire.

—Excerpt from *Book for Cooks to Excel as Do Chefs*

After a weeklong slog across partially flooded spring countryside, Ada and Brillat at last arrived at Lutecia's gates. The requisite graft was paid to the guards, who eyed the Camarga with disturbing interest. Once inside the city, Ada left behind the busy avenues for the shadowed manure- and garbage-fragrant byways that were far more preferable than thronged humanity.

"I've never held fondness for Lutecia as a whole," Ada muttered to Brillat, whose ears swiveled to listen. He'd been receptive to many soliloquies in recent days. "But I did love the quartier we lived in for years." She'd learned routes to get where she needed to go, avoiding the crowds that made her mind confuse the current cacophony with the Battle of the Tents from so long ago—and now there were even more people in the city than before. They camped beneath overhangs and clustered on stoops, faces haggard. She perceived the absence of food on their persons and within their bodies.

"We need the latest official news of court," Ada told Brillat, though she dreaded what they may find.

A roving bread vendor shouted out the day's wares from some unseen alley nearby as Ada brought Brillat to a stop before a notice board. Her tongue tingled with awareness of the remnant yeast used to paste papers to the thickly layered wood. She scanned the twenty-some sheets in search of relevant news amid a smattering of advertisements and, as Yanik had mentioned, broadsides from the Blessed, calling for Caristo's execution and Merle's ascension. Most of those had been ripped or marked to obscure text, but bold words of rebellion shone through.

Brillat's high-pitched snort and gesturing muzzle jerked her attention toward the far end of the board, where crisp ink filled a new notice.

TODAY

THIS SECOND GYSTSDAY OF THE MONTH

WE EXECUTE THE FOUL BRAIZIANS

WHO POISONED PRINCE RUPERT

5:00

No location was mentioned. None was needed. All such events took place in the plaza before the palace.

Her breath frozen, heart racing, Ada had the horrible realization that after weeks of near-constant travel, *she didn't know the day of the week.*

Whirling Brillat around, they almost bowled over a man on horseback.

"Sorry!" Ada gasped, and then lunged forward to grip him by a ratteen sleeve. "Tell me, please, monsieur—what day of the week is it?"

The young dandy, his mustache neatly curving like a miniature black smile, recoiled with such alarm that only Ada's grip kept him astride. "Why, it's Gystsday! The second!"

"Thank you," she said, easing her hold so that the fellow could retain his seat. She put her heels to Brillat, directing him to the only place she could think to go—the nearby ruins of the Golden Horse, where she needed to find their old friend Emone.

Five o'clock. Scarcely two hours away. Verdania liked to do executions—and glossectomies of Chefs—right before sunset whenever it occurred throughout the year, embracing the sordid symbolism of a day ending along with a life or a life as it had been known.

Her mind couldn't articulate words. She just knew they had to hurry, hurry, hurry. Brillat needed no prompting, leaping carts and taking corners as if he were winning an urban horse race. At the lot where the Golden Horse once stood, charred timber and brick had been carted away, new walls just beginning to take shape. There among the workers was a familiar broad figure.

"Simon!" Her voice was a hoarse roar.

Emone's loyal doorman recognized her urgency and bounded over stacked wood to meet her. "Madame Adamantine!" He took in the presence of the Camarga with wide eyes.

"Emone. Where is she? I need her." Because if she didn't have Emone to ground her, she'd throw herself headlong into an escapade that'd be exactly what Erwan—and Solenn—had advised her to avoid. Emone had been a fellow officer of the Thirty-Fifth Division, known for her stiletto-sharp wit and ocean-deep empathy. Not the kind of empathy imbued in rare Chefs, but the emotional sort, which in her case was paired with a sparkling charisma that misanthropic Ada had always found baffling and admirable.

"She's at our storehouse. It's nearby." With a wave to his companions, he set off hurriedly on foot, Brillat following with huffed breaths.

The wattle-and-daub building looked damp and old, its thatched roof swaybacked. As they neared the open door to the lower floor, Simon upheld a hand to keep Ada back.

"I hear horses, but ours are away." He pulled a long knife from his belt.

"Have you been having trouble since the fire?" she asked in a low voice as she quietly dismounted. Brillat remained utterly still. "I did send a note—"

"Which was received with gratitude, madame." Ada had posted the letter from Rance. She couldn't go into detail about what had happened with their homicidal, cannibalistic old peer Mallory Valmont, but she did need Emone to know that there would be no more arsonists or other varieties of assassin in her pursuit.

Simon gestured for quiet and crept forward. His build reminded her much of Maman's man Ragnar, but while Ragnar had moved with an old soldier's confident swagger, Simon crept like a large dog who'd been kicked and abused as a pup, and now years later still regarded human legs with fear. Even so, he didn't hesitate to engage with this new threat to Emone. Such was the devotion that she inspired.

He peered through the doorway. "Madame!" he yelped. "What are you doing?"

"I scraped together coin to let horses." That was Emone's voice. Ada advanced to look as well. Emone stood between two tacked chestnut horses. "A crier was shouting that the Braizian prisoners were going to be executed, and I—*Ada?*"

"Emone. Don't tell me you're going off on a foolish escapade to save them. You were supposed to temper *me* from making a suicidal effort."

Emone planted her hands on her slender hips. She wore a tailored pantsuit in lavender, the color complementing her pale complexion and blonde hair. "I suppose we're doomed, then. So much for that." Brillat released a soft snort, gaining her attention. "Who's your friend here?" She'd always held Camargas in high esteem.

"This is Brillat," Ada said as they entered the stable. Simon closed the door behind them. "What do you know about the execution?"

"It's in two hours. The crier didn't elaborate." Because much of the population in the city was illiterate, criers were relied upon to spread everyday news, whether from court or regarding sales on scented walking sticks. "I'd heard last week that the Braizian contingent was being held, so I made sure to listen on Gystsday in case Caristo took the next terrible step."

Ada had forgotten that Caristo favored executions on Gystsday. Such a perverted tidiness in killing people on the day designated for the God who would then escort the dead across the veil and resolve their mysteries.

Ada took a steadying breath. Her rapid heartbeat made her a touch faint. "What weaponry do you have? I have knives, a pistol—"

"I have this rapier—and more, as Claudette stored several here— two pistols, powder, these two horses—"

Simon loudly cleared his throat. "Mesdemoiselles, what of *sense?*" His words were harsh, but his tone tentative. The two women froze, gawking at him. "I'm aware that these Braizians mean much to you— I've heard your stories for years now, Madame Emone—but you both need to consider these terrible circumstances with logic."

"Logic? We don't have time for logic!" Ada said, and knew the foolishness of the statement as it met her ears. "Oh, Five. I don't want to die. I don't want Erwan to die." She pressed her hands against her face, Brillat's head warm and supportive at her shoulder.

Simon faced Emone, his pale skin flushed. "Madame Claudette tasked me with watching over you while she was away. I can't—I can't let you act the fool."

Ada walked a few feet to plop down on the lower steps of a long staircase upward. She needed to untack Brillat, but some part of her wanted him ready to go, even though she knew she couldn't take him in horse form to an execution. The city guards wouldn't be alone in eyeing the rare horse with interest. She let her thoughts drift as she willed herself to calmness. From upstairs, she perceived food being prepared: previously parboiled beef that had now almost cooked to tenderness, undoubtedly in a large pot over a fire. Along with that were bread crumbs—an effective thickener in many soups—with salt and pepper. Nearby were other ingredients to be added when the meat was ready: eggs, grated bofor cheese, fresh herbs now limp on their stems, and verjuice. This was the making of a decent soup, one she could improve upon, if she survived the next few hours.

She *would* survive. Solenn would need her even more if Erwan . . . if he . . .

"There'll be a heavy presence of guards at this execution, because otherwise, the angry crowd would tear the Braizians apart themselves. The palace wants people to enjoy the execution, not participate in it," Simon said with slow thoughtfulness. "People are worried, angry, hungry. If they tear apart these prisoners, the bloodlust will carry onward from there."

"'Enjoy the execution,'" Ada repeated dully. "Oh, Five. I spent the last week planning out, in detail, how I was going to free the musketeers from the bastille. By this hour, they likely aren't even being held there, but closer to the noose."

"By Hester's flame, I wish Claudette were here," Emone muttered.

"Where is she?" Ada asked.

"She hurried back here the week after the Golden Horse burned, but I told her to continue to the fabric market at Toulo. We need to keep at least one side of our enterprise alive. I *thought* she'd be safer away." For years, Emone had managed the Golden Horse Tavern while Claudette had continued the fabric business founded by her late husband.

"We could use her sword about now," Ada said. Claudette was among the best civilian swordfighters she had ever known. Seeing Simon's cheeks grow pinker, she raised a hand. "We're not dunderheads.

I know we can't go at fifty guards with bared blades and smoking barrels, but . . . we need to do *something*."

Grief steeped Emone's face. "We may need to witness."

"You're suggesting we stand there and witness Erwan and his beloved companions *die* and do *nothing*?" Ada asked.

"A witnessing isn't doing nothing, madame," Simon added softly. "It's important."

"I know it is, but . . ." She gestured with both arms, unable to sally more words.

To witness meant to attend a death, to see the light leave someone's eyes as they crossed the veil to gaze upon Gyst, and to love and pray for them through that time of transition. One of the vital aspects of witnessing was informing loved ones of what had happened, removing any ambivalence about their death.

The idea of facing the Corres and Solenn with the burden of such news . . .

"We're going to arm ourselves," Emone said, grasping Ada by the shoulder. "We'll look for opportunities. If there are none, we'll bear witness, and honor them in that."

Ada couldn't speak through the tightness of her throat, but she comprehended the wisdom of this flexible plan. There wasn't time to contrive anything more. The palace was on the far side of town. They needed to leave within minutes if they were going to get spots near the head of the rabblement.

There would be a full audience at the execution.

Emone seemed to realize this problem at the same time as Ada, as she looked at her with blatant concern.

Ada moved to untack Brillat. As she worked loose the girth, he turned, worry in his black eyes as well. She'd talked to him about her issues within crowds during their long ride.

"I'll deal with the masses." Ada set aside the saddle and panniers.

"'Deal with them'?" echoed Emone. "Last time—"

Meaning when they'd been caught in the multitude that came for Prince Rupert's death declaration. When Ada had recognized the Braizian princess as her daughter. "I dealt with my anxiety then too. You helped me through. I'll rely on you again."

Simon took in this talk with a furrowed brow, not prying for context.

Emone released a long breath. "No time to dither, in any case. Simon, I originally was going to ask you to come with me. We could still get another mount, or—"

"I'll attend on foot, madame. You may need an additional ally in the crowd."

Emone stared into the distance, nodding. "Yes. Yes, that's a good idea. Ada, do you remember how to wield a rapier?"

"I've practiced moves using sticks perhaps a handful of times in the past fifteen years."

"Very well. Maybe you can avoid impaling yourself. Your body remembers the terror of battles; maybe it'll remember some more useful skills as well."

Grand-mère had somehow retained her own fighting reflexes, even as her memory of recent events faded. Perhaps that would also prove true for Ada.

Ada settled Brillat in one of the empty stalls, and as she moved away, his teeth snagged her sleeve. She tried to interpret the gleam in his eyes.

"I'll be careful," she murmured.

He didn't appear to believe that, as his ears flattened. Simon and Emone jabbered across the room as they made their own preparations.

"I've worked through my foolishness—for the time being, at least. I intend to make it back to Solenn and my grandmother—and I must help Braiz and the kin. That's what Erwan would want." Her words were as thick as desiccated bread in her throat.

With a snort, Brillat released her. "Thank you for looking out for me," she whispered, giving his face a quick stroke as she turned away.

Minutes later, she and Emone rode out on the chestnut mares.

A few civilians had already gathered on the broad expanse of flagstones, most of them children, barefoot and huddled in little gangs. They carried bags of rotten produce, and they were excited. The sight of children, eager to toss fruit at Erwan and his comrades as they—

"Don't." Emone's voice stopped her, sure as a boulder dropped in her path. "Don't speak to them. Don't even look directly at them."

Allowing a few seconds for sense to seep in, Ada knew Emone to be right. Scolding the children, trying to correct the error of their ways, would likely lead to an early deployment of their rotten produce and also attract the attention of soldiers. They were already present as well, forming a short human wall from the palace gate to the platform of the gallows, where a single post and rope stood ready. More rope lay coiled in wait nearby.

They would hang the Braizians one at a time. Erwan would be last; commanding officers always were in such circumstances. They'd torture him, force him to witness each death in sequence before his own turn came.

Oh, Five. Gyst, Melissa, Lait, Selland, Hester.

"Ada, lean close and tell me what happened with Mallory Valmont and how you knew about this execution."

Emone had a special knack for saving people, for knowing what they needed most to endure and thrive. Ada had never been more personally grateful for her empathy than at that moment. Ada had to focus on her telling, omitting details that were too dangerous and too private to be known even by one of her oldest, dearest friends.

More and more people arrived, some on horseback, some with wagons, but most on foot. The voices, the bustle, the very energy of the increasing crowd began to press against Ada. With her tale done and the noise level prohibitive to extended whispered conversations, she began to pray. As confused as she was about the Gods, as betrayed as she felt by Hester and Gyst, she craved their solace, their blessing. Their mercy.

For Erwan. His musketeers. Her friends with her in this venture, new and old. Solenn.

Ada kept thinking of Solenn. They'd had too little time together. She'd only had the chance to cook her one meal, only one! That felt more wrong to her than langra cheese without sparkling wine atop.

"Ada, how are you?" asked Emone, her voice barely audible. They were trapped by the crowd at this point, the time past five. Verdania could do nothing in a timely fashion, including murder.

"Sweaty, but I'm enduring."

Emone's broad hat cast her face in shadow, but Ada could read her concern in the tilt of her head. "There's movement through the gate. It won't be long."

"Hey! Hey! Where's the king and all?" a jack in front shouted at the guards milling on the platform.

"Gone to Versay," answered a woman nearby. "Took most of court with him too." This provoked a series of jeers.

"Versay, Versay, beautiful Versay, as the rest of us starve in squalor," said another man.

"Versay won't be as pretty once the Blessed get there," added someone else.

Ada perceived a smattering of food around her and also—a friend about ten feet away, nearer the gallows. The figure wore a black cocked hat, long silver hair loose upon velvet shoulders. Where had Brillat found such a suit, the sort very much to his fine tastes? Her brain foggy, she needed a second to answer herself: the storehouse was used by Golden Horse Mercantile. The upper floor was likely a sartorial fantasy land.

As if sensing her attention, he turned to meet her eye. His face was impassive, his nod small, but she felt his support like an all-encompassing hug.

A trumpet blasted from the palace balcony, the surprise sound causing Ada to jump in the saddle. Her horse quivered, ears back, but retained discipline, as did Emone's mount. The metal gate opened and more soldiers came through. Ada couldn't see the street children any-more, but knew their positions by her perception of their ready fruit.

"Attention! Attention, good people of Verdania!" shouted a reader from the balcony beyond the wall. He wore satin palace livery as he stood beside the trumpeter. "Today we send to Gyst the Braizians behind the foul plot to murder our beloved Prince Rupert." He paused. After a few seconds of apparent indecision, the audience began to boo and cheer in a messy roar.

Ada's soaked clothes stuck to her like a second skin. The evidence that Erwan had presented, the surrender of Madame Brumal, it all had meant nothing. The king had made his decision and nothing else mat-tered. By the Five, she loathed that chancre of a man and every lackey of his who nodded because he nodded.

She studied the guards, the wall, the positions of everyone around. She saw no openings for attack, no vulnerabilities. A glance at Emone's grim face informed her that the situation looked as dire through her eyes.

Five, please, grant me the means to save Erwan. Don't force me to witness his demise.

A Verdanian musketeer came through the gate, his peaked hat and tall feather high above the crowd. Behind him came a man with messy brown hair and soiled prison garb. The fruit was flung, and the target—

Oh no. Oh, by the Five Gods, no.

The prisoner was already dying. His innards experienced a horrific cascade of failure as his stomach digested an epicurea that she had only encountered in her tour-days.

Singing mushroom. The very epicurea that had brought Prince Rupert to an excruciating end. It had been eaten—forced in him, undoubtedly—about two hours ago, judging by his progressive condition.

The prisoner who emerged next was already dying as well. A soured, mushy apple smacked him in the side of the head and would have knocked him down if not for the guard forcing him onward.

Ada gripped Emone by the arm, then with her other hand made a silent signal, drummed fingers against her thigh: epicurea. As officers, they had learned numerous signs to use while conducting quiet urban operations. Emone recognized the gesture with pursed lips, her gaze jerking between the soldiers and the prisoners. The question left unsaid: Who was the degustator?

Ada made another low sign against her thigh, a flat hand angled to naturally curve. A sign to indicate the sea. Braiz.

Emone mouthed something that was profane or a divine appeal, or both.

Out came the third prisoner.

Ada could now clearly see the first man as he walked right ahead of her, his hands bound at his back by a heavy rope. His face was flushed, not simply by poison, but by heavy bruising. His eyes were purple puffs. If she had known this man in the Thirty-Fifth, she likely wouldn't recognize him now.

The fourth man emerged.

The children in the audience were out of produce.

Erwan would be next. Oh Gods, Erwan would be next. Ada could scarcely breathe. Rage and futility threatened to make her incandescent. She suddenly regretted stopping Mallory Valmont's plot to raze Verdania. These people were past redemption. They deserved the sorrow and war to soon engulf them. Drop Graecian fire on the lot. Extirpate them from the earth.

A Verdanian musketeer came next, white plume bobbing with each step. The gate closed behind her.

There were four dying Braizian musketeers ready to meet a dramatic end for show.

Erwan wasn't here.

CHAPTER TWELVE

SOLENN

Some of Gyst's unknowns become somewhat more known if one uses a convex lens to make small objects appear much larger. Make a study of aging cheeses in a cellar. If a cheese is covered by tiny brown specks, and when the cheese is dusted, these specks simply transition to another cheese, this is evidence of cheese mites. Utilize a convex lens to make that which is small appear large, and you will find that these specks are akin to tiny spiders. To safeguard cheeses from an infestation, cover them with things such as oil and cloth—though the mites do aid the affinage of some cheeses, creating a desired pebbled rind.

—Excerpt from *Book for Cooks to Excel as Do Chefs*

On their last visit to the crater where Hester stood, with her tongue intact, Solenn had perceived the fiery potency of the God at a distance, along with the disturbing aura emanated by the ruins of Ys. This time, she experienced naught but worry about whether her idea could bear fruition.

As she and Aveyron reached the basin, a baritone growl rang out from the woods ahead. The tilted arena that held Hester's statue lay just beyond.

"Stop. Name yourselves," came a deep voice.

"I'm Ambassador Solenn de Braiz." She introduced herself in Verdanian, the language in which she'd been addressed. "With me is my friend and companion Aveyron Silvacane de Camarga. Who might you be of the Coterie?"

"I am Monsieur Gervaise." A beast emerged from the brush. He easily stood seven feet in height, walking upright like a human. He had long flat feet adorned with broad black claws. A small felted hat rested between his ears, the deep green in contrast to his ruddy brown fur. He wore a rapier attached by a belt.

"Monsieur Gervaise." She bowed. "I'm honored to meet you. Are you a guard assigned watch over this place?" Queen Abonde was making sure that no further humans trespassed here and committed sacrilege.

"I am." She noted that many of his words emerged from the throat, as hers did now, though he had a long tongue. "This is not a place to be casually visited. Why do you come?"

Aveyron stepped forward. He wore a tailored purple pantsuit, the lapel embroidered with green vines. "I bring a sealed letter from the queen's secretary. As you will see, our permission to visit was granted by Queen Abonde herself." He extended a small envelope toward the beast. Monsieur Gervaise sniffed as if to verify the identity of the sender, then stepped back to open the letter.

After a moment, he nodded. "Why do you come?" he asked again.

Aveyron looked to Solenn for that answer.

"I bled here. I want to understand why." A vague reply, but also honest.

Monsieur Gervaise considered this for a moment. "You may continue, but do not tarry."

"I'm grateful for your vigilance, monsieur," she said, bowing again. Truly, she was. She looked around, nodding several times to acknowledge anyone who might be in the shadows. Beasts, like wolves, were said to travel in packs. Monsieur Gervaise withdrew into the forest.

They reached the ruined amphitheater and paused to take in the sight below them. The crooked stone seats and steps. The centuries of wear upon the rock; the accumulation of grass, shrubs, and trees. The broad, broken stage where she had fought for her life, her existence, against two Gods as they also fought each other. The pit where she'd fallen, and feared Erwan had died.

Her fists clenched. No, she wouldn't dwell on those renewed fears now. She had work to do.

She and Aveyron continued down to where Hester stood. Her face was in a permanent grimace, birds' nests creating furry tufts between her teeth. One thick knee met the ground while the other stayed propped at a ninety-degree angle. A fist was upraised in defiance. The pose had previously seemed mighty to Solenn, but now it struck her as sad—a statue that memorialized what may have been the worst moment in a God's existence.

Solenn placed a hand on top of Hester's bare foot. Despite deep shadows, the rock contained heat that wasn't solar in origin. Aveyron followed her example.

"So much power," he murmured.

Solenn nodded. Much power indeed, for a God made immobile.

"What *are* you hoping to find here, Solenn?" he asked as she studied ground covered with blast marks and shrapnel. Blood smears had dried in dark trails on the pale stones. She was grateful that the Coterie had taken care of the bodies of the Albionishmen and the servants of the comtesse.

Solenn crouched before a fragment of Hester that was roughly the size of a melon. Mallory Valmont hadn't been judicious in his fireball-flinging and had damaged Hester's larger body, though it wouldn't have been damage in his eyes. After all, he'd intended to grind down her entirety to eat as he took on her divinity. Hester's cursed nature bore a great similarity to that of rupic.

Rupic. Ugh. Such a foul thing. That ingredient came about because of another epicurea, stony owl stomach. When a person ingested that— either forced to do so or doing it in ignorance—within hours, the person began to slowly, agonizingly turn to stone. Their remains were called rupic. Mallory Valmont had apparently cannibalized people in such a way for decades. The magic had made him a battlefield hero in his youth and, after his conviction and imprisonment, had sustained his life during what should have been a fatal prison sentence at Mont Annod.

She pressed both hands to the stone. They felt strangely sensitive, almost as if the pressure of her own touch could shape the rock, if given time.

"This is what I hoped to find," she said to Aveyron, hefting up the stone with a grunt. It weighed no less than a normal rock of such size, that was for certain. Even separate from the whole, the chunk had lost none of its heat, but that made sense. Hester's powder had also been imbued with the God's might.

Aveyron looked on her with alarm. "What are you doing? You can't mean to—is that why you brought a pack?"

"Yes. What did you think I was going to put in it?" She slid the sack's straps from her shoulders. She'd asked Aveyron to find her a pack built to carry a heavy load, and he'd brought her one that was constructed of some kind of thick leathered skin, smooth to the touch, the base and strap attachments reinforced by extra layers of leather. It was the perfect size for this rock. She forced the opening wide like a gaped mouth and gingerly lowered the stone inside.

"I was at a loss, really. I resolved to wait and find out." By his grimace, he didn't like the conclusion. "What are you hoping to do with such a rock? It is, in all truth, epicurea, though derived from a God." When Hester had made determinations about what flora and fauna were to be food to humans as perceived by Chefs, she hadn't excluded herself, though she was essentially a more potent form of rupic. "We can't take that back to Arcady. Hester is the God who cursed our existences."

"Hester is always in Arcady." She cleared her throat to forcefully swallow spittle. She was going to lose her voice if she talked much longer. She left the bulging pack between her feet as she straightened. "She's in every fire, every oven, in the essence of everyplace there that feels like a home, whether it's a cottage, tree, or den."

"Well, yes, but this is her very *body*. It's dangerous."

"Of course it is. I'd break my foot if I dropped the rock on it."

Aveyron shook his head, his queued hair lashing his shoulders. He showed no appreciation for her joke. "This is part of Hester. Because of her, we continue to suffer."

"Hester lives with the consequences too. She's suffering even now. Listening, but unable to speak." Solenn's throat produced sounds that were increasingly hoarse. "If the kin and Braiz are to survive, we must ally, but we needn't stop there. We know Gyst stands against us, but Hester—"

"If she regains power and movement, what's to keep her from assaulting us again?" Aveyron gazed up, more toward the sun than the looming statue.

"What indeed?" boomed a familiar voice from above.

Solenn spun around, gasping, her hair lashing free of her braids beneath a wind powered by broad, flapping wings. Queen Abonde drifted downward. Her pale dragon form extended some fifty feet from nose to tail. She was the size of Hester, though a far different shape. Really, Abonde was like a thick white snake with four legs, spikes of a deep gray intermittently lining her spine from the horned crest at the back of her skull to the distal point of her tail.

Her golden eyes fixated on Solenn as she landed on the other side of the stage, facing the defiant, paralyzed Hester.

"I, too, would like to understand your motivations, Ambassador Solenn," said Queen Abonde, her needle-adorned tail lashing around to encircle her feet—like a cat—as she settled down. This wasn't a pose that spoke of relaxation, but indicated a serpent poised to strike.

Solenn and Aveyron dropped to both knees, prostrating themselves before Queen Abonde. Solenn had anticipated that her plot to bring part of Hester back might raise questions, but she hadn't expected Abonde herself to come here in all her dragon might. She doubted that the visit boded well.

"Majesty," Solenn said.

"I've listened to much of your discussion." Her neck angled to regard the God. Solenn wondered if Abonde had come here before. "You represent us well, young Silvacane."

He bowed. "I'm honored, Majesty, though I do wish to add that I'm not adamantly opposed to Solenn's effort. I simply don't understand her ultimate intention."

"Yes, that is yet unstated." Queen Abonde's voice sounded deeper than in her human form, but the cadence remained the same. "Ambassador, you hope to bring this segment of Hester Incarnate to Arcady?"

Solenn nodded as she pulled out her table book.

"Even knowing how she tore asunder our world, tore asunder the inherent nature of the kin? Made us food, made us prey, all to better humankind?"

I don't hold her in fond regard myself. She tried to immolate me and almost succeeded in doing so. I bear substantial scars upon my body. Solenn felt the tautness of the broad burns across her thighs even now.

"Yet you also sympathize with her."

I do, Majesty. She's the God of Hearth and Home. As she said through Mallory Valmont as we fought here, she's been able to interact with the world only through brief touches. That's the same level of engagement she has with her fellow Gods. Hester compared her experience to being in the cold, staring at a warm, cozy family through a window. She's been isolated for thousands of years like that—yes, an imprisonment of her own making. One that Gyst was fine with leaving her in indefinitely. I refuse to agree with Gyst on many matters, especially this. She flipped to another sheet.

Queen Abonde cocked her head. "What do you intend to do with that rock within Arcady?"

I hope to present it to a master carver to see if they would be willing to work with the stone to make some kind of form capable of speech.

"Why propose this endeavor to one of the Coterie? Why not a human?"

Foremost, because I've never met a craftsperson who could work with stone and wood as Aveyron's companion can. Beyond that, my intuition tells me that this choice is right. That it gives the Coterie control over Hester, and that Hester herself will need to acknowledge, accept, and respect that.

Queen Abonde studied Solenn with her inscrutable gaze. "What do *you* feel as you touch the stone?"

Aveyron had warned her before that Abonde could sense lies. Solenn had no desire to test that theory now. *Inherent power of Hester.* She paused, then resolved to write an uncomfortable truth. *Inherent power within myself.*

"Your tongue was a direct conduit to the Gods," Abonde said with deliberate patience, "but your entire body descends from the holy."

That echoed what Ada had also told her. She struggled to speak. "But I couldn't sense Gyst when he confronted me in Braiz." Solenn knew that Aveyron would have reported this incident to Abonde. "Are you saying that if Gyst really tried, he could—"

Fear made her stressed throat completely clench. Gyst couldn't control her again. She couldn't, wouldn't, let that happen. She tried and failed to force out words, and even though she knew her own anxiety was the cause, her panic worsened. Sudden sweat soaked her body, her heartbeat galloping as if to outrace the threat of a God.

Aveyron's hand brushed her trembling fingers, and she nodded to give him permission to speak on her behalf.

"Her deep fear is that Gyst could possess her again," he said. Had she been able to speak, she wasn't sure if she could've confessed a terror that deep. Thank Selland that she had a friend such as Aveyron.

"A wise fear." Queen Abonde cocked her head. "We kin do not know the Gods with intimacy, but I don't believe Gyst could do such a thing. Not simply because of the loss of your tongue, but because of the inner fortifications you have built against him."

Solenn bowed her head in an expression of gratitude.

"If a Coterie carver takes on this task, what then?" asked Queen Abonde, redirecting their conversation.

Solenn was suddenly glad she needed to write on her tablet. That gave her the opportunity to think through her presentation. *We know that Hester could speak and walk in her stone form.* She flashed the page to Abonde, who nodded. *We know that Hester accumulated power for her attack on the kin by hoarding blessings for a prolonged time. This stone fragment holds inherent power. It can hold more. I plan to take the carved version to the Grand Pentad in Nont to place it in her designated hearth.*

"Directly feeding the stone," murmured Aveyron, eyes wide. "But will it work? If the stone has a face or mouth, could she eventually talk?"

"Gyst saw no possibility for Hester to communicate again, and he is the knower of many unknowns. It's likely Hester has no idea either," said Queen Abonde, thoughtful. "She wouldn't simply be pulling in power from the pentad hearth, but in a more direct flow from any prayers and offerings within the immediate area. Her awareness wouldn't be as distanced, as diluted, as it is now."

"That also means that she would have an easier time releasing power in an attack upon you or someone else," Aveyron pointed out to Solenn.

An easier time, yes, but if she wanted to attack me now, she easily could. All she needs is to send one spark onto my clothes, a blanket, a curtain.

"What is your ultimate goal, once Hester can speak?" asked the queen.

Most of all, I don't want her as an enemy for my family, for Braiz, and for the Coterie. If the relationship can develop further, we will not spurn blessings.

Queen Abonde bared her teeth. "The bias of Gods is dangerous. Favor may be temporary."

As if Solenn didn't already know that intimately. She furrowed her brow, pencil tapping on the book for a moment. *That's true with any relationship.*

"The stakes are somewhat higher with a God," Aveyron said with a wry smile.

"Would you ask her to be a weapon on your behalf?" Queen Abonde asked, no mirth in her tone.

Solenn regarded the question with proper sobriety. *Hester is God of hearths and homes. Braiz and the kin need their homes protected. I wouldn't ask her to aid in the destruction of Verdania and Albion.*

Now that she thought about it, Solenn realized she had no overwhelming hatred for either place. The people there suffered at the whims of their rulers. If she were to target anyone in particular, she would choose Lord Whitney. He had known just how to provoke King Caristo of Verdania and set tragedies into motion.

Queen Abonde pulled back her head, considering the giant statue and Solenn. "You continue to be a curious human, Ambassador. I will permit you to bring the fragment into Arcady, but I place guidance upon you. If Hester presents herself as a threat to you or the kin, the stone must be shattered, all remnants adulterated so that there is no risk of consumption by a human. Monsieur Silvacane, you are my agent as well as her aide. You will keep me apprised of developments."

Aveyron bowed his head. "I will be observant and dutiful, Majesty."

"I trust you will be." With a sinuous arc of her long spine, Queen Abonde lifted upward. The beat of her wings created a violent blast that smarted Solenn's eyes. She lifted an arm to cover her face, but by then, the dragon was out of the crater. Abonde's power was evident in her graceful movement, by the sheer maturity indicated by her mass.

The way in which Albion was utilizing dragon epicurea seemed all the more disturbing after having met Queen Abonde in her native form.

Solenn released a long, relieved breath. *Now* she felt like a more productive diplomat. Not only did she have permission to move forward in her plot, but she was alive and unharmed. A successful day all around.

She packed up her table book and reached for the heavy pack.

"Solenn, you needn't take that alone," Aveyron said softly.

She paused. She'd taken for granted that she would carry Hester Incarnate herself. Weeks ago, she would've insisted on it as a point of pride. She wasn't the same person now.

Solenn smiled and beckoned Aveyron over.

She gripped one handle. He grabbed the other. Walking closely, as a team, they exited the crater, a portion of the God's body swaying between them.

CHAPTER THIRTEEN

ADA

In recent centuries, the Camarga region of Verdania has begun to cultivate rice. The even temperatures, bright light, and drying wind make the area ideal for this crop. Even so, far more rice is still imported from Hesperia. Taste the different varieties offered by each place. Detect the subtle variations and consider what food pairings will accentuate or clash with the natural goodness of the rice.

—Excerpt from *Manual for Tour Chefs*

Where was Erwan?

Was he not present because he was already dead?

The crowd before the palace quieted as the speaker from the balcony began to spout words about foul Braizians and the noble virtues of Prince Rupert. Ada leaned to whisper in Emone's ear. "They are dead men walking. No cure."

Emone took this in for a moment. "Selland preserve memories of them among those who will grieve. Their hangings will be mercy."

Horrible as the statement was, it was true. Otherwise, their remaining hours would escalate their agony. Ada thought again of how Solenn had been forced to sit with Rupert and his friend, perceiving everything as they similarly succumbed. Ada would well understand why Solenn would take a knife to her own tongue for that reason alone, not even considering the direct manipulation of Gyst.

"We'll try to retrieve them, after," Emone whispered. "Guard your reactions. Remember, we must blend in."

Blend in with these vile people who took in death as entertainment. Again, she wondered if she should've let Mallory Valmont and Hester carry out their vengeance upon this country. Maybe—

No. No. She had to remember that there were a few hundred people present here out of the seven hundred thousand souls who resided in the city. She couldn't let the few, vocal representatives of humanity at its most horrendous cause her to cast judgment upon the entire city.

The mob cheered at something bigoted, and Ada forced herself to grin. Erwan would understand.

Oh, Five, where was he? Was he still held elsewhere, as the more valuable political prisoner? Could Emone find out?

The first Braizian couldn't make the climb to the gallows. He tripped on the steps, flopping forward like a drunkard. People hooted and jeered. A soldier dragged the Braizian to meet the rope.

Ada looked at the other musketeers in line rather than the lead man as he kicked the air. They showed no reaction. It was all they could do to stand upright as their organs festered.

"Gyst," she mouthed for his ears alone. "Whatever your grudge against Solenn and me, be kind with these men as you guide them through their revealed mysteries. Tell them that this injustice is being witnessed, that word of their dignity and duty will be carried back to Braiz."

There was no blatant dankness or scent to indicate Gyst was present, not in the fading daylight of this terrible day, but she knew he'd heard. She retained belief in his omnipresence, if nothing else.

The second man died. The third. The fourth had to be carried all the way up the stairs, people howling that he was a coward, a weakling, that he couldn't face death like a man—what did that even mean? What difference did such small body parts make at moments like this? Anger and grief rocked her in waves, but she did cheer when his body stilled upon the rope. His suffering was done.

Ada and Emone slowly rode away as soon as permitted by the decreasing mob. She saw Simon far, far ahead, his tall form looming above most everyone else. Of Brillat, she perceived and saw nothing. He must have wormed his way through the throngs quickly.

"How are we going to get them?" Ada asked Emone. It was too dangerous to clarify of whom she spoke, but Emone's nod showed that she understood.

"I know people," she said simply. They rode slowly, both with an occasional casual eye around them to make sure they weren't being followed. "The greater problem will be money to pay for access and shipping. My pockets aren't making much music these days. I've put everything into rebuilding and taking care of my people."

Emone collected the orphaned, shunned, and lost the way that some older women had the propensity for taking in cats—but knowing her and Claudette, they likely saved cats as well.

Ada remembered something she hadn't thought about in weeks— the jewels she'd lifted from Mallory Valmont's estate, still in an interior pocket of her coat. "I can take care of that."

Emone arched an eyebrow in blatant curiosity. "It won't be cheap. Many of the executed, they go to . . . well."

Ada sucked in a breath. "That's right. The physicians' schools." The dead musketeers would be highly desired for anatomical study because rare singing mushroom had been part of their demise. They'd be cut apart, subject to modern chemical analyses, their organs weighed. Butchered, not unlike magical beings, though consumption wouldn't be the end goal. "I think I have more than enough to cover the cost, though. Whatever is left can go toward the Golden Horse."

She delved into her pocket to find the filled bag of rings and other jewels. "Examine them when you have some privacy," she said, passing the bag to Emone as they reined up. She nodded and tucked it inside her own overcoat.

The swaybacked storehouse was visible a block away. "While I still have a horse, I'm going to utilize speed to make inquiries after Erwan and his peers. I hope to be back before sunset."

"Be careful," Ada said.

"Unlike some people, I *have* kept in practice," she said, a hand glancing the hilt of the rapier at her side. She trotted away.

Simon had returned first and awaited Ada at the entrance to the stable. His face was flushed and sweaty from his fast walk. "Madame Adamantine. I'm sorry—"

"Thank you," Ada said softly. "I still—"

"Your Camarga is gone. I asked our neighbors, and they only saw—"

Ada swung herself out of the saddle. "He'll be back. Camargas do as they will."

"If he's wandering the quartier, he'll be nabbed. I can call upon—"

"Simon, if he's not back within an hour, I'll worry then. I trust him."

That was a partial lie. She did trust Brillat, but she'd also fully expected him to be blithely idling in his stall. His lack of a return was vexing, one worry to stack upon others like pebbles in a tenuous pyramid.

"Is that Emone riding away?" Simon asked. "Is she—"

"She's going to make inquiries. Here, I'll feel better if you're with her. Gods know, last thing I want is for something more to befall those I love."

"I understand that sentiment, madame," he said in a soft, sincere voice.

She handed over the reins of her horse, but he didn't mount up—he'd need to adjust the stirrups before doing so. Instead, leading the horse, Simon jogged in pursuit of Emone.

That left Ada alone at the storehouse. If her thoughts were allowed to macerate, she'd surely go mad, so she did the healthiest thing she could think of: she grabbed a handbasket left by the door and set off to buy provisions for supper.

The surrounding quartier hosted the resident poor, mostly immigrants from beyond Verdania. The buildings were tall and teetering, shingled roofs mottled with obvious replacement patches. Running children and dogs poured through narrow byways. Muddy hogs rooted in the drainage trenches along the street. The smells from open windows evoked far-distant locales such as Hesperia: hot oil, cinnamon, oregano, the uncommon but delightful smell of cooking rice. The sweet blooms of a potted orange tree on a high balcony made Ada's tongue tingle with awareness.

Erwan had expressed curiosity about traveling to Hesperia. As a man raised in a climate cold, gray, and damp, he held an inherent curiosity about places that were said to be warm and sunny, with a vastly different color palette within the natural world. Hesperia had hosted a thriving artistic scene these past fifty years too. She could imagine Erwan going there for a brief study of the masters and then practicing his own amateur talents with a canvas set to overlook water flecked with colorful sails.

Did he still sketch and paint as he once did? Had he shared his joy of art with Solenn?

She was blinking back the sting of tears as she recognized wrongness upon her tongue. The taste reminded her of meatiness, coppery blood, and rich marrow.

Her first thought was that she had never before encountered this epicurea—then she realized that wasn't true. Something of this very nature had flown high over the sea cliffs of Braiz.

A hand to her rapier, she rounded a corner. A dark cat scampered away. Down another block, around another corner, she reached the dirt bank of a canal, where a few men fished and others sold wares from carts, lamps already lit in anticipation of the coming night. Ada's dark skin and worn clothes blended in more here than in most quartiers of the city, nor was she the only person to openly carry a blade and pistol. Leaving the makeshift tents behind, she ducked under a broad, droop-branched willow tree to find two girls circling each other, three-foot-long sticks in their hands. As Ada watched, one girl rushed the other, their sticks meeting with a resonant hollow clatter.

Whatever those sticks were, they were among the most potent epicurea she had ever encountered. The only thing more powerful: Hester's powder.

The girls, both around ten, were oblivious to her presence. Both had golden-brown skin, their black hair pulled into pigtails tied by ribbons. Their white skirts flared above the knee as they twirled, lunged, and thrust. By propriety, such skirts should be midcalf, but in a quartier like this, they were fortunate to have clothes in good care at all. They screeched at each other in words Ada didn't know but readily comprehended to be insults.

Each tap of the sticks sent tingles up Ada's spine, as if a little power reverberated through the air with every impact. She needed a closer look.

One of the girls backed up and, glancing over her shoulder, saw Ada. She froze, mouth gaped. The other girl then observed Ada as well but, instead of being fearful of the stranger, stalked closer with her stick brandished.

"Who are you and what do you want?" she challenged in accented Verdanian.

Ada bowed. "My name is Ada. I'm a former soldier. I couldn't help but admire your swordfight. I started my own formal training when I was about your age. I had a sponsor," she added as an afterthought. Even the poor could learn to duel or ascend to an officer program with a benefactor. She certainly couldn't state that her training had been part of her tour days as a young Chef.

The first girl relaxed, but the second furrowed her brow. "Why are you here? You're not one of *us*."

"No, I'm not. I'm on the way to the market. My mind is full of sorrows, and I just . . . kept walking." Sometimes the truth, minus details, was best. "Would you like me to show you some moves?"

At that, both girls gasped. "Give her your stick," the second girl ordered, and her friend promptly complied.

Ada set down her empty basket and, unbuckling her own rapier, held it out to the first girl. "I'll trade you," she said with a smile. As a dark-skinned orphan child, she'd known her share of bossy peers and bullies. Ada would forever look out for the meek. "But do not draw my blade or this lesson ends."

The girl mutely nodded and made the exchange. The second girl looked enraged for a second, then calmed again as she seemed to remember she wasn't holding the sword, but she would be the first trained in its use. "Show me your moves, madame. Please," she added.

Ada's fingers twitched on the stick. It was warm, but not because of the girl's body heat or sunlight. The thing still contained ambient life—and it was about as heavy as the plume of a hat, despite its length and its roughly two-inch diameter.

"Where did you find these poles?" she said in blatant admiration.

"It was floating on the river," said the first girl. "When we waded in to grab the thing, we found it was almost broken in half. We broke it the rest of the way."

Indeed, the top of the stick had a jagged edge, as did its mate. But farther down on her stick, a hole had been drilled through, which still held a loop of leather. This had been attached to something.

She recognized the hollow structure, the smooth yet porous feel. This was bone. Like a bird's bone—a large magical bird, the stuff of legend—or something else that could fly.

She thought of her brief conversation with Solenn, Brillat, and Aveyron, and of the existence of Caldian dragons. Whoever had used this wing must have crashed in or near the rivers or canals around Lutecia.

"Well?" said her opponent, her tone challenging.

Right. A lesson in dueling. This would foremost be a test of what she remembered. "My first advice—don't do the move you just did, trying to cut the torso and shoulders. Modern rapiers don't transmit enough blunt force to make such attacks effective. Swing at me as you did your friend."

She did, and Ada immediately found a wide opening to prod the jagged edge of her "sword" against the girl's upper arm, above the pulse of her brachial artery. "See? You made yourself vulnerable. You must learn defense first if you want to survive." The girl nodded, beaming in pleasure despite her potential death. "Now, your guard positions. This pose is prima. Do this as you unsheathe."

Ada went through the guards in sequence. The current fighting style across the continent—in practice for about a century—arose from Lucania, and kept Lucanian words for terminology. Once Ada ran through those poses, she had the girls switch spots. She kept a closer eye on the brash girl, who now held her sword, as she was the most likely of the two to unsheathe it, but she was too busy correcting her friend's posture like an instant adept.

A few adults came by and hovered at the fringes to make sure nothing untoward was occurring, as was only right. Ada acknowledged them with nods.

After some twenty minutes, with both girls given equal time, Ada requested her rapier's return. "Now, keep in mind you must behave responsibly with what I've shown you. You're not experts. If anything, you can now hurt yourselves with considerably more finesse."

"When I become a champion duelist someday, I will credit you as my first mentor, Madame Ada." The bolder of the two girls said this with absolute sincerity.

"You honor me." Ada bowed. Because the girls wore skirts, they curtsied. As Ada picked up her basket and walked away, she heard one girl say to the other, "Now, be on guard—ha!"

Ada smiled and shook her head.

She went about her shopping, Erwan heavy on her thoughts, but on good memories more so than fear. Back in the days of the Thirty-Fifth, they'd sparred often to maintain their skills. He would love that, on this day of grief, she had taken the time to instruct two girls on swordplay.

She soon carried already-cut chicken breasts, an array of produce, a hefty chunk of bread, and a passable bottle of red wine plugged with an oiled rag. Not far from the storehouse, a silver-haired man came alongside her, matching her stride.

She looked sidelong at Brillat. "I was worried about you."

"My apologies. Matters took longer than anticipated." His brow furrowed, his nostrils flaring. "There's a faint scent about you—"

"Dragon?" she asked softly. Before he could judge further, she quietly explained what she'd found. His face turned contemplative.

"There's no point in feigning ignorance now. You found the remnants of dragon wings rendered into a form that humans can use. There are ways that Chefs can attune the wings with related dragon epicurea, enabling a human to, with practice, use them as if they were natural to the body."

Ada stopped in the walkway to stare at him. "I've never encountered anything of the like in Verdanian texts."

Brillat released a wry laugh. "Were you favored? Obedient? Of utmost loyalty? The kind of person who'd be granted access to the rarest of knowledge?"

She grunted. "No, I was an incessantly questioning brat who never broke under their near-constant disciplinary efforts. I see your point. There are probably whole libraries of privileged books I never saw." She glanced at her hands gripping the basket. "There must've been some residue shed from the bones. Will scrubbing my hands be adequate to remove that taint?"

"It should be, yes." They were quiet as they entered the stable of the mercantile building. No voices or footsteps carried from within. They stopped before the gate of his stall. "Good, we have privacy to speak more. You needn't worry about the bodies of the Braizian musketeers. They will make it home to meet Selland in the sea."

Tears immediately came to her eyes. "You—how—"

"To all, a return home," he said, repeating a phrase she'd heard weeks before, when the kin were emptying Maman's manor of epicurea. "Thousands of my kin will know dignity and peace due to Erwan's help. This was the least I could do, to afford the same courtesy to his comrades."

"I can't thank you enough, I—"

The door across the room banged open. "Ada!" Emone stood there, Simon her stalwart shadow. "We came back and you were gone, and we searched for you but—"

"We saw you from a distance, madame, and that you walked along with someone."

Ada glanced within the stall. Brillat was quietly shedding his clothes. She set her basket on stacked crates and walked closer to the door. "I was in polite dialogue with someone, that was all." She looked between them, reading the strain on both their faces. There was a reason they'd searched for her. "You found out something." Icy cold trickled through her veins.

"Caristo had choice royal prisoners brought with him to Versay a week ago," Emone said. "Erwan was included."

Ada's fists clenched and unclenched, their rhythm slow in contrast to the new thunder of her heart.

As of a week ago, Erwan was alive. But then, a week ago his fellow musketeers had been hale as well.

"Prisoners at Versay are often there because they are friends of court," Ada said slowly. "But they're also there for the sake of royal oversight during interrogations."

"Yes," Emone said simply.

"If he's still there, his classification would mean that he's likely being tortured or otherwise deprived." Ada's heart beat fast, her breaths deep. Her mood could only be described as murderous. "I'm leaving in the morning."

"Ada, the Blessed are the worst around Versay. They know the king is there, and they want him dead. You're going to have to fight through them *and* Verdanian forces to get to the palace."

"You say that as if you think it'll stop me."

Emone's grin was tired. "No, no, but as you said earlier, you usually rely on me to deliver sense in dire circumstances. I want you to be careful, that's all. We already lost Didina because of Valmont's attacks on us, and Erwan is in danger, and Claudette . . ." She shook her head, unable to broach further possibilities. "I don't want to lose you too."

"Do you want . . . help?" Simon asked as if he felt required to do so.

"I have my Camarga, and we make a good team." On cue, Brillat's head emerged over the half door. She'd sensed his change as Emone was speaking. "Your people need you here," she said to both Emone and Simon.

"I know they do, but I still wish I could do more for you and Erwan." Emone's face skewed in dismay. "I made inquiries about accessing the musketeers, but I may not hear back until tomorrow or—"

"It's been taken care of," Ada said. At Emone's arched brow, she continued. "I can't say more than that. Keep the jewels and use the funds however you wish. Make the Golden Horse better than ever."

"Five be praised," Simon said with reverence, flaring his hand.

Ada resisted the urge to argue about the Gods being grouped together in thanks. This Gystsday brimmed with sorrow, and yet, hope still glowed like a stubborn coal amid the ashes. She would rely on that modicum of warmth.

CHAPTER FOURTEEN

SOLENN

Some fragile cheeses gain structure and flavor from being wrapped in a bark such as spruce. Leaves serve a similar protective function, those of chestnut being among the most popular to use across the continent. Wrapped cheeses can be washed in eau-de-vie to eradicate impurities. Lait and Gyst are beseeched to safeguard the food as it matures.

—Excerpt from *Book for Cooks to Excel as Do Chefs*

Hope. Fear. Strange how those two emotions often snarled together these days, like yarn batted about by cats. Solenn stood at the entrance to . . . not a building, but a grove of trees that had a distinct sense of place. Surrounding oak trees boasted trunks five feet wide, gnarled by time and exposure. Their branches formed a high, complicated ceiling backed by blue sky. She heard whispers around her, beings unseen.

"I'll be waiting right here," Aveyron said, reassuring her with a smile. She had insisted that she alone parley with the dryad, and he'd volunteered to wait outside with the stone. The plan made solid sense to her. She'd always been told that it wasn't good manners to surprise a host by bringing along dogs and small children; surely that was also true of toting along a living fragment of the God who'd cursed your kind to an exploitive double-existence.

Solenn stepped beneath the shadows of the twined vine archway that formed an entry. "Greetings! I'm Ambassador Solenn de Braiz. I've come to speak with Dryad Lyria, if she will be so generous as to meet with me." Solenn bowed, though no one was visible before her.

"Lyria." The name echoed, spoken at a high pitch.

"Lyria!" again, in a deep base.

"Leeeer-ee-uh!" came another screech, followed by jumbled repetitions.

Solenn glanced back at Aveyron, who didn't act surprised at all. "The neighbors are helping," he said.

After a moment, leaves to the side of the archway rustled. A knee-high being that looked like a spiraled beige root emerged. They had the large-headed look of a toddler, with two large green leaves sprouting from the top of their head.

"Lyria asked me to take you to her," said the root-child. "Both of you."

Solenn hesitated. "Monsieur Aveyron was intending to wait here with a rock, as we were unsure if—"

"Bring it," said the root-child.

Aveyron shrugged and hoisted the heavy satchel.

They took a winding, narrow path through a dense forest to enter a small grove some five by ten feet in diameter. It had the very feel of a room, complete with a ceiling of newly budded branches.

The root-child giggled and bounced back up the path.

"Dryad Lyria?" Solenn called. Aveyron had told her that dryads didn't favor honorifics. "I beg your pardon, I'm—"

"I know who you are." The deep baritone surprised her, and Solenn chastised herself. Who was she to assume how a tree would speak, whatever their name? A thin figure entered the room through a wall of leaves. Lyria wore no clothes as humans understood them. She was a walking tree with coarse brown bark, elongated dark-green leaves as her hair. Her mouth was a black slash, her eyes like glossy pebbles polished by waves.

Solenn bowed. "I hold great admiration for your work. I . . ." She stopped speaking, as she couldn't help but stare.

Lyria didn't walk so much as she crept on a countless number of wriggling roots—like a crab, but with far more appendages.

"This rock. You've brought me a God," Lyria stated in a deep monotone. No need to delicately introduce that issue, then. The kin's perception could be helpful in such ways.

"Indeed. Greetings, friend," said Aveyron, setting down his burden.

"Salutations." Lyria's smile was brief. "Draw it forth and tell me your story."

Her bluntness didn't seem to faze Aveyron. As he folded back the leather to reveal the stone, Solenn explained how they had come about the rock and why they had brought it to her. The dryad bowed over the stone, her twiggy fingers stroking the sides with delicacy. As if she might be burned.

Despite her statements to Queen Abonde, Solenn knew a sudden spike of fear—if Hester wanted to directly attack the Arcady, she now had an avenue. But Lyria didn't seem to experience any similar concerns as she lifted the stone.

"Most rocks I encounter are far more aged, but none before has been a God." Lyria spun the rock on her twig-tips as if it weighed nothing. "She speaks to me, Hester does."

"Can you hear her?" Solenn said, jaw gaped.

"Not as we talk aloud." Lyria motioned to her own mouth with a free hand. "She speaks to me as other stones do. She wishes to be carved."

Solenn bowed her head, momentarily overwhelmed with relief.

"Do you comprehend *how* she wishes to be carved?" asked Aveyron.

"I won't know until I set my tools to their tasks. I can make an effort later today, but I don't know how the work will progress. Some of my projects take hours. Others, years." Solenn guessed that Lyria did her carving elsewhere. This grove had to be akin to a bedchamber, a private place for her to catch sun and rain. "You say that you wish for Hester to be capable of auditory speech. I don't know if such a thing is possible."

"Neither does Hester," Solenn added softly.

Lyria nodded. "The one thing I can say is that this rock *aches* to speak. She's hungry. Needy. She craves as no other rock can, but then, few other rocks were once human beings."

"Because Hester is much like rupic, her debris is especially dangerous." Solenn couldn't help a shudder of revulsion.

"Queen Abonde herself bid you to take care," said Aveyron.

Lyria swayed like a tree in a wind, though only a soft breeze rustled the woods. "Yes. Any fragments will be pulverized and mixed with large quantities of dirt to adulterate the accursed holiness." *Accursed holiness.* Such a fine phrase.

Lyria rotated the stone on her twigs again. "This will prove interesting. I will send word when the work is done. Leave the bag there, Aveyron. I may find additional uses for it."

"Very well." He bowed and backed away.

"Thank you again, Lyria." Solenn barely managed the words, but Lyria's full focus rested on the stone, as if already seeing the possibilities. Solenn left without a sound. She knew how even the easygoing Erwan could become grumpy if he was interrupted during a creative spurt. Artists were like snakes, best left undisturbed.

Though she could no longer sense magic, Solenn felt strange once they were outside the grove, as if she'd forgotten something important. She also recognized her deep restlessness. Back home, when moods such as this struck, she'd set off riding for hours along the cliffs, inhaling that glorious wind and trying to spy distant krakens. The creatures didn't favor Malo—sailors said that was likely because there were too many ships—but every so often, she'd see the flail of far-off tentacles. Krakens were always much closer at Land's End, where the Sleeve Sea met the endless Blue.

"Solenn, you have that look on your face. You're pondering."

"Yes." She needed to speak with krakens. Solenn thought on Mamm-gozh's advice. Sometimes proper diplomatic channels were not only unnecessary but detrimental.

Her throat felt strained after speaking with Lyria, so she pulled out her table book. *Queen Abonde scoffed at the idea that I begin my alliance with krakens, but has she forbidden us from making an attempt?*

"No." He cocked his head. "I don't know where we'd even find them, though."

I do. Is there a dolmen out near the equivalent of Land's End?

"Land's End! I've never been there, but I know it's what we call an 'anchor place,' where the geography is the same on both sides of the veil."

Good. We won't need to cross over if krakens lurk there in Arcady. How far of a ride do you think it'll be?

"A few hours. Long enough that a saddle would be best for you." Aveyron's grin portrayed his readiness.

A quick stop at the cottage gave her time to pack food, both water and piquette, and to pull a thick coat from the tailored wardrobe that'd been waiting for her in the remodeled cottage.

Outfitted for the trek, she mounted Aveyron in his stallion form, and he set off at a steady canter.

Solenn had visited Land's End almost every year during her life, sometimes several times within a short span, as cousins died as babies or accidents happened or old age took its toll. Land's End was imbued with the innate thrum of Selland's might, and therefore the place where the corpses of Braizian royalty met Selland soon after their souls met Gyst.

Miles upon miles of Arcady passed beneath Aveyron's gray hooves. They skirted towns humanlike and decidedly not, traveling the road only when it aligned with their need. Solenn recognized the gradual uplift of terrain as they crossed the equivalent of the Verdanian and

Braizian border. Through hills of gorse and broom they rode, the greenery deepening, the settlements sparser. She somehow sensed the nearby ocean before she could even smell it, and then she caught a glimpse of the blue-gray water. Her heart lurched with joy. It looked like Braiz. *Home.* The skies were suitably pink and gray as dusk neared. Aveyron's steps slowed. He walked the last stretch, giving his muscles time to cool before he came to a stop.

At his signal, she dismounted and proceeded to untack him. He promptly changed form.

"Do dolmen exist below the water as they do above?" Her voice was stronger after hours of rest, but the relentless wind here would tire her throat fast.

"That's my understanding, yes. There's supposed to be a submarine shrine just beyond the rocks." He pointed to the eroded, rounded pink granite that made up the jutting cliff of Land's End as he pulled on his clothes, shivering. He'd chosen one of his thicker outfits to bring, a suit with velvet green and slim black breeches beneath the skirt. It would warm his more temperature-sensitive human form.

"I hope I have enough voice for this and that they can understand me," Solenn said.

"You needn't worry about that." Aveyron finished up his buttons. "Krakens don't vocalize speech. They don't change form at all."

Solenn stared at him, suddenly wishing they'd discussed this in more detail before committing to the journey. "Don't speak? What? Am I—do I need to get in the water?" She'd never been scared of the ocean, not even when she'd almost drowned as a child, but these waters were the most vicious of the northern coast.

"No. Very few emissaries meet with krakens, but those that do engage them at the tip of Land's End. A kraken extends a tentacle upward, you see, and when they touch someone, they then share thoughts—"

"No." She took a step back.

Aveyron blinked, stunned. "No? But this is—"

"You're saying krakens communicate mind to mind. Like Gyst." Icy-cold dread made her shiver.

"Similar to Gyst, yes, but they can't *control* their conversation partner, it's just—"

"How do you know? Have *you* spoken with them?" Her words were so slurred and inarticulate that his expression stayed blank for a moment as he deciphered her speech. She already knew he wouldn't have spoken with krakens. They resided in colder northern waters.

"I know by what I've read and been told. Of course I've not parleyed with them myself." He kept his voice level. "I believe you can do this, Solenn. You won't even need to speak aloud. Krakens share and read pictures in the mind. My understanding is that many land concepts baffle them, though, so you'll need to work with slow—"

"I can't do this." She couldn't let someone into her mind, not again. What if they didn't let go? What if she couldn't regain control of her body? What if she couldn't even control her *brain*? She'd already lost her tongue—what else would she have to cut off, a hand? An arm? What if their direct physical touch let them penetrate her mind deeper than even Gyst, truly delving into her mysteries, her fears, her shames?

"Solenn, krakens are regarded as holy by your people. You already have a close relationship with them."

She'd thought allying with krakens was a grand idea, but if she lost her sense of self, she couldn't save Braiz. Or Erwan. Or her parents and Adamantine. Even Hester relied upon her for aid right now.

"I'm sorry. It didn't occur to me that this would be so challenging for you." Aveyron positioned himself to grip her hands. Her body felt limp with new despair. "Would it be acceptable if I did this in your stead?"

That aroused her from the churning maelstrom of her terror. "What?"

"I'll engage with krakens on your behalf, if you should trust me with such a vital task. I'm not an ideal representative for Braiz, but I'll do my best."

She felt both relieved that he would take on such a risk and burden and disgusted by her own weakness. "I want you to be safe too." Her voice barely existed.

"Other kin confer with krakens. Queen Abonde has herself." He squeezed her hands. "I'll survive and be well."

She knew that the fact that Queen Abonde had used this form of communication should comfort her, but it didn't. There was no way for Solenn to know if the queen had somehow been altered as a result. Solenn's own scars were private.

"Solenn," he said, the wind buffeting his loose silver hair over his shoulders, "do you trust me?" She nodded without hesitation. "Will you still come with me?"

He was nervous, she realized, and yet didn't hesitate to step forward to do what she could not. She certainly couldn't let him go forward alone. She needed to make sure that he was well—that he was still Aveyron.

The dirt underfoot soon ended. The rest of the trek involved jumps from pink boulder to pink boulder, each one smoothed like rising balls of dough. Most of the gaps between rocks were small, but the way was dangerous. She'd known people who'd broken ankles and legs on these strangely colored rocks.

Land's End narrowed to a triangular point. She glanced down the cliff's edge to see black water twenty feet below. She'd never been allowed at the edge. Her parents and Erwan would've been aghast. Strangely enough, she wasn't scared of the perilous height, though a fall from here would almost certainly be fatal.

Aveyron stepped to where land ended. The wind blew his hair almost straight back. Solenn had to brace her legs on two different boulders to maintain her balance as she joined him. There was just enough space for them to stand side by side. Water stretched out before them, as if to the ends of the world.

She saw no sign of krakens.

She and Aveyron looked at each other. He shrugged, clearly at as much of a loss as she was. If krakens didn't speak, yelling at the ocean wouldn't work. Selland alone would know what to do.

Selland! She and krakens were cousins through the God. He could mediate.

Solenn pinched her fingers, focusing on the brisk wind, the salt, the very power of this place. Land's End was always imbued with a sense of gravitas, but here in Arcady, she felt it even more.

Selland, she called in her mind.

His presence immediately prickled at her senses.

Rattled by his quickness, she took a deep breath before continuing. The other Gods often reciprocated when given offerings, but Selland did as he willed. As suddenly as he had arrived, he could also leave. *We've come to speak with krakens. How can we beckon to them? Could you kindly help us?*

Even as she asked, she wondered if she truly wanted this meeting to happen. Could krakens be trusted? Should she tell Aveyron to not continue? Without him—and with Erwan gone—she would be bereft.

The wind flicked tears from the corners of her eyes, as if with a gentle fingertip, and Selland's presence faded. That was it? Had he—

"Look!" Aveyron said with a gasp.

Several hundred yards away, the water churned. The boiling movement drew close, quickly, and then a massive body breached the surface just below them. The kraken had to be as long as five wagons lined in a row, its turbulent tentacles longer yet. One such purple-black tentacle rose higher and higher, its base thicker than many trees. As the end flexed up, she saw big pink suckers; the lower ones were larger than her head and probably deep enough to fit her like a tall hat. She'd been told that krakens were more massive than a premier ship of the line, and now she fully believed that. This one could even be grander than Queen Abonde in her dragon form.

She knew she should motion to Selland with gratitude for his quick response, but the closer the tentacle came, the more her horror increased. Not because of what it was, but because of what it could *do*.

"I'll be fine, Solenn," Aveyron said, but his smile for her was tense.

The tentacle extended above the cliff, the thick protrusion hovering at Aveyron's height. No suckers lined the very tip, which was good, as the ones right at cliff level seemed to have serrated edges like tiny blades.

The tentacle remained poised in space. Waiting for her.

She stepped back, slipping on the curved surface of a boulder in her haste. She caught herself on one hand, angling her leg so she landed on the fleshy outside of her thigh rather than her knee.

"Solenn?" Alarm rang in Aveyron's voice, but he couldn't turn to help her.

"I'm fine," she said, or tried to. She pushed herself up as the tentacle thickly bent, the dark tip pressing into Aveyron's head. She couldn't see his face, but his posture remained straight.

A low wail of terror escaped her throat.

"It doesn't hurt," he said. Krakens could make him say that. "We're beginning our conversation."

She was afraid to even grip his hand for support, lest the kraken's pervasive force travel through his body and into her.

When Gyst spoke through Solenn, her voice, her face, her mannerisms also shifted to a minute degree. She couldn't tell yet if there was a change in Aveyron. She wanted to trust this kraken, she did, but Gyst, Gyst, Gyst, he was all she could think about, his control, his words, how he could so gently advise her and a moment later force her to stand upright to accept a lash of Hester's flames.

"Krakens know of you as an ambassador, Solenn, and they accept me as a liaison on your behalf. They . . . I need to stop thinking in words." He paused. "This is a lot to work through. Give me a moment."

His silence tormented her. When he spoke again, it was slowly.

"Many kin don't understand political boundaries. The kraken don't at all. They are showing me what they see, and their vision isn't like that of humans or equines. Everything has a rainbow cast. That somehow enables them to detect light, even deep within the water. They . . . I'm sorry, I know I'm babbling. I'm also trying to continue conversing with them."

Solenn tried to tell herself that a continued palaver was a good sign. If the kraken wanted to control him outright, it might have done so already . . . or might not. Gyst hadn't immediately exercised absolute control over her either.

"By talking to one kraken, I'm speaking with many. Within the waters of Arcady, they can share images across a great distance, but on the other side of the veil, they must touch to communicate. Ships . . . they don't fully understand ships, beyond that they carry people, which they find . . . tasty." He grimaced. The accompanying image must not have been pleasant. "War is also a foreign concept. They don't engage in violence for fun or diversion. They attack to eat. I'm trying to . . . you said they never attack ships from Braiz. I want to understand why."

Good, good. This would be an excellent starting point. Solenn was frustrated, however, that krakens understood so little. She'd been raised with the idea that they were brilliant beings, gifted so by Selland; perhaps the truth was that they were still brilliant, but in a different way.

Aveyron continued. "Krakens understand that ships come from different places. To them, ships from Braiz are good because they don't attack them, so krakens don't attack the ships either. The vessels also carry less epicurea, which makes them friendlier. That's their full concept of your country," he said, succinctly destroying much of Braiz's beliefs in krakens. "They don't understand Albion as a separate entity, only that . . . ships from the colder water tend to attack them and carry more epicurea, which makes them more viable as food. They don't eat epicurea or people who've ingested it, though," he clarified. "Such people they kill and leave for Selland."

By all the salt in the sea! Had no one ever noticed that ships that left Braiz were never attacked? That had to include trade ships, including those from Albion. Why, if Albion ruled Braiz and began to hunt from there, *all* vessels could become potential "food" for krakens.

Solenn edged closer to Aveyron. She'd never before been disturbed by octopi or squid, but the size of this tentacle upon his head repulsed her. Viscous gel dribbled around Aveyron's ear and darkened his fine coat.

Even so, she bent closer to his head. "Show . . . flags?" she forced out, then repeated the words in an attempt to be clearer.

"Flags? I don't know if that will help. Krakens don't usually picture ships above the water, it seems. For them, breaching the waves means profound vulnerability and is best avoided." There was a long stretch of silence but for the sounds of birds and the constant orchestral crash of waves below. "Gods help me. I'm trying, but they don't even see colors as we do, much less the fine details on flags."

Solenn made a frantic gesture to Selland. *Please, let the kraken understand.* Braiz and Albion had distinct maritime flags—at least, to human eyes. Braiz used bright-blue and purple bands, the edges fringed with silver lace. Albion featured a red rampant dragon—oh, how much more terrible that symbolism seemed now.

"They are . . . so happy to chat with me. I'm being flooded with images. I think—oh. They—oh. The tentacle has been straining out of the water for too long, they need to—"

The tentacle released and retreated to the water in a blur of movement.

Aveyron wavered in place. She immediately gripped his hand.

"I—the full return to myself is disorientating." His smile for her was weak but looked sincere. Was he truly still himself? "Come, let's get out of the worst of the wind."

She gave the water a last desperate glance. They'd come all this way, for what?

She and Aveyron continued to hold hands as they made their way back to land. The process was slow and careful, as little light remained.

Once on solid ground, she gestured to the waves, to him, and shrugged. Her confusion needed no words.

"I don't know, Solenn." His own frustration came through. "Their way of experiencing the world is vastly different than ours. More foreign than I ever could've imagined. Queen Abonde was right to doubt that we could ally. I can say that krakens love each other, they love the ocean, and they fully feel Selland's embrace in every moment—there's an intensity of *life* to them I can't help but envy. But the way they see the world—quite literally—is alien to us, as is their idea of culture, ritual. I don't even know how I could put into words some of what I saw." He shook his head, his hair lashing his face.

But what of an alliance, of krakens aiding Braizian ships? Did krakens have any sense of how much more fiercely they would be hunted if Albion dominated the continent?

"I don't know what else to tell you," Aveyron said, his own voice hoarse from the wind. "I'll transform, and we'll ride to find shelter for the night. You'll be able to write in your table book then."

Aveyron sounded like himself. Even more, she believed he was himself. That was one comfort, even as she drowned in despair.

There would be no alliance with krakens. She couldn't think of any other mighty sea-kin who could be helpful allies either. The Braizian navy was on its own.

As Solenn rode Aveyron into the night, she knew coldness that seeped far deeper than skin.

CHAPTER FIFTEEN

ADA

Fromage frais is a light fresh cheese made using whipped cream. The flavor is mild and sweet, and much improved by adding herbs, spices, and fruits. It is a favored accompaniment to caviar. Serve with a wine that is white or fortified.

—Excerpt from *Book for Cooks to Excel as Do Chefs*

Refugees clogged the roads just south of Lutecia, but the farther south Ada and Brillat traveled, the more they were able to ride cross-country over the rolling green hills interspaced with tilled fields and forests. Columns of smoke were visible far in the distance, the mood eerily quiet as they jumped fences and avoided people. The wind carried the scent of distant rain as the clouds grew darker, as if to match her increasing dread.

The closer they drew to Versay, she knew, the likelier it was that a confrontation would take place. After hours of vigilance, the moment at last arrived.

Three riders in Verdanian blue were almost invisible beneath trees upon a hillock but left no mystery to their intent as they spurred their horses downhill toward Ada and Brillat. Not a friendly approach—she'd bet an almond pan-pie that they'd accuse her of being a Blessed just because, or they'd avoid any verbal justification entirely and simply kill her in an effort to claim a Camarga as their own.

She and Brillat had discussed such dangers on their journey, and upon sight of the soldiers, he released a sharp sound that came across as an acceptance of a challenge. His canter shifted to a gallop as he followed the curve of a verdant creek.

The skies above growled.

Of course a storm would choose to break now after hours of placid gray. Ada motioned to the Five in appeal. Without reins to grip, her hands kept a light touch on Brillat's neck as she bowed forward.

One of the soldiers blew a whistle, long and low: a sound that civilians knew from an early age as an indication to stop, or else. She checked their distance. The slope had sped the cavalry's approach.

The clouds rumbled again. Lightning flashed out of the corner of her eye. This wasn't a time to be out in the open or sheltering in the woods. They needed a village or shed or barn, one not already occupied.

Brillat bounded over a fence, then through a stand of trees. A lightning bolt struck close enough that Ada felt her scalp prickle. The boom shuddered through her very bones, like the report of a close cannon. She glanced back. A tall tree they'd just galloped by now lay across the path. The soldiers reined up on the far side.

Twenty seconds ago, Brillat would've been *under* that tree. By what grace had the timing been so fortuitous? Seaborne storms were the domain of Selland, but those of the interior had no distinct divine affiliation.

The wind picked up with a howl as they exited the woods, a stretch of marshland ahead. Water glimmered at the base of the reeds. Brillat drew up short, snorting. Which way to go? Neither of them knew, and the nearest bridge or road was the likeliest place to find more soldiers.

Then a narrow section of grass dead ahead bowed opposite to the wind. It fell as flat as oil-slicked hair to form a zigzagging path.

A small sound of alarm and surprise escaped Ada's throat. The last of the Gods was no longer neutral. "My thanks to you, Lait," Ada said, bringing her fingers up in the distinctive motion of growing grass. Brillat, ears alert, took the provided path. The ground sloshed underfoot but supported his hooves. The grass to either side stood as high as his belly; the water would likely be deeper yet.

Ada glanced back. Five feet away, the grass began to stand tall again—or as much as it could, beneath the wind. The three cavalrymen came into sight at the far side of the marsh. Ada didn't look back again, but smiled as she heard splashes and yells. They hadn't been graced with a path.

Brillat climbed up an embankment into the lanes of a vineyard of just-budded vines. They rode on a few miles farther through more vineyards and a grove of chestnuts. Finally, spires arose over a distant hill. A town. But who held it? Blessed, Verdania, or townsfolk? None were inclined to be friendly.

Rain began like a sigh.

Ada squinted at the view, the particular rooftops, trees, and hills. "I think I recognize this place. Viflay. They make a fromage frais that's sweet and light. Their butter is fine too." Cows grazed in a nearby corral. That was a good sign. They hadn't been slaughtered or driven away.

At the edge of the village, Ada dismounted at a barn door. She'd intended to make a subtle entrance, but the wind caught the door the instant she unlatched it. It swung back to smack the wooden wall with an incredible clatter. She yanked it shut, causing even more racket.

Cursing beneath her breath, she drew her rapier and ducked behind a wooden support post. It was better protection than none. Brillat sidestepped into the deep shadows cast by stacked, baled hay. He would be well aware of how his white hide made him a target. Faint gray light shone through high, open windows.

Ada was unsurprised to hear a door creak at the far side of the barn.

"I know someone's here," hollered a deep voice. "What're you about? Who are you?"

"I'm a traveler in desperate need of refuge from the storm and conflict, monsieur," she called out. "Are you the owner of this barn?"

"I am. If you're one of the Blessed, you'd best show yourself out. Better to take your chances with the lightning than with me." He moved closer. She moved the opposite way. Sailcloth covered a carriage in the middle of the barn floor. She used that for cover as she circled around the man, her ears alert for the sound of anyone else. This fellow could well be a distraction.

"I'm not with the Blessed," she said, "nor have I had the misfortune to meet their ilk yet."

"You can remedy that in the morn, madame. They're camped just on the other side of the main bridge."

Oh, Five. She pictured what she remembered of this place. She'd essentially approached from the back; the main road to Versay came right through town and included a beautiful stone bridge over the river. The Blessed would strive to control that thoroughfare.

"Are Verdanian soldiers here?" she asked.

"No, and I can't decide whether that's good or bad. Gyst knows that answer better than me. I just don't want anyone to slaughter my milkers."

Yes, he spoke like a true resident. "I'm not seeking any trouble, monsieur. My rapier is in hand, but I'd rather not use it tonight. If you can provide me and my horse with shelter, I'll be glad to shovel manure or do other labor on your behalf."

He snorted, sounding amused. "Madame, I'm holding a pistol and I'd also rather save my shot for the morning. If you're against the Blessed, we welcome you among us. If you know how to use a rapier and a gun, maybe the Gods delivered us what we need."

She released an exhausted exhalation. Had Lait helped her and Brillat or directed them here only to help her favored dairyman? Both could be true. "I should hope you have more than a handful of fighters, or this'll be a quick quarrel at daybreak."

"There are many travelers caught here, and a number are helping defend the village. We're feeding folks in the tavern right now."

The wind banged at the door as if demanding entry, rain pelting the walls. Shelter, food, company, a chance at death amid a noble conflict— that sounded like a fair option about now.

"You may count me in, monsieur." Even so, she kept her blade unsheathed as she rounded the carriage to present herself to her bene- factor. He likewise still held his pistol, though aimed away. He was a short man with a cocked brown hat. A manicured, curved mustache stretched from one side of his face to the other. Appraising each other, they nodded and put away their arms.

"I'm Terrell," he said. First names were appropriate; after all, they very well might bleed together soon.

"I'm Ada."

"Former soldier?"

"A lifetime ago, yes."

"You should bring your horse into the interior of the village. We're keeping them together to better protect them."

"A good strategy," Ada said. On cue, Brillat emerged from the shad- ows to regard Terrell.

The man's eyes widened. "A Camarga. You should've mentioned that from the start! I'd know you to be a person of character."

"Unfortunately, many aggressive individuals also want to be people of character, and so it's best to wait for such introductions."

He barked out a laugh. "Sadly true. I worked the ports in the south during my youth. I've seen such horses more than once." He genuflected to Brillat, profound sincerity in the motion. Brillat nodded in return, which didn't seem to surprise Terrell in the least.

"Follow me," Terrell said, beckoning to them both. As she came around the wagon, she noted the sailcloth didn't fully cover this side. Against yellow paint, black calligraphy read GOLDEN HORSE FABRIC MERCANTILE.

Ada stopped. "Golden Horse Mercantile! Are these people in the village right now?"

"Why yes, in the tavern. Do you know—"

"Please, lead the way, monsieur," Ada said. Brillat cast her a questioning look, to which she nodded.

Lait hadn't just brought them here to help the dairyman. The Gods had been nudging many people to converge here, it seemed.

Ada situated Brillat in a smaller covered corral central to the village. She trusted that he could defend himself if anyone attempted to acquire a Camarga to escape town. From there, she followed Terrell through a burst of rain to a raucous tavern.

Sudden sweat doused her worse than the rain had as she stopped inside the dark hallway, brightness ahead. The place exuded warmth and good cheer, a party atmosphere she'd known before in the hours prior to a battle. She barely heard Terrell as he encouraged her to partake in victuals and wine. There had to be forty people present, attired in everything from stained hemp to court finery as they shared tables and drinks. A fine sight indeed, if one could tolerate packed humanity.

Glass clattered, a pot rattled. The air reeked of cooked chicken, broth, burned oil, sweaty clothes, dankness, damp leather. These were tavern smells, not battle smells, and yet . . . and yet . . . Ada's fists twitched, the burble of voices ringing tinny in her ears.

She breathed fast as she scanned the tables, trying to make out faces by firelight, when—there! The person she sought sat at the closest table on the far side.

Ada approached. "Claudette," she called, then again louder as a man's booming laugh drowned her out. "Claudette!"

The black-haired head turned her way, eyes widening with recognition. "Adamantine!" Emone's partner rose and rushed to her before they embraced. "Many years has it been, my dear." Claudette kissed each cheek in the warm Lucanian fashion. Unsurprisingly, a rapier bobbed at her side. "What brings you here amid this mayhem? Surely my Emone didn't send you."

"I left her only today, and while she's worried for you, the Gods were the ones who provided guidance. Can we speak outside?" Ada was trying not to visibly quiver.

Claudette nodded in understanding. "Emone told me," she said simply, giving Ada's hand a squeeze. "You must be hungry. You step out. I'll get you food and refreshment. I'll try to choose well." She winked, knowing full well that Ada was a Chef.

"I trust you," Ada said, and did. Not only to choose food that would be relatively edible, but to be her companion in battle.

The Gods had cursed her in some regards but blessed her as well. Tomorrow, with Claudette in her company, she might just survive. Versay was not even an hour's ride away. Erwan was there. He must be.

Unable to put her emotions into words, she gestured to the Five. She was so close.

CHAPTER SIXTEEN

SOLENN

Cheese makers who use rennet usually utilize one derived from young calves to coagulate their milk, but in northern Lucania, there are villages that use pig rennet and have done so for centuries. Stranger yet are tales that in more remote areas in the hills and mountains, people even use the stomachs of rabbits in their cheese making. Keep this in mind as you create your own cheese; Gyst's unknowns are myriad, as the saying goes, so rely on methods that are known and adapt from there.

—Excerpt from *Book for Cooks to Excel as Do Chefs*

Solenn awoke to bright sunlight and a profound sense of failure.

She and Aveyron had stopped only briefly for succor before continuing to their cottage the previous night. She wouldn't have been in a mood to talk, even had she a voice, but she did try to reassure Aveyron that she wasn't mad at him. The lack of a union with krakens wasn't his failure. Truly, he'd probably handled the conversation better than she would have if she'd tried to push through amid her terror.

For months, she'd accepted the responsibility that her marriage to Prince Rupert would save Braiz. She'd had so little control of what happened in that arrangement—and then lost control completely when Gyst wielded her like a puppet. Logic told her that Rupert's death, the dissolution of diplomatic relations between Braiz and Verdania, and the burgeoning war with Albion weren't her fault. But that didn't change how she felt.

The oppressive weight almost felt physical. Like Gyst's mantle, but formed of her own knowns and unknowns.

As she broke her fast with foods from her magically restocking cabinet, she had the odd realization that she'd never once regretted slicing off her tongue to evict Gyst. Allowing him to keep control wasn't an option. Nor had she liked her other option: to become God in his stead.

She didn't understand why she'd had such access to divine power, but she did comprehend the intense might she could've utilized. Might that could have been used to protect Braiz.

But she would've been dead. Never again able to ride a horse, to feel the sea wind upon her cheeks.

Deep in her personal darkness, she at first ignored the tap-tap-tap at her front door. Aveyron was away to report to Queen Abonde, and he didn't knock like that. She set her empty bowl back inside the cupboard, resolute in ignoring the stranger at the door.

The knock repeated, louder. Incessant. She glared at the offending door.

"Go away," she rasped, and could barely understand herself.

The knock repeated, impossibly louder. Seeing no other choice, she grabbed her table book and went to answer.

Lyria stood there, head tilted to one side, her black eyes unreadable. Why was she here? Had something gone wrong? Had the rock crumbled?

"Ambassador Solenn. I've brought you the completed work." She dipped her body, indicating the obviously heavy leather bag in her grip.

"What?" How could Lyria be already done?

"I completed work with the rock," Lyria repeated in her deep baritone.

Solenn had enough presence of mind to step back, gesturing Lyria to come inside. She did, ducking her leafy head, and as she entered, Solenn experienced a new sense of alarm. This was a stone building reinforced with wooden planks—and she held her table book in her hand.

Lyria followed her line of sight, head tilted.

"You can use your paper and pencil to communicate with me. I will not take offense. I can read Verdanian, which is where my home-tree stands." Apparently, she wasn't offended by the wood in the household, either, as she moved to stand in the small central room. Solenn belatedly remembered that Lyria had been here before and even worked with the materials around the fireplace. Perhaps all the wood here had been salvaged; that would be in keeping with the ethics practiced by Aveyron.

Solenn again realized her inadequacies as an ambassador. Should she invite Lyria to sit? Should she offer liquid refreshment? Aveyron had yet to advise her on how to handle social calls. Now that she had permission to use her book, though, she could ask. She jotted down her questions and showed the page to Lyria.

"I do not sit and I prefer water in either of my forms. If it is acceptable to you, I will remain in this spot." Lyria gestured with a branch-arm. Solenn understood why this was a favorable place. The nearby window shone bright light upon Lyria, her green leaves edged in gold.

Pardon my shock at your arrival. I didn't anticipate that you'd finish so quickly.

"Neither did I," Lyria said. "I began, thinking merely to test the density beneath my chisel, and then I couldn't stop. The stone was eager to find its form."

Eager. Solenn felt a desperate welling of hope.

"It shed slivers of stone with the enthusiasm with which many long-haired animals shed fur," Lyria continued. "It *needed* making. I am honored that I was the artisan invited for this task, but I can't take credit for the work. I shaped this only as the wind and water carve the shore. The difference is that I worked faster."

Her trunk bowed forward to pull open the leather bag and hoist up the new avatar of Hester.

It was a humanlike head formed of gray, mottled stone. The face featured full cheeks, a bold jaw. Thick eyebrows acted like eaves above wide, round eyes with pupils fixed forward. Tendrils of hair escaped from coiled braids reminiscent of antiquated Braizian court styles. All she needed was a tall coiffe.

Actually, Hester looked Braizian overall. That eye shape. The bold, thick nose—not unlike Solenn's own. Was Hester trying to look Braizian, or was this how she'd looked thousands of years ago, before she became a stone God?

Below the jaw was a stout, strong neck. To that had been fastened a broad leather collar, like those associated with aggressive dogs, with a thinner strap bracing around the forehead. Two long, looped straps from the collar made it easier for Lyria to carry the head without constant need for the accompanying bag.

"In a forest, there are many things that speak but cannot use words or even make sounds," Lyria said softly. Gripping both straps by one strong branch, she sprawled a twig-hand atop Hester's head. "A tree that is thirsty, that has stifled roots, that is diseased—you can tell much by the texture of bark, the dryness. This stone was much the same. Most stone, you must understand, is stolid, never in a hurry. Not so with this remnant of Hester, which looks old but acts young in its impatience."

Lyria extended her burden to Solenn. Setting aside her book, Solenn took the straps with both hands, bracing her forearms against her body to compensate for the dense weight. Her throat felt tight with terror of dropping it. The head weighed a bit less than it had before, having shed maybe a quarter of its mass, but was still heavy. With a grunt, she lifted it onto a low table facing the fireplace. Only when she was certain the balance was right did she set down the straps.

Hester's stone face didn't change expression—it couldn't—but the fire revealed more nuance in the carving. The thick-lipped mouth was neither smiling nor frowning, but there was a quirk to the corners, a readiness to react. The eyes had an intelligent focus. Tiny creases in the corners indicated this wasn't made to look like a young woman, but someone of experience and years.

Solenn wiped tears from her eyes. Minutes ago, she'd been drowning in despair, and now *this*.

After drying her hands on her justaucorps, she picked up her writing implements again. *Thank you. Is there any way I can show my gratitude to you?*

Lyria swayed her whole body side to side. "I didn't do this for *you*," she said, not unkindly, then pointed to the carvings around the hearth. "That work, yes. That was my own expressed gratitude toward you, shown in a form that I hoped would bring you pleasure on nights when you were homesick for Braiz."

That raised a question that Solenn had to ask. *Why did you choose a fireplace to showcase your work? I would think a place of fire would carry bad associations for you.*

"On the contrary. Among dryads, we say, 'All fires take us home.' This is not a fatalistic view. Some trees will die in fires and this is a cause for mourning, but many more rise from the ashes. There are some trees and plants that can only grow if the woods are scorched on occasion. But more than that, I know your kind—like many of the kin—requires heat to warm your bodies and food. This would be a place for you to find solace for needs physical and otherwise."

Solenn had heard that saying about fires before. It was featured in an old tale about a Chef whose tongue was so Hester-blessed that he could enter any large hearth or bonfire and emerge at the destination he desired. This didn't work out for him in the end, as he'd surprised his parents in the night and was slain as an intruder. Solenn had never been sure what the moral of the story was supposed to be, beyond warning one's parents of an impending visit.

My gratitude remains.

Lyria accepted this with a bow of her trunk. "This, I appreciate, but understand that you owe me no favors, Ambassador. This was no transaction, as you humans are so inclined to engage in with your Gods and each other."

Solenn had a sense that pressing further would bring offense, so she only bowed again as she walked Lyria to the door. The dryad said nothing again until she was outside. A breeze rustled her leaves as she looked away and then back at Solenn.

"I will say this now as well. I cannot speak for half the year, when I am one with my tree. That is a peaceful time, in many ways, and yet, I miss words. You understand. As does Hester, as a result of her long deprivation. When we experience such empathy, it is only right that we act upon it." With that, she ambled away on her graceful root-feet.

Solenn was still standing there, tears in her eyes and a fist to her heart, when Aveyron returned. He wore a dapper suit of red today, but his grin was brighter yet. It was quite a contrast to the somber mood with which he'd departed earlier. "I just saw Lyria on the road. She said the carving is done. Truly?"

He came inside, and she wrote to him of the meeting with Lyria. He studied the carved head, his expression thoughtful.

"Ever since we saw the gigantic statue, whenever I think of Hester, I cannot help but think of that frozen sneer. That face and this one do resemble each other greatly, but here there's softness. Nuance. This Hester feels like less of a God."

Like less of a God.

Solenn pressed her fingers to her mouth, ruminating. Hester had relished in being able to move and speak again through Mallory Valmont, even as his consumption of her form would have led to her eventual death. Gyst had likewise rejoiced in experiencing the full range of human senses when he possessed her body. She knew his delight when she felt everything from her excruciating burns to a simple, common fart. For all the Gods' power, they still missed what they'd once known and taken for granted as humans oh so long ago.

Solenn had taken things for granted too—control of her own body, the ability to use her tongue to swipe crumbs from her upper lip. But more than that, not unlike the Gods, her perspective was still confined to her human experience. She was working with beings that weren't human; she had to think beyond herself.

Would krakens be willing to speak with us again soon?

Aveyron looked surprised by the shift in topic. "I read nothing otherwise in their mannerisms. They were happy to engage with us."

Why would they be happy? *How often do they communicate with other kin?*

Aveyron's silvery brows furrowed, thoughtful. "Not often, I think. They are . . . intimidating, to say the least, especially for ground-based beings. Not simply in their size, but in their manner of communication. You wouldn't be alone in your hesitance. That might explain some of krakens' joy—they were able to talk with someone new."

Krakens had each other but were otherwise lonely. Solenn nodded to herself with a new sense of resolve. Her and Aveyron's first effort with the kraken may not have made progress, but it was a starting point. They could continue from here and needn't do so alone.

Were you able to talk to Queen Abonde about our meeting with the kraken?

"No, she was occupied. I recited events for a clerk to relay."

I'm going to write my own letter to the queen requesting her advice. Maybe she can point us toward other beings with more familiarity with krakens, or other resources. She could hint that the queen herself could aid them, but she'd need to do so with care. As Aveyron nodded, she continued to her next important point. *Can we travel to Nont today?*

"Of course. No point in waiting to place the head there, is there? But how best to go about that . . ." He drummed his fingers on the wall for a moment as he mulled. "We can travel to the approximate area of Nont in Arcady. There I can try to find an empowered cat who can escort us across the veil, sparing us the much-longer trek to and from the dolmen."

Solenn liked that idea, but hesitated. *Would the cat wait for us so we could have a quick return?*

"A cat is a cat," said Aveyron, rising. "But they are more likely to linger if we promise them fish or whatever else they reasonably desire, to be paid if they will wait for us in a safe place."

That sounded like a perfectly valid transaction. Solenn looked past the back of Hester's head to a fire that was low on logs, and yet, if she could personify the mood of the flames, she could only describe it as enthusiastic.

She now felt the same.

CHAPTER SEVENTEEN

SOLENN

Mackerel can be found in the Sleeve Sea, the Blue, and the Southern Sea, and are of different kinds and sizes. The most popular cooking methods remove most of their oil, which is what gives them a taste that is boldly "fishy" in a way that some people do not like. Of course, you will always have diners who prefer strong flavors.

—Excerpt from *Book for Cooks to Excel as Do Chefs*

Aveyron secured the aid of a cat who looked like a common feline-about-town with soft orange stripes and a bright-pink nose, but whose regal bearing reinforced that he was a local vicomte of considerable power. The promise of fresh mackerel ensured his services to cross the veil.

Therefore, in a matter of hours, Solenn found herself in Nont. The northern skies over the Sleeve Sea were blushed pink and gray as the sun began its eastern rise, the colors reminding her of a healing bruise. With a hood pulled over her lace-capped head, she walked steep steps that provided a shorter route to the pentad. Planters of flowers sat by most private and business doorsteps, bees painted on the sides of the troughs and vases to make clear that the blooms were there as offerings to Melissa.

This was Aveyron's first time walking the city in human form. He gazed about with curiosity, glancing back so often that he almost tripped a few times.

Solenn smelled the Grand Pentad before she could even see its high spire over the other roofs. The Chefs always cooked through the night to prepare victuals for the needy to break their fasts. There was something homey about the fragrance of baking bread against the sea air that made her smile, even amid her worry. Her sweaty hands kept an especially tight grip on the leather bag that contained Hester.

Solenn and Aveyron entered the pentad, their steps echoing in the broad emptiness of this early hour. A few people—fishers, from the look of their clothes—were kneeling in Selland's room overlooking the sea. Aveyron murmured to an attendant acolyte that they needed to urgently speak with August Chef Gurvan. When they were politely denied this access, as Gurvan was busy in the kitchens, Solenn pulled back her hood to show her face. The acolyte's pale shock made it clear that she was recognized.

"Your discretion is necessary," said Aveyron.

"Of course, monsieur." The acolyte spoke Verdanian, as had Aveyron; in a major port city, most everyone in a Grand Pentad knew several languages and patois. "I will inform the August Chef immediately. Pardon."

Aveyron and Solenn continued to Hester's chamber. A crackling blaze filled the ten-foot-high hearth. Fast footsteps echoed through the pentad, drawing closer. Solenn cast a questioning look at Aveyron. There was no way that the acolyte had reached Gurvan in the kitchens yet, but here he was, entering the chamber with wide eyes. His gaze went from Solenn, still bare of hood, to the strange silver-haired young man beside her, to the covered bundle in her grip.

"Princess. What have you brought here?" He flared his fingers to appeal to Hester.

Of course. He was an empathetic Chef. He'd probably sensed them coming from outside. Ada would have.

After setting down her burden as gently as possible, Solenn wrote in her table book in Verdanian. *We require absolute privacy.* She hated forcing others from the building, but the chambers had no doors, only broad archways, and sounds carried far too well.

"Of course." Gurvan gave them all another dazzled look, then hurried away. Distant voices and footsteps echoed.

With Aveyron's help, Solenn lifted Hester free of the bag to sit on the flagstones immediately before the hearth.

Gurvan returned, out of breath. "We've escorted out the few people present and shut the doors, pleading the need to cleanse the grounds. We feed breakfast outside at this time of year, anyway, praise the Five." He stared at the back of Hester's head, cast in shadow.

What do you sense? She wanted his honest reaction.

The old man's laugh was high and giddy, a pitch she'd never heard from him. "Something blessed, and yet—my pardon. You're writing in Verdanian." He switched languages. "I'm sensing Hester herself, the brief awareness I experience when I draw upon her benevolence or extend offerings, only . . . *more.* And increasing even as we stand here together."

Solenn glanced at Aveyron. He couldn't show a major reaction and reveal his own perceptive skill, but he inclined his head. He must have sensed a flare in Hester's power too.

Gurvan forced his gaze to Solenn. "I should note that I'm glad to see you again, Princess. I heard a *rumor* that you'd left the city without permission soon after we spoke. I was left wondering about the subtext of our last conversation, which focused much on Hester. I thought your return would answer questions better than Gyst, and yet, I'm left with deeper wonder. Pardon, I should introduce myself to your companion as well. I'm August Chef Gurvan." He bowed to Aveyron.

Solenn couldn't help but be amused by Gurvan's flustered ramblings. *My companion is named Monsieur Aveyron. His care saved my life when I lost my tongue. I trust him absolutely. He will be able to explain difficult matters faster than I can with my pencil.*

If she'd been told late yesterday that Aveyron would need to represent her again, in another vital meeting, her despair would've risen like floodwaters and threatened to drown her. But here, she wasn't shut out of the conversation as she'd been with the kraken. Even more, Hester was physically with her. Solenn's spark of hope had fresh tinder, and was ready to ignite.

Selland himself arrived, his strong breeze stroking her hair, his presence evoking prickles across her skin.

Gurvan acknowledged Selland's arrival with pinched fingers as the hearth fire leaped higher, encouraged by the new rush of air. "May your meals be perfectly salted, Monsieur Aveyron, for the kindness with which you've regarded our princess."

"She's my friend, August Chef. We've helped each other. Now, I understand that you are busy, and we cannot tarry either. Give me leave to explain our situation, as best as I can."

Aveyron proceeded to reveal the truth about the City-Eaten-by-the-Sea that once existed off Braiz and how Hester's destruction of the place had damaged her as a God. He omitted mention of the kin entirely, but even so, Solenn was amazed at the information he'd recently been granted permission to share. Her words to Queen Abonde had made some impact, it seemed. Aveyron said to Gurvan that antiquated references to Hester being cursed with divinity were true—she was akin to rupic. This was an especially important point to raise, as Gurvan needed to understand the epicurean responsibilities of keeping Hester Incarnate here.

"I have indeed encountered ancient references about Hester being cursed, but I never would've considered that interpretation," Gurvan said. "And this . . . this *piece* of her, so beautifully sculpted. You intend to leave it here?" He had moved to where he could regard Hester in profile. He seemed too shy to look her directly in the eye.

Aveyron explained that Solenn had promised Hester that she would find means for her to communicate more openly with the world again, with the hope that Hester would aid in the defense of Braizian hearths and homes in the fight to come. As he spoke, Solenn wrote, elaborating on her idea of feeding Hester with direct offerings through this very hearth.

"This concept . . . it honors us, but also brings considerable risks." Gurvan's expression was grave. "Detailed stone is fragile. If Hester's face were to chip or break, the debris itself would be holy and dangerous. I am the only empathetic Chef in attendance at the Grand Pentad, but there are others in the realm. They come here regularly to worship, contribute, and exercise. I would trust them with my life, but to trust them with the sordid temptations this might offer . . ."

Gurvan was imagining the horrific sacrilege that could come of Hester's body; he didn't know that it had already occurred. His thoughtful consideration verified Solenn's intuitive belief that he could be charged to safeguard Hester.

We don't know if this ploy will work to imbue full life into stone, much less how long it might take. What I can guess is that the more worship, offerings, and attention Hester receives here, the more power she will directly take in.

Gurvan looked thoughtful for a moment, then spoke quickly. "I'll take responsibility for feeding her fire, removing ashes, and handling the full cleaning on Hestersday. We'll encourage penitents to visit her hearth and increase the offerings from our own kitchen as well."

I'm sorry to place extra work on you, August Chef.

Gurvan regarded her with outright reverence. "Please don't apologize, Itron."

Solenn recoiled. The word "itron" placed too much honor on her. It was a word reserved for the most respected of women and for the Gods themselves. Not her.

At her reaction, Gurvan's smile softened. "I'm sorry that the word makes you uncomfortable, but if you think on the meaning, you will understand why I use it. We Braizians, we are not as formal as you residents of Verdania," he said as an aside to Aveyron, "which means that when we *do* use such a word, there's more meaning."

Aveyron inclined his head. "I've noted few uses of this word in my time here. Even with my limited understanding of your language, I agree, it's appropriate. Even more, Princess, if our plans go forward, you may need to get more accustomed to having it apply to you."

If their plans went forward—if she could become public in her role as ambassador. That idea felt too fanciful to consider right now, but then, there was a time when she had ignorantly daydreamed of owning a Camarga of her own too.

Shall we place Hester in the hearth?

With that course agreed upon, the next question was how to safely do so.

The large hearth had sets of iron tools at either end. Aveyron gathered two ash shovels while Solenn used a poker to move burning logs around the central point, where most offerings were placed. Gurvan stepped away for a moment to acquire additional supplies.

Solenn wrote to Aveyron. *After we place Hester, we need to address the delicate matter of epicurea with Gurvan.*

Aveyron grimly nodded. "I almost hate that we must do so. I cannot help but like the man, even though he's a Chef. If he's resistant to relinquishing epicurea, however, my respect would've been misplaced."

He's a trained Chef. He has been raised with the idea that using ingredients is the godly thing to do. Nor was that idea wrong; it had been Hester's very intention to bless humans, to the detriment of the kin.

"Madame Garland seemed to change her mind quickly."

Solenn had to smile. *She already had rebellious inclinations.*

The echo of footsteps signaled Gurvan's return. Solenn pulled her two filled sheets of paper from their tacket binding. They blackened and curled the instant they met the fire.

"Here we are." Gurvan carried packing paper and rope. "We'll bind the head in flammable material, and then it will simply burn away.

Fetching the head out later—well, we have time to give that predicament some thought."

Aveyron aided him in removing the leather carrying holster from the head, and together they swaddled the God in cushioning cloth. Even though Hester couldn't see or breathe, Solenn hated to see her entire face smothered. Gurvan used the two shovels like tongs to grip the padded sculpture and shove it far back into the flames. He'd knotted ropes to indicate which way Hester faced too. If and when her eyes became functional, she would oversee everyone who came to her hearth.

"There's something more that we must address with you, monsieur," Aveyron said as Gurvan put the hearth implements away.

"Something more?" Gurvan sounded faint at the very idea.

"The princess has a request of you, August Chef, something of immense importance. It connects to her unusual relationship with the divine." Aveyron paused to give Gurvan time to absorb this introduction. "She asks that you cease use of epicurea."

Solenn placed a splayed hand against her chest, indicating that she knew the gravity of this request. She was stunned when he promptly nodded.

"I will also make you and Monsieur Aveyron privy to certain matters, Princess. Foremost is that I heard of your escape from Nont from a particular source: your grandmother. Queen Privela wanted my insights on the request you made for her to stop using rose fairies. I had no immediate explanation for her. The next day, before I even had time to research the issue, our epicurean larder here caught fire. It began spontaneously. The full contents were lost, no one injured." He gestured gratitude to Hester.

Solenn glanced at Aveyron. His eyes widened in shock as he took in the revelation that Hester had apparently done such a thing for the benefit of the Coterie. Solenn knew that the kin preferred to take their dead back to Arcady to return them to their families, but preventing the ingredients from the indignity of consumption was most important of all.

Gurvan also was studying Aveyron's reaction. Solenn smothered a gasp. Gurvan had to sense the epicurea-like miasma that Aveyron exuded while in his human form. She surmised that few empathetic Chefs would have that capability.

"I resolved to accept the God's not-so-subtle hint along with the princess's own advice," Gurvan continued, picking up Hester's brace straps. "We've made no effort to replace the cabinet or what was lost. Our additional stores remain where they are. Have I acted rightly?" he asked Aveyron.

Solenn marveled at this moment: the highest Chef of all Braiz, looking to a peculiar young man for advice on a holy matter beyond his comprehension.

Aveyron dipped his head. "I understand that abstaining from epicurea is asking much, especially as your country is immersed in war, but please either burn the rest upon this hearth or sink it into deep water with an appeal to Selland."

"We will do so this very day," said Gurvan, bowing.

Solenn heard a distant bell pealing for dawn, then realized that could not be. Such bells should have already tolled, and this sound carried a different pitch.

More bells began to ring. Gurvan whirled away, headed toward the Grand Pentad's entry doors. Solenn followed, Aveyron at her side.

"What do they mean?" Aveyron asked.

"Emergency," she said hoarsely.

"August Chef!" A woman in white acolyte's garb panted at the top of the steps as Gurvan opened the door wide. "The bells began at the watchtowers!"

Solenn cried out, a hand to her mouth, as the Grand Pentad's own bells began to ring. The noise vibrated through her bones.

People began to fill the streets, jabbering, many residents still in night attire. The sun had just risen above the horizon.

Aveyron looked to Solenn, but Gurvan answered before she could write. "We've had several enemy ships sighted in recent days, but these bells indicate one—or many—have entered the bay itself. My pardon, but I now have duties to attend."

Of course. People would soon flood these grounds in search of solace and companionship. Solenn nodded, giving his sleeve a light touch in gratitude.

"We thank you, August Chef," Aveyron said, then joined Solenn. She pointed toward the water visible past the rooftops of the few buildings that still stood on the lower slope. With a wave to Aveyron to follow, she began to run. He fell into an easy stride beside her.

A crowd had already begun to gather at the seawall. Solenn pulled up her hood. Though a greater variety of complexions could be found here than at court, she might still be recognized, and that would be bad. Bells continued to ring. The people of Nont continued to come.

A gray-haired man in loose sailor's garb had climbed to sit atop an isolated, high stone wall. He had a spyglass in his hands. Solenn didn't need such a device to see the line of ships at the opening of the bay but couldn't identify their size or flags.

"What d'you see?" yelled an impatient man to the fellow on the wall, followed by a chorus of agreement.

"Albion." The confirmation jolted Solenn and the rest of the crowd. Even in the last war, no Albionish ships of the line had made a direct assault upon Nont. They'd attacked farther east, taking smaller port towns and disgorging their invasion forces there—as they had recommenced in recent days. "Five three-deckers."

Five! They'd each have a hundred or more carriage guns. "How many of ours meet them?" questioned a higher-pitched voice.

"Use your eyes!" came the retort. "There are two two-deckers." Even though most everyone could indeed spy the ships in the distance, giving voice to the dismal circumstances caused cries of despair to rise from the crowd. Those two-deckers had no more than seventy guns each. Solenn had to imagine Braiz's nearest remaining three-deckers had been sent east to fend off the landing forces there. Albion may well have lured them away.

Solenn muffled a sob. Hester hadn't been in her hearth a half hour. She couldn't lend additional aid, even if she so desired to. Solenn gestured to Selland, pleading for his winds to favor Braiz, knowing that in a sea battle much depended on the wind. She looked to Aveyron, whose eyes were clouded by worry. She could guess that he was thinking of their failed effort to recruit krakens.

Solenn had tried to find help. Tried, and failed. Now all she could do was gaze upon the horizon and pray.

CHAPTER EIGHTEEN

ADA

If you are encountering cockscombs for the first time, you may assume they are tough or like gristle, but no. These ornamental bits from roosters do require tedious preparation, but the result has a mild chicken-meat flavor that is tender to the teeth. They also make for a magnificent garnish for the platter.

—Excerpt from *Book for Cooks to Excel as Do Chefs*

Many sins lurked in the world, but one of the most prevalent, most aggravating, was that cooked chicken was constantly undersalted and underseasoned. It didn't matter whether the chicken was stewed, roasted in a pan or by rôtisserie, or wrapped and cooked within a firepit. Cooks simply couldn't do the dead birds justice. Ada mourned the repeated inadequacy as she chewed a meaty thigh. The resident cooks had otherwise done a fine job too. The meat wasn't undercooked—another frequent sin with chicken—and the skin was well plucked and had crisped up beautifully.

"We've been here three days," Claudette was saying. The two of them sat in a vacant tack room fragrant of damp wood, horse, and leather. "We've tried to depart five times, only to be turned back by nearby fighting. Only two in my crew have fighting experience. The rest can sew a fine suit in a day or identify dozens of fabrics by touch alone, but they're no use in a scrap, unless they can stab the attackers with needles."

"If the enemy is that close, they have bigger problems," Ada said, hovering a hand over her mouth as she chewed. She wished she had more of the cheese that she'd eaten first.

"Indeed." Claudette pursed her lips together. She was a beautiful woman with sparse age lines, probably nearer to sixty than fifty, but no one would ever guess that. In contrast, Ada was forty-two and would be rich if she could transfer her silver streaks of hair to silver metal. "Most of the people trapped here are cloth merchants like us, fleeing the spring exposition."

"How about the villagers?"

"Some twenty experienced marksmen and brawlers, young and old, all firmly aligned with Verdania but experienced enough to know the presence of *any* soldiers bodes poorly for their material possessions and families. A number of the younger women and children fled a few days ago. I can only pray to Lait that they found a refuge." She motioned to the God, which Ada immediately repeated, her own gratitude to Lait fresh. She took a long drink of a cider that was clean and bright, made from local apples.

"How many of the Blessed are waiting across the bridge? And who *are* they exactly, does anyone know? I've heard everything from peasant uprising to Merle Archambeau's private brood to Albionish agitators goading a peasant uprising." She purposefully held back which of those was her personal opinion.

Claudette took a swig of the cider as well; Ada perceived that she preferred drinks less sweet, heartier. Her shadowed face frowned. "Archambeau hasn't lacked time to act like a stallion at stud, but if he's produced the three hundred Blessed out there, I doubt he's had time to play tennis as much as we've been told. I'm inclined to believe this is a peasant uprising encouraged by the Albionish, who are riling people to their benefit."

Ada was relieved to find more agreement. "Have you seen direct evidence of Albionish involvement?"

"Yes. I defended our wagon as we turned back yesterday. Five Blessed tried to hold us up. Excellent fighters, all. Five men died, none ours," she said with an air of satisfaction. "We searched the bodies to strip them of arms and funds. The best fighter of the lot had carried Albionish money. I don't mean a souvenir coin or two, as some old soldiers possess, but a pouch that announces they're ready to hit a tavern once they return to their familiar shore."

"Did they have any epicurea? I've heard they've raided military storehouses and espoused an 'epicurea for all!' message."

"The same rallying cry is on notices posted from here to the coast, but I haven't seen epicurea in use, not that my viewpoint means much." Many ingredients had subtle effects. Even the foulest of them all, rupic, showed no outward symptoms unless a manic rage flared. That could come across as a mere personality trait in a stranger. "I just realized, Ada, that we've jumped right into battle planning. We should make a proper start of this conversation. Greetings, old friend. What brings you to this quaint country village?"

Ada laughed and gave her the basic story as she finished eating. That done, Claudette checked with her crew, then joined Ada near the central livestock corral, where she introduced her to Brillat. Claudette had been around Camargas before and regarded the horse with the sincerity one would a human being.

"We're going to fill our guard post now," Ada said to Brillat. She didn't need to explain the importance of holding this place. If Viflay fell, Verdania would have more difficulty holding Versay, and their own trip into and out of King Caristo's country château would be all the more challenging. Ada faced Claudette. "I do rather like the village, even if their chicken was lackluster. The cheese and cider were exquisite. I consider that solid justification for a death-defying stand."

"I killed a man because of cheese once," Claudette mused.

"Only once?" Ada murmured as they continued through the village. The rain had stopped.

"I'm only counting deaths, not maimings."

"An important clarification."

Claudette was Verdanian-born, but her mother had remarried a Lucanian merchant and moved the family there. Claudette had thus been trained in Lucanian rapier techniques from an early age by native experts. Ada trusted her as a fighting companion *and* as an adviser on fashionable clothing, if ever she needed such opinions.

After a quick walk of the perimeter, Ada and Claudette ensconced themselves in the lower floor of a three-story bookshop right at the bridge that the bulk of the Blessed would soon cross. On the floor above, the undeniably feisty elderly booksellers were armed with muskets; the tavern across the way was likewise guarded from upper windows.

Ada peered out an open-shuttered window that overlooked a paved path, a low stone wall, and the broad, glimmering river. The silhouettes of tall trees acted as a sporadic wall between her post and the waterway. The bridge was barely visible, its wet gray stones almost obscured by the darkness. Claudette sat feet away, near the door that opened onto the avenue. While she had a pistol, she readily admitted she had no talent for striking her target with projectile weaponry; she would rely on her blade as much as possible. Just outside, a rain barrel would provide the door with waist-high cover as invaders came from the bridge.

From that direction carried distant voices and a waft of smoke, but no fires were visible. Some dogs barked as horses whinnied.

"How does it feel to be fighting on Verdania's behalf again?" Claudette asked softly.

Ada cocked her head as she considered the statement. "I don't think I am, really. As much as I hate Caristo, I dislike Albion far more. My interests are simply aligned with the king's."

Claudette did raise an excellent point, though, and Ada continued to mull the matter over as her companion dozed. Ada *was* aiding Caristo, even if indirectly. The man who'd had the Braizian musketeers executed. Who would do the same to Erwan and imprison Solenn for life.

Which put Ada's own need for petty revenge in perspective. If the Blessed killed Caristo, Merle Archambeau would be an even worse leader, even if he weren't being used as a puppet by Albion. The entire continent would suffer, including Braiz. Braiz, the place beloved by Erwan and Solenn, where her grandmother was now.

Ada had her priorities right, uncomfortable though they were.

When she began to struggle to keep her eyes open, she gave Claudette a nudge. They switched places so Claudette could keep watch. Ada took probably an hour to fall asleep. Voices from the floor above, a hooting owl, a barking dog: everything made her jolt awake again. Of course, deep sleep claimed her nearer to dawn, and Claudette had to shake her awake with the strength of a pâtissier beating egg whites to stiffness.

"The Blessed are moving."

Ada didn't spare time to rub her eyes. She promptly loaded her turn-off pistol, so named for its twistable barrel. She could've done so in the absolute dark, but milky light now filtered into the room. "I'll take the window. Can you alert our neighbors above?" She couldn't recall the floor creaking in some time. Claudette nodded and crept upstairs as Ada peered out the window. Sure enough, figures were skulking about on the far side of the river.

"The bookshop owners fell asleep," Claudette confirmed as she returned, positioning herself by the ajar door out to the street. "Do you feel like you got enough rest?"

"No, but it'll do. If I meet Gyst today, I'll be awake and fighting." And ready with words harsh enough to make a sailor whistle in awe.

Several men in red tabards, creeping low, acted as the vanguard. Ada could make out their bobbing heads but had no direct line of fire—but the nearby tavern did. Shots rang out as the Blessed made it to the high point of the bridge. One of the men fell, the next two going down in a barrage a moment later. A roar emerged from beyond the river.

Some twenty-odd Blessed came in a rush. Muskets fired from both sides of the bridge. A high scream wailed from nearby. Smoke fogged the passage, briefly, but Ada caught movement in red. She fired as the fighter dashed along the downslope of the arched bridge. The body flopped down with a screech.

Ada loaded again, spinning the warm barrel off with her calloused fingertips, then loading again in time to take down a bearded man. He rolled down the town side of the bridge, coming to rest by a post. Before he could move again, one of the booksellers from above fired. His skull erupted like a melon dropped from height onto flagstones.

Ada dryly swallowed down her gorge and aimed again, but several Blessed found shelter behind the bridge's parapet; a couple more made it across. That meant it was Claudette's turn to act. Ada couldn't watch but heard the movement at the nearby door: the whisper of a blade, the gasp, the thud of a body.

An acrid fog drifted over the bridge, and from beyond it came another off-chorus roar. A second wave approached. Ada loaded, fired, loaded, fired—the pistol jammed. She hissed and grabbed her backup, loading and missing on her next shot. A man lunged toward her window, a rapier in one hand, a knife in the other. A blast from above sent him sprawling over the low wall. A splash in the river followed.

"Gods bless booksellers!" Ada yelled. The thump-thump of a stomped foot indicated she'd been heard.

"Ada!" Claudette called from outside. Ada glanced through the open door to verify that Claudette had crouched behind the rain barrel to gaze directly up the bridge. "A group's advancing close together, slowly."

Ada hissed. They both knew what that meant: the Blessed had a light cannon, likely looted from some local depot. They'd try to pose it atop the bridge to fire upon town, drive them back from their point of defense. Foolish of them to advance with cannon this early, though. They should've waited until they fully controlled the bridge.

Over the smatter of gunfire and yells, she could now hear the heavy grind of wheels on stone.

"Cannon incoming! Stop them!" she shouted to the booksellers and tavern folk. A musket ball sang her way, impacting in the windowsill just as she ducked. She pinched her fingers to Selland. Saltpeter placed gunfire in his domain.

She loaded again, glancing out her window to see three red-clad figures throwing themselves over the stone wall mere feet away. She wasn't sure where they'd come from, but Gyst had made unknowns known, and now they needed to die.

"Claudette!" she yelled, pulling her rapier, but the older woman was faster yet. She leaped through the broad windowsill to land in the walkway. She engaged the first of the fighters, rapier to rapier.

Ada had no such grace. She sat on the sill to pivot around. As soon as she had her feet, she lunged. The man and his knife had no chance—and no hand. She sliced it off at the wrist. With no need for immediate defense, she utilized narrow measure to attack again, slicing the man across the neck. Blood gushed. He crumpled.

She turned to find Claudette had gripped her opponent's rapier by the forte—the dull and wide point of the blade, unlikely to cut—and kicked another approaching man in the gut. He flopped backward over the wall with a comedic, undulating yell, and seconds later met the water with a loud splash. Claudette released the blade, retreating from her opponent.

Ada gazed past her to the bridge, where a knot of people approached. Another attempt to bring forth the cannon. She switched weapons. Loading her pistol, she advanced to the street, edging out enough to look up the slope and fire. She struck a woman in the chest at the same time the muskets from the tavern fired. The incoming Blessed scattered.

The cannon rolled back with a loud clatter. Someone screamed. Ada cringed. A terrible thing, to be crushed by a rolling cannon.

She retreated to the bookshop again to find that the riverfront scuffle was done, and Claudette was hopping back through the window.

"Are you well?" Ada asked.

"Barely scratched." Claudette's bloody nose attested that more than that had happened, but far be it for Ada to quibble with a swordswoman.

She caught a strong whiff of smoke and looked up.

Smoke plumed from the upper level of the bookshop. A spark from a musket, a ricochet from an incoming shot, a knocked-over lamp—the causes were myriad, but one certainty was the flammability of the building's contents. While not as spontaneously combustible as a flour mill, this was a place of organized, legible tinder.

Most every building in this village was connected or mere feet apart. If the shop burned, all of Viflay could be razed.

"Hester, hold your flames," Ada murmured, then gasped. "The rain barrel!"

She grabbed a bucket she'd seen near the stairs. Claudette knocked the lid off the barrel as she stood in the doorway.

"It's half-full," she said, reaching for Ada's bucket. Her rapier was sheathed. "You maintain your position. I'll take the water."

The strategy was sound. Claudette's feet pounded up the wooden stairwell as Ada returned to the window, and just in time. The Blessed were making another attempt to station the cannon, and this time, no muskets defended the village from the story above. She moved to the doorway to deliver direct fire. She struck a man in the shoulder. He didn't fall. She reloaded, trying to ignore the dismaying clamor above, and shot again at the same time as a neighbor from the tavern. The injured man went down, as did the woman next to him. Who hit whom didn't matter.

Claudette bounded down the stairs, flushed with exertion, empty bucket swaying. "The fire put itself out."

Ada paused in twisting on her gun's ornate barrel. "Pardon?"

"The fire had already spread up a bookcase, flames licking the ceiling. The booksellers were trying to smother it at the base with blankets. I threw the water and—" She flared her hands open and then drew her blade. "The water shouldn't have had such a widespread effect, but it did. Blessed be Hester!"

Why had the God demonstrated such generosity after weeks of forcing cold upon Ada? Was Hester setting her up for a worse calamity? Immersive theological deliberations would need to wait. Standing in the doorway, Ada fired at the Blessed on the bridge again, missing— and behind them came another group with the light cannon again. The commanders apparently didn't care how many people fell in this particular effort.

"Ada!" Claudette barked.

She whirled around to find two Blessed in the open window just as one of them brought up a pistol. Ada dropped flat. A boom resounded over her, the acrid stink of gunpowder filling her nostrils. There was a screech, and a body thudded beside her—a blank-eyed man, bleeding from a cut throat. Ada rolled up to her feet. Claudette had engaged the second man through the open window. She lunged, delivering a blow. As he recoiled with a cry, Ada fired her pistol, striking him in the chest at close range. He crumpled.

The sounds of musket fire came from above. The booksellers had belatedly resumed their position. "The bridge!" called one of them. "They're pouring over."

With no time to reload, Ada dropped her pistol into her pocket and drew her rapier. Claudette saluted her with an upraised sword, and together they met the flood.

Ada confronted a soldier as he ran into wide measure, strikable within a stride. She attacked primo tempo, a blow with a single move: one slash, and he was down. Claudette engaged in her own fights in quick succession. Blessed without swords scrambled back. Ada grimaced, well aware that she and Claudette were vulnerable to pistol fire, but that could hardly be helped. A man aimed his blade at her legs—bad form in swordplay, and it left him vulnerable to a jab to the chest.

A gun fired nearby. A bullet whizzed by her ear. She recoiled a second later, with the heart-lurching awareness that if the shot had been an inch closer, her movement would've been too late. Times like this, empress bee mead came in useful, but such epicurea wasn't an option now.

Nearby, the townsfolk from the tavern had joined the fight in the street. The fog increased, as did Ada's heartbeat. Any order to the battle had been lost.

A man came at her. She feinted, scarcely having the presence of mind to parry. Claudette whirled over, a figure of grace, and the man fell.

Claudette. How was Claudette here? Erwan—where was he? Ada gazed around, frantic, every clatter of sword and knife and blast of gun amplified in her ears.

"Ada!" Claudette had gripped her arm. "Are you all right?"

Ada felt no heat from blood and injury, but no, no, she wasn't all right. Where was she? What was happening? She shook her head.

"Stay with me," Claudette said, positioning herself to defend her, just as more fighters in bright red rushed forward.

The red tabards. The Blessed. Not Albionish—not all of them. Ada blinked fast, as if that could ground her more in the present, and she engaged in combat. A minute later, she and Claudette had the Blessed down, either dead or moaning.

Everything was suddenly quieter, though the foul fog remained. Ada looked toward the bridge. No more of the Blessed approached.

She was in Viflay, near Versay.

Erwan was there, imprisoned.

She was in this village with Claudette. Bodies littered the street.

"Ada, your mind, are you *here*?" Claudette asked quietly.

"Mostly." But she was shaky. Drained. The street brawl had taken all of two minutes, probably, but she felt like she'd been engaged in vigorous fighting for an hour.

Unsteady as she was, when her foot found a puddle near the book-shop door, she skidded. One second she was upright, the next she was down, air shoved from her lungs. The pain in her right calf was sudden, excruciating. Her first thought was that she'd been shot, but when she gripped at her injury, she found metal jutting from her flesh just above her boot. The meat of her calf was impaled all the way through.

"What—" she began, then understood. She sat in a large puddle of water. The nearby barrel had been shattered in the close fighting. One of the rusted hoops that had bound it now stabbed through her leg.

Oh, Gyst. Rusted metal. The danger of infection was bad enough, but lockjaw . . . She'd seen such deaths, people curved double as their muscles clenched in excruciating agony.

"Ada—oh, by the Five. Did it go all the way through?" Claudette leaned over her. "It did." The curved metal was about eight inches long.

As terribly as it hurt, Ada felt eerily calm. Her brain no longer drifted to the Battle of the Tents. She was very much here. Bleeding profusely.

The sound of a trumpet rang behind her, and she twisted to look toward the bridge.

"I know those notes. That's Verdania." Several of the nearby villagers cheered.

"I can see them coming over the bridge," said Claudette.

This was a good development, and yet also very, very bad.

"Claudette, please. Leave me here. Go to my Camarga. Put my saddle on him—he'll verify you have the right one. Let him free. Once the soldiers come in—"

She scowled, nodding. "They'll take all the horses, and yours especially—of course. I don't suppose he could herd the Golden Horse's mares somewhere nearby?"

"Ask him." Her voice rasped with pain. It'd been a while since she'd been in pain like this. She didn't fancy the reminder of how it felt.

Claudette sheathed her rapier. "But what will happen to you?"

"I'm on their side. There are witnesses. I'm a useful veteran. They'll likely see further use of me." She'd come into more than one village like this while wearing that blue finery. She knew how the procedures should go; now she only hoped such order was maintained.

"Likely," Claudette muttered. "Emone will tan my hide if anything happens to you."

"Claudette—"

"Fine. You get word to us soon of your whereabouts, understand?" she added with ferocity.

"I'll do my best," Ada vowed. Claudette planted quick kisses to her cheeks and dashed away.

Not a minute later, Verdanian soldiers surrounded Ada.

Her conversation with a captain went as anticipated. She described herself as a traveler stranded in town, and that as a veteran, she had aided in the fight against the Blessed. Her testimony was backed by the booksellers, who gushed praise at her efforts and horror at her injury.

"Madame," said the mustached captain, "as a show of thanks, we'll bring you back to camp to be treated by our physicians."

Exactly as she'd anticipated. She made a show of furrowing her brow. "How distant is camp?"

"Not far. We're guarding Versay on behalf of our Gods-blessed King Caristo." He said this loudly and with pride; Ada resisted the urge to roll her eyes. "We defended the grounds yesterday, and expect a renewed assault this afternoon, as a large force approaches from the south." He gestured to her leg and its unpleasant jewelry. "You'll be promptly treated upon arrival and made well enough to join us in our defense. Will you raise your sword again for king, country, and Gods?"

In other words, they would clean her leg and prop her against a fencepost, where she just might kill a few more enemies before she died herself. And they wouldn't even owe her livre for the service.

She didn't mind under these circumstances. She had her entry to Versay.

"I would be honored—" she began, then purposefully lurched herself free of the metal hoop, her agonized scream saving her from the need to lie.

CHAPTER NINETEEN

SOLENN

We of Braiz call Selland our father and mother. No matter our work, Selland's touch is upon us. Our sailors feel this pressure most heavily, to be sure, but seaweed even fertilizes our farmers' fields.

—August Chef Gurvan of the city of Nont
in Braiz

"Selland, Selland, fill our sails and rend theirs."
"Selland, keep our sailors strong and safe."
"Selland, grant our cannons power and accuracy."
"Selland, blast the Albionish into tiny bits to feed fish!"
So many prayers around Solenn, some quiet and many aloud, but Solenn knew hers were distinct in their plea. The Grand Pentad was likely filling up now as well, the people there principally praying to Selland and Hester as they sought protection for their homes and loved ones. Though Solenn was frustrated that Hester's head had only just been placed within the hearth, the strange benefit was that people would now directly feed her in their need. How the God would then use that power . . . that was a blessing or curse to contend with at a later time.

The ships' maneuvers seemed excruciatingly slow to those watching from the shore, but by the many stories she'd been told over her life, Solenn knew the activity aboard was anything but passive.

"Hey, hey!" yelled the man with the spyglass. "There're ripples in the water."

That started a buzz louder than Melissa's largest hive of bees. If Solenn had tried to speak, the words would've been lost in the noise. She could only turn to Aveyron, tears stinging her eyes.

Ripples in the water meant at least one kraken had emerged between the ships of the line and Nont. She'd never known a kraken to be this close to the city before. This couldn't be a coincidence, so soon after their conference, but at the same time, what did it mean? The kraken had been so oblivious to human intricacies.

"Solenn." Aveyron spoke loudly to be heard as he leaned close. He tugged at her arm, pulling her away. Away? She shook her head, gesturing to the sea. He expected her to leave, now? But again he pulled on her arm, his mouth a determined line. She trusted in his reasoning and followed, the anxious crowd parting to let them through.

"What?" she croaked once they'd retreated to an area of razed lots.

"Follow me," he said, briskly walking upslope into Nont. With a frustrated huff, she joined him. The streets were packed with people who seemed to be headed to the shore, the Grand Pentad, or their neighborhood pentads. Those who weren't going somewhere had simply stopped to stare out at the water. A bread baker with floured forearms and pained eyebrows stood on his stoop, studying the sea. Children crowded a balcony, their legs swaying through the rails, while a woman behind them watched with her apron skirt pulled up to hide her mouth.

After several minutes, as Aveyron occasionally paused to test the air, she realized he was following someone. Another of the kin, she supposed. They reached a flatter area along the slope, the château not far above. A stone-paved intersection ahead lay broad and empty, the usual morning wagons gone. A willowy figure in hooded gray stood in the shadows beneath a wall of verdant green and fierce pink blooms.

Queen Abonde in human form, *here*. Solenn looked to Aveyron in shock.

"She followed us across the veil," he said softly, wonderingly. "I only knew because she let me glimpse her a few times. She beckoned us to come this way."

Solenn shook her head. The queen was far too vulnerable to be here, in the middle of the city. If her hood blew back when she was around people, anyone would know in an instant that Abonde wasn't human.

"Majesty," Solenn murmured as she approached. She and Aveyron couldn't make any show of public obeisance.

"Ambassador, Monsieur Silvacane." Abonde spoke Verdanian as a courtesy to Aveyron; another reason for them to keep their voices low. "I have contemplated your words in recent days, in particular your observation that for the Coterie to continue on its present course will doom us as it has our cousins abroad. Your effort to communicate with krakens struck me as particularly profound. They are likely the kin most stark in difference to you, and yet you still made an effort." She paused, frowning as she looked away. "As you have likely noted, I do not rule the Coterie as your human nobles lord over their subjects. The Coterie understand the symbiosis of nature. We practice cooperation, negotiation, and sometimes, sacrifice. I will not ask anything of the kin that I will not commit to myself."

Solenn's heart pounded, a new spark of hope catching light.

"Even more," Abonde continued, "I'm well aware of the risks you've personally undertaken. I acknowledge that I placed you in an impossible predicament wherein you could say nothing of the kin to your royal relations, even as I demanded everything. For that, I apologize, and have only been impressed with the progress you've made despite the restrictions placed upon you."

"Queen Abonde," Aveyron said, voice hoarse with emotion, his head bowed.

"As rulers who act with responsibility and honor, we make ourselves vulnerable foremost." Abonde's phrasing stunned Solenn: she classified the two of them as peers. "I scouted out the advance of the Albionish ships and took it upon myself to personally request that krakens come here so that we may provide them with blatant examples of who is an ally or an enemy. Ambassador, I will convey you as we do our part to contribute to this sea battle."

Convey you.

By all the salt in the sea, Queen Abonde was offering to let Solenn ride her. Had this ever been done before? How would she stay on? Riding a horse bareback was one thing, but a dragon . . .

Even so, Solenn had to nod. There were many risks here, necessary ones. But there must also be faith. Abonde, likely one of the last dragons in the world, was placing herself within range of cannons. Solenn wouldn't shirk in her own responsibilities.

Her mind returned to the frustrating parley of Aveyron and the kraken. Solenn wouldn't be able to speak or write once she was astride. She had to communicate their alliance without words, and she knew how to do so.

She gripped Aveyron's arm. "Flag." Solenn pulled off her cloak, motioning to her back.

"You want it . . . tied to you?" Aveyron asked. "Yes, of course. If you can get a Braizian flag, Queen Abonde, with rope still attached, I can quickly secure it to her."

Solenn experienced a spike of new anxiety at the reminder that she must leave behind Aveyron as she attended to this duty, but that also comforted her, in a way. She'd placed him in frequent danger. Today, he'd be safer, but not completely safe. None of them could claim such security.

Queen Abonde strolled into the center of the intersection and, facing Solenn and Aveyron, changed. As when Aveyron shifted, the process occurred over a span of seconds. Her dress didn't shred away; instead, Solenn could only wonder if the garb was much like Gyst's ethereal cloak of unknowns, her wings and scales given new form. Abonde's body stretched, arcing outward from both ends. The tail lashed into existence, the neck stretching as tall as nearby three-story buildings.

Then there were the wings, the diaphanous gown gaining solidity as it flared outward, the resultant bat-like wings even larger than her sinuous body, which contained a silvery sheen in the morning light.

Screams and cries lit up the surrounding buildings as Abonde pushed herself from the cobbles and flew away. Wind and dust blasted Solenn's face, the nearby vines lashing about wildly.

"Solenn." Aveyron gripped her by the arm to gain her attention. "Once I have the flag affixed to you, I'll boost you onto her back. There's a gap in the spikes along her spine, right behind her mane. That's the only place where I could guess that you would sit, as it correlates much to a horse's back. Just . . . hold on, please."

Abonde returned with another gush of wind punctuated by alarmed screams from witnesses. In a front claw, Abonde carried a Braizian flag, the rope dangling. Aveyron and the claw were nearly the same size as he approached to pry the flag free. He flapped it a few times to untangle it, then motioned Solenn to turn around. Abonde's broad wings cast a cool shadow over them.

Aveyron wrapped the rope around her waist, securing the stout rope with a sailor's knot, then cinched it again over her breasts and under her armpits. He stepped back, satisfied.

"To many homecomings," he said to her. She splayed a hand on her chest, nodding, then advanced to Abonde's torso. Aveyron stooped, forming a stirrup with his twined hands, and boosted her up. Abonde's slick scales were surprisingly not that different in texture from the coat of a groomed summer horse. She gripped the joint where the wing and shoulder met and used that to propel herself to the dragon's back. She had an odd, vivid memory of when Aveyron helped her to climb to the roof of the palace in Lutecia. That had been one of the most terrifying feats in her life, and now it felt scarcely of note.

Her body fit perfectly in the gap along Abonde's back, and she was relieved to find that the vertical spikes on either side tapered down to be low and blunt. Abonde's deep-gray mane, not much different in color from that of a young Camarga, draped to around her thighs. Solenn applied a firm grip to the tendrils, trying not to yank them.

Abonde lurched upward. Solenn's stomach felt like it had heaved somewhere it ought not for a smattering of seconds, the movement of flight strange and disorienting. The wings moved with synchronous power to either side. Below, people had begun to flood the edges of the intersection. She could no longer see Aveyron. He'd slipped away to avoid public notice.

Solenn had no such option.

Abonde angled to fly toward the sea. Solenn gave the mane a quick tug. When Abonde glanced back, she pointed toward the cliff-top château.

The dragon's broad brow furrowed for a moment, but then understanding dawned on her features. "Ah yes. We must establish our alliance with your own kindred foremost." While Abonde's words were fainter against the wind, she was still easy to understand as she flew toward the château.

In mere seconds, the dragon reached the castle atop the slope. She glided a low circle over the courtyard. The few horses below scattered. Solenn hoped the stables were far enough away that the horses there wouldn't hurt themselves in a panicked response to Abonde's presence.

With one hand holding on to Abonde, Solenn waved with the other. The rope, tight with strain, stayed secure, the weight of the billowing flag at her back. Guards with upraised crossbows lowered them as she was recognized.

Throughout her life, Solenn's brown skin had set her apart from much of Braizian court. She had been sneered at, judged, and advised not to spend too much time in the sun, or she'd become darker yet.

A laugh erupted from deep within. Let court see her now, fierce, resplendent. Let them know her, not simply as the princess who'd sliced off her own tongue but as the woman who rode upon a dragon.

Abonde swooped around the towers in a figure of eight, giving more denizens a chance to behold them. People gawked. Solenn waved back, but when she recognized her father upon a balcony, she pounded on Abonde's shoulder with a fist. The elongated, serpentine head glanced back. Solenn pointed. Abonde flew closer to Prince Morvan. Musketeers to either side of him started to pull him back, but then they all seemed to recognize her at once, freezing with their mouths agape. She waved with the full power of her arm, and then Abonde turned away, arcing over the city.

For the first time, Solenn had a bird's-eye view of the scar left by the port fire.

If her eyes weren't already streaming with tears from the constant cold blast, she would have wept. A third of the city was gone, the very heart. Like the seeded center scooped from an apple. The Grand Pentad looked all the more grand since it was also fairly lonely, its steeples and bell towers higher than anything else on the lower edge of the city. She could well imagine August Chef Gurvan pulled outside by the new strangeness he perceived, and she waved as if he were indeed down below. The crowds along the sea wall were incredible, the colorful people like swarming ants from this height. She grimaced to see them point upward and scatter in fright.

They had nothing to worry about from Abonde at the moment. Albion did.

Striking back at the country that had butchered her cousin-dragons was unquestionably part of the dragon queen's motivation as well, but she had no need to state something that personal. Solenn understood.

The row of ships reminded her of the toy models that her cousin the young heir had owned when he still had all of his baby teeth. They used to play together, the two of them, with Solenn always taking the role of some adversary like Verdania or Albion. Prince Janik never considered playing as anyone other than Braiz. The one time Solenn suggested otherwise, he burst out crying. She had been baffled at the time. Shouldn't someone, especially the heir, try to think from other perspectives? That didn't make a person disloyal—it made them wise.

Strange, how a childhood incident could be prescient of her bur-geoning skills to see as others saw and be a diplomat.

Ripples extended from the surfaced kraken, its turbulent tentacles visible. The kraken was still some distance from the ships, where repeated cannon fire had created a low, thin fog. Three of Albion's massive ships advanced on Braiz's smaller pair.

Swooping low, Abonde roared. The deep, terrible sound caused Solenn's heartbeat to knock against her breastbone, her legs and fingers clutching the dragon all the more tightly.

The water below boiled and frothed as the kraken's head became visible above the water.

Artistic depictions did no justice to krakens, their bodies some amalgamation of a gigantic squid and dragon. Round, glistening eyes angled up to see them as Abonde flew lower. Solenn felt the flag at her back pulled taut by the wind. She was a symbol.

Abonde flew toward a ship that Solenn recognized, the Braizian *Varville*, already engaged with an Albionish ship. Other nearby vessels maintained distanced positions, watching the fight the way tomcats gathered to take in a set match, ready to jump in if a foe demonstrated vulnerability.

Solenn bowed lower over Abonde's neck, clutching the queen's mane with both hands. She hoped she wasn't causing pain through her hold, but by the Five, she was unnerved whenever Abonde turned and her legs started to slide, and she was *cold*. Cold as if she stood naked in an outdoor privy during a snowstorm.

She felt Abonde's muscles coil, the way a horse might gather itself before a jump, and was braced as Abonde dived at the premier Albionish warship. The cannons and cannonade couldn't angle upward to attack, but the sailors and marines carried pistols and muskets aplenty. Shots whizzed by, Solenn breathless, as Abonde tore through layers of sails. Cloth briefly snared and blinded Solenn, then flapped past. Strange pressure rang in her ears as Abonde whirled up and away. Solenn had no time to prepare herself as the dragon lashed back around, her body colliding with the top of the mast to grip it with all four legs. Solenn sprawled to cling to Abonde.

The dragon's wings ceased beating.

All Abonde's tremendous weight bore down on the mast. The wood of a ship, even the mast, needed to be flexible to endure the ocean's heaves; therefore, there were several prolonged, terrible seconds where Abonde was perched like a cat on a fencepost as the mast slowly, slowly curved. The sailors below ceased firing as they scattered across the deck. Wood snapped with a resounding *crack*. Solenn felt her stomach begin a perilous lurch downward, and then Abonde's wings beat again, soaring up as the top half of the mast came down upon the deck. More snaps and screams rang out as Abonde lifted away.

Solenn, numbed with cold, couldn't be sure if she'd been hit by a shot. Abonde acted fine too—no, she acted angry. Her body throbbed with exertion. She seemed beyond speech.

Had the Braizian flag attached to Abonde and Solenn made their representation clear to the kraken? Solenn studied the waves with desperation, but she could no longer see the creature amid the churning sea.

And then it attacked.

There were no ripples of warning, no chance for the Albionish to rally, had such a thing even been possible after Abonde's surprise attack. There was a magnificent wrenching of wood as tentacles hugged the hull from beneath and began to sway the vessel back and forth, a sordid version of a parent rocking a fussy child to sleep. The kraken's head didn't emerge. Sailors slipped and slid across the deck, screaming. People began to freckle the waves. Solenn sent a fervent, wordless prayer to Selland. The near nine hundred Albionish sailors and marines aboard would mostly be conscripts. They hadn't asked for this doom. She could only hope that Selland would send them to Gyst quickly.

Nearby movement caught Solenn's eye: the *Varville* was drawing alongside, her cannons ready to fire. After a long minute, the tentacles slithered back into the sea, and no sooner than they had, the barrage began. The Albionish didn't answer. The hull was almost certainly perforated below the water, every deck littered with debris and bodies.

Abonde drifted behind the action, swooping low over the other Braizian two-decker. Solenn recognized the masthead and flags of this vessel too—the *Malo*! Why, a few years ago, when the ship was ceremonially launched, she'd brought sand from the Malo beach aboard in a glass saltcellar and presented it to the captain. Now, as she flew above, she could hear the cheering men and women aboard. These were her people. This was, in a sense, her ship.

As Abonde lifted up, the view showed Solenn the other Albionish ships of the line, growing smaller. They were retreating toward the visible shore of Albion.

"Look," said Abonde, turning.

The ship they had attacked was sinking, and the kraken had emerged again, the tentacles plucking sailors and dragging them below the way a person might pick berries from a bush.

Solenn dryly swallowed. This was the balance of nature, and that was often a terrible thing.

Abonde swooped lower, gliding over the *Varville*. Sailors danced upon both decks, waving. To her surprise, Abonde came around again, lower still. They were within musket range. Solenn felt a spike of fear for Abonde, then understood why she'd taken this risk. The dragon queen wanted the sailors to recognize Solenn. As Abonde hovered for a moment, those powerful wings flapping, Solenn waved. The tumult below increased. Abonde rose again, pointed toward Nont. Home.

They'd done it. The Braizian navy, the kraken, her, Abonde, Aveyron—all of them, allied. Oh, Selland! Hester! Without releasing her full hold of the mane, she gestured to the two Gods, but thoughts of landing brought something new to mind.

She was no longer a mere princess to her people. She was a symbol. A warrior. A direct ally of Selland and his krakens.

Her relationship with her people, her family, would never be the same again. She'd earned the respect and recognition she wanted, but at a cost.

Solenn would never again freely ride the countryside on Maiwenn, not even with two musketeers as her company.

She felt Selland's tingling touch upon her cheeks as fresh tears dried upon her cheeks before they could join the greater salty waters below.

CHAPTER TWENTY

ADA

Verjuice is a pungent acidic liquid with a sweet-tart flavor. It is usually made of the juice of unripe grapes or other fruits, such as crab apples, and may or may not be fermented. Red verjuice is made from mostly red grapes and is earthier in flavor, while white is derived from white grapes and is crisper. Sorrel juice is sometimes added for both color and flavor, making verjus vert. Verjuice heightens the flavors of sauces, mustards, and salad dressings.

—Excerpt from *Book for Cooks to Excel as Do Chefs*

Ada would've been happier about her successful entry into Versay if less pain were involved. She sat in a wagon surrounded by other injured soldiers, studying the layout of the cantonment with experienced eyes even as she took long, slow breaths to manage her agony. She had already bled through the booksellers' hastily tied bandage.

The expansive lawn at the front of Versay had been turned into a military encampment. There were about one thousand soldiers here, she estimated, but her companions in the wagon had said the nearby

Blessed boasted three times that number. These were small forces compared to the tens of thousands she'd overseen in her previous service days, but as Yanik had noted over a week before, the Blessed had proved terribly effective, even with their low numbers. After all, in the end, it took only one person to kill a king.

Ada was helped from the wagon by a soldier young enough to be her son. His excited grin showed he had yet to be jaded by the truths of war, even though a bloodied bandage crossed over one eye.

"Never thought I'd visit the palace of Versay," he said, gazing about as if he could see glittery delights, not mere tents, cookfires, and bustle.

"Hester keep you warm," was all she could think to say. If he survived, she wondered how long it'd take for the war nightmares to start.

She was living her own nightmare right now.

Ada yearned to flee, but beneath her pain and panic pulsed stubborn logic. She had to retain her wits, and that meant going *through* the camp to make her exit.

Erwan was on the other side. She had to envision him as her goal.

In the surgery tent, the stench of iron and gangrene lingered, a stubborn stain within the air. One surgeon's tools remained out on a small table, the arrayed blades ranging from delicately narrow scalpels to broad bone saws. Her stomach twisted, and she made herself look away. If Gyst wanted to attack her now, he had his opportunity. She may well end up at such a surgical table soon, but not now, not today.

Fortunately, her physician didn't bring up the possibility of amputation or even say much at all. Nor did Ada; she was proffered a brandy bottle, took a mighty swig, then bit down on a leather strap. Muttering in a low Ricardian accent, the man cleansed the two-sided wound and added stitches. The injury bound, Ada was waved off, though she could still scarcely apply pressure on her right foot.

Ada was told to speak to a lieutenant just outside. She knew what would come next: a quick issue of food, ammunition, and a watch post, where she'd be planted to keep shooting until she died, all in the name of the divinely ordained King Caristo.

She asked after a latrine and exited out the other side of the tent into the full activity of camp.

Just walk, she told herself. *You're not trapped. Not under attack. You understand this place the way a watchmaker comprehends the innards of a timepiece. Think. Walk.*

She carried herself, limping as she was, as if she knew where she was going, and maintained an adequate presence of mind to say the right things when she was questioned time and again. She did pause to grab an oversize Verdanian enlisted soldier's jacket from a pile. It had bloodstains and minor holes, but she wasn't about to quibble. The jacket granted her easier passage through the rest of camp. She soon entered the palace itself, where she called upon memories of past tours to find the austere corridor designated for special prisoners of the crown.

There were no guards posted at the door. Or in their office. No one moved about the corridors at all.

Something was very wrong here. She drew her rapier and prayed she wouldn't need to use it.

The guards could've abandoned their posts—or been called else-where—or everyone here could've been moved—or—

Someone coughed in a nearby chamber, the sound echoing. Some prisoners remained, at least.

She checked the logbook for arrivals and found the information she needed dated a week ago. Captain Erwan Corre, Braizian. Room 21.

Also listed was one Comtesse Esme Alarie. Her mother. Room 27.

Ada should have expected Maman to be here. As a lower noble-woman, she wouldn't be in a grimy dungeon, though the crimes of which she was accused were grievous by Crown standards. They'd get a poor immigrant executed. Instead, here Maman could still be visited by her remaining friends from court.

She grabbed the single bracelet of keys hanging on the wall and held the collected metal in her palm to prevent jingling, but her heavy limp made subterfuge impossible.

"Hey, hey, is someone there? We need food, monsieur!" yelled a deep voice, the person pounding on the thick wooden door of their cell as she passed by. Her heart was pounding almost as hard.

At room 21, the view-slot showed a mostly dark room, the barred window admitting little light. A sheet was drawn up to cover a long lump in the cot. Blood soaked the length.

No. No. No.

With a gasp, she unlocked the door. She used the tip of her rapier to pull the sheet back, to find two mustached men in palace guard uniforms nestled together like spoons, bodies bloodied.

Not Erwan. Erwan wasn't here.

She sheathed her rapier and covered her face with both hands, allowing herself a moment to lean against the wall and moan in grief and frustration, then made a brief assessment of the men.

One was missing his rapier, knife, and pistols, while the other remained armed. The blood was freshly red.

She tried to picture the scene. Erwan had disarmed a guard and slain both. Blood spattered the floor and wall; he could well be injured, but he was likely alive. She clutched that hope as if with slippery hands.

He'd head toward the stable for a horse on which to escape these extensive grounds. She'd do the same, with the goal of finding him and Brillat, after some quick work here.

She filled water carafes at the pump just outside. Birdsong had ceased, gunfire instead punctuating the air. The battle had been brought to Versay. Two twelve-pound rounds of bread remained in a cupboard, harmless white mold flecking the crust. She sliced them up into thick chunks. With sloshing strides, she delivered bread and water to each occupied room, shoving the goods through gaps in the stone wall. Some prisoners cursed at her or yelled questions, but she said nothing.

Ada saved room 27 for last.

She peered through the slot. Maman sat at the end of her bed, facing a small table. She'd always been a thin woman, but now she had a frailty to her that reminded Ada of how Solenn had likewise wasted away in recent weeks. Her brown hair draped loose around her shoulders, a kerchief holding strands back from her face. She looked twenty years older without her finery and powder, as if she could actually be Ada's mother by age.

On the table before Maman were two rocks about the size of an adult thumb, both standing upright.

"I'm not sure if we should do that today," she said, tapping one of the rocks. Her voice shifted to a higher pitch. "Sometimes we must do things we do not want, Ragnar. I know that. I'm a Chef."

Ragnar—a Chef—what? Ada stepped back as if slapped, almost knocking over the carafe. Ragnar was dead, what was Maman—oh, Five. The rock-Chef was portraying Ada. Maman had the two rocks waddle across the table, talking as they went. She was treating them like dolls.

Ada blinked back tears as she faced away. She'd known military prisoners to entertain themselves similarly to stave off the loneliness and madness, but this . . .

She couldn't bring Maman with her or even set her free. Not only did Maman need to remain ignorant of the fact that Ada was still alive, but she had the survival skills of a baby bird fallen from the nest. A cell offered some safety.

She shoved the water and bread through the gap. Maman continued her play, oblivious. Ada opened her mouth, then closed it, backing away.

She needed to find Erwan.

Ada limped with steady determination into an outer wing of the central palace. Even though she wore a soldier's jacket, the domestics who dashed through the corridors regarded her as one might a strange roving dog. She kept her rapier sheathed, even as closer gunfire split the air. She could scarcely tap her foot on the ground now. Sword fighting wasn't an option unless her rival was kind enough to let her sit.

Many fast-moving feet approached. Ada took shelter behind a large potted plant. Seconds later, a dozen Blessed came into view. Their red tabards flapped over the sorts of coarse clothes worn by laborers and farmers.

"This way!" cried a leader, continuing the charge.

Ada waited for their steps to grow fainter on the new-styled oak parquet floors before she hobbled out again. She was sweating profusely despite the chill of the day.

"Behind the central keep," she murmured. "That's the nearest barn. It's not far."

She passed a dead soldier, then another, then two dead Blessed. Another Blessed bled out as she emitted soft whimpers. Ada motioned Gyst's X as she continued along. "Grant her quick peace, please," she whispered to the God, exiting to a broad garden courtyard.

Beautiful blooms dazzled her eyes as nearby gun blasts caused her to hunker, her leg jutting out at an awkward angle. Her tongue recognized edible rose petals and hips and numerous other things, nearby rose fairies included. They fluttered in lazy circuits over the thriving bushes.

At a crossroads around a central fountain were more dead—Blessed, palace guards, and musketeers. None were injured or dying . . . someone had already finished off the lot. As she moved past a musketeer, a patch of gold upon their dark breast caught her eye.

It featured a five-point crown within a shield. The insignia of the royal musketeers, always close by King Caristo and Queen Roswita. She checked the other musketeers, lifting arms and rolling bodies to identify three more. One, she recognized as a peer from twenty years ago.

Why hadn't the royals gone back to Lutecia when it was evident that the Blessed were gathering here? Once the king and queen were in the capitol palace, they were fairly secure from a physical assault unless they were intimately betrayed. The grounds here were far too open and vulnerable. The walls were more intended to retain drunken courtiers than hold off attacks.

"This way!" someone shouted. Feet pattered closer. Ada didn't know which way they were coming from or who they were, and she couldn't run. She dropped to sprawl face down, straddling the bricks and damp earth at the edge of the path, praying she blended in.

Footsteps thudded to a stop about ten feet away. "I think they went that direction," said another, deeper voice. "Yes—you hear that?"

Ada's upturned ear detected a clash of rapiers somewhere dead ahead.

"Yes, you're right," said the first speaker. "We'll get her, by the Gods! This'll be fun." He tittered in delight.

The group—there had to be five or so—ran around Ada toward the other battle. Only after they'd passed did she turn her head enough to see their red backsides. More Blessed.

Ada needed to press onward to the stable. And yet, and yet . . .

She released a soft groan as she pushed herself up to stand again, her view upon the fallen royal musketeers. The Blessed soldiers were pursuing a woman. They were regarding the effort as "fun." Judging by the sheer numbers of dead royal musketeers, their target may well have been the repugnant Queen Roswita herself.

Selland preserve her, but Ada could abandon no woman to the whims of soldiers in their bloodlust, not even Roswita.

Movement caught her eye, a rose fairy hovering a few feet away. Its focus was on her, and foolishly so. If Ada had a net, she could scoop it up for the pickling jar. But then, who was she to criticize another being for foolishness in light of her own recent decisions?

"If you're like Brillat Silvacane, you can detect something strange about me," she whispered to the fairy. The fairy was about as long as her thumb, its body like that of a naked human but for the humming-bird-fast colorful wings upon its back.

The fairy tilted its head. Had it recognized the name?

Ada leaned closer. "Do you know Brillat Silvacane? He should be nearby." She trusted that he'd follow her to Versay. "Can you find him and bring him here? I'm Adamantine—"

The fairy flitted away, probably to another rosebush. Ada sighed. Even if it did know Brillat, she could hardly expect a fairy to aid a Chef such as her. Five knew, she'd netted such fairies from the time she could toddle, and though she'd never been fond of eating them herself, she'd preserved too many to count.

She limped around the bodies in slow, steady pursuit of the Blessed.

A low building ahead sat in the middle of the garden and had the peaked wooden roof one expected of a mountain chalet. The front door was open, voices carrying outside. No guards lurked on the porch. The Blessed's ineptitude was showing, and Ada was grateful for it.

"We should burn them out," a high voice declared.

"Nah, we need her alive for Merle's bounty. A charred corpse could be anyone."

Ada sucked in a breath as she leaned against the wooden wall. They *were* after Roswita. Why was she still here? Had she retained any guards?

An argument broke out, voices overlapping in disagreement. Ada edged into the doorway to better assess the numbers inside. The room was a parlor, one end filled with a piano and other instruments, the other with sofas and cushioned seats in the latest fashion. Some dozen Blessed had gathered to either side of a gleaming white door flecked with damage—and, judging by the splintered wood, some shots had come from within. Considering the presence of flanking doors, she surmised this room to be entirely interior, lacking a window egress.

"We can kick it down—" said one mustached fellow.

"And get shot as you stand there, aye, there's a good idea," countered another. There was one Blessed already dead on the floor, a crimson pool expanding around them on the parquet.

"We can get an axe or even some furniture to knock it down."

Ada withdrew, retreating to shelter behind a tall-backed wooden chair upon the porch as she loaded her pistol. The odds before her weren't favorable. Desperate for any advantage, she extended her perception in hopes of finding some mundane ingredient nearby that she could utilize.

What captured her attention wasn't in the garden, but within the chalet: a wealth of epicurea all in one spot, the variety encompassing everything from pickled rose fairies to unicorn derivatives to quick-hare jerky. The items weren't in the considerable quantities one would find in a royal pantry, but within a palace Chef's traveling satchel.

A Chef attached to the palace would be adept in matters of offense and defense, and was probably a reason why Roswita had made it into the chalet at all.

Then she sensed fast movement—a familiar waft—

"Ada." Brillat, his panting breaths quiet, crept to join her. The man was naked but for armaments strapped to his person: a powder horn, pouch, and long knife, of which the scabbard bore a Verdanian cavalry emblem. He held a pistol in his hand.

"Hester burn us all," she hissed under her breath, her heart racing impossibly faster. "You were almost a bit too quiet there, Brillat. I might've shot you."

"Yet you didn't. Why do you linger here?" he asked without judgment in his voice, which she appreciated.

"I believe these Blessed have trapped Queen Roswita inside. She's either carrying epicurea or accompanied by a palace Chef." The Blessed had resumed their loud argument inside. They clearly had no commander in their company.

Brillat's face twisted in disgust. "And yet you feel you must—"

"You know what it's like for kin to be regarded as prey. I will not leave any woman to suffer by undisciplined soldiers, even her."

"That's a considerable stash of epicurea inside. The people trapped within could be ingesting it now to aid their survival, and yet they're not." He was right. That *was* peculiar, especially if a Chef was present to enhance the inlaid blessings. His cool gaze drifted downward. "I can smell that your wound has turned."

"I can feel that it has turned. Praise be to Gyst," she said bitterly. "I don't suppose you encountered Erwan on your gallop here and he's about to pop out as a pleasant surprise?"

"I did not, though I did take a direct route as I followed our fairy friend," he said. Five forgive her for doubting the fairy. "How many Blessed are within?"

"A dozen, all look to be men. A range of ages."

"Some likely veterans, then." He loaded his turn-off pistol with quick movements.

"Yes, though as you can hear, they lack cohesion." The argument had now gone to whether they should fetch more allies, which was resisted as that meant the promised monetary reward would be further divided. "If we wait long enough, they might start eliminating themselves, but I fear more Blessed will arrive soon, whether this group wants them or not."

"Agreed. If you're not in the mood for swordplay, I might make use of your weapon?"

He didn't need to vocalize their strategy. She could readily surmise it. "By all means." She passed it to him, the strap joining others upon his milk-pale body.

He tipped his free hand, as if doffing an imaginary hat. "Shall we?"

Nodding, she followed him to the open entrance. He dashed to position himself on the other side of the doorway. They shared a nod of readiness, then, as one, opened fire upon the Blessed.

CHAPTER
TWENTY-ONE

SOLENN

*We Braizians appreciate simple things. "Giving leeks" is what we call
the act of paying compliments. Why? Because everyone likes leeks!*

—August Chef Gurvan of the city of Nont
in Braiz

Abonde drifted lower and lower over the château to indicate her intention to land. Therefore, by the time claws scraped the broad courtyard, musketeers and soldiers had assembled in the company of Prince
Morvan. Jean and Talia were within the group.

As the mighty wings stilled, Solenn felt limp, afraid to move lest she
slide off to land on the ground like a puddle. Perhaps it was a blessing
that her cold muscles were still incapable of unclenching.

"Solenn." The queen's voice was quiet, tired. "Do you require aid
to dismount?" She asked this in Braizian.

Solenn's first reaction was denial. She needed to be strong and
confident in this moment—but she also had to accept her limits. She
wouldn't aid their cause by falling on her face.

"Yes. May my musketeers approach?"

Queen Abonde made a slight nod of assent.

Talia and Jean stepped forward without hesitation after Solenn beckoned to them, though their faces were pale. Their movements became more cautious as they moved underneath Abonde. The dragon had crouched to almost rest on the stones, but even so, Solenn was some ten feet high. She pivoted her hip to slide over the slope of Abonde's belly and into Jean's arms.

"Princess." His eyes shone. "Selland preserve you."

"Are you well?" Talia stood a foot away, her eyes scrutinizing her from head to toe.

"I—" Solenn had to nod, tapping her throat. She shivered.

Talia walked from beneath Abonde. "Piquette! Piquette for the princess!" People dashed away to fetch refreshment. As Talia returned, she pulled her cassock over her head. Both musketeers wore their full daily regalia. "Another layer will help," she said, lifting the cloth to rest over Solenn's shoulders. She then left to meet the drink bearer.

Talia's body heat within the cloth seemed to soak right into Solenn's chilled layers. She rested a hand on Abonde's pale belly. The dragon was cool, her form still slightly heaving from the work of flight. Solenn was left to assume that the dragon's quiet meant that she was awaiting a proper introduction. That's what a visiting human would expect of their mediator.

"When you departed with Aveyron, I knew such worry and fear," Jean said in a low voice. "But for you to return, with a dragon—to witness your actions out there—oh, Princess. Itron." Emotion broke his voice, and startled Solenn. They'd known each other for years and had no need of constant formality. This level of reaction—this respect— from him was new and unnerving. It was one thing to be given leeks, quite another to be buried in them.

"Princess." Talia returned. She carried a flagon and a cup. Abonde's wings provided partial shelter from curious eyes as Solenn took small sips to help her throat. With her musketeers in her shadow, she walked to stand between the dragon and the awaiting Braizian assembly. With a beseeching gesture to Selland, she spoke, projecting her voice as best she could.

"You know me as Priñsez Solenn ar Braiz, and I hold that title still, but I am also acting ambassador between Braiz and a collective of beings known as the Coterie. Queen Abonde is their noble and ancient leader. I respect her as I do few in this world." She motioned to the dragon, who bowed her head in acknowledgment. People at the fringes of the courtyard gasped and murmured even as the musketeers remained stoic. Tad's head tilted in consideration. "The Coterie and Braiz share common enemies in Verdania and Albion. For this reason, we propose a military alliance to preserve our citizens, but this union places disparate conditions upon Braiz and the Coterie. Queen Abonde?" Solenn could only pray that most of her words had been understandable.

"Thank you for your introduction, Ambassador Solenn." Queen Abonde's clear voice in flawless Braizian created a ripple of exclamations among the humans. Her head turned to take in everyone. Solenn had a sense that she was amused, though this also had to be frightening for Abonde, revealing herself after thousands of years in hiding, well aware that these people could and would butcher her if they weren't currently so awed.

Solenn extended an arm toward Tad. "Queen Abonde, I introduce you to my father, Priñs Morvan ar Braiz, who often represents my grandparents in diplomatic matters."

Prince Morvan advanced beyond the musketeers to bow before the dragon. She returned the gesture in spirit with an undulation of her neck. "On behalf of King Myles and Queen Privela, I welcome you to Nont and to Braiz. We're grateful for the aid you offered us in battle this day. May I confirm that the kraken acted in accordance with you?"

"The krakens' involvement is more due to direct mediation supervised by your daughter," the dragon replied. "She sought out krakens and proposed this cooperative effort, in Selland's name."

Solenn bowed, grateful that the queen's wording didn't deny Aveyron credit even as he was left unnamed.

Tad blinked, his brow furrowed. "Princess Solenn has stated that she's an ambassador. We require a greater understanding of you and the Coterie, Queen Abonde, so that we may reciprocate in this relationship."

Queen Abonde's neck reared up. The pose could only be described as intimidating. "I will state my situation bluntly. I am a dragon, one of the last in this part of the world. Albion has infiltrated Braiz using epicurea derived of dragon. They are among your people, even now, as they seek to destroy you and then proceed to Verdania. Dragon epicurea empowers them in extraordinary ways, but my dragon cousins and I are far more powerful alive." This created murmurs anew. "*Everything* that you know of as 'epicurea' is derived from living, thinking, intelligent beings who love and hate and experience the world much as you do. We are more valuable as cooperative allies for your cause than we are broken down piecemeal when dead."

Abonde paused, her silence powerful. Solenn spoke up to give her a chance to recover. "The Coterie is willing to ally with us if we cease use of epicurea. We surrender what ingredients and derivatives we have to them, and they will return the remains to the families of the slain." People exclaimed in shock. She waited a moment before continuing. "The Coterie acknowledges the Gods as we do. They undertake their own rituals to commemorate and say farewell. We need to respect them in their grief, just as we ask for respect as we send Braizian souls to Gyst and our bodies to Selland."

Many of the people present had never used epicurea or had done so only in urgent circumstances. Even so, this information shook them—though Prince Morvan's reaction was more blatant. He looked vaguely ill as he looked between Solenn and Abonde.

"Cease abuse of our kind, and we will be your allies against our shared enemies," said Queen Abonde. "Perpetuate your use of epicurea, and you become our open enemy."

Solenn hadn't anticipated the latter statement, but she realized she should have. It only made sense. The Coterie had made themselves—and kin worldwide—vulnerable in new ways. Blatant aggression was their best recourse, one that they hadn't dared to enact since Hester's assault upon Ys three thousand years ago.

"I see," Prince Morvan said slowly. "This is no easy thing you ask of us, but—" As Queen Abonde's neck reared back, high tension in its coil, he upheld a hand to plead for the chance to continue. "I understand how you've exposed yourself to danger today, in both battle and through your forthright words. This must not have been easy for you. I also recognize that you, as queen, have taken on this risk foremost. The breadth of known epicurea is staggering, but you didn't ask the more vulnerable among your Coterie to contribute today. You and the great kraken did so instead. I respect that."

Oh, Selland preserve her father. He *understood*. He truly did.

Queen Abonde's neck relaxed. "I likewise understand that this isn't a change your people can undertake overnight. At this time, we won't assault Braizians who still possess epicurea. That said, we will only directly ally with and aid soldiers and sailors who are not carrying or using epicurea. I know that the specific ship that we assisted today had no epicurea on board, and so presented itself as a ready beneficiary of our support. I will be forthright. We love and mourn our dead just as you grieve for your own dead. Eating the flesh of our kin, forming their wooden bodies into aging barrels, adorning their feathers as ornaments, and harvesting them in myriad other ways is to us the most abhorrent sacrilege. It is intolerable."

Solenn could read the shift in Tad's posture as he took in the implication that Abonde could sense epicurea as did an empathetic Chef. He would understand that there'd be no hiding ingredients from the queen—not that he would engage in such deceit, but others would.

Tad gave Solenn thoughtful consideration as well. She'd never told him that her tongue had awakened—but now her tongue was gone, and here Solenn had revealed that she was an ambassador to beings who regarded Chefs as anathema. She could tell his brain was putting pieces together, but without glue. She would need to lend assistance later.

"Thank you for your bluntness, Queen Abonde. Our ships contain little, if any, epicurea as a matter of practice," Tad said. "Therefore, our navy will easily adapt to this new procedure. We can discuss details as we draft formal documentation."

To Solenn's surprise, Queen Abonde reared back her head and laughed. Prince Morvan took a step back, perhaps more awed by the revealed rows of teeth than by the sudden expression of mirth. "The Coterie is already at work on different documentation, as requested by Ambassador Solenn, to clearly define her role and benefits. As she has apparently learned much from *you*, Prince Morvan, it will be interesting to work with you in this alliance. For now, however, I must depart. I will fly for Albion."

Solenn made a sound of surprise and concern. Abonde turned to face her.

"I have revealed myself here as an ally. I will reveal myself there as an enemy. I will send word to you of any relevant reconnaissance. Perhaps our kin there will be able to contribute to our effort as well, though I hate to ask more of those who've already lost much."

Solenn thought of others who had also lost a great deal. "May I make a request, Queen Abonde?"

She tilted her head. "You may."

Solenn approached to quietly tell her about what had befallen the sailors from the *Everett* and of the need for proof of Albion's complicity. Abonde said she would see what might be found.

"One more thing," said Solenn. "Is it possible that the returns of Brillat Silvacane, Captain Corre, and Adamantine Garland might be aided and expedited? They may still be apart." Or injured or dead. She couldn't vocalize such possibilities.

"I will see what may be done." Her tone was strangely gentle for such an imposing figure. "Farewell for now, Ambassador Solenn, Prince Morvan." With a powerful pulse of her wings, she was airborne. Solenn tilted her head to watch her make another circuit around the château before flying northward.

"Solenn." Prince Morvan hurried forward to wrap his arms around her, his chin against her head. Tears stung her eyes. This was almost like the closeness that they knew in the old days. "Oh, my daughter," he whispered. "I'm so proud of you. I'm sorry. I'm sorry I didn't better support you before. I didn't know."

"You couldn't know. I wasn't permitted to tell you." People began to talk and move around the courtyard, but Morvan's and Solenn's musketeers formed a protective ring around them. "I had to—"

Solenn stopped, coughing to clear her throat. An odd, increasingly loud rumbling came from beyond the walls. She was certain she heard the distinct wail of bagpipes.

She pulled out her table book and wrote. *I had to leave, to talk to Queen Abonde. She needed encouragement to change strategies before the Coterie was butchered to extinction, like their kin in Albion.*

"To think, all epicurea is like *her*." Tad shook his head in awe. "Actually, no. I don't want to think of that at all, not when I consider what I've eaten over my life."

I've been coping with this new knowledge for weeks.

"I'm sorry you've had to do so alone," Tad murmured. "Or perhaps, mostly alone." He glanced at Lieutenant Talia with an arched eyebrow.

"We knew—and still know—very little, Your Highness," Talia said. "We certainly weren't party to the reasons for her recent departure."

"Prince, Princess," said one of Morvan's musketeers, her brow furrowed. "People have gathered outside the château as they celebrate our victory today. They call for Princess Solenn." That explained the loud rumble she was hearing.

She felt a sudden twist of nausea. The last time a crowd outside a castle had chanted her name, they'd called for her death. These people would be no different if circumstances changed.

"Oh dear. They'll want you to speak." Tad misread her visible flash of fear. "I can order white fluff for you—actually no, I can't." He shook his head. The drink used magical egg whites from golden chickens. King

Caristo had relied on it for his public speaking in Lutecia. "We've taken magic for granted."

Rethink everything, including how Albion can attack us. I've seen the dragon wings they've used to fly into Braiz. They could attack anywhere. She gestured to the spires around them. *As for the crowd, I may not be able to speak, but I can be seen. Talia, I need a tall coiffe.*

Talia's eyes lit up as she understood. "Of course. There's no better way for you to look Braizian from a distance. I can get one promptly and pin it for you, Itron."

In Verdania, Solenn had been forced to fit her feet into shoes that were too small. Now in Braiz, the word "itron" felt too big, too holy, to apply to her.

She withdrew into the château briefly. Talia, with her practiced hands, tidied her braided-up hair, which had been snarled by her flight. She then replaced Solenn's flat lace cover—it seemed like a minor miracle that it had stayed attached at all—with a tall one more suitable for a woman Mamm-gozh's age. A woman alone might need near a half hour to fully prepare her own hair and coiffe, but Talia had it done in minutes. Solenn had to smile. Such a contrast to the aggravating hours she'd spent being made to look presentably Verdanian during her brief time in Lutecia.

With Tad and their musketeers, she walked up the long stairwell to the castle wall. Outside, every avenue was packed with bodies, thousands of voices and bagpipes cheering at the sight of her.

"Itron," said Jean, leaning close that she might hear. "Look there, downslope. The Grand Pentad's banners approach." Hundreds of people stood between the gate and the retinue lodged in the crowd.

The last time she'd seen those tall, bright banners—five in a row, each depicting a God—had been during her escort from the city as she left to become a bride. They only emerged for official circumstances. Now, amid the buildings and bustle, she could see only the lead two, which quite appropriately were Selland's blue and Hester's red. Selland

was always first in Braiz, but the order otherwise varied. Hester's place-
ment would be no accident, however, not with Gurvan's oversight.

They need help to get through the crowd.

"Yes, Itron." Jean didn't look to Prince Morvan for approval. He
simply left.

Not a minute later, she gazed directly down as Jean led a cadre of
peers into the throng. They used shrill whistles to encourage people to
move and make room. As the banners advanced, she saw they acted
as an escort for a Camarga—Aveyron! He would've had no means to
readily reunite with her. He must have gone to Gurvan for help.

Once the retinue had made it within the grounds, Solenn went
down to meet them. Jean intercepted her.

"Your horse is returned to you." There was a knowing sparkle in his
eye. "A Chef came in escort, bearing sealed correspondence. He begs
your apology that the August Chef couldn't come himself." He handed
her the sealed packet.

Within, she found two sheets. On the first was a scant paragraph
in Aveyron's handwriting. He stated that the matter of payment for
their passage to Nont had been addressed—good, that cat deserved a
fine meal!—and he was admitting Gurvan into his limited confidence.
Aveyron had seen no other way of promptly returning to her vicinity.
Nor could she, now that she thought about it.

The second sheet, in Gurvan's calligraphic Braizian, explained that
work at the Grand Pentad had increased a thousandfold and he must
attend matters there as people worked through their fear and relief
around the day's battle. He was making certain, he said, that people
didn't simply thank Selland for the kraken's aid, but that Hester was also
given her due for the protection of their homes through the dragon's
intercession.

I entrust you to burn these while calling upon Hester. Solenn pressed
the papers into Jean's hands. He bowed.

How quickly would these offerings supply Hester with vigor?
Could the stone God be trusted once she regained a modicum of life?

Solenn kept asking these questions over and over, even as she knew the Gods themselves had no answer.

Unable to speak, unsure of what to say, she advanced to where Aveyron waited and pressed her face against his neck. His mane rustled against her lace headdress, his breath a reassuring huff as he leaned against her, an embrace that provided more support than a thousand words.

CHAPTER
TWENTY-TWO

ADA

The siege dragged on and on, and soon the desperate residents of the walled city had no more cannonballs. They still had plenty of food stores, though, including the five-pound dense cheeses for which they were famous, the rinds literally as hard as rocks due to the work of cheese mites. "We will fire cheese upon the invaders!" declared the mayor, and so they did, and the battle was won. When people ask why mimo cheese is so expensive, cheesemongers explain using this story: the cheese is not only delicious, but useful.

—Apocryphal tale of mimo cheese

Honor is not absent in war, but by necessity, its application is selective. Ada's shot struck a tall man directly in the center of his back, his companion a stride away downed by Brillat's blast to the skull. The other soldiers screeched alarm as they pulled their own weapons—rapiers, pistols, knives—but there was no cover nearby. Ada, her body braced against the wall, reloaded a few seconds slower than Brillat. Her shot crunched through one fellow's leg, while Brillat got another in the arm.

Return fire arrived as they ducked back outside. Wood chunks and splinters exploded from the doorframe as it caught pellets.

"Times like this, I wish I'd taken a moment to don clothes," Brillat said. His side nearest the door was freckled with blood—he'd caught shrapnel.

"As you're such a natty dresser, I thought you hadn't encountered anything to your liking," Ada said, fast fingers twisting on the warm barrel. "Though it'd also be a shame to ruin a good outfit in a battle."

The men inside were barking at each other as they tried to foment a new strategy. Ada hoped that this plan included an utter fixation upon her and Brillat, leaving their backs exposed when the occupants of the room chose to open fire.

"Sometimes, sacrifices must be made for just causes." Brillat recoiled to avoid more shrapnel from the doorframe.

"I feel that way about my coat," she said, unable to give the ragged green thing a fond glance at the moment.

Brillat peered out, fired, and withdrew. Another shot zinged between them. "Two dead, two injured," he murmured. "Still poor odds as we strive to save a person we both have reason to loathe."

Ada had never liked Roswita simply due to her proximity to Caristo, and also understood that her judgment was unjust. Someday, she'd like to know how Solenn had gauged her in more personal circumstances.

As for Brillat, well, Roswita had a well-documented delight for epicurea and a tremendous amount at her disposal even now.

Ada poked her head out and fired. As she stepped back, tapping her injured leg, it buckled. With a hiss, she caught herself against the wall and flinched as a shot reverberated through the surface.

"This might drag on all—" she began.

Simultaneous pistol blasts inside the chalet caused her and Brillat to flatten as they gazed at each other, questions in their eyes. Several screams rang out. Then a thud, another thud, more yells. Brillat moved fast, firing into the room, then dropped his pistol to draw the rapier as he advanced.

No time to question, no time to dither, Ada finished reloading and followed him into a room acrid with powder.

Brillat disarmed a Blessed by slicing off most of his fingers. Ada then shot another soldier as he lunged toward Brillat with a knife. Three other Blessed stood nearer the interior door, which was now open. A stout woman adorned in the highest regimental garb of a palace Chef was using a silver platter as a shield as she and another Blessed fought with knives. Behind her, rapier ready, stood a tall man wearing a loose Verdanian guard jacket over soiled gray pants. Shaggy hair coated half his face, but Ada recognized him all the same.

Erwan.

In a show of celebration, she walloped a Blessed with the butt of her pistol. A heavy blow to her back sent her staggering on unsteady legs—the Blessed whom Brillat fought had bumped into her. Forced as she was to balance on her bad leg, pain snared her attention and her breath, her ears ringing. The chaos of the scene clobbered her all at once: too many people, the clatter of rapier and knife, harsh odors, the yells and grunts and the cries of the injured on the ground.

In an instant, Erwan was there, hooking her left arm to keep her up while guarding her with his right. A breath later, Brillat defended her as well.

"Ada," Erwan greeted, a smile in the word. "It's good to see you."

"Likewise," she said, hoarse with pain. "We do need to stop meeting in battles like this. Might I suggest a good boulangerie or fromagerie next time?" A red tabard flashed close, and she remembered to strike again with the butt of the pistol, just as Erwan wielded his blade against the same foe. She smacked him upon the skull while Erwan impaled the fellow through the gut, causing him to collapse with a deflating screech.

They gazed around, ready to intercept the next threat, but there was none. No Blessed remained standing. The new quiet helped to clear Ada's mind. She assessed Erwan at a glance; he was gaunt and filthy but uninjured. Brillat had sustained no further wounds. The Chef took up a protective pose in the doorway, her level gaze meeting Ada's.

"Chef Sidonie Pedroza?" Ada asked in both surprise and horror. She hadn't faced one of her peers since she'd gone rogue sixteen years prior. They'd been in the same tour group as teens, traveling the realm, learning its ingredients and eccentricities. Never friends, but fair companions. This woman, by her level regard, clearly recognized her. With a word she could have Ada jailed and sent to Guild prosecutors, who, upon verifying Ada's continued recalcitrance, would have her tongue removed.

Like mother, like daughter, Ada supposed, but she also knew Erwan and Brillat would do what they could to save her from such a consequence.

"Adamantine Garland Corre," Pedroza replied with a glance toward Erwan.

Ada couldn't recall Pedroza and Erwan ever meeting years ago, but she had evidently made the connection between Ada's old surname and that of Erwan. Before Ada could speak, a colorful form appeared behind Pedroza.

"Oh my," said Queen Roswita in a tone more curious than anything. Her embroidered blue-and-green robe volante shimmered as she moved forward. "There were a lot of them."

Ada knew she was supposed to kneel before the queen but wasn't feeling particularly respectful this day or decade. Without any acknowledgment of the royal presence, Brillat began to make the rounds of the fallen Blessed, killing any who still lived.

"And a naked man assisted. That was not anticipated," said Queen Roswita with a tone of dry amusement. As Pedroza emerged into the parlor, Ada had a better view of the queen and was surprised to see a rapier in her hand. She held it with the fluidity that came of experience. "But then, little today has been anticipated. Thank you again, Chevalier Corre." Of course, Roswita would know Erwan as Solenn's advocate.

He bowed. "As was only right, Your Majesty."

Oh, Erwan. Ada's heart made a distinct pang. Despite all the injustices done to him and his comrades, he had still risked himself for the queen. But then, hadn't Ada done the same?

A strange look passed over Queen Roswita's face—grief, anger, pain, all in a flash. She sheathed her weapon. "I do not take honor for granted. I know better, having lived in Verdania as long as I have. You could've continued your escape. You chose to join our fight, and for that reason, I'm not a captive of the Blessed." She still spoke with the slight guttural accent of Grand Diot.

"You may wish to lock yourself in that room again as you await reinforcements," said Ada. "The fight's not done. The Blessed are everywhere here, like midge flies at a summer fete."

Queen Roswita cocked her head, her smile faint. With the full Chef's satchel left in the other room, Ada could now perceive a faint remnant of the epicurea Dobie's Wort within Roswita's body. The sweet stalks were used to treat migraines, usually as a tisane. "A wise consideration, from one who obviously hates me so. I remember your name, *Chef* Corre." Pedroza, who'd gone to close the front door, froze when she heard Ada's title spoken. At that moment, Ada realized that Pedroza had purposefully not identified her as a Chef. She'd been ready to abet Ada's continued desertion. "I've heard rants about you over the years, the empathetic Chef and officer gone rogue. My husband probably doesn't know the names of any of our three resident Chefs, but he knows *yours* because you've slighted him and the very Gods."

Brillat caught Ada's eye, his face one of tight-lipped concern. No doubt not only because of the flow of this palaver, but because of how they tarried.

"Ah yes. 'To serve the king is to serve the Gods,'" Ada said with blatant bitterness, feeling light-headed as she tapped her bad leg on the ground. She must have tottered, as Erwan was there in two strides, an arm around her waist.

"So is said of Chefs, and good queens," said Roswita in a tone that didn't include herself in the latter category. She looked between Ada and Erwan, her striped skirts swaying. The redness in her eyes seemed to be not from tears but from lingering pain. "Have you been together throughout your desertion?"

"We were reunited briefly only weeks ago, madame," said Erwan. His fingers held Ada secure and close.

Roswita released a long breath, sending loose tendrils of silvering blonde hair adrift around her face. "That dissolution of Braizian marriages. Another sorrow created by my husband's piques. Well then, may you be together now in a reunion worthy of troubadours. Go, before the naked man has a tantrum because you're lingering here overlong." She waved them away with a slender, ring-laden hand.

Pedroza turned to Queen Roswita. "I'll get them to the back door. I've secured the front entry, but please, lock yourself in the garderobe for now, madame."

Roswita looked on the verge of arguing, then sighed and nodded. "I should probably sit again. Don't be long. Monsieur le Mousquetaire," she said, addressing Erwan crisply. He straightened. "Extend my sincere apologies to your princess for her poor welcome to this country. May Selland fill her sails." With that, she returned to the inner chamber.

"She knows Princess Solenn is innocent?" Ada asked softly as they followed Chef Pedroza deeper into the re-created mountain chalet. Heavy wooden furniture and simple fineries decorated the place. Ada had a vague recollection of having heard that Roswita had a favorite chalet from her youth rebuilt on these grounds a few years ago. This must be it.

"Many in the palace, even those who hate Braiz, can see that there's a clear lack of proof," said Pedroza, glancing back. She had a commanding stride that matched her fitted justaucorps with double-rowed gold buttons and braid. "Roswita has no more influence over the king than a child blowing a dandelion puff has over the sea wind."

"He abandoned her here yesterday, taking most of the royal guard with him," Erwan all but growled.

"Roswita's been leveled by a migraine these past three days," said Pedroza. "Until a few hours ago, she wasn't able to move from her back without retching. Dobie's Wort, potent as it is, only helps her to sleep during these bad bouts."

"I'm glad she's better now," Ada said. "But, Chef Pedroza, I must warn you—epicurea isn't what we think it is. Cease your use of it in all forms, I beg you."

Brillat stared at Ada, agog at the implications she presented.

"Captain Corre already requested that we not utilize epicurea to our benefit during our fight and provided no justification as to why." Pedroza's brow furrowed as she faced Ada. A heavy wooden door awaited them five feet away. "Now you're implying it's, what, poison? That can't be true across such a breadth of ingredients. We Chefs have been using them for thousands of years."

"And we've been *wrongly* using them for thousands of years," Ada said heavily. "Please, keep my words in mind."

"Very well." Pedroza shook her head in clear disbelief. "Before you go, do please tell me, your grandmother . . . has she—is she—"

Under other circumstances, Ada wouldn't have admitted her grandmother was still alive and therefore vulnerable to Guild prosecution, but Pedroza had proved herself to be an ally. Ada found it comforting that the friendship that Pedroza and Grand-mère had shared in the palace apparently hadn't faded with time. "As of last week, she lived. Her body is hale, but her mind . . . she's often confused."

Pedroza's brows furrowed as she accepted this news with grief. "I'm sorry. I've known others to endure similar. But she has . . . you've . . ."

Ada understood. "She's enjoyed her freedom greatly, but she still speaks of her time in the palace kitchens with fondness." Had this Blessed attack happened twenty years ago, Grand-mère would've been in Pedroza's very role, perhaps with the same close relationship that Pedroza had with the queen. Not a friend but not fully subservient either.

"I'm glad," Pedroza said softly. Brillat had gone ahead to the door, opening it to scout. "Are you clear to leave, monsieur?"

"Yes," Brillat said. "No Blessed or Verdanian soldiers in sight."

"Monsieur, I don't suppose you'll explain why you're gamboling about mother-naked?" Pedroza asked.

"No," he said, a trace of a smile on his lips. Ada suspected he took deep joy in confusing humans. "You'll need to relish in the mystery."

"I assure you, we will," Pedroza said wryly.

As Ada and Erwan approached the door, Ada realized she had one more thing she must say. "The royal jail. The prisoners are locked up without care. Once you have Roswita secure—"

"I'll make certain they're attended to." Pedroza looked curious but contained her questions. "I would never let anyone starve. I'll inform the command promptly."

At that, Ada and Erwan followed Brillat outside and into a tidy grove of young apple trees in regimental rows. Beyond that were more trees and greenery.

"The gardens sprawl behind the palace for a mile from here," Brillat said. "As my weapons may be needed this next while, I'll stay as I am." As if to reassert that possibility of more conflict, nearby gunshots rang out in a quick cascade. They moved as fast as Ada's leg allowed, though Erwan's aid did much to help her speed.

"Thank you for bringing up that matter of the jail." Erwan looked pained. "I regret that I had to leave the people there without defense." He addressed the matter of Ada's mother with delicacy even though Brillat knew their familial connection. Sometimes known secrets were best not voiced.

"I understand," Ada said, her fingers giving him a light squeeze. She could feel his ribs through his coat.

Brillat gazed around; if he'd been in horse form, his ears would've been pricked. "Hide," he hissed, pointing them behind a hedge. They swiftly sheltered there, Ada woozy with redoubled agony as she crouched. She could now feel the swelling in her calf against her boot shaft.

Some twenty Verdanian soldiers ran past, headed toward Queen Roswita's chalet.

The trio's trek continued. They hid behind a wall to avoid more Verdanian soldiers, only to find a band of sneaking Blessed a few minutes later. Ada used her pistol while Brillat and Erwan utilized blades. The next group of Blessed, however, they avoided by ducking inside a building. After that, they seemed to leave the current battle behind as they continued through the outer gardens. Ada wanted to talk to Erwan more but instead breathed heavily from exertion, each step requiring gritted teeth and focus. Brillat and Erwan whispered together to relate what had happened over the past few weeks. After learning of his comrades' deaths, Erwan briefly paused to grieve, his head butted against a wall as he wept. He wasn't surprised by the news, though. He'd been told they would die, and that it was his fault for not admitting that Solenn was complicit in Prince Rupert's death.

With slow deliberation, Ada told Erwan that Brillat and the kin were ensuring that the musketeers made it home to Braiz. Brillat shifted in discomfort at Erwan's tears and gratitude.

"We believe in reciprocating kindness, that is all," he said with a shrug. "As part of that, I'll guide you to an abandoned cabin in the woods that I found as I fled Viflay. You can stay there while I cross the veil to acquire medical aid."

Ada frowned. "No. We can't waste time resting here. We need to head northward. We'll find another horse somewhere and—"

"Ada," Erwan said in a gently chastising tone she remembered all too well. "You have a fever that's been worsening since we were reunited. You soon may not be able to ride astride at all." When she continued to glare, he tried a different tack. "If you press on, you'll only let Gyst's unknowns continue to attack your body." On Ada's behalf, Brillat had related how Gyst had confronted Solenn in the cellar. None of them had a doubt that Gyst was exacerbating Ada's injury out of spite.

"The medicine I bring cannot stop that attack of unknowns either," said Brillat. "But it'll help you engage in this battle."

"Fine," she said, grumbling, with a grudging sense of relief. Her fever was beginning to worry her too. Even her good leg was beginning to drag as exhaustion set in.

Minutes later, Brillat reached beneath a tall shrubbery to pull out the saddle he'd hidden there. Ada had been too distracted to ask after her gear and was relieved at its reappearance. Brillat changed form. Minutes later, they continued with Ada slumped in the saddle, Brillat at a fast walk while Erwan jogged alongside. Every so often, rose fairies swooped around them. As Ada had no idea which one may have helped her, she tried to give them all a little smile and nod of gratitude.

The back wall of the grounds stood only some six feet high, its stone structure topped with iron spikes. That height wouldn't have been hard for the Blessed to surmount, but the open gate was where most of the dead and injured lay. Uniforms of blue and red were rendered dark.

"A Camarga?" an injured Verdanian soldier whispered in wonderment as they passed, the words forming a bloody bubble on his lips.

Ada had a harder time focusing as they entered the woods. Shadow and light seemed to swirl over her. Brillat's purposefully gliding walk would've lured her to sleep but for the uncomfortable heat arising from her body.

She blinked, disoriented, when Brillat finally came to a stop. Beneath the deep shade of old-growth trees stood the cabin. There was no door—no, there was, but it lay on the mud, its surface furry with bright-green moss. Wooden shutters dangled loose from their panes. The floor creaked moistly as they entered; holes in the ceiling revealed glimpses of pink evening sky. Erwan helped her lie down on the floor. Half closing her eyes, she let her senses drift.

"There's a well outside. The water is pure," she murmured.

"I'll refill your canteen, then," Erwan said, his fingers glancing her cheek. "Brillat—"

He'd followed them inside in his human form. "I'll try to be fast. This is by no means a safe place."

"I'm well aware," Erwan said with grimness. "Selland preserve you, my friend." The two men clasped arms. Brillat stepped outside. A moment later, Ada's sense of him vanished. He'd reverted to horse form.

Erwan sat beside her. "Ada, how does your boot feel?"

"Tight. You'll need to cut the leather." Slitting the stalk would allow the lower portion to still protect her foot, at least. She didn't need her vulnerable sole attacked too.

His long, unkempt hair dangled loose around his shoulders as he bent over her leg. His soft touch to her calf made her gasp. "I'm sorry," he murmured. "I'll be gentle."

"I know," she whispered, smiling at him even through her pain. Strange how she could be so happy and miserable all at once.

"Do you have bandages in your saddlebags?"

"Yes. I have the clean bandages for my monthly, and I shouldn't have need of them for weeks yet—though my body hasn't been as timely as it once was. Perils of my age."

He cast her a somewhat shy look that gave her a pang. They used to talk with frankness about such things. "I'll cut these bandages off, then, as they're soiled through." He did so, and she just managed to stay conscious as he tugged the crusted cloth away. "There's pus, and it looks like your stitches ripped out on one side."

She detected his unasked question. "Drain the wound. Maybe the release of pressure will make it easier for me to walk."

"Very well," he said with resolute grimness.

With a waft fragrant of hot whey and damp moss, Gyst's presence strengthened in a shadowed corner of the old cabin. He had no visible form. He said nothing. He was just there, watching.

A respectful Chef would signal his X and murmur his praises. Instead, out of Erwan's line of sight, she directed a lewd gesture the God's way and resisted a hysterical giggle as his presence faded.

She wasn't afraid of irritating the God further. She could smell the rot within her own flesh.

Tears seeped from her eyes. Under Erwan's touch, she was so happy. So miserable. So *scared*, all at once.

CHAPTER
TWENTY-THREE

SOLENN

A boiled oatmeal pudding is a warming, restorative meal. Mix together oats, minced herbs to preference, and pepper and salt. Tie everything together in a bag and place it in a pot full of water. Bring it to a boil. Open up the bag. Add butter, and enjoy.

—Excerpt from *Book for Cooks to Excel as Do Chefs*

Solenn was provided minimal respite. She requested food and privacy, eating a simple bowl of boiled oatmeal pudding with honey with such haste that she almost choked twice. Piquette helped her to wash everything down. Refreshed, she continued to her next confrontation.

A full dozen musketeers escorted her through the castle, all of them familiar, most of them from the contingent that had first traveled with her to Verdania. They knew her best, but even so, she recognized new nervousness in how they regarded her. Some of these same people had been awkwardly gentle with her since the loss of her tongue. Now, she'd become someone even more strange to their thinking.

They went not to her grandparents' private audience room but the war council chamber. High ceilings of dark wood loomed overhead, the drapes heavy with embroidery and lace. At the long table sat generals, admirals, and subordinates representing ships and units already deployed. She'd known many of these men and women amid polite society. Now they looked upon her with ambivalence.

Her family's reaction wasn't so restrained.

"My girl." Mamm-gozh wrapped her in a hug. The cheek that pressed against Solenn's head was wet with tears. "Welcome home." She paused, her voice lowering. "I set my rose fairy jar in the garden. Within the hour, it had been emptied, a snipped rosebud left beside it. I wish I'd known—I wish—"

Solenn gave her an extra squeeze of wordless support.

Her grandfather was again elsewhere—under heavy guard in a safe place, she imagined, with the heir and his immediate family in a different locale—and so Tad was present to conduct this meeting. He stood to embrace her, causing everyone else in the room to stand as well. "Welcome home, Ambassador Solenn." His movements were stiff, unfamiliar, which meant she was even more surprised when he continued: "A chair close beside me, please, so I can watch as she writes."

There was a collective gasp within the room. Whenever one of the princes sat at the head of the table, they were acting as an immediate representative of King Myles. Not even Mamm-gozh had ever sat at the side of the king in such a place of equality.

Attendants also brought out a standing easel and large sheets of paper on a backing of smooth wood. Ink pens and a full bottle were set on the table. Some thought had been put into how best to accommodate her in this meeting, for which she was incredibly grateful.

That positivity faded as her interrogation began.

What was the Coterie? What was their domain? To what had she committed Braiz? Were the sources of all ingredients *truly* like the dragon? On and on, the questions an unceasing flow. She wrote large so that most people could see her answers when they were set upon the easel, and she went through pages in rapid succession. As she did not speak, several men began to comment aloud as she wrote rather than wait to respond; Tad squelched their rudeness with a few abrupt words of his own, but Solenn couldn't deny that the restless silence of the room felt strange. It drove her to write faster. Several people had difficulty grasping that they must relinquish all epicurea; many of those present were among the few in the realm with easy access to magic and were undeniably resistant to losing their privilege. Could no middle ground be found? What if ingredients were kept only for emergencies?

She finally lost patience. *Put yourself in the position of a selkie. Your son dies. How will you feel when his body is butchered, his skin removed? His few magical internal organs will be processed by a Chef to later be eaten, but his skin will be sold to a haberdasher, his fat used for lamps, his meat salted for consumption. You request the entirety of his remains back. You get a remnant of skin. Are you satisfied?*

Her displayed answer made some people visibly squeamish. Good. Tad considered the words with a thoughtful hum.

Messengers entered on occasion to deliver military updates to those present. When a Chef in Grand Pentad livery began to lurk at the back of the room, their direct gaze on her, Solenn requested that Talia intercept the message on her behalf. Heads turned to take in their murmured exchange. Talia's face held tense composure as she approached to whisper into Solenn's ear.

"August Chef Gurvan requires your immediate guidance. Hester has awakened. The Grand Pentad has been closed out of necessity."

"What?" The squawk escaped Solenn's lips. Hester's head had been empowered, already? But then, how many thousands had fed her offerings in person, how many tens of thousands had appealed to her to safeguard their homes this day?

Necessity? she wrote small, only for Talia's eyes. Had the pentad been set alight? What had happened?

"The Chef said only that the hearth fire now had an overwhelming presence," she whispered in reply. Questions were evident in her pale eyes, but Solenn had no answers, not when she was likewise awestruck.

Now, how could she explain her departure to the council? She couldn't tell them of her hopes. She couldn't presume what Hester would say or do. Solenn resolved to keep things honest and simple.

She wrote a message to her audience on a fresh sheet of paper. *August Chef Gurvan urgently requests my presence. I apologize, but I must go.*

As she finished the sentence, Tad laid a gentle hand on her forearm. "Solenn? What is . . . ?" he murmured.

Solenn glanced at the fire. She yearned to trust Hester as she did Selland, but faith wasn't something she would place upon the God blindly. It required mutual respect.

She wanted full respect from her father too. No, not just respect . . . acceptance.

"I must go," she whispered. His lips parted as if he was going to question her again, but then his eyes briefly met hers. He gave her a curt nod, then stood. He waited for everyone to rise and spoke.

"Ambassador Solenn requires a full contingent to accompany her to the Grand Pentad. Quickly." His request provoked musketeers into motion and sparked whispers around the table.

Talia and Jean joined Solenn. "You require your Camarga readied, Itron?" Talia murmured.

Trying not to visibly cringe at the application of that word, Solenn nodded. Jean hurried ahead.

༄

Night draped the world in black, stars like jewels set in the span above. Crowds lingered outside the château and through the streets. Judging by the cups and bottles raised to her in toast, the city had stayed up late to celebrate the day's victory. People chanted her name and "Itron, Itron,

Itron." One shrill voice proclaimed love for her. Some people fell upon their knees to prostrate themselves. Solenn was unnerved. She wasn't a figure to be worshipped. Her company kept people back even as they surged. Her heart raced. Aveyron was agitated as well, his ears and eyes taking in everything, a herd creature aware of surrounding predators.

The empty lots around the Grand Pentad had provided more space for people to gather. Word of the building's closure—and rumors of why—had likely drawn many citizens, like midges to ripe fruit.

She was relieved to dismount before the steps of the Grand Pentad. Another Chef emerged, a lamp revealing profound relief on his features.

"The August Chef extends greetings to you, Ambassador Solenn, and permits the entrance of your Camarga within the pentad." He recited his strange message as calmly as if describing the fish found in an average day's catch.

Solenn caught Aveyron's side-eye. His entrance to the sanctuary would fan wildfires of speculation, but then, he had already come to the château with a full pentad escort. The extraordinary nature of Camargas, often rumored despite their uselessness as epicurea, had likely already been speculated about today.

Aveyron followed her up the steps to raucous cheers. His hooves echoed strangely as they stepped within the sanctum. Solenn motioned to her company, indicating her desire to keep Talia and Jean close while the others could maintain guard at the doors alongside Chefs.

Gurvan awaited at the broad archway to Hester's chamber. He murmured greetings to Talia and Jean, and welcomed Aveyron by name. Gurvan had been born with a complexion like milk, but he now looked impossibly paler.

"Hester began to speak a half hour ago, Itron," Gurvan said to Solenn, his voice shaking. "I was staying near her fire to supervise and assist supplicants. She . . . she called to me by name, then asked that I summon you here." He flared his hand, head bowed. "When I could move again, I helped other people to exit."

"Move again?" Solenn shoved syllables from her throat. Out of the corner of her eye, she noted Aveyron tug on Jean's lacy sleeve, the two of them stepping into another chamber. She could only hope that Aveyron was changing form.

"There's power to her words. It is . . . humbling."

"Is it safe for Ambassador Solenn to approach?" asked Talia in a sharp tone.

"There's no . . . purposeful offense in Most August Hester's words. This isn't an attack. She simply . . . is." Silence lingered as those present took in Gurvan's statement. In the quiet, Solenn could make out faint yet steady jabber from Hester's chamber. At her perplexed look, Gurvan took a deep breath, then continued. "She has spoken without ceasing, commenting on everything within her sight and about various other circumstances as well. She apparently could see for some time before her voice could function. From a distance, her soliloquy is tolerable, which is why we—"

Solenn walked around him and into the room, ignoring Talia's urgent gesture that she wait.

Thirty feet away, the fire was barely contained within its wide, charred alcove. It resembled the outdoor bonfires on holiday Hestersdays. Even at this distance, heat lapped her skin.

She didn't need to sense magic to recognize the welling of power in this room. Hester could readily set fire to this building, could raze what remained of Nont. Solenn took a steadying breath as she walked onward. Selland's fluid nature was proof that Gods could change. Hester could also change, for the better.

She'd made it a few more feet when emotion crested over her like a tidal wave, bringing with it a memory of water.

Home. Braiz. Water eddying around her ankles and eroding the sand beneath her soles as she stood on the misty beach.

The crunch of flaked salt between her forefinger and thumb as she pinched seasoning from the nef on her family's table, smiling as Tad and Mamm teased each other about some silly thing that had happened earlier in the day, their laughter even sweeter to her ears than the rollicking play of oboe and bagpipe during a party.

The warm huff of Maiwenn's breath against her flat palm as the mare took up a proffered carrot with her gray lips.

Through the flash of memories, Solenn's eyes were still open wide, taking in her view of the room before her. Overwhelmed by vertigo, what she truly felt beneath her fingertips was the well-worn stone floor as she crouched down. A step behind her, Talia's moan also came from near the ground. The musketeer had also been leveled by an emotional onslaught.

Home, home, home. Coziness. Familiarity. Voices. Touches. The deep rightness of being in a place she loved, with those she loved.

This was the sensation that Gurvan had described. Hester was blasting everyone in her immediate vicinity with profound emotions. No wonder the Grand Pentad had been evacuated.

"Hester." Speaking was even more difficult than usual, as her more urgent need was to sob with sheer longing and gratitude. "Can you hear me? You are *too much.*" Telling a God they were too much struck her as ridiculous after the words emerged, but they remained true nevertheless. Hester had been isolated for so very long that perhaps she had no sense of her effect on people.

"Solenn." The voice was high, feminine, not at all like the distorted tone that had emerged from Mallory Valmont when Hester had spoken through him. The single word reverberated through Solenn as if she stood beneath the mighty Grand Pentad bells as they tolled, something she'd done only once in her life. That was enough. *"Whatever do you—"* As Hester stopped speaking, the power of her presence dimmed. Solenn's head was suddenly clearer, though tears still streamed down her cheeks. *"Oh. I see. Yes, Hester sees, Hester understands."*

Solenn remembered her last sight of Malo as she rode for Verdania, the village and sea blanketed in gray fog. While she would've liked for her parting view to have consisted of bright sunlight and clear buildings, the perfectly Braizian gray, moody day had made her laugh at the time. It still made her smile now.

"Power is outwardly flowing with my mighty breath, the breath of Hester, enhancer of life-sustaining heat. I have been . . . preoccupied, yes, by thousands of queries and appeals for my generosity. I didn't fully realize the magnitude of my puissance," said Hester. Only the faintest of feelings fluttered through Solenn's mind. She pushed herself to stand, then turned to Talia. The musketeer lay face down, her shoulders heaving in sobs.

"Talia?" Solenn asked softly.

"I'm sorry, Princess. Ambassador." Talia pushed herself to her knees as she wiped her face, regaining her composure as she picked up her feathered hat from where it had fallen beside her. "My first husband. I remembered him, as if he lived anew."

Not all memories of home would be gentle, that was certain. There was a reason why Gurvan still lurked at the doorway; Solenn viewed this not as cowardice, but wisdom.

She offered Talia her hand and helped her rise. Together, they approached the fire as emotion eddied around them, like seawater teasing at toes at the end of dry sand.

"Most August Hester," Solenn said. "I am here to parley."

She walked to treat with the God who, when they last spoke, had tried to burn her alive.

CHAPTER TWENTY-FOUR

SOLENN

While Braiz makes wine, it is not the equal of its cider and brandy. Indeed, Braizians themselves will joke that partaking of the wine made in the Reez Peninsula requires four people and a wall—one person to pour, another to drink, two to hold on to the imbiber, and a wall to keep the person from escaping. For wines, rely on Verdania.

—Excerpt from *Book for Cooks to Excel as Do Chefs*

"I congratulate you, Solenn. I harbored little uncertainty that your plan would come to fruition, that your land's savior of hearth and home would be rightfully released . . ."

"The fire speaks? The fire is Hester?" Talia murmured, her breaths labored.

Solenn looked back in concern. "The emotions . . . ?"

"Are dimmed, but still clouding my brain," she murmured.

Solenn felt only a trace of the feelings now; was she bearing up against them more because she was descended from Gyst? As Ada and Abonde had pointed out, Solenn still retained her divinity, even if the conduit of her tongue was gone.

"Hester, can you please dampen the flow more? No one else will be able to tolerate your presence otherwise." Solenn hoped that Hester could understand her.

The heat from the mighty fire didn't decrease, but the holy presence did. Solenn had that confirmed when Talia gave her a nod. She beckoned Gurvan to approach as she again faced the hearth.

"Thank you, Hester. Is now a good time to pull your head from the flames?"

"I desire more power, for truly, this piece of rock could hold more energy, but . . ." She paused, seeming to gather herself. *"I forgot how sensitive mortals can be, how unsuited they are for celestial conference. I now understand why this sacred pentad was closed. Yes, yes, Hester recognizes the grief and curiosity of those denied their place of worship. Remove my head if you must, royal Solenn of Braiz, for I will still know the prayers and offerings of mortals through this fire and so many others in the city. For am I not mercifully divine? Am I not rightfully free? Free! Oh, how exquisite . . . an offering of bread by a magistrate, and fine bread at that, unburned, tender, fragrant, a crunchy yet malleable crust, worthy of my attention, worthy of my divine favor."* What was Hester talking about? *"And now an eager Chef to the north has called upon Hester to bless his roasting chicken, ah yes, and a fine bird it is. So many prayers, voices, all hailing my wondrousness. I am with you, Solenn, I am with magistrate and the distant Chef, and with many here in Nont, so many in Nont."* The God released a small cry of delight. *"Hear Hester's voice at long last! Yes, yes, my voice freed after so long. Hester, long starved, long deprived, now is the time to feast . . ."*

Hester continued to jabber on as Solenn realized that the God's presence was both here and everywhere, and that she was using her voice to acknowledge all those who called upon her, who fed her power with their entreaties. Hester's unbridled yearning, her relief and euphoria, pulsed through the air like a heartbeat.

Solenn pulled out her table book and angled it toward Gurvan. *Have we decided on how best to safely remove the head from the flames?*

"Ah. Yes. That." The coolheaded elder looked ready to bolt if emotions flooded the chamber again. "I'm still unsure of how best to go about that. I cannot bear the idea of using metal tongs that could chip her, though I'm not sure she would permit such a contrivance at that."

Aveyron pulled a shirt down over his head as he entered the room. He wore breeches but no shoes. Jean set down the saddle by the door and joined them, the intense illumination revealing his awe.

"By all the salt in the sea," Jean said breathily. Hester's attention had shifted yet again as she narrated about a party near the seawall where people sang and danced around a bonfire. "What's going on?"

"Please, I would very much like to know," said Talia.

Solenn gestured to Aveyron.

"Hester's very body is made of cursed stone, monsieur, madame," said Aveyron. He had picked up the gist of the question asked in Braizian, answering in Verdanian. "We presented it to an artisan. In her hands, the stone took the form of a human head. Ambassador Solenn brought it here with the hope that direct offerings and prayers would imbue it with the power to speak and interact."

"With what intent, Monsieur Silvacane?" asked Talia in Verdanian.

He hesitated, looking to Solenn. She tapped her pencil as she considered how best to explain her recent interactions with the Gods, but she would need a book to do so in a way that made sense. *Hester was recently my enemy. I have strived to improve our relationship.*

"An enemy?" Talia gestured to the Five and to Hester. "You haven't merely sought an alliance with the Coterie, then, but with the very Gods. *A God.*"

Hester's current tangent stopped. *"That is truth, Madame la Mousquetaire,"* she said, her tone imperious. *"I will speak in the standard language of Verdania, as it will be most universally understood by those present, and my voice, long silenced, must be understood. My choice of tongue is no mark of favoritism on my part, I assure you, for glorious Hester is called upon across the sprawling seas, on lands far beyond your imagination. Ah yes, in a domicile to the south, I taste burning words as parchment is fed to my fire, yes, Hester knows your secrets now as does Gyst, but he will enjoy them far more than I. Better to be given—ah! Cheese, dripped into the coals. Such an exquisite delight, this fat. An accidental offering, but one accepted with eagerness—child, Hester will remember this cheese, oh yes she will. My sweet dear Solenn of Braiz, princess and ambassador both, come closer so that Hester may better view you with these eyes."*

Solenn recognized the wonder in her musketeers' faces as they considered that "these eyes" remark. She wrote, and Aveyron spoke for her. "Do you see as if with flesh, God Hester?" he asked.

"Yes, yes, but Hester remains based in stone, always stone, solid and yet ever vulnerable. You queried as to how this beautiful head of mine might be removed from this proud fire. The good August Chef, oh very good, his offerings and attention ever pleasing, should know the answer to this dilemma."

Gurvan looked momentarily flustered by Hester's praise. "I should? Oh. Do you mean blessed skin, Most August One?"

"Yes, August Chef, tell the tale, tell the tale, so that Hester's own ears can hear the recounting of her generous actions."

"Of course." He faced the others. "Some Chefs are born Hester-blessed and can endure more heat than most or understand its working at a deeper level." Solenn nodded, remembering that Chef Pedroza in the Lutecian palace had mentioned such a gift. Aveyron didn't nod but listened with a thoughtful expression. "We have no such Chefs in Nont, unfortunately, but anyone can make a request of Hester for a temporary endowment. I myself knew a woman whose house was burning with her babe inside. She pleaded for Hester to bless her as if she'd eaten fire salamander—pardon for the epicurea reference," he said as an aside to Aveyron, "and was so blessed. She dashed in and saved her child right before the building collapsed. Her arm was burned and some hair was lost, but she knew only gratitude."

"Yes, yes, Hester has saved many through her beneficence over the years," Hester said with an air of satisfaction.

"A temporary blessing," Jean murmured. "One that doesn't make a person impervious."

"This is truth, deep truth, for not even Hester is impervious. Ah, a romantic couple huddles close to my fire, calling for me to help warm them as they warm each other . . . ," Hester murmured.

Solenn stepped closer to the pentad hearth.

"Solenn, have you even considered that someone else could grab the head from the flames?" asked Aveyron, stepping alongside her. She gazed at him, chagrined. "As a representative of the Coterie, I should fetch her. I don't believe she'll do me harm."

Solenn considered his words for a moment and then nodded. Hester and the Coterie needed to establish a new relationship. That needed to begin now.

Without hesitation, Aveyron lunged into the flames with an out-stretched arm, his silver hair flaring at the abrupt movement. Solenn could scarcely breathe as she waited for him to start screaming as he caught fire. He advanced on all fours into the ten-foot-high hearth, flames coiling around him, and then he pulled back. Pivoting around on his knees, he cradled a large oblong object against his chest: Hester's head. He set it down on the flagstones beyond the fire and then flipped around on his buttocks and limbs.

His shirt was smoking—and then caught fire.

Solenn surged forward, but her musketeers were faster yet. Jean grabbed the shirt, yanking it over Aveyron's head, while Talia used her gloved hands to pat at his pants and exposed skin. The smell of burned fibers filled the room—but not the scent of cooked meat.

"Aveyron!" Solenn cried.

"I think I'm well," he said, rolling to sit up as he checked his own body. Talia peered around him, scrutinizing him front and back. The hearth's glow showed Aveyron's pale skin was reddening across his face and chest. He grabbed at his hair, patting at the ends, and sighed in relief. Solenn knew that burned hair smelled horrible, but she detected no such stench.

"Do you need water for your burns?" Talia asked.

"No. I think my human skin has fared worse from being too long in sunlight," he said, but winced as he palpated his chest.

Hester laughed, high and giddy. *"Burns happen, yes, people underesti-mate Hester's intensity, but you, colt of the Coterie, you respected my poten-tial. Your fast movements spared you much pain. I know your gratitude, sweet as Melissa's celebratory bells, and you should know my own for your stalwart aid to the ambassador and your care in handling Hester's head. Yes, yes, I comprehend the vulnerability I experienced in your hands. For that, Hester shows appreciation by quelling the rising heat within your body . . ."*

Jean, who had been stomping on the burned shirt, shook his head in blatant awe. "I did not expect such experiences when I awoke today."

"Thank you for your aid, August Hester," said Aveyron, turning on his knees to bow to her.

Solenn had been so concerned for Aveyron that she hadn't regarded Hester's head. The God had been set down with haste, but mostly faced the people in the room.

"The tales, oh, so many tales speak of the arrogance and might of Hester, and they hold truth, and yet—and yet—I have also come to know humble-ness and regret. You were assisting me, Aveyron of the white horses. Hester owes gratitude, not harm. Not to you."

Solenn shivered despite the nearby fire's heat, reminded again that it was not prudent to be an enemy of this God.

"Most August One, will you be able to restrain your heat again so that you may be taken to the château for safekeeping?" asked Gurvan.

"Can Hester hold back her searing presence within her celestial self captured in stone? Can she? Can I? Yes. Yes." Hester sounded more con-fident with the last word. *"Even a God must learn again, must . . . aha! The lightning struck a dry tree, and it burns, it must burn. I will bless the fiery flow, yes, so the forest may be razed and grow anew . . ."*

Solenn recalled what Lyria had said of such fires as she scooted to sit before Hester. Streaks of black darkened the gray. The neck couldn't move, but her face certainly could, as she smiled when she saw Solenn. Her eyes were fully gray, but the pupils had gained an intelligent black sheen that reminded Solenn of an animal.

It had worked. The ploy had truly worked.

"Hest—" Solenn started to cough. The fire was aggravating her throat. She motioned to her table book.

"I am celestial. All the languages of the world are known to me," Hester said. *"Such is my power that I comprehend your intent even as your tongue doesn't form words as it once did. I discern even the prayers of nurslings."*

Hester could understand Solenn, even when she could scarcely decipher what she had said herself? She thought of when Gyst had confronted her in Malo, how he'd seemed to comprehend her with ease, even when her great-grandmother had not. Such must be the way of the Gods . . . which meant Selland also knew her intentions. She took heart in that.

When we go to the château, you must try to keep quiet and constrain the emotions you create all the more. The crowd will riot if they know you're present. She motioned to Gurvan. *Have you the leather bag?*

"Yes, it's nearby. I'll fetch it, Itron." Gurvan bowed to Hester as he stepped aside.

"People, people are such sensitive things. Flesh and sinew, so readily broken, readily crisped. Quick to react with no thought to think," Hester muttered, as if she hadn't a reputation for behaving with such haste in her time as a God. *"Hester has gone centuries without speech. Words, words, swirling forever in the lake of my mind, never an outlet, never the pleasure of hearing my own voice aloud, not until now. You ask Hester to hold back her heat, and to be silent? Will next you ask her to dampen the sun as if with a wet blanket?"* Her tone held not anger but frustration. No, not frustration—fear.

"Over three thousand years of imposed silence—staying quiet now is an understandable challenge," said Aveyron. An incredible statement of sympathy, one that Hester herself seemed to recognize as her eyes briefly fluttered shut, expression pained.

Solenn hesitated a moment, then wrote. *Please don't take offense at this, but would it help if you were temporarily gagged?*

She was glad Gurvan was out of the room as she showed her offensive suggestion to Hester. To her surprise, the God laughed. A glimpse within her mouth revealed the presence of teeth and a tongue. How did such things even exist? Lyria couldn't have carved anything internal, and yet Hester could speak. Solenn was awed and somewhat envious.

"Offense! Dear Solenn, you who have sacrificed much effort and care on my behalf, Hester is not a fool. She sees that you suggest this from the depth of your compassion. Even so, Hester also comprehends this to be a ludicrous suggestion to make of a God. Hester, the destroyer of Ys, whose breath fuels thousands of fires in this very instant, submitting to a mere cloth gag! But yes, yes, I concede to this temporary measure."

Solenn released a low, slow exhalation of relief.

Gurvan returned and pressed down the sides of the leather bag. "I will open the doors again after you depart, August Hester. Your fire will be well fed, I assure you. Our gratitude is immense."

"As is mine, good August Chef, whose bread and praise have graced my fires as reliably as wood and coal," she said with new softness. Gurvan blinked fast to hold back tears.

Solenn reached for the head. It radiated little heat, but she still paused. If her hands were burned, she wouldn't be able to write. That fear hadn't struck her earlier when she'd intended to reach into the fire, but it arrived now like clarion trumpets in her brain.

Hester seemed to read her hesitance and smiled with a hint of sadness.

"Solenn, dear Solenn, my attention is in thousands of places at this very moment, but right here, here, here, within this ancient pentad, I feel alive. The longer that I am awake, the more I see, the more I remember, the more I am a God, not separate, but existing with renewed intimacy within the world. Perhaps you understand what I mean." Recalling her experience

within Gyst's holiness, Solenn nodded. Hester continued, *"Hester is a grand God, the grandest in many ways, but even she knew despair, the deepest of despairs, the craving for the absoluteness of death. This head, my holy form known again, is of impossible value. It exists, and I have the ability to speak anew, all because of you. You have restored my faith in both myself and the world. Please, place your own faith in me."*

Taking a deep breath, Solenn pressed her fingertips to Hester's forehead. It was as warm as a rock in afternoon light during summertime. Reassured, she put away her table book and cupped the heavy head with both hands. She lifted it into the bag, even as her musketeers shuffled in unease.

Solenn motioned to her mouth and looked at the others in the room.

Aveyron shrugged. His pale chest bore a broad red blush in the center. "I have nothing for a gag unless we use my burned shirt."

"Pardon, but a gag?" asked Gurvan. His expression showed horror as the matter was explained to him, but after a moment he understood the wisdom and nodded.

"If I may offer my own handkerchief, Most August One?" asked Gurvan, brandishing a white cloth with a lace edge. "It's clean."

"Birds have sat upon my stone and bred and shat for centuries, yes, yes, they have, and oh they do so even as we speak, but Hester appreciates your consideration, as ever," she said with brusqueness. *"I accept your offering, August Chef, though this cloth will not taste as well as the bread and cheese from your kitchens."*

Gurvan passed the cloth to Solenn. "Are you ready?" Solenn asked Hester.

"Yes, Itron, yes."

Solenn froze. The regal God Hester had called her *that*?

"Come closer, closer still, so you know my words as you'd know a normal fire's heat on a cold morning," Hester said, and Solenn leaned forward. *"I, too, have been called 'Itron,' and I know the full weight and honor of its syllables. Think on the meaning, yes, and accept that the word fits you*

better than 'princess.' Doesn't Hester, most august and noble God of Hearth and Home, know of what she speaks?" As a divine being, Hester of course knew Solenn was not royalty by blood. *"And this is a title you have earned by wit and sacrifice, have you not? Own these syllables, kind ambassador. Accept them without shame, without modesty. As one Itron to another, I speak. Now, gag me so that my silence will be brief, for in the interim I will burn with withheld words."*

Solenn sat back on her haunches for a moment, absorbing the advice, then nodded. She folded the handkerchief and wedged it into Hester's mouth before drawing up the sides of the bag.

"Itron," Lieutenant Talia said. "I must ask, may one of us carry this burden for you?" She gestured to herself and Jean.

After a moment of consideration, Solenn shook her head, holding the bag close. There was an element of symbolism to her carrying Hester—a host, personally bringing an important guest to their home.

"I'll step aside to change now," said Aveyron, approaching to touch Solenn upon the arm. When she looked him up and down, frowning, he countered with a smile, "My skin is sensitive no more, and my back burned least of all."

He stepped away and returned a moment later. Jean saddled him. With a bracing breath, Solenn led the way as they stepped onto the portico.

Thousands upon thousands of cheers greeted them. People filled the streets and lots as far as she could see. Many of the rooftops, steep as they were, were adorned with people rather than birds.

The entire musketeer contingent conferred briefly, Solenn in their midst. Word had spread that Hester herself had manifested in the temple, but far more wanted to catch a glimpse and plead the favor of the princess who'd ridden a dragon. Some musketeers argued that it might be best for Solenn to stay in the Grand Pentad overnight, as it would be easier to guard her on the street during the daytime. This was an important consideration, especially since they all knew that Albion had spies present in Braiz. Even so, Solenn used her table book to request that they return to the royal château. They mounted up. Talia and Jean flanked Solenn on Aveyron.

Their progress was steady. Cheering people lined the avenue for what looked to be the entire route to the château. Notes of bagpipes and oboes carried over the raucous voices. Solenn tried to act nonchalantly but was unnerved by the sheer number of people calling to her. One woman screamed that she wanted prayers. There could be Albionish agents present, she knew, ready with guns or prepared epicurea, but her most pressing fear was of her own people. Solenn's thoughts fluttered back to the Lutecian mob that had called for her death. Sentiments could turn in an instant, but the rabblement didn't need to hate her to kill her. To them, she was now Gods-touched. Dragon-touched. Akin to epicurea. These people could rip her apart in their loving zeal, as if she were an ingredient to bless them, piecemeal.

Her musketeers understood the threat. They studied the crowds with grim resolve.

Vigilant Aveyron, however, was the one to signal alarm. He stopped, ears perked as he stared upward. The procession halted, and even the surrounding people quieted as they also stared.

"Dragon, is it the dragon?" piped up a small, high voice, which was then shushed, but not before a murmur of panic swept through the onlookers. A few people ran, but most waited, watching.

A soft screech wailed from above, vaguely like a bagpipe. Solenn's heart pounded fast in worry, but she could tell by Aveyron's attentive posture that whatever came was no threat.

Only when the stars were blocked time and again in a swirling pattern did she realize what approached was a bird, a massive one with an ebony body that glistened as it came within reach of light from torches and lamps.

"A seasweeper!" Talia said with a gasp. "I haven't seen one since I was a girl." With reason. They'd been hunted to near extinction, as their succulent white meat was said to calm ill stomachs as nothing else could.

The large seabird, its hooked beak a bright orange, held a satchel in its talons. It looked like something one of her grandparents' messengers would carry. As the bird glided low over the street, it released the packet. Jean dipped almost out of the saddle to snare it.

People around them broke out in applause, whoops, and queries about what the satchel held. Solenn's companions shared a look of concern and sped their progress. Jean carried the delivery, as Solenn was already burdened.

Solenn understood why the delivery had been made public—such shows by the Coterie would be necessary—but the timing could've been better. They were only halfway to the château, and now the crowd was more agitated than before. Fortunately, armed royal cavalry met them partway to provide a greater escort.

They reached the château with no further interruptions. Tad met them in the courtyard, his face haggard but relieved. Solenn gestured for Talia to speak on her behalf. "Prince Morvan, a seasweeper just delivered a parcel for the princess—the ambassador."

"Would you like privacy to review the contents, Ambassador Solenn, or would—" Tad began to ask, but she shook her head at the idea of privacy and pointed to both herself and him. "You would like my company? Very well." He offered her a tremulous smile.

Solenn felt a small lurch deep within her chest. Awkwardness remained between them.

Solenn dismounted and addressed Aveyron, her face pressed to his. "I'll come down later and tell you the news," she said in a raw whisper. He nodded.

Solenn and her father, with their musketeers, went to their residential corridor and the personal library therein. Hester's bag was gently set upon the table.

Solenn had no idea how urgent the message was from Abonde, but she knew foremost that Hester couldn't remain gagged and blinded for a prolonged period. She'd already endured too many years of such deprivation.

Lieutenant Talia, please introduce our additional guest within the bag so that we may then read the missive.

Talia took in the immense order with a resolute nod. The silver-haired musketeer straightened, meeting the gazes of Prince Morvan, Jean, and the prince's three musketeers within the closed room. "You are in the presence of a living piece of Most August Hester, God of Hearth and Home."

With precise timing, Solenn pulled down the sides of the bag, then quickly adjusted Hester's position so the God could look upon the people present. A second later, she pulled away the gag.

"Ah!" Hester's profound sigh of relief sent out a wave of emotion. Solenn gritted her teeth as she remembered the death of her beloved pony when she was five, of how, as she had watched the grooms finish covering the grave, she had taken comfort in that Guillaume would forever be in one of his favorite hills outside the village.

Around her, Tad and the musketeers crumpled beneath the weight of their emotions. Only Solenn remained upright in her seat.

"Hester," Solenn said in a tone of warning.

"My divinity, my might, naturally expands as does a spark within a library lined with ancient scrolls." The God, at least, sounded chagrined, as she apparently made a conscious effort to restrain her power again, causing the emotional pressure to recede. Nearby, Talia shook her head as if trying to recuperate from vertigo.

"Most August Hester is still adjusting to her new form," Solenn said, speaking slowly.

Tad and his musketeers looked shaken as they reclaimed their tall postures. Tad's expression tightened as he looked between the God and his daughter. Solenn had to wonder at the thoughts going through his head.

"Most August One," said Tad. "Your arrival here is . . . a surprise." His brow furrowed as he studied the gag still in Solenn's hand.

"Prince Morvan, the gag was an agreed-upon measure for the period of transit," Talia said. "I think you now understand why."

By Tad's expression, he had a hundred more questions, but he showed restraint. "Yes. That kind of . . . effect could unintentionally be dangerous. On behalf of my parents, King Myles and Queen Privela, I welcome your . . . physical self to Nont, August Hester. I am Prince Morvan, Ambassador Solenn's father."

"Prince Morvan, yes, yes, I know you well, you who as a toothless lad would sneak hard sea biscuits into my flames to spare you from eating them yourself on Sellandsdays." Solenn's father looked mortified, even as Hester good-naturedly laughed with her head tilted back as much as her stiff neck allowed. *"You know this already, yes, you do, that your daughter is an extraordinary young woman, one of tact and acumen. Indeed, she possesses compassion superior to that of my own sibling Gods."* Her soft tone and kind words surprised Solenn. *"She has asked me to support your defense of Braiz. Most August Hester, God of Hearth and Home, readily agrees to bless your defense. Verdania claims me as their native deity countless times each day, and after years of such declarations, yes, yes, even a God begins to believe in what people say. But many years ago, beyond the memory of most trees, there were no borders, and Braiz was as much my home as Verdania. My home, my land, a place where Hester's true feet tread. Hester is glad to look upon this place again."*

"Your favor comes as a . . . profound relief, August Hester." Tad looked pale and overwhelmed.

Solenn wrote in her table book. *Everyone in this room must keep Hester's presence in confidence. I will either carry her with me or leave her within my room. Feign guarding me, but guard her most of all.*

"Feign guarding you, Itron?" Talia challenged, gently chiding.

You understand what I mean. Solenn was glad that Talia, at least, could still offer fond criticism.

"Indeed, they should guard you to their utmost, dear Solenn, ambassador to both the Coterie and the very Gods," Hester said. *"By the light of my fires, and I have many fires, I will know if they do not."* Her smile had a sinister edge that reminded Solenn of the giant statue's frozen sneer.

"Now, now, read the missive from the seasweeper, as I am not Gyst, and I retain a limited awareness of the world's mysteries."

Solenn reached into the courier's bag to pull out several pages. The first sheet bore the now-familiar cursive writing of Queen Abonde, in Braizian.

"Queen Abonde confirms that thirty Albionish two- and three-deckers are deploying imminently." She spoke with slow care to be understood, her sense of dread increasing as she read. "The queen says she shredded the sails and rigging on three others but could do no more under a barrage of fire. *Thirty ships.*" She paused to absorb that terrible number for a moment. "They also have readied dragon wings and other epicurea for their attack."

That wasn't a surprise, but the news chilled her nevertheless.

Solenn skimmed onward. Queen Abonde stated that the kin of Albion, though their numbers were scant, had offered assistance in fulfilling Solenn's request.

She shuffled to the next sheet, which felt coarser to her fingertips. Tight ink lettering filled the paper top to bottom, front and back, all of it in Albionish—which she could scarcely read. She handed that sheet and its mates to Tad, whose eyes lit up as he recognized the language. He'd learned Albionish as part of his war duties and had kept in practice through diplomacy.

"This is—" He gaped, then flipped to the back of the page, then to the next. "These are from Lord Whitney's very bureau. Intelligence on Braizian navy ships stationed at Nont, dated early last year." Paper crinkled in his hands as he read fast. The musketeers shared looks of grim eagerness. Even Hester was quiet as she read the mood of the room.

As for Solenn, she felt a sense of weary satisfaction. She had a strong feeling she already knew the contents.

Finally, Tad rested the papers on the table, tears in his eyes. "The fire. They did it." His voice was quiet, deadly. This revelation felt larger than the very presence of a God. "These papers addressed to Lord Whitney summarize the completed deed. Who they hired, how they set about it. They even celebrate that we blamed our own sailors, as they intended." He looked almost ready to cry in his rage. "You were right, Solenn. Ambassador."

"Free the sailors of the *Everett*. Take care of them." She could barely manage the words.

"We will. Tonight. They will see care, and justice."

Solenn nodded, her eyes partially closed. Now she could only pray that the maligned sailors of the *Everett* wouldn't be freed just in time to suffer anew in Albion's next onslaught.

CHAPTER
TWENTY-FIVE

ADA

While fine white bread is best with sauces and butter, the buckwheat bread or so-called black bread of Braiz and northern Verdania is considered the best pairing for the salt pork that many peasants there rely upon. It is considered even better when stale and is a trustworthy staple for travelers. Perceive the flavor of black bread with different meats and with the bread at different ages, and contemplate how it seems to change.

—Excerpt from *Manual for Tour Chefs*

Existence hurt. Moving *and* existing hurt more.

Ada was being carried, scooped up with arms beneath her thighs and around her back. She recognized the particular huffs of exertion too. Erwan. Erwan was carrying her. This would've been the start of a thoroughly enjoyable fantasy if not for the throbbing agony in her leg that was getting worse with each jostle.

"Ada, shh. You must be quiet."

She hadn't even realized that she'd made a sound. He certainly was, with noises of physical strain and the scratch of leather and hemp. She opened her eyes to find darkness. Nighttime. Erwan carried her into woods that emanated the dankness that followed heavy rain. She felt an object sway against her and realize he'd strapped the saddle and bags around his body as well. This daft, wonderful man. He'd make sure she could ride in comfort whenever Brillat returned.

Ada tapped his arm, gesturing downward.

"Are you sure?" he asked in a low voice.

She nodded. He set her down as gently as he could, allowing her good leg to find the duff first. Her fever hadn't left—her wobbliness made that clear—but a brief nap had brought her more clarity.

She leaned against a stout tree trunk and flared a hand to indicate Hester's fire. She followed that with a hand chop to symbolize a sword: Were they avoiding Verdanian soldiers?

He paused to listen before answering in a bare whisper. "Yes. I'm sorry I couldn't carry you with more grace. I'm not at my physical best."

Verdania had probably sustained him with water and old bread for the past week, at minimum. There was a gauntness to him she'd never seen before, and she didn't like it. By the Five, they needed to survive this so she could feed the man.

Glancing around, she spotted a rotting log lying across the forest floor. With Erwan's aid, she sat there. He crouched beside her, studying the forest for threats.

A bird whistled. No, that particular bird shouldn't be whistling in the dead of night, only during the day. Another whistle came from their other side. They were surrounded by soldiers—fool soldiers, probably city-born—but that signal didn't indicate they'd found anything of interest.

Erwan waved her to come down off the log. She eased her buttocks to the mossy ground. The two-foot-high trunk now acted as cover at her back. Erwan shifted the saddle, angling his body so he could draw the rapier if need be.

About a minute later came another whistle—a pause—and then one at a higher pitch. She and Erwan shared a look. The soldiers had found something, likely the cabin.

Erwan motioned to ask if she was ready to get up; she was. Together, they rose. He helped her walk, and they did so with slow care, not daring to speak again until the woods were quieter.

"How long did I nap?" Ada whispered.

"Perhaps an hour. Not long."

"Brillat never said how far he needed to go to cross to his other realm?"

"No, only that he knew of such a place nearby."

"Cats seem to have the ability to cross at their whim, but they must be special in that way." Which, as a cat lover, didn't surprise her. "We don't need to wander in the dark woods all night or cause Brillat to come in pursuit."

"Do you think you can find his . . . doorway?"

"It must have *some* sort of miasma about it. By the Five, I wish I'd had more chances to talk to Solenn about what she's experienced with magic."

"Whether she could sense a gate or not has no bearing on what *you* may sense," he murmured. "She also experienced death by epicurea in prolonged, excruciating detail."

Ada grunted acknowledgment. Solenn's abilities had indeed been more potent in peculiar turns, her Gyst skills heightened in a way that reminded Ada of how a sprinkle of salt could enhance inherent flavors in food. "I'll focus and see what I can find. At worst, I'll observe the positions of more soldiers."

She rested her shoulder against him, his height still comforting in its familiarity after all this time. Closing her eyes, she concentrated on the tingle of her tongue, awakening its divinity as she called on the God most closely tied to the kin's divided nature.

Hester. I'm still hesitant to trust you, but I also know that you must discern the cleft between worlds better than even Gyst. Please, help me to know it so that we may meet Brillat there and be spared additional dangers.

She felt Hester's warm, prickling presence for scant seconds, and then the most gorgeous, ethereal music suddenly teased at her ears. Notes like those from a flute, a piano, a bassoon, pipes, all melded in perfect harmony—and yet, the instruments weren't quite the same as those she knew, not unlike the way that voices sounded different when heard below water.

"Ada?" Quiet concern rang in Erwan's voice.

"I hear the gate. I think." Her ears tickled inside in an almost maddening way, but she knew no finger could ease this itch.

"You *hear* it?" Erwan asked. He had to remember what she'd told him long in the past about how she rarely discerned the holy by sound. She'd heard Gyst speak a few times and on occasion had an empathetic awareness of the texture of food by its crunch, but no more than that.

"It's like faint music in the distance. I asked Hester for help, and it's like she . . . opened a window in my ears."

"Can she be trusted?"

"By all the unknowns in a cheese cellar, no! But I can say with certainty that this music isn't human, or not by any humans I know." She couldn't ignore that she'd seen very little of the world. "You fear this could be a trap?"

"I fear many things, my beloved Selland included."

"I rightly fear some of Brillat's kin taking their vengeance upon me. Most won't be as generous as the rose fairy was, and for good reason. A gate would be a logical place to find such beings too." Ada released a long exhalation.

"And yet, here we walk, right toward the music." Erwan sounded dryly amused.

"Here I am, on a walk with the man I love on a brisk night," Ada said, laboring to walk and speak. "I can't think of anywhere else I'd rather be."

He snorted. "You still have a tendency for sentimental babble when you're feverish, I see."

"I'm the same person in many ways, but I'll keep you guessing sometimes."

"Good," he said softly.

They entered an area of older trees, their trunks broader than draft horses, the moist smell becoming deeper, danker, underlain by the kind of rot that told of new growth and possibility through Gyst.

"The music is getting louder as we approach," Ada said.

And, indeed, it became more beautiful. The sound alone could've made her weep—oh, the strings! Their distant quiver seemed to make her heart quake in her chest.

Erwan kept her upright when her good leg started to slide on slick leaves along a slope. Branches crackled nearby, movement making them both start.

"A deer," Erwan said with a hiss. "I saw the hide."

They reached a basin that was sodden underfoot. Saving her breath, she engaged in battle gestures to let him know they were close to the gate and needed to be careful. He signaled that he understood.

Her feverish brain idly wondered how long it'd take for Solenn to pick up on these old hand signals for times when she needed to express thoughts without a voice or paper. They'd need to teach her, later.

Please, Five, but Ada wanted to survive this and spend such time with her daughter.

The ground sucked on their boots, giving little subtleness to their approach. Ada was glad her bad foot scarcely touched the earth, or her slit boot likely would've been pulled off by the greedy mud. A tall structure stood in silhouette ahead—stone columns in a close row. Some were halved or otherwise diminished, but all looked to be white marble, the vertical ridges almost eroded smooth.

The music seemed to seep from the stone itself, and having listened to it for some time now, Ada realized the same snippet of song was playing over and over again. It couldn't have been more than a minute in length.

"It's a dolmen," Erwan murmured. "There are places like this all around Braiz. Hester's crater could probably be classified as one as well, though that is a hundred times larger than any other such site I've seen." Leaving Ada to lean against a plinth, he walked a few feet away. The ground here was solid. Ada suspected that dirt and grass had formed a carpet over a marble floor. "Do you suppose a gap between columns acts as the doorway or—"

The music twisted, the horns belching, the strings screaming, everything growing horribly louder as her tongue burned and her stomach—oh, Five—

Erwan returned to her in seconds, just in time to prevent her from collapsing. He pulled her away from the column as his right hand drew his rapier. "Where do you sense—"

"There," she said with a gasp, gesturing with her head rather than release the grip she had on his body. Past the columns on the flat parcel on which Erwan had just walked, there was a distortion in the air, like what occurred on an extremely hot day in far southern Verdania. A blink later, Brillat appeared, crouched with one hand on the ground as he faced the columns. He stood, tugging down a fitted dark jacket, then whirled on his heel to face them, a hand going to the twin pistols he now wore on his hips.

"What—how—" His surprised face looked disturbingly pale by starlight.

"Soldiers were searching the woods. We had to leave our shelter," Erwan said, sheathing his blade to better support Ada.

"I asked Hester to help us find the gate so that we might all be spared the dangers of the darkness." Ada's nausea eased off some, but a waft of the otherworld scent lingered and caused her tongue to burn as if she'd licked a palmful of ground pepper. She supposed it made sense for a place made of magic to overwhelm her senses. Through it all, however, she still perceived that Brillat carried food and medicinal items upon his back, including something especially foul. "I found this place by the music that repeats. I don't know why Hester was so quick to help or how she even had the power to enhance such a thing for me, but—"

"I know why," Brillat interrupted. "Erwan, do help her to sit over here. She's swaying like a sapling in a storm."

"I am not," Ada muttered as she was helped to a downed section of column. She hadn't even been aware she *was* swaying. The stone's chill through her clothes felt good with her fever. Erwan sat beside her and set down the saddle. "Are all places like this imbued with such heartfelt music?"

"No. Every such shard of the old city is different. What you hear is the music that was playing near these columns when Hester tore our city asunder." He reached into a small knapsack. "I brought food for you both. Ada, you must eat before I supply you medicine, as that will leave you more unsettled." He also set aside some clothes, presumably for Erwan.

"Understood. Why did you return, dressed as if you didn't anticipate becoming a horse again?" she asked. Brillat wore his full regalia as a comte now, a purple satin outfit embroidered with dandelions, complete with a matching feathered cocked hat.

"I have much to relate to you, quickly, as you eat." He pulled out two small buckwheat bread loaves already split, luscious butter and honey forming a creamy core. The combination made her mouth water in want. "Solenn has achieved the extraordinary with both Queen Abonde and Hester. Our worlds are changed in ways not seen since the kin's nature was split asunder."

Brillat summarized his news as Ada and Erwan ate. She listened with a furrowed brow. Solenn had actually provided Hester with a new body. How had she even conceived such an idea? Brillat couldn't conceal his own concerns about the arrangement.

"Hester has helped us recently, and yet . . ." Ada shook her head.

"I trust in Solenn's judgment," said Erwan. "I've been raised with an understanding of Selland's fluid nature, so it comes as no surprise to me that other Gods also have their whims. The fact is that Braiz needs Hester as an ally, even if temporarily."

"But if she turns . . . ," Brillat said.

"Then she turns," said Erwan. "We have other enemies who are certain in their ways. They worry me more. Albion undoubtedly aims to crush us. Lord Whitney has plotted everything with incredible care for years to get to this point. Acquiring Verdanian epicurea to bolster Albionish forces. Arranging for Solenn to take the blame for Rupert's murder. Sending an oddly timed new marriage offer to Solenn, to stir up rumors around Braiz in collusion with Albion. The quick rise of the Blessed to instill chaos in the very heart of Verdania . . ."

"Indeed," said Brillat. "Whatever else may be said about Albion, they aren't fools."

"We need to get back to Braiz, fast, to support Solenn," Ada said. "Could another Camarga possibly be called here to expedite our return? Or do you have something else in mind?" She gestured again to his dapper clothes. She felt a little better since downing the bread and his vial of gin-like medicine.

"I do indeed have something else in mind. The queen has granted special permission for you both to cross Arcady to reach Braiz within the day."

"Arcady." Erwan tested the name on his tongue. "This is your otherworld across the veil? Where Solenn was almost killed because she was born a Chef?" His gaze went to Ada.

She guffawed. "I had concerns about following the music here because I knew some nearby beings may not take kindly to me. I can only imagine the reception I'll get *within* your realm. I should note that my tongue is intact *and* I intend to keep it that way."

Brillat's smile was tight. "Your tongue is under no permanent threat."

Ada had a sudden terrible suspicion about the horrid-tasting thing he still carried. "Only temporarily?"

"You're guaranteed safety. I will escort you the entire way. You'll both be blindfolded, and you, Ada, will partake of this root here that will taint your tongue for the duration of the journey."

She remembered the shadow beings she'd seen when she utilized cat magic—the walking trees, ambling quadrupeds larger than cottages, and other things she couldn't even try to describe. "You want me to remain ignorant of the vast array of kin that exist."

"Yes. Many mysteries have been revealed today, but not all, and it should stay that way. Also, treating your tongue should largely eradicate the nausea and disorientation that the inherent magic of Arcady would cause."

Ada grimaced as she nodded. "I've already had a sample of that. Very well. I'll cope with the horrible flavor if it'll get us to Solenn faster."

"To see Solenn, within the day." Tears glistened in Erwan's eyes. "Will she even know me, with this?" He touched his beard and cringed. Ada could only imagine how that hair aggravated him. He'd never liked to go a full day without shaving.

"She will. I did." Ada stood, wavering only a tiny bit. Her fever had diminished, but she knew that was only because of Brillat's treatment. The infection was likely continuing to rage with enthusiasm, courtesy of Gyst. Even Chef-blessed epicurea—not that Brillat would ever use such an abomination—could do only so much against a wound in this condition.

But no matter. If she needed to crawl back to Braiz, she would. Solenn awaited them.

CHAPTER
TWENTY-SIX

SOLENN

The most masterful and respected of cooks in Braiz are crêpe makers, and once you have attempted making these yourself, you will understand why. The batter is light and thin, which does not require much strength, but the cook's every move with their rozell and spanell must be precise. A crêpe can burn in the time it takes to gesture to Hester.

—Excerpt from *Book for Cooks to Excel as Do Chefs*

Hester didn't sleep. Nor did she cease talking.

Perched upon a table in Solenn's chamber, Hester murmured her way through a thousand observations and stories ongoing around the world. Solenn didn't mind. There was something soothing about the cadence of the God's voice, even when it sometimes arose in excitement and awakened her. Mostly, though, Hester's mild emotional incandescence currently evoked the sense of when she was sometimes sick as a small child, and Mamm would keep vigil by her box bed with a candle and a book, which she would read aloud to comfort Solenn and keep herself awake.

"Find sleep, rest, know the comfort of home, home, home. You needn't feed more food to my beautiful fire again, no. Your family, I hear their stomachs, I feel their hearts, too fast with hunger, I know that even in their relief over your return, they suffer. Hester understands, she will make the wood endure longer than it ought, yes, because Hester is kind and magnanimous and loves you as you love her. Another sailor! Praise and yearning, yes, ever welcome, ever deserved, as you deserve your own peace and sleep." Though she continued to praise her own good works, Hester's tone had become less imperious. Gentler. Perhaps the God's greater connection with the people of Nont had softened her quite literally hardened heart, or maybe the sound of her own voice was lulling her after she had existed in such prolonged silence. Whatever the reason, the God of Hearth and Home truly did sound more at home. *"Hester is sorry to have awakened you again, dear Solenn, yes, she burns with apology."*

Solenn needed a few seconds to realize that Hester spoke to her, not to another person; her name wasn't uncommon across Braiz. She sat up to regard the God through the open door of her box bed. Hester's head was angled to face the fire and her bed, a broad, arched window at her back. The wooden shutters were open enough to admit fresh sea air but not birds. Faint angled rows of light adorned the floor. Dawn, already.

"Your voice isn't bothersome, truly. How are you feeling right now? You're not tired?" Solenn swung her legs through the box bed entry.

"Tiredness is the stuff of mortals! Hester is a God, the greatest of the Gods, long divorced from a fleshy form. Within this gorgeous body that I now know, this head with an artful nose and full cheeks and a strong jaw, a glorious face, I absorb the fire's heat within my surface." Her gray brow furrowed. *"Hester will be candid, noble Solenn, ambassador to those who have never known such mediation. Your promise to give me means to speak was a strange one, yes, one that I had no cause to believe genuine. Hester sees much, knows much, but she cannot understand why you took such a risk. Hester's booming celestial might, though limited right now . . ."*

"Limited"! If Hester left her presence unchecked, she could level thousands of people in an instant, miring them in emotions both joyous and tragic.

". . . is daunting, immense, beyond human understanding. With a thought, I could annihilate your family—and Braiz—yes, yes, because encouraging flames is easy, the simplest of tasks. Destruction is natural, graceful, the way of small children if left alone. But even Hester, aglow in divinity, struggles to counter something such as a wildfire, yes."

Two months ago, Solenn would've been overwhelmed by the very idea of being in an intimate conversation with a God. Now, she casually moved to pour herself water from a carafe, her head tilted toward Hester as the God continued.

"Hester, God of Home and Hearth, sought to help humans by hurting the kin, yes, this was a plan with much thought, and yet, and yet, Hester couldn't truly comprehend the damage such an act would do to her incredible self. Some sacrifice was expected, certainly, but so much? So very much." Her arrogance softened to chagrin.

"That's a very human attribute, to act without full understanding of the consequences, but the kin are the same. I suppose it's the way of all aware individuals."

"Solenn, you who also ponder deeply but do not see all, have you realized," Hester said softly, "that Queen Abonde, that most ancient of lizards, or another winged kin could fly me, yes, this very stone head, over to Albion, where I could, with glory and ease, obliterate the royal family, Lord Whitney, and much of their nobility? Oh, so many dead and bleeding and suffering, with Albion left vulnerable, their soft underbelly exposed to the blade. Weakness so profound that even Braiz, yes, weak as it also is, could cross the sea and seize control?"

Solenn sucked in a breath. She could imagine that the war council would soon broach the possibility of the kin conducting offensives. They would undoubtedly find it easier to ask for non-Braizian lives to be sacrificed. There was much they didn't think through. She made an effort to be otherwise. "That would leave you on their land. Your stone is too dangerous to trust among people, especially in Albion, where they'll harvest anything and everything."

"Oh, such an attack would obliterate a stone of this size, this beautiful head, shattered to dust, yes. My most August Self, the statue long idle within the broken amphitheater, survived my attack on the Coterie because of its intense mass, yes, its capacity for energy and power. Even as incredible as Hester's body is, however, much integrity was lost in that effort, and in constant exposure ever since. The piece that became my head wouldn't have broken away so easily otherwise, noble Solenn."

Hester had again expressed her potential for violence, but not in a threatening way. "Do you *want* to expend your power like you did before?" Solenn sat at the table, staring at Hester as if they were companions for a meal.

"Oh, the stories, the stories, so many tales of me, recounted near fires. Do they do justice to my magnificence? Do they focus on the kind works done by Hester, how often she tries to assist humans, petty as they are, hobbled as she is compared to her sibling Gods? No, no! Too many stories do her dishonor, make her sound like a petulant tot. That Hester gets angry cannot be denied, but penance has been served, a long and fraught penance." To Solenn's surprise, the stone at the base of Hester's eyes darkened. She seeped tears, the way a stone cliff does as snow melts above. *"I want . . . yes, I want very much to continue to experience the world as I am now. I want to . . . I want to help, to feel like I'm part of homes, not apart. I want people to know Me."*

As Hester became emotional, more of her power seeped into her words. Solenn recalled sitting upon Erwan's shoulders to pluck an apple from a high branch as he chattered about how apples, cider, and brandy were important to Braiz, and all she could think was how beautiful the apple was and how wonderful it'd taste—only to bite in and realize that apples for cider weren't necessarily appropriate for snacking.

Solenn smiled ruefully as she pushed aside the memory flash and took a sip of water. She wondered how much of Hester's repetition of her grandness and goodness began during her long isolation as she fought to ward away the despair that almost overtook her. "Your very response is why I took the risk to help you. I know what it's like to be apart, to be misjudged. To be unable to speak." She needlessly motioned to her skin, to her mouth. No one else would likely understand her right now. "You committed a terrible wrong. You can do better. We can all do better. We can live alongside the kin. They can live alongside us. Albion . . . I don't want Albion destroyed. I just want them to mind their own loaves!"

"*Mind their own loaves.' Yes, yes, that saying existed when I walked with legs of flesh. Ever strange it is, how some things do not change.*" Hester's gaze shifted. "*No, no, baby, don't reach for the fire, no—I must douse my— oh good, that gave the mother enough time to grab the child. Yes, praise me for sparing the babe's flesh, but recognize also your own speed, as you . . .*"

Solenn heard a soft scratching noise at the door. "Pardon me, Hester," she said, and walked across the chamber. Her musketeers slept in a neighboring room; one of them normally would have taken the extra box bed in her chambers, but Hester's presence required new precautions. Tad had worried about Solenn even sharing a room with the God, not because of a fiery attack but because of the potential flow of emotions. Solenn had countered that, insisting that she wanted Hester to have company as much as possible. The God had been alone for too long.

The scratching noise came again, and it sounded like it came from near the floor. Voices spoke in the hallway. She slid open the view-slot. "Pardon, but what is going on?"

"My deepest apologies, Itron." Jean came into view. Behind him was one of Tad's loyal musketeers; he peered past Solenn as if Hester might be looming over her shoulder. "One of the palace cats is at your door, one we know well, but she—she's carrying a note in her mouth, the way a cat would carry the mouse."

When Solenn's effort to speak emerged as a croak, she released a frustrated huff and ran for her table book. She hurriedly wrote and then opened the door to show him the sheet. *The cat is a messenger. Do no harm.*

The courier, sitting before the door, was a small black cat with bright golden eyes.

"Mew." The meow was muffled by the scroll.

"Tiffen." Solenn genuflected as she crouched, her nightgown rustling around her legs. She accepted the note. "Thank you." At least with cats, she knew her tone would come through even if articulate syllables did not. Pinning her table book and the note against her thighs, she rubbed Tiffen's chubby-cheeked head. The cat began to purr.

"Jean, have you any milk or meat that a cat would like?" Solenn spoke with slow care.

After a moment, Jean nodded, and motioned to his companion, who dashed to an adjacent room. "Our peers had breakfast salt ham delivered minutes ago, Itron." An instant later, the musketeer returned with a hand-size slice. Tiffen hurried to intercept her payment, her purr impossibly louder.

Just as human couriers are promptly rewarded with food and drink, so must other messengers to me, if they stay long enough. She would need to inquire about the seasweeper later and express belated gratitude.

"But we . . . we *know* that cat," blurted out the other musketeer. "Tiffen was born in this tower." The brawny man looked on the verge of faintness at the idea that a familiar feline was something *other*.

Reconsider what you think you know, but do not speak of what you have seen or treat cats differently. Keep their secret. Tiffen's loud, happy smacks made her smile.

Both men nodded, Jean's smile wry while the other man still looked addled. "Would you like to break your fast now, Itron?" asked Jean. She indicated yes. "Good. Food will come promptly."

"Thank you," she managed aloud, closing the door.

Hester ceased her murmurs as Solenn returned to the table. *"A message sent from the Coterie? Mayhap from the queen herself?"* She'd become more composed in the interim.

Solenn nodded. "You really have no idea what the message could be?" She took another drink.

"So many fires, so many homes, even Hester in her greatness cannot heed them all. Calls, prayers, gather my attention, just as a voice from the crowd does so by calling your name. Even more, a dragon has no need of fires for warmth, and while Hester can feel sometimes when Abonde experiences a sense of home, such moments are rare, yes, sadly rare." Hester paused in thought. *"As with some people, she has come to reside in houses more so than homes."*

That truly was sad. Solenn had never considered that Abonde might be detached in such a way. She pulled open the scroll. It was not in Abonde's hand, but the Braizian words were crisp and tidy:

Chef and captain together.

She flipped the page over. That was it. No context, no information about how Ada and Erwan were or where. She released a huff of frustration.

"Feed the words to my flames, yes, so that I may know them," Hester said with new softness, seeming to understand that Solenn was in little mood to try to speak. Solenn threw the scroll into the hearth; they blackened to ash in an instant. Hester promptly made a thoughtful sound. *"Dear Solenn, you are vexed by your ignorance of their whereabouts? Through my omnipotence, I can say they are deep within Verdania."*

"Are they near a fire?" Solenn asked, desperate to know more.

"No, no," Hester said. *"But together, oh such sweetness. They exude a sense of home that captures my attention, yes, as they take great comfort in that they are together again."*

Solenn blinked back tears, still selfishly yearning to know more, but relieved to be informed of that much. "Thank you." After their years of separation, Ada and Erwan deserved such time together.

A loud knock shuddered through the door. "Itron? Your breakfast."

Normally a maid would bring in the tray, but no such staff were permitted in her room now. Jean himself brought it in and placed it upon the same table as Hester. He bowed to the God, backing away. Hester effectively restrained her emotions, and he exited without issue.

Solenn sat and lifted the cloche that had kept the food warm in its transit through the château. On a platter was her favorite breakfast, crêpes with spiced apples. She took in a deep breath of the glorious scents—this could very much be a dish that came to mind when Hester exuded power—and to her surprise, Hester also audibly inhaled.

"You can smell this?"

Hester's own face showed wonderment. *"My sense of smell has long been dominated by fire. Even when I recognize bread and such victuals, it is through smoke. But this, this—Solenn, strange Solenn, as you breathed in a comforting food, a remembrance of home, I smelled it myself, free of taint. Through you. You!"* Her voice rattled.

"How?" Solenn asked with a sudden spike of fear. How was she so bonded with the Gods, even after the loss of her tongue?

"You seemed to share it with me, yes, but not through the fire. You were the mediator," Hester mused. *"So like when my power touches that of my siblings, but purer. For even through their touch, there is smoke."*

"Have you even had crêpes before—truly tasting them?" Solenn could imagine Hester had known many through her fires.

"No, no, not upon my tongue, even in my mortal years so distant. Buckwheat is new to Braiz, yes, not common until these past five hundred years."

An idea solidified in Solenn's mind. She used her knife to cut and spear the end of the crêpe. She extended it toward Hester's head, a wordless invitation.

Hester's lips parted in shock but she nodded, speechless. Her mouth took in the food, her tongue visible as it maneuvered the morsel in ways Solenn could not. Solenn idly wondered where Hester's intake was going, but she supposed it was digested in the same way as food offered through the fire.

Solenn took her own bite, placing it on her teeth so she could chew. *"Taste. As a God, as a mighty God, I know much, but not flavor. Not in so very long. I can taste it as it should be tasted, unburned,"* said Hester. *"The crêpe so thin, the buckwheat nutty. The cinnamon—a spice unknown in my human years, one I didn't encounter until I became God and experienced all the world. Salt is there, too, yes, salt! Brother, I recognize you. I do."*

Hester's eyes didn't merely seep tears. She wept as she swallowed, trails darkening her granite face.

Solenn cut a piece of apple next. If Hester could have leaned toward it, her lips working like the beak of a baby bird, she would have. As the God took in the fruit, focusing, savoring, Solenn ate the other half of the slice. The apple was tender yet toothsome, its flavor diminished compared to what she'd known in the past, but still pleasant.

"Solenn, Solenn, your breakfast is yours. Hester knows your recent deprivation, yes, and that you cannot deny yourself sustenance." Hester tried to sound regal, but continued to cry as she chewed another bite of crêpe.

Solenn paused to write on her table book. Jean stood at attention as she opened the door.

"Itron?" he asked, then leaned closer to read her message. "You request another of the same breakfast? Of course!" Both musketeers looked thrilled, and the cooks would likely be even more delighted. All would assume that Solenn's appetite had increased. That wasn't untrue.

She returned to her seat, sharing the rest of her meal—and the next—with the God of Hearth and Home. Solenn experienced no self-consciousness as they shared the food and spoke, as with a friend.

CHAPTER TWENTY-SEVEN

ADA

Verdanian biscuits are a fine treat that will keep for as long as a year, have you the temperance. Take half a peck of fine flour, two or three teaspoonfuls of ale yeast, the yolks of two or three eggs (dependent on their size), and a chunk of sweet butter, and mix it up into a paste, thick as that of a manchet (this being the finest of breads). Form it into a long loaf and bake until done. The next day, cut it into slices, then rub them in powdered sugar before baking upon an elevated wire mesh or basket maker's rods, until the biscuits are dry top and bottom. Rub them again in sugar while they are still hot.

—Excerpt from *Book for Cooks to Excel as Do Chefs*

The root provided by Brillat was truly among the worst things Ada had ever tasted, and as she had an empathetic awareness of a diverse range of terrible foods, that was saying something. Even so, she couldn't complain much, not even when the mysterious diligence they sat in swayed and jostled as badly as any wagon made and driven by humans. She was with Erwan and Brillat, returning to Solenn. Ada counted herself blessed.

Between bouts of dozing, she and Erwan conversed about Solenn's beloved mare Maiwenn and last fall's apple harvest in Braiz and the various establishments that Ada had worked in across Lutecia in her years as a cook. Even blindfolded, with the circumstances as they were, it felt weirdly wonderful to just . . . talk with him. Brillat also sat in the enclosed cabin, quiet, unintrusive, the magic of him strangely absent thanks to the flavor in her mouth.

Pleasant as the conversation and company were, there was still the matter of her leg.

She tried to angle it so she didn't bump into Erwan or the wall, but it was impossible to gauge the jolts in the road ahead. On occasion her mind returned to the surgical tent in Versay. The smell of gangrene and iron. The specialized blades upon the table. Their functions.

By the time they debarked, the taint upon her tongue had begun to wane. Using a walking stick and Erwan's arm, she traveled through tall grass that made her hiss as the leaves brushed her leg. Brillat guided them both to a large, flat rock, where they sat. Ada needed help to do that as well, since her knee was being less cooperative as the swelling worsened.

"The medicine should've done more," Brillat muttered.

"And Gyst should've done less," Ada said.

The disorientation of transit lasted mere seconds. A brisk briny wind greeted them.

She heard Erwan take in a deep breath. "I smell the ocean," he said, joy in his voice.

"I can smell it too," she said, with considerable relief. She could even detect a hint of Brillat's presence now.

By the singing of nearby birds and a caressing breeze, they were definitely outside. She reached out with her perception, detecting lettuce, chervil, cauliflower, and broccoli in early stages of growth.

"We're in a potager," she said, using the Verdanian word for a kitchen garden.

Brillat exchanged indiscernible whispers with someone else, then spoke up in a low voice. "You may remove your blindfolds now. Captain, I would ask you to dampen any exclamations, for reasons you'll soon understand."

Ada pulled off the cloth. The cloudy skies were deep gray, the light indicative of early morning. Tall stone walls surrounded a garden with greenery in tidy rows. Nearby scaffolding upheld curling shoots of pea plants.

"Selland preserve us." Erwan spun in place. "We're at the royal château in Nont. We're *within* the fortress." He kept his voice down, but his alarm was clear.

"Indeed." Brillat was dryly amused.

"You kin would make for terrible enemies, Comte."

"Yes," Brillat said. "But we are not, so that is not for us to dwell upon. Our arrival here is convenient in that we need not travel farther, but I also realize the burden this places upon you."

Yes, how to explain the method by which they'd penetrated one of the most-protected places in Braiz. "I suppose it's a good thing we left behind those Verdanian coats," Ada said. "Has the existence of Arcady been revealed to other humans?"

"No, and I doubt that it will be. We don't want to tempt people to intrude."

"Well, my task isn't as impossible as the one that was placed upon Solenn, and she has endured," said Erwan.

"Actually, use her experience for our explanation. Say the dragon dropped us off," said Ada. Low clouds surrounded the spires of the castle, a mist granting a moist, earthy flavor to the air. There'd be no view of Nont from the parapets. The whole bay was likely blanketed by deep fog. A dragon *could* sneak in during this weather.

"A useful lie, one that I'm confident Queen Abonde herself would endorse," Brillat said. "There's something more I must tell you both, of which I was just informed by our kind gatekeeper just now. Much has happened during our prolonged travel today. Ambassador Solenn succeeded in bolstering Hester's power, enabling her to speak."

"How?" asked Erwan.

"I don't even know the details yet, but—"

"Hester *burned her*," said Ada. "She tried to kill her!"

"And you," Erwan added softly.

Ada waved that off. "That's not what grieves me. Solenn was hurt."

"Solenn also contains the immense capacity to forgive and to inspire others to forgive." Brillat sounded more thoughtful, less doubtful.

Ada considered how Hester had dampened the fire that would've destroyed the bookshop—and Viflay entire—and also helped her find the gate, and still stubbornly shook her head.

"Place your faith in Solenn," Erwan said gently. "In this, she knows more than we do."

Ada felt the need to argue. Their daughter was *sixteen*, placed in extraordinary circumstances, and yet . . . Ada also knew she couldn't coddle her daughter. She'd witnessed how Solenn had chafed under such well-meaning protection in Malo. She couldn't commit the same error.

"I'll try to withhold further judgment," she said gruffly.

"Shall we move on, then?" Brillat asked. "Captain, I daresay, you'd best lead the way and reduce our chances of prompt death by zealous guards."

"But of course," said Erwan. He tugged down the simple tunic provided by Brillat. The clothes had a homespun appearance, but he wore them with the dignity of his formal skirt.

They entered through the kitchen, where the staff granted them curious looks until someone looked hard at Erwan. A gasp rang out. "Captain? How—"

"Greetings, Salowa. We're just passing through," Erwan said, his tone casual. And they did, to murmurs and stares. In the corridor, two musketeers recognized Erwan with far less restrained reactions. There were tears, hugs, questions, chatter. Erwan exercised polite authority to keep him and Ada and Brillat moving forward, which was difficult as word of his arrival spread.

"Can you tell me where I might find Princess Solenn at the moment?" Erwan asked.

"War council meeting," someone answered to a chorus of agreement. "Prince Morvan is there too. Hey—send a runner, they need to know of the captain's return—"

Ada stayed close to Brillat; musketeers and soldiers eyed them with caution and some asked questions, but they received little attention in comparison with Erwan.

"Do you expect your son to be here?" Ada murmured to Brillat as they lurked, waiting for Erwan to again press through a happy throng.

"He shouldn't be far from Solenn," he said in a low voice.

Ada's awareness of Hester's presence grew as they climbed stairs and as the barriers of stone and distance were reduced. That taste of smoke and char returned to her tongue, that residual minerality as if she'd licked a statue. She had to repress a grimace. So much of Hester's miasma reminded her of rupic, the epicurea she had long regarded as most repugnant. The stone powder, after all, had once been flesh. The texture had changed, but to indulge in it was still cannibalism. She could tell Brillat had noted Hester's radiance too. His nostrils flared, his eyes narrowing. His recent words had professed open-mindedness, but positively accepting Hester could be no easy thing for him either.

They reached the royal residential tower at last, and most of Erwan's greeters were held back due to increased security. They advanced up the stairs with new swiftness, Ada relying heavily on her walking stick. It went without saying that the family's private quarters, where Erwan would also keep a room, would be the best place for their reunion.

They reached the topmost floor, Hester's presence a deep warming glow just down the hallway, when a vaguely familiar taste assaulted her tongue. Meatiness. The chalkiness of bone. Power strong enough to assert itself against the presence of a God.

Dragon. But this couldn't be Queen Abonde. It carried the distinct potency of ingredients prepared and enhanced by a skilled Chef.

Ada and Brillat shared a sudden look of intense alarm. "Erwan!" Ada yelled. "To arms!"

She and Brillat took off running. Every step stabbed agony through her leg, but she forced herself to move. Erwan hesitated only to command the musketeers who still accompanied them.

"What do you sense?" Erwan yelled, catching up as they rounded a corner. Far ahead, musketeers lurked in the corridor, coming to attention as they noted the approaching commotion.

Ada fought to maintain movement and couldn't answer, but Brillat did after a beat. "Dragon wings. Albion." Erwan had been told of Ada's recent discoveries.

"The wings converge with Hester's location," Ada managed. Tears streamed from her eyes. Oh, Five, but she hurt.

"Open the door! Albion has infiltrated Solenn's room!" Erwan yelled to the musketeers awaiting them with drawn rapiers. Jaws gaped as he was recognized.

The musketeers acted without hesitation, yanking the double doors open. The incredible potency of Hester and the dragon wings rolled over Ada's senses like thick smoke, causing her to gag as she forced herself to slow down to make the turn into the room. Her leg collapsed, dropping her to a knee with a ragged gasp.

Both Erwan and Brillat turned to assist her, and that's what saved them.

Heat and power blasted outward, sending Brillat and Erwan down to the floor beside her. Ada had a glimpse of a figure standing near an open window, a human torch with a blackened body fully wreathed with flames. As parts of their body crumbled—literally crumbled, like a dry bread crust crushed in a strong grip—something large fell from their grip, striking the ground with a magnificent crack that Ada not only heard but felt.

Hester's presence diminished as if it'd whirled down a drain. The change left Ada dizzied, but even so, she grimaced and pushed herself to stand alongside Erwan and Brillat.

Another figure moved beyond the window. They wore a gray uniform suit bundled thick like someone in a winter caravan to Mont Annod, a hat strapped on, their face covered but for the white skin around their eyes. They pushed off the window, granting Ada a view of broad wings, satiny gray membrane, and yellowed bone.

"Halt, in the name of Braiz!" Erwan yelled. He dropped his rapier as he pulled his pistol, loading it even as he moved. Leaping over the charred flesh and bone, he caught himself against a smoking wooden shutter and fired.

Lowering his arm, he turned. "There are more fliers!" he shouted. "There are fires on tower roofs—I see at least five from here. Where are the king, queen, and heir?" His attention went to the other musketeers and the growing emergency for the château, but as Ada reached the window, her attention stayed on the person with massive flapping wings.

Her close-up glimpse of them had been brief, but she had seen gold braid and ornamentation. Even more, she had a hunch as strong as the presence of dragon epicurea.

"Lord Whitney!" she shouted at the top of her voice, gesturing to Selland to carry her words. "You knave!"

Far away as the person was, they paused, regarding her from afar.

"Brillat—" Ada began, sensing him come alongside her.

"Whoever it is, they're a powerful Chef," he said as together they watched the flier continue into the deep fog.

The attacker had been Lord Whitney himself. She was sure of it. She could criticize him on many points, but he wasn't a commander who shirked danger. She'd seen him at a distance on the field of battle more than once. He wouldn't shun a chance to make a surprise attack on the minor power that acted as a barrier between him and his greater goal of Verdania.

Ada turned. In her haste, she'd dropped her stick. Even relying on it again, her limp was worse as she walked to where Hester Incarnate lay in pieces. The largest chunks were the size of a thumbnail, but most of her stone form had disintegrated to powder that radiated energy with more potency than the granules utilized by Mallory Valmont. This powder acted as though it'd been enhanced by a Chef. Solenn had somehow achieved this incredible accomplishment—only for it to be destroyed.

Oh, Five. How hard would Solenn take this loss?

Erwan's gaze raked over Ada in concern before he continued to the hall, giving orders. Brillat stood beside Ada. With a crimson boot, he nudged the charred corpse. The incredible conflagration had largely reduced the person's head and hands to fragments amid ash, but the uniform attire was so thick, only the outer woolens had been blackened and continued to smolder.

"Albionish tailoring," she muttered, pointing to the high collar and single-row buttons. The full gray was obviously camouflage perfect for an attack on Braiz, especially on a day like this.

"The Albionish were going to take Hester," Brillat murmured. "She didn't cooperate."

"Her remnants are powerful, but nothing compared to what they embodied when she was intact." It was impossible to tell what Hester had even looked like minutes ago.

Ada gazed out the window. Fires still burned on the other towers, but they were strangely small. People moved near the conflagrations, bucket brigades being coordinated to fully douse the flames. "It doesn't look like it's rained here in the past day. Usually old buildings go up in an instant."

Brillat pointed at the hearth. A vibrant fire burned there. "Hester hasn't the power to squelch the arson fires, but she's constraining them, best as she can. That feat alone is extraordinary. However did Solenn empower her this quickly?"

Ada understood the question he couldn't voice: How had Solenn imbued magic like a Chef, but better than any Chef, even with the loss of her tongue?

She looked between the corpse, the broken stone, and the window, thinking as would an army officer in an investigation. "Either the flier or the dead soldier here, or both, were empathetic Chefs. They probably flew here to this tower to set a fire but perceived Hester in Solenn's room. The passenger then came inside to grab the mysterious epicurea." She shook her head. "How are the dragon-winged fliers even able to carry a person? Those wings are large, but the mass involved . . ."

"Epicurea." Brillat's mouth was tight. "They aren't merely using the wings. The flier is also empowered with incredible strength."

"Also dragon-derived?" she asked, as she hadn't sensed familiar strength-boosting ingredients. He granted her a small nod. "The huge wings would prevent the flier from coming inside buildings or even landing atop certain structures. The passenger was the arsonist."

"And possibly a would-be assassin. This is known to be the royal family's tower. I'm certain Solenn and Queen Abonde warned the château about the breadth of Albionish epicurea, but this weather provided an ideal cover for a sneak attack. They could've even flown in during the night and hidden in some nook on high."

Solenn could've died just now. Ada took in a rattling breath.

Voices rang out in the hallway, Erwan's included. Ada limped to the doorway and leaned there, taking in the beautiful sight of Erwan hugging their daughter. Prince Morvan lurked a step behind. Under other circumstances, this reunion would have been a joyful one, but Solenn stared over her captain's shoulder with wide, dread-filled eyes. They pulled apart.

"Princess," Ada said, bowing her head as she stepped forward.

Solenn's smile for her was tender, frail, a second of hesitation reveal-ing the desire for a hug that couldn't be. She continued into her room and stopped. A wordless wail escaped her throat as she dropped to her knees, both hands over her face as she stared at the fragmented remains of a God.

CHAPTER
TWENTY-EIGHT

SOLENN

Though Hester is known for her all-consuming rage, the oldest canon also refers to her as the most hopeful of the Gods. The two concepts, after all, do not cancel each other out. No matter what happens, Hester is said to hold on to a spark. This may not provide warmth, but it may later grow into a fire that does. Think on this as you cope with the hardships of your training. Maintain your own spark.

—Excerpt from *Manual for Tour Chefs*

Everything had felt more possible this morning, the light bright in Solenn's mind as a contrast to the gray outside. Not even the annoying questions of the war council had dampened her mood as they persisted in seeking out what they considered to be justifications for epicurea. Then word had come from a breathless messenger—Captain Corre had returned! Solenn had rushed through the château with her musketeers. Surely if Erwan was back, Ada was with him. The last missive had said they were together, after all.

Now this. Now this.

Solenn's hopes had shattered along with Hester's head.

"Priñsez." Ada's voice sounded forced when she spoke Braizian. "Please, come sit. I can bring you water."

Solenn shook her head. Her throat was clenched too tight for her to even attempt drinking. She'd only choke.

"Pack the princess's most important belongings," Erwan was saying to Talia. "She'll need to reside someplace safer."

Safer? What was safer? Braiz was under attack. Her country had the aid of Queen Abonde and krakens, yes, but that wasn't enough. Albion was actively assaulting them, nor could the threat of Verdania be forgotten. Only minutes ago, the war council had relayed the information that the Verdanian army had mustered to march on Braiz within the week.

Braiz still had no official word regarding the musketeers who had accompanied Erwan, and the fact that he was here alone said much. He never would have left behind his comrades if they lived.

People spoke around her, their noises melding like the drone of bees. Solenn walked to sit on the carved wooden bench on the outside of her box bed.

An instant later, Ada was there with a water carafe, Talia and Jean a step behind. "Here's water. Ah, sorry." She'd spilled water on the floor. Solenn blinked as she realized why: Ada had a terrible limp and was even using a stick.

She pulled out her table book. *You're hurt?*

"Yes. There was a battle." Ada dismissed the incident with a shrug. "It's already been treated, Princess, but running toward your room strained it anew." She made an effort to sound nonchalant. Solenn didn't believe it.

"Itron." Solenn first thought that Talia had spoken to her, but her murmur was aimed at Ada. "Princess Solenn's high honorific is now 'Itron,' though 'Ambassador' is also acceptable."

Ada's face looked blank for a moment. "Itron. Oh. Of course. My pardon."

Discomfited, Solenn wrote to change the subject. *Soldiers mentioned arson on other towers. Can we please find out about the damage and injuries? What of my family?* She directed the page toward Jean, who hadn't been with her initial party to enter the room. She could only hope he had more current information, but he shook his head.

"We're seeking verification of your family's safety. Everyone was scattered across the grounds, which was for the best, truly. If they had been able to catch you all in one place . . ." He motioned to the Five.

"I was watching the fires from the window a moment ago. Hester was blatantly curtailing the spread," Ada said softly.

Hester still had some power to help, then, but her distance and diminished strength would limit what she could do in a full attack. Solenn blinked back tears, realizing that her own grief must be small compared to the horror that Hester had been returned to, again left distant and mute.

Unlike Hester, Solenn wasn't alone. She had her family. Braiz had not yet fallen. From an early age, Erwan had taught her that she must know where she entered a room and five places by which to leave. She needed to think ahead. The loss of Hester Incarnate was devastating, but it wasn't the finale of this suite.

We know Albion's fleet is on the way. This attack today is to sow chaos. Adamantine and her musketeers nodded in grim agreement. *I need to return to the war council.*

"Your father is in the hallway," said Talia.

Good. I need to talk with him. She stood, straightening her justaucorps over her hips.

Bells began to ring. Solenn froze, as did everyone else in the room. Talia motioned to the Five. Adamantine and Brillat glanced at each other, expressions puzzled.

"That means enemy ships have been sighted," Talia said in Verdanian for their benefit.

Everything was happening too fast, too fast. If they'd had another week, Solenn could have gone to Hester's full form for another rock and begun the imbuing process anew. Her hand trembling, she wrote, *Queen Abonde may return soon. I need winter garb ready near the courtyard.*

Talia made an abrupt bow. "I'll have that prepared within minutes, Itron."

Solenn approached Erwan, who faced her with a smile that could be described only as tender but exhausted. His mustache and beard were disturbingly strange. They made him look *old*.

"I need to report to the war council—" he began to say, and paused as she nodded vigorously. "Ah, you wish to go there as well? Let us go together, then."

Movement across the room made her turn. Two musketeers were bundling and sweeping up the maimed corpse. Good. But that left a more serious problem. She motioned to the remains of Hester's head.

"We can—" Erwan began.

"I'll handle it," said Ada, her brows furrowed as in deep thought.

Solenn felt a profound sense of relief. More than even Brillat, Ada would know precisely when the divine powder would cease to be regarded as food. She'd make sure that no one committed a sacrilege in the way of Mallory Valmont.

Thank you, she wrote to Ada, then faced Brillat, writing in Verdanian. *I'm sorry we haven't gotten to speak. Aveyron is in the stable. He's well. He's been an incredible help and friend.*

Brillat's face, often haughty and severe, softened as he bowed. "I'm glad to know that. I'll go to him now," he said, then faced Erwan. "I'm a stranger here. If I might—"

"I'll have a trusted musketeer assigned as your companion as we head downstairs." Erwan clapped hands and forearms with Brillat, a gesture of close camaraderie. She wondered what they had endured in Verdania, and when or if she would ever know the full story.

"Itron," Ada said softly, bowing her head to Solenn. "Be careful."

Solenn nodded again, propelling herself forward. She couldn't linger here, not in her despair, not in her need to savor another scant meeting with Ada.

She gestured to Hester as she passed the hearth. The flames steadily burned.

CHAPTER TWENTY-NINE

ADA

Dogs and pigs can be trained to find truffles, but their skills are mild compared to those of empathetic Chefs. One such Chef from the royal palace has in recent years been seasonally deployed to Peribord to acquire the royal family's personal stash of these blessed fungi. It is a joy to see such a professional at work: audibly sniffing the air, eyes closed, drawing on divinity to find something likewise divine.

—Excerpt from *Manual for Tour Chefs*

Ada was left alone in the room. The blackened shutters had been drawn together and bolted. The stench of a partially cooked man remained.

Prince Morvan had ordered that she be given as much time and assistance as required to attend matters. His embrace had been brief, formal by appearances, his whisper fast. "Thank you for bringing Erwan back. Thank you for bringing yourself back." He paused. "Vicomtesse Corre has sent word that your grandmother keeps asking after you but she's well. She's decided to make a dessert each day. I sorely wish I was in Malo to visit." He'd always had quite a sweet tooth. He used to eat honey from the jar in admirable quantities.

"As do I," Ada replied, voice thick. They parted.

There was no sweetness within Solenn's room now. It was unfortunate that the window must stay closed for security, as the stink would be slow to dissipate.

She avoided stepping on the blackened floor as she paced around the remains of Hester, her tongue tingling with flavor and power. Few things in her life repulsed her the way that rupic did. As a child, she'd thought it sounded horrible when she first read about it in Guild canon. Mallory Valmont's profound sacrilege had then validated her feelings a thousand times over. After realizing his newfound powder was the essence of a God, he hadn't hesitated to heartily indulge with an aim of immortality, godhood, and vengeance.

Ada considered the powder before her, and did indeed hesitate. But she thought of how Solenn had collapsed as she entered the room, her hopes as pulverized as this rock.

Solenn and Erwan needed a miracle, or their home would be lost.

She went before the fire and thought to crouch, but realized that if she went down, she wouldn't be able to rise again.

"August Hester," Ada said, drawing on the power channeled through her tongue. Even though Hester's powder still contained a weighty presence, she sensed the difference as the God's direct attention rested upon her. "I will admit, I'm reluctant to trust you. Not a month ago, you would have seen me dead, despite my devotion to you over the years. Even more, you would have killed Solenn. You *burned* her. But she believes in you, and I can't deny that you've tried to help me in recent days. I can no more ignore that than I can the aid also offered by Selland, Melissa, and Lait, or the machinations of Gyst.

"I don't ask this lightly. Can I . . . use you as an ingredient?" Ada said, the words foul on her tongue even though the food was yet unmade. Utilizing Hester within food wouldn't be sacrilege if the God gave her blessing, but oh, it was still *disgusting*. "If you consent, please grace me with more of your presence." Bells continued to ring outside. Albionish ships drew closer by the minute.

Tingles slowly escalated across her tongue, the flavor of smoke and char briefly canceling out the presence of the stone powder. As quickly as the presence had arrived, it departed, leaving no aftertaste.

"I suppose that's an affirmative," Ada said, almost wishing that Hester had refused.

She checked a few bureau drawers in the box bed and found an unsoiled, empty leather bag a little larger than her hand. Using a clean cup, she filled the bag with the most powdered remnants of Hester. She tucked that in an inner pocket of her stained coat.

With that amount reserved, the cleanup was forthright. She used the hearth tools to sweep the rest of Hester's remains deep into the fireplace, where she utilized a shovel to mix it with ashes. For good measure, she poured water onto the floor to further distribute what dust remained.

"What am I doing?" she muttered to herself, the presence of the bag heavier on her conscience than within her coat. Mallory had been *possessed* by Hester. The God had controlled his voice, his movements, everything. If Hester did the same to her, Ada could become a Chef-trained weapon to harm those she loved—or even kill herself. Ada could be forced to defenestrate herself from a high window.

So long as Ada wasn't killed outright, Hester's influence would be short lived, based upon the cycle of digestion. This sort of potential possession wasn't like what Solenn had endured with Gyst. He had established a residence that he intended to use at his whim. Hester would be more of a brief squatter, she—

Ada *tasted* dragon.

She whirled to face the shut window again, for an instant fearing the Albionish had returned with their dragon wings, but no—this was a living, breathing dragon. Her tongue didn't merely tingle; it throbbed as if it were swelling. Queen Abonde was not only powerful—she was . . . immense. Ada had an eerie awareness of the sheer quantities of meat, fat, bone, and viscera. The muscle tissue radiated the strongest, like hearty beef with a gamy edge.

If Queen Abonde was here, she was either going to confer with Solenn or leave with her. Ada's daughter would do her duty for Braiz. Ada would do hers.

She opened the door and greeted the musketeers who awaited her there. "I'm done in here."

"Our thanks," a young musketeer said. Sudden clamor rang from outside—trumpets. The musketeers shared wary looks.

"The dragon has returned," Ada said simply as she moved on, leaving them to attend to the room and guard the window.

It was time for her to do what she did best. Cook.

CHAPTER THIRTY

SOLENN

Civilians often believe that Chefs commissioned in the army spend much of their time preparing foods to be used for battle. While this activity is indeed necessary, their greater role as Chef is in ensuring that food and water remain safe. Gyst can work mischief in minutes that can destroy a division more thoroughly than any cannon.

—Excerpt from *Manual for Tour Chefs*

The anxious tedium of the war council meeting was interrupted by a trumpet's blast of five notes in sequence, playing a newly agreed-upon signal: dragon sighting.

Solenn stood, everyone else standing in response. Tad, the lead commander present, as her other family was secured elsewhere, faced her with grief and pride upon his face.

"I may see you in a few minutes, or a few hours," he murmured. "Go with the knowledge that we love you and we want you home soon."

She'd expected him to say farewell with stiff formality. His personal, emotional farewell brought tears to her eyes. "I love you," she whispered near his ear, hoping he understood. His tightened grip said he did.

She left, Talia and Jean at her side. People in the hallways parted to let them pass.

She entered the courtyard to find Queen Abonde hovering in wait.

"Ambassador Solenn," said the dragon. "Are you able and ready to fly with me into battle?"

Solenn nodded, her heartbeat as powerful as the dragon wings above her.

"Prepare yourself. I will circle for reconnaissance." Queen Abonde lifted up and away.

"Your clothes are in the gatehouse," Talia said, taking the lead.

In a small, private office, Solenn changed her coat for a thicker one. Her lace headdress was replaced with a fitted leather cap that fastened beneath the chin; jockeys wore such garb for horse racing. The pressure on her bound-up braids felt strange, but if it kept her head warmer and her hair contained, then good. Riding gloves were next. Talia secured a scarf around Solenn's mouth. Her breath was hot against the thick wool.

Noise from outside—exclamations and the rattle of gusty wind—indicated that Abonde had landed. Solenn exited to find Erwan in wait. Her heart panged, remembering how he'd dutifully waited for her so many times before. He'd changed into his musketeer attire, the continued beats of Abonde's wings causing his cassock to flare up around his hips.

"The dragon is beautiful and fierce," he said with reverence, then faced her. "But so are you, Solenn." His smile looked as it should on his clean-shaven face. A few nicks provided evidence of his haste.

She wanted to tell him how overjoyed she was that he was here, but bells continued to ring and the people of the château didn't contain their raucous reactions as they had on the dragon's first visit. He wouldn't be able to understand her speech, and she knew that would grieve him. She pulled out her table book.

My captain, I'd like to introduce you to Queen Abonde. I will also need help to mount her back. Her anxiety showed in her shaky handwriting.

Erwan pressed a fist to his chest and bowed. "I will be honored."

Solenn saluted both Talia and Jean. They somberly reciprocated. "Selland fill your wings," Talia quipped, a play on the familiar farewell.

"Have you any orders for us in your absence, Itron?" Jean asked, his hat held to his chest.

She considered asking them to look after the Silvacanes, but she had a feeling the proud Camargas would not be pleased by the aid. *Guard our home, and I pray I'll see you soon,* she wrote, then put away her table book.

Solenn and Erwan walked into the courtyard.

Abonde continued to slowly beat her wings. Solenn imagined the dragon was keeping her muscles warmed, just as a horse would continue moving before a race.

"Erwan Corre, Mouskeder ar Braiz," said Abonde, her great head bobbing. She spoke in eloquent Braizian. "I have heard much of you." Her voice grew soft, for their ears only. "Your aid and consideration toward the kin is known, and we thank you."

He bowed again. "Your aid and consideration is also known. Comte Silvacane has become not only an ally, but a friend."

"Your slain musketeers should arrive three days hence," Abonde continued quietly. "Let us hope that their arrival is not lost amid deeper mourning."

The news drove a gasp from Solenn. The other musketeers truly were dead. She had known them. Loved them. Raced them on horseback. Exchanged snowballs with them. They'd stayed behind in Verdania on her behalf, and now, their mysteries had been resolved. She motioned Gyst's X and then pinched her fingers, a silent plea for Selland to preserve her memories of them.

Tears filled Erwan's eyes. "We will speak more of what occurred later," he said to Solenn, "but I can tell you that Adamantine witnessed their deaths. They died with prayers upon them."

"Would that I had more time for you to linger and mourn, but the longer we wait, the more of your people will die," said Abonde.

Solenn confirmed that she was ready.

Erwan gave Solenn the necessary boost to reach the notch between the queen's spines. He looked strangely small below her—then smaller still as Abonde pushed off. So many people stared up at her, waving, cheering. She was their symbol of hope this day, even as her own representation of hope had been dashed to bits.

"Solenn, Brillat Silvacane sent word of what occurred to Hester Incarnate," said Queen Abonde. She must have sensed Solenn's grim mood and surmised the reason. "You have not lost Hester's favor. From the words relayed to me, it seems clear she sacrificed herself, lest she be employed as a weapon by Albion. Even in that act, she worked in your defense. This battle, this war, is not a hopeless one. Look." She rose higher and higher. Clouds frayed and tore around Abonde, and then they rose above the layer of white. Cold seeped through Solenn's thick clothes, tears smarting and drying at the corners of her eyes.

Out across the water, through more thin clouds, she could see Braiz's fleet and the advancing line of the Albionish. Beyond them—she could see the very shore of Albion! And there were more clouds—no, not clouds, but plumes. She leaned against Abonde's mane, squinting.

Queen Abonde glanced back to confirm Solenn's line of sight. "That's smoke. The surviving kin of Albion have emerged to wage outright war. They cannot do widespread damage, as many remaining kin are diminutive and thus limited in power on this side of the veil, but I assure you, there is chaos and death."

Queen Abonde lowered over the water, the Sleeve Sea dark below. As they neared the Braizian line, sailors erupted in cheers. Solenn clutched Abonde's mane with one hand and waved with the other, but only briefly. In the space between two ships, a long purple tentacle extended above the waves. The nearest ships cheered all the harder.

In her mind, Solenn beseeched Selland to be with her and his other children this day.

Ahead lay the Albionish, their ships spaced out in rows. Even at this distance, she could see the open gunports along each deck. There were also other crafts—galleys, powered not by sails but by people upon rows of oars. Strange objects littered the decks and, as she watched, moved upward.

Queen Abonde released a wordless roar.

They were dragon wings, she realized, spates of them. These were what Abonde had sent warning of last night. Fliers were beginning to fill the air, and more looked to be ready on deck. Some of the fliers hauled cages, too, that looked to be loaded with people. An invasion force, coming in by air. Solenn imagined that the flier had to be using some kind of epicurea to make them unnaturally strong, in addition to whatever helped them to fly and control the dragon wings.

As she stared, she realized the soldiers in the cages had to be using epicurea too. The best available. Otherwise, flying such few numbers to shore would be pointless. These soldiers would be like Mallory Valmont had been in the Thirty-Fifth Division, back before she was born—a superior soldier, nigh invincible, trained in ruthlessness and destruction. He'd been regarded as a one-man army on the battlefield.

Horror and fear made her heart pound as if she'd been running uphill, but she reminded herself that not even Hester's powder had made Mallory Valmont invincible. These invaders could, and would, die.

Solenn bowed low over Abonde's neck, hanging on for dear life as the dragon plunged to attack the first of the fliers.

As they swooped downward, Solenn recognized that the flier held a pole in their hands. It extended outward into a lance.

Oh, Selland. Abonde's rage-fueled attack on Albion the day before had given them time to prepare.

Nevertheless, Abonde veered close to her opponent. Solenn felt a sudden lurch and, looking back, realized that Abonde's long tail had lashed outward, striking an enemy's wing near the tip. The flier faltered, lurching in midair, but didn't go down. Abonde whirled around, giving Solenn a brief view of even more fliers taking to the sky. How many dragons had been slain for this effort? How many years had Albion prepared for this very moment? Their cursed fleet was bad enough.

How was Braiz to survive against these forces? *How?*

The flier continued a persistent track toward the shore. Abonde dived at them from behind, but the caged soldiers proved to be armed as well. Pops and smoke emerged from the bars. Abonde tipped, left, right, left to dodge. Solenn ducked almost flat against the right side of Abonde's neck to make herself a smaller target. All she could see was pale dragon scale and water, and then—a brief flash of dragon wings and a thick gray figure. A magnificent ripping sound filled the air.

As Abonde banked away, Solenn risked a glance over her shoulder. The membrane of an Albionish wing had been shredded. The flier swirled downward. The hatch on the cage opened, figures dropping out. They could have epicurea that would help them make it to shore. The threat they presented wasn't over.

More fliers with cages approached Braiz.

The lines of ships drew nearer. Solenn ached to exchange dialogue with Abonde—were they going to attack Albionish ships? Take down more fliers? Did krakens need continued guidance?

Another flier approached, no cage hauled beneath, their wings beating fast. They flew not toward the shore but at Abonde, who accepted this direct challenge with a new roar. Her body rumbled beneath Solenn.

Solenn tapped at the base of a wing, trying to get Abonde to speak, to look at her, to communicate. Instead, the rumble grew louder, but Solenn suspected this was the very opposite of a cat's purr.

The dragon was *enraged*.

Abonde showed no awareness of the rider on her back. Her entire focus rested on the new flier. Their wings were especially large, the membrane tinted gold. Solenn thought that must be the natural color but then noted that the human's uniform wasn't plain gray, but glinted with gold edging. Not a subtle uniform to wear during an attack, but such was the way of commanders, seeking to inspire by their visible example.

Was this Lord Whitney himself? Whoever they were, they also carried a lance. It extended in mere seconds, the barbed tip sparkling in a rare sunbeam. This didn't deter Abonde. If anything, she seemed to move faster.

Wind whistled past Solenn's ears. Her scarf yanked from her head and almost took her cap with it. The commander dodged, somehow making their wings move upward with strokes that were beautiful and sinuous. How the fliers directed the wings, she didn't understand, but this person had particular control, spinning, diving, attempting to come up behind them with the lance.

Abonde spun in the air. Solenn's seat and legs lifted up, gravity gripping her, and then Abonde twisted around again. Solenn slammed down on the dragon's spine, air jolted from her lungs.

In a rare view of the level sky, she saw no more dragon wings rising from the Albionish galleys. However, the existing fliers had almost reached the city.

"Abonde!" Solenn couldn't even hear herself when she yelled. She yanked on the mane, to no reaction. They dived close to the commander.

The lance reared upward, almost striking Abonde's wing. Solenn saw the whites of the commander's eyes set against pale skin. They wore a helm unlike any she'd seen before, a cap and face scarf fused, an inner layer of wool visible at the edges.

Solenn kicked at Abonde again, trying to arouse awareness in her, but the dragon was as blinded by rage as Hester in the old tales.

Roaring, Abonde came around again. The commander passed their lance to their left, lunging at Abonde with folded wings. Solenn felt the tip strike true, Abonde's body jarred by the impact. The dragon screamed, the sound shrill and terrible, and she plummeted. Solenn clutched the mane but couldn't hold on.

She fell. Wind whistled past her.

Her limbs flailed in the air. She saw Nont. The fog had dissipated, granting her a distant view of its white tiers along the cliff, the background hills a comforting deep green.

Braiz. Home.

She tried to hold her breath, but as she struck the water, that mattered little. The violent impact shoved the breath from her mouth. A horrible, burbling roar filled her ears. She opened her eyes to see darkness and bubbles. The heavy clothes that had kept her warm during flight now dragged her down like an anvil as everything became darker. Was Gyst about to take her by the hand? She would have much to say to him. He'd know some more unknowns by the time she was done.

Her lungs burned with the need for air.

She thought of everyone she loved. Mamm and Tad. Erwan. Aveyron. Ada. Maiwenn. Her grandparents.

Selland.

She recognized the tingle of his presence even amid the cold pressure upon her body. He was the very water that drowned her.

She didn't want to die but was so heavy. It'd be easier to sink and soon know peace, but she'd never been one to take easier paths. Her arms flailed outward just as she felt a nudge from below. The movements in concert weren't enough to propel her upward, but they arrested her downward progress. Her arms, already up over her head, waved downward as if she could fly. She flapped them. Her legs scissored.

A definite force nudged her from beneath. Strident, but gentle. Encouraging. Solenn made her limbs move again. She had to fight to live. She'd done this before—oh, by all the salt in the sea, she *had* done this before, years ago.

She'd still had her full set of milk teeth when she nearly drowned as a child. It'd been a high holy day, and Mamm had dressed her in a layered, lacy gown. She'd gone close to the shore in Malo, something she'd been nagged not to do time and again. A wave snared her. She was pulled down. She fought her way upward. *I'm like a seal,* she remembered thinking. Erwan had met her as she neared the surface. Together, they crested the waves.

"You should have drowned!" everyone had cried in disbelief when they reached the shore, motioning their gratitude to Selland. Solenn had motioned her thanks, too, but with the cockiness of a child had announced, "No. I decided that I wasn't going to drown."

She had decided.

Erwan wasn't with her this time as she emerged. She had a moment to take in a deep breath, and then a wave tried to dunk her. Her arms fanned out as if she could clutch the whitecaps. The shore wasn't far— nor was Nont. She had a jostled glimpse of partially constructed buildings. Then blackness again, another wave. She sputtered and struggled to stay up. She wanted to find Abonde in the sky, to know that she was still aloft, but she didn't dare tread water here among the riptides. She could easily be dragged under and away. The shore. She had to make the shore. It wasn't rocky here. The piers and wreckage were gone.

She made her limbs move, sodden and clumsy though they were. Gyst had once described the actions of the Gods as nudges, and she felt Selland's nudges now—his waves at her back, relying on her to do the rest of the work herself.

She had decided not to drown now, just as she had resolved as a child.

Had she the energy and breath, she would have laughed. She understood now why Gyst had been able to possess her, why she'd been powerful enough to choose or shun her own divinity. Or perhaps more accurately, one facet of her divinity.

She was a child of Selland, just as she was a child of Gyst.

A wave covered her again. Selland couldn't stop the waves, couldn't fully contain their might. She didn't need him to. Solenn emerged again, choking, the sensation worse without a tongue, as it was harder to propel water from her mouth.

Sputtering, fighting, immersed in Selland's violent embrace, she swam for the shore.

CHAPTER
THIRTY-ONE

ADA

People who assume that cooking is entirely about heat have never been in a château kitchen with its marvelous offices for confections and pastry. There, Hester's coziness means cold, not warmth. Frequent deliveries of ice keep the works chilled. The floors are slick with melt-off and sawdust, fallen flour rendered to mud. Here, on even the hottest summer's day, a cook requires layers of clothes, which must then be shed when it comes time to confront the ovens and welcome Hester's full might.

—Excerpt from *Book for Cooks to Excel as Do Chefs*

Ada loved cooking.

Years of training had emphasized to her that Chefs were defined by more than their tongues. They needed to hold an inherent understanding of and appreciation for food, as it did more than supply nutrition to fuel the body. It was history, culture, memories of the dead, memories built with the living. Ada had always enjoyed every aspect of the cooking process. Harvesting from the garden, tugging a hide from flesh. Breathing in the scent of dank greens, slow-roasting chicken, tending a daylong stew. The very feel of a pinch of salt between her fingertips, granules scraping the whorls. Discovering how lavender honey from the south tasted different from chestnut honey from near Lutecia.

The ritual of cooking meant joy through practice and discipline, whether that meant a simple plate of fresh cheese topped with just-picked figs and a drizzle of honey or fare as labor intensive as beef à la mode. Ritual meant comfort. The cooking or assembly process required that certain things be done in certain orders, and not even the oversight of the Gods drastically altered that process.

Ada needed the ritual. She needed something familiar and cozy as she set about doing something that violated her beliefs at their most intrinsic level.

She couldn't eat rupic raw as Mallory Valmont had. The very thought made her throat clench. No, she had to cook something fundamentally repulsive into edibility. Therefore, she turned to a recipe she had applied similarly in the past.

The oatcakes that she had used to draw upon cat magic.

This time, she incorporated not a handful of hair from the nearest cooperative feline but the powdered remnants of Hester's living stone.

The basement kitchen of the Nont château was large and set just behind the main keep. Tables, shelves, and modern raised stoves lined the whitewashed walls, along with several broad hearths centuries in age.

Ada didn't work alone in this space. The kitchen bustled with nervous activity. Soups simmered. A rôtisserie cooked several portions of lamb. Other people cleaned vegetables and meats, chopped herbs, washed dishes, and contributed in their own ways to the war effort.

Ada had informed the head cook that she was a rogue Chef from Verdania and that she needed to cook an urgent meal for the battle. Her reputation had preceded her.

"You know better than to cook with any magicked ingredients, right? Because of the dragon and all?" she'd been asked by a cook clearly nervous about confronting a Chef on such a subject.

Yes, Ada knew.

She had been offered space at a stove, but deferred, saying she'd instead claim a hearth where a cauldron of soup also bubbled. Chefs had debated for years about whether a fire or a modern oven was better blessed by Hester. Ada normally shrugged off such pedantic drama, but today, she decided that an old hearth would be imbued with more of Hester's divinity than a decade-old stove. The spot also gave her the isolation she needed. She was in no mood for idle chatter.

As the divinity of the ingredient would not spare her from breaking a tooth on a pebble, she first used a mortar and pestle to grind down a handful of Hester's powder.

From there, she assembled the normal ingredients. Oats, lightly chopped. A sprinkle of salt, with a plea to Selland. She felt his presence, a strange sea breeze rustling the room. Honey next, collected by bees near buckwheat. Ada called to Melissa, hailing her for her past aid through mead and bees, and requesting her help again. The God promptly heeded, her touch amplifying the sweetness. The butter had been made that morning, the milk from cows that fed on green spring grasses within the very walls of the château. The sea breeze had imbued it with a delightful salty edge. Lait didn't bother making herself known. Water came next, poured from a carafe in a slow drizzle. Using her hands, Ada began to mix everything together by feel, knowing when she needed to add a touch more moisture.

Gyst lurked nearby. He was a pest like that, sure as a fly. She hadn't even called him through any specific ingredient, nor would she have in this newly modified recipe.

"Haven't you done enough lately?" she muttered. She was mostly standing on one leg; her injured calf pulsed pain with every heartbeat. "But while you're here, notice the powder I'm using. You thought Hester should stay stuck where she was forever. Solenn found a way around that. She found a resolution to a mystery that even *you* had given up on. How about that?" Her pride reinforced her low voice.

She couldn't see Gyst. His presence was a mere enhancement of the existing scents in the room, and it quickly faded. She wasn't so arrogant as to assume he'd left because of her chastisement, but she was relieved he was gone.

She patted the oat dough into an even layer and used a knife to cut perfect rounds.

The next God she addressed was Hester, and Ada had no worries about gaining and maintaining *her* attention.

A large flat stone sat in the middle of the fire, years of use forming a shallow basin in the middle. The first batch of oatcakes sizzled as she dropped them onto the surface. She guffawed to herself. She was using Hester to cook Hester. There was something amusing about that. Something horrible.

Ada was going to eat rupic. Not merely perceive it but ingest it. She shuddered even as she flipped the oatcakes over. The top of each was perfectly browned.

The ceiling overhead creaked. The room above was used for plating and preparation, fewer workers there than here, but it took few feet to make a great deal of noise. A reedy boy with a faint mustache dashed down the stairs, panting heavily.

"Hear, hear!" he cried in a bold, insistent voice. "More of those Albionish dragon wings are coming toward Nont, and they're hauling soldiers with them!"

Exclamations broke out all around. "How's that even possible?" asked a deep voice.

"How's any of this possible?" The shrill voice verged on hysterical. "Gods talking, dragons flying about."

"The musketeers say they'll likely try to attack here!" the boy continued, enthusiastic in the way of the innocent. He waved farewell and then bounded up the stairs again, no doubt spreading the word in other nooks and crannies of the palace.

"What? *Here?*" exclaimed a young cook. "Our kitchen?"

"No, don't be so literal! He means the château whole, but any tactician worth their salt knows destroying an enemy's food is a smart way to strike," added the head cook. She was right.

Dread and anxiety surged in Ada.

"Hester," she whispered. "Your might is already mixed into these oatcakes. Enhance them, please. Help me help Braiz. Help me help Solenn."

Hester heeded her plea. The drizzle of power was nothing like the molten flow the God could've poured forth when her avatar was intact and nearby, but her approval was evident yet again. Ada gestured gratitude and tried not to vomit in revulsion.

CHAPTER THIRTY-TWO

SOLENN

The salt deposits of eastern Verdania are fortuitously placed near much firewood, which over the centuries has aided in the extraction of Selland's mineral deposits. The pits are flooded to raise the salt-saturated water, which is then boiled until only the salt remains. In this way, Hester refines her brother deity's gift.

—Excerpt from *Manual for Tour Chefs*

Solenn found sand underfoot.

She shoved herself forward, the weight of her waterlogged clothes worse on land. She fell, her face dipping into the shallow water again. That made her mad. She would not make it this far to drown on the beach! She dragged herself out of the water. Waves lapped her feet as she lay stretched out like a beached seal.

Distant bells caused her to roll to her side. Nont. The battle. She worked onto her knees, teetering. Smoke rose from across the city above her. What was burning? Had the fliers carried incendiaries?

Nont had already survived a devastating conflagration in the past year. What remained couldn't now be lost.

"Hey. Hey!" Atop the rocky cliff twenty feet distant stood some dozen Braizian soldiers. "Are you—"

"She is," declared one of them. "I saw her fall from the dragon!"

"The dragon!"

"She sure doesn't *look* Braizian." Whether that was an assessment of Solenn's clothes or skin color, she knew not, and didn't have the energy to be irritated about such things. She fumbled to remove her sodden coat.

"You dolt, she's a princess," hissed a woman soldier. "Do you need help, dimezell?" she called out, louder.

Solenn nodded, waving. Three women split off from the rest, taking a path down to the beach. A year ago, one of the major piers had stood here.

"That's right, she lost her tongue. Cut it off herself," said a soldier on the cliff, his tone making that sound more admirable than falling from a dragon.

They didn't seem to be speaking loudly, but she heard them with strange clarity. How was that possible? If anything, with water in her ears, she should be hearing worse, and yet, and yet . . . Realization made her suck in a sharp breath. Pentad canon said the Gods always tilted an ear when they were invoked. Was she hearing them because she was the focus of their conversation? At least she wasn't party to *all* talk about her—surely word was spreading about her plummet into the bay—but even this insight was too much. The last thing she wanted was to be privy to all the surrounding gossip about her.

The women, hands and voices gentle, helped her remove her soaked layers with quick efficiency. Tugging off her boots required several hands to hold the footwear and brace her body.

"However did you make it to land, Prin—Ambassador?" one of them wondered aloud, gesturing to Selland.

Solenn shook her head, deferring the question as she glanced back at the sea. Far-distant smoke indicated cannons had been firing, but she couldn't even see the ships from her low point. To her profound relief, she saw that Abonde still flew. The dragon was making a circuit over Nont, trying to attack two fliers still aloft over the city. Where was the dragon-winged commander?

She tapped the soldier who'd seen her fall. "When I was on the dragon, we fought a flier." Solenn spoke with slow care to make herself understood. "Where did they go?"

There was a long hesitation as her words were interpreted. "Oh! The dragon slashed one of the flier's wings. The fellow crashed into the water. Couldn't see more than that, not even with my spyglass."

Solenn gestured gratitude for that much information.

The more she considered it, the more right it seemed that the commander was Lord Whitney. He was the kind of man who'd make sport of hunting dragons, and practice using their parts until he'd become nearly as agile as Queen Abonde.

"We'll get you to a post to warm up, send a rider to—"

The woman's voice ended in a squawk as a massive shadow moved over them. The soldiers on the cliff yelled. Solenn looked up to find Queen Abonde's legs extended as she prepared to land on the beach. Thanks to the low tide, there was just enough room for her to do so without resting in the shallows.

The soldiers ran back for the cliff. Abonde landed heavily, sand spraying up as her claws found purchase.

"Solenn." Queen Abonde sounded ragged. "Are you hurt?"

Solenn assessed herself. Her chest ached as if there were still water inside, bringing to mind Gurvan's concern that she could swallow liquids wrong and develop pneumonia. Well, water had definitely gone where it ought not, but there was nothing to be done for that now.

She shook her head. "You?" The garbled word inspired her to check her pouch, though she knew what to expect. Water sloshed inside. She supposed she should abandon the whole thing, as the table book was ruined, but she *liked* her pouch. She would feel strange without it. Therefore, she removed it, only to dump out the liquid inside. She carried her shoes as she walked closer to Abonde. She could smell blood over the scent of the sea.

"Oh," Solenn gasped in quiet horror.

Shots had punctured the membrane of Abode's wings. There was a slash to a back haunch, and several more along her neck. Grazing bullets or a lance could've caused those. Moving around the dragon, Solenn found the injury that worried her most. The commander's lance had scored a foot-long trench through her scales. It was hard to gauge the depth through the blood. The white sand beneath contained a growing red puddle.

"You need treatment," Solenn said.

"No one else can offer Nont an aerial defense as I can."

As if Solenn didn't know that. "You can help no one if you're dead." She coughed. Soon she'd have no voice at all.

"A rider's coming downslope!" shouted a soldier. "A musketeer!" More townspeople were gathering to gawk at the dragon. The crowd parted to let the rider through.

At the cliff, Erwan dismounted a chestnut horse and, leaving it with a soldier, hurried down to the beach. Erwan, oh, Erwan . . . he must have been watching her entire flight.

He slogged through the sand with commanding strides. "Princess Solenn. Queen Abonde." Erwan studied them both with worry.

"Captain Erwan. How fares the city?" Abonde asked.

"The winged attackers have employed what we can only surmise is Graecian fire. Conflagrations burn across the city." He gestured to the land behind him. "This is probably one of the safest areas of Nont, as there's little to burn."

Graecian fire. That stuff was as legendary as the City-Eaten-by-the-Sea. Solenn thought the recipe had been lost long ago. She looked questioningly at Queen Abonde, who bowed her mighty neck and sighed.

"It uses dragon oil," she said simply.

Erwan's nod was grim. "Water doesn't squelch it. People are gathering to fight it however they can, Majesty. On my way here, I passed a building being knocked down to create a firebreak."

"Smothering the flames with large quantities of dirt will help contain it, though the buried debris may still sizzle," said Abonde, gazing up at Nont. "But that advice helps little when multistory buildings burn."

Tears stung Solenn's eyes. Hester could have done much more to help if she were physically here. If Solenn could talk with Hester again, that alone would be useful—but she was only one of the Five, and they had more allies besides.

Time and again, she'd heard of Lord Whitney's brilliance. How he thought through most every possibility. They needed to engage him in ways he'd never anticipate.

An idea formed in her mind. "We must go to Arcady."

Queen Abonde gazed at her, neck cocked. "What have you in mind, Ambassador?"

Ambassador. Solenn was an ambassador. The title that felt like a wistful secret days ago now adorned her like a heavy crown. She moved closer to Abonde, her battered body trudging with drenched stiffness. She had a sense that she'd aged too quickly in recent weeks, endured too much of life packed into mere days. "Many things. You're seriously injured. You must get care." She spoke slowly to try to do so with clarity. "Then we need to confer directly with the Gods. We need divine aid to pursue Lord Whitney and end this war."

CHAPTER
THIRTY-THREE

ADA

People may argue that the best technological innovations of the past century are guns and other artillery, but these people know not their own households and the blessing that is the raised stove. For time untold, Chefs and cooks have labored stooped over hearths, causing immense damage in their bodies. Now, for much of our work, we may stand upright as we govern four to six burners hosting various pots. Those other people can celebrate their guns—me, I will attend my fricassee and omelet in comfort!

—Excerpt from *Manual for Tour Chefs*

As much as Ada wanted to check on the progress of the battle, she didn't think it'd be wise to risk Hester taking control of her body while she stood on a high parapet. Therefore, she entered the vacant patisserie office near the kitchen, using crates to block the door behind her for privacy.

Natural chalk walls kept this room cooler, nor were there ovens here. All such warm work was done in another room. Here, butter lined shelves in great blocks, while dough slowly rose in cloth-covered vats. This was a zone fragrant of Gyst, Melissa, and Lait. She liked to think that the two female Gods, though they'd extended only infrequent aid, might balance against Gyst if he decided to be unruly again.

Ada sat in a wooden chair, hissing in both relief and pain as her leg changed position. A dozen oatcakes, loosely wrapped in a clean cloth, sat on the table before her.

She stared at them. Despite the urgency of battle, she procrastinated, loathing herself for it. Her daughter was out there right now, probably risking her life. Erwan would be doing the same.

Ada needed to help. She needed to eat.

She picked up an oatcake. To her nose, it was fragrant of toasted oats. The holy powder carried no blatant presence in color or smell. She focused on the inherent presence of Hester and beckoned to her, as if opening a flue within her mind.

She took a bite.

The oatcake burned her tongue, not with heat, but with potential. She'd known divinity channeled through epicurea throughout her life, but never like this. Never with such eagerness.

Hester questions your intelligence, but is grateful nevertheless. The mental voice was soft, feminine, with a hardness that denoted maturity.

"You're not exactly known for intelligent decisions yourself," Ada retorted aloud. Mallory Valmont hadn't been able to communicate with Hester until he'd eaten handfuls of raw powder. As ever, a Chef could amplify not only the flavor of food but its very soul.

A light laugh filled her mind as Ada took another bite. *That is true, yes, a fact I know all too well. One would think thousands of years of personal experience, of watching others endure life, would help in that regard, but no, no. Slow down your ingestion, Adamantine, mother of dear Solenn.* The voice took on a no-nonsense brusqueness. *My power is one of the mightiest in this world. It is not to be ravened.*

Ada's head swam as if she'd guzzled down a pint of apple brandy on an empty stomach. Her tongue *vibrated*. Her entire body tingled. She'd felt exhausted minutes before, but now she knew energy the way she hadn't since childhood. She felt *good*.

"Thank you for asking me to slow down rather than forcing me to do so." Ada held half an oatcake in her hand. Incredible. She'd had a few bites and she felt like *this*. Mercy.

I am not Gyst. Never, ever am I like him. Hester's resentment carried through her tone.

"You controlled Mallory Valmont."

Never against his will, you must understand. Hester promises you, from the depths of her flames, that she would only act in such a way to save your life. Such is her respect, yes. Never will I control you. I want . . .

Yearning burned in Hester. She wanted to simply *be* with people, Ada realized. She was sociable, long deprived.

Chef Ada, you are much like your daughter, yes, your compassionate and wise daughter, but perhaps you're the greater fool. You've taken a terrible risk, a dire one indeed. I wouldn't trust me if I were you. You've doubted me, rightfully, oh so rightfully. I was ready to let you die weeks ago, and I let Valmont burn Solenn. I burned her. I burned her. Agony and guilt rang in her tone.

You were ready to die yourself. Ada experimented with speaking to Hester within her head. The switch felt right.

Yes, the all-powerful, all-aggrieved Hester was ready to die, for there was no hope, none at all, of truly experiencing the world beyond her crater. Not even my brother Gyst thought such a thing was possible, but Solenn . . .

Solenn is special.

I know every human in this world, yes, as none can live without my fire to warm them and to cook their food, and not another is like Solenn. She believed in me when I didn't believe in myself. How incredible is that statement? That she believed in a God when a God did not? She's helped me . . . live again. To speak, oh, to speak, a thing I once took for granted, but never again. The imperious tone softened to reflect wonder and gratitude.

In that moment Ada understood that Solenn had been absolutely right. Hester was a God, but fallible. She made mistakes. She could also make amends. Solenn's solemn kindness and willingness to act when even the Gods had not had made all the difference.

You're very different from Gyst. Ada took another bite. She felt strangely warm and cozy in such a cold room. She hoped that she didn't cause the nearby butter to melt.

Gyst, ah Gyst. My brother, he cared for me—still cares. He understands mercy, yes, but kindness is a separate concept, one he has forgotten, if he ever knew it at all. But Solenn, she possesses kindness beyond compare. She has asked Hester to defend Braiz, but not to remove her blessing from Verdania and Albion. Such temperance! Solenn knows a thousand reasons to hate those places and people, yes, a depth of hatred I know myself all too well, and one that has motivated me toward destruction. But not her. Not her.

Ada remembered how she had burned with grief and rage against all of Lutecia as Braiz's musketeers died and people cheered. For the callousness of those hundreds, she would've condemned hundreds of thousands in the heat of that moment.

Hate can be valid, but we still shouldn't act on it in our most irrational moments, Ada said.

Such restraint has been as foreign to me as coldness. Hester paused. *The battle. We must gaze upon its progress.*

Ada, feeling less dizzy, finished the oatcake. *Why? What's going on?* She stood, tucking the remaining oatcakes into her pockets.

A fire long lost to the world, recently rediscovered, has been deployed upon Nont. Graecian fire. A terrible thing, its burn like no other. You, a Chef of long practice, will know its true nature as soon as you breathe its smoke. It's made of dragon oil and other things, in amalgamation terrible.

Dragon oil. It made sense that the fat of a dragon would have a use. Most any oil did, whether from pigs, hazelnuts, butter, or olives.

Ada passed through the kitchen. Scarcely anyone paid her attention. She'd done what she wanted to and cleaned up after herself. She hesitated a second, taking in the scene as she hadn't before. This place exuded coziness that she felt with all the comfortable solidness of a bellyful of stew on a cold night. It hadn't carried that sense a short time ago, though it had been a decent enough workspace.

She continued up the stairs and through corridors. Dull pain and tightness burned in her leg, but she moved with incredible fluidity. Her limp was gone. Even more, she'd forgotten her walking stick in the office.

Ada emerged onto the flat roof of a lower tower. Guards studied her for a moment, then turned their attention to the sky. Ada did as well, then down upon the city and the bay beyond.

"Oh, Five," she said in an exhalation.

Much of the lower city was still gutted after last year's fire, a scar just starting to heal. Across the remaining city were at least a dozen fires, spreading fast. One of the far towers of the château burned at its highest point, like a torch held high to the clouds. Her tongue pulsed with awareness of the potent epicurea in use.

But that wasn't all that she sensed. A new layer had been added to her perception.

She sensed *homes.*

Across Nont, thousands of times over, places exuded light that her sight couldn't fully comprehend. She felt emotions: coziness, familiarity, love. Desperation. Need.

Ada felt eerily aware of the pounding of her own heart, the frailness of her form. She was so small against this city, this world, her emotions mere specks of sand on a beach, but they were part of a whole. Each of these entities *mattered.* Not simply to her, but to Hester. The God had no heartbeat, and yet she pulsed with life and devotion for these individuals who turned to her amid their terror and turmoil.

People were scared and praying. Ada couldn't hear their pleas like sounds. Their words were . . . presences.

This was what she'd felt in the kitchen just now too. It felt like home to cooks who'd worked there for years. They pleaded for its protection.

Hester exuded a reaction as she recognized what Ada was detecting too: awe.

Through your own inherent divinity, daughter of Gyst, you've enhanced what Hester could even feel through her beautiful, now-shattered stone head. Incredible, incredible.

Smoke arose from far out in the bay as well. The naval battle was underway. Fires burned there. Sailors prayed to make it home, for their families to be safe in their absence.

Tears streamed down her cheeks. She understood their fears so very well. She also understood that within her multitude of powers, she could do more than ever before.

I saw Mallory Valmont create fireballs, Ada said. *What can we do to stop fires, especially the Graecian ones?*

Hester made a thoughtful sound. *I burn with ideas.*

CHAPTER
THIRTY-FOUR

SOLENN

Never forget that something as simple as flour, if exposed to a spark, can cause an explosion that will level buildings.

—Excerpt from *Book for Cooks to Excel as Do Chefs*

"Queen Abonde, would it be permissible for Captain Corre to travel with us to Arcady and act as my support, as he has for much of my life?" Solenn turned aside and coughed. A day before, she might not have dared make such a request, but Erwan had been able to murmur to her in the château earlier that he and Ada had traveled a shortcut through Arcady. That Erwan had made such a journey was extraordinary, but that an active Chef had done so and lived said a great deal about how much human and kin relations had changed in little time.

One thing that hadn't changed for Solenn: a need for companionship. Aveyron was inaccessible, and Erwan had long been her support. She'd learned the hard way that asking favors of the Gods could be dangerous on her own, as they made their own demands in return. At least Selland wasn't transactional like the others. He would help her communicate with krakens again, of this she was sure. She sent him thoughts of gratitude.

Abonde tilted her elongated head, considering. "Yes. I will allow Erwan Corre to accompany us. Captain, approach so that I might tell you where to meet us."

He did so, kneeling. Abonde leaned close to speak for his ears alone. He rose. "I will see you momentarily," Erwan said. "Queen Abonde. Ambassador. Thank you both for placing your trust in me." He bowed to them and hurried up the cliff.

Solenn felt a pang of love for him. Weeks ago, she'd been furious when she'd found out that Erwan and her parents had lied to her about her origins throughout her life. Her trust in him had been broken. Now, with time and perspective, it had been restored.

Solenn looked to Abonde with a furrowed brow, shrugging to indicate that she had questions.

Abonde's head loomed close to Solenn. "I cannot carry him. When we leave, we will be followed by your people and perhaps even the Albionish. Captain Corre requires an edge to reach the meeting place. By leaving now, he appears as a messenger and is not likely to be pursued."

Solenn nodded as she sat to pull on her boots again.

"I must apologize to you, Ambassador," murmured Queen Abonde. "During the battle, I lost reason. I endangered you, myself, and the kin who depend upon me. That human . . . wore my brother's wings. I knew he was dead, not that he'd been . . . harvested."

Solenn shook her head, making her sympathy clear upon her face.

Abonde looked toward the city, baring her teeth. "We must away. Too many humans are gathering, and fighting approaches us as well." Blasts of nearby gunfire punctuated her statement.

With no one trustworthy available to boost Solenn aboard, Abonde had to lower her belly onto the sand and awkwardly roll to one side.

Her ragged breath revealed her pain. Solenn scrambled up as quickly as she could. At least, with fewer layers of clothes, she had more mobility.

Abonde took off promptly, exertion evident in her faltering wing-beats and grunts of effort. They glided low over the shallow water, then up to the western edge of the city. No Graecian fires burned there, but smoke lay thick and cloying. Solenn could only imagine how much more horrible the smell would be if she still had her Gods-touched tongue.

Abonde landed within a recess formed of trees and tall buildings. Solenn promptly slid off. Not a second later, Abonde shifted form and crumpled to the ground.

"Majesty!" Solenn bent to grip her across the shoulders. Even though Solenn had been upon Abonde's back as a dragon, touching her in such a way felt like a kind of violation. The queen, however, didn't shrug off her aid to stand. Her entire torso was bloodied, the ephemeral robes tattered and dark.

"Where are we going?" Solenn asked, then repeated the words twice to try to make them clearer. She suspected the fault was not solely her impaired speech, as Abonde had the dazed look of someone grievously injured.

"An abandoned bakery. Please, pull up my hood."

Solenn did so. Abonde bowed her head, her inhuman face hidden by shadow. Together they walked along an upward-sloped alley, Abonde's steps labored. Pain seemed to affect her more in her humanoid form, or perhaps the very act of shifting had exacerbated her condition.

The port fire had touched the old bakery, scorching one broad wall black. Part of the steep roof looked to be collapsed, causing Solenn to give the place a chary eye even as Abonde proceeded. Inside awaited Erwan; he must have set his horse free, as none had been outside.

Erwan blinked as he took in the identity of Solenn's companion. "Queen Abonde." He genuflected. "Is there any aid we can offer you before we journey farther?"

She pushed back her hood and glanced down at her body, grimacing. "No. A quick exodus will be best." She gazed past Erwan to the darkened shelves beyond the bakery counter. "Lord Emperor?"

"Queen Abonde." Gold eyes glinted from the shadows. A sleek black and white tabby cat stepped into view, stretching with a raised tail. "I suppose my fish payment will need to wait. Blasted *war.*"

Erwan glanced at Solenn, wide eyed. She had to look as stunned. She hadn't expected such a normal-looking cat to speak Braizian or any language at all, not on this side of the veil. This Lord Emperor must be powerful indeed.

In Arcady, they arrived on a gorse-covered slope like so many in Braiz. Gray skies admitted little midday light. Around them was what could only be described as a small encampment that aroused to a frenzy at the sight of the injured queen. All manner of creatures descended upon them—birds large and small, beings somewhat human, others shaggy or serpentine and decidedly *not.* This had been an agreed-upon meeting place for Queen Abonde and her retinue, Solenn realized, a wise precaution indeed.

"Get her to the tavern," said a silver-haired woman of statuesque, stout build. Solenn gaped—this person was surely another Camarga. Her voice carried evident authority, as the group agreed on this course. A dryad far taller and broader than Lyria scooped up Queen Abonde in their arms and carried her away on fast-moving root-feet.

The silver-haired woman turned to Solenn and Erwan, curtsying. "Ambassador, we have clothes and food for you there as well. We stationed such things at various depots, should the need arise. And you, I presume, are Captain Erwan Corre?" She spoke with an eloquent Lutecian accent that reminded Solenn of Brillat.

"I am." He bowed, doffing his three-cornered hat. "May we have the honor of your name?"

"I'm Lunel, Aveyron's dam. Come, the walk is short. We will take care of you."

"I'm glad to meet you," Solenn tried to say, and shook her head in frustration.

"The paper you usually carry. As you are wet, I can guess it was ruined?" Lunel asked, and when Solenn nodded, she smiled. "We'll bring you more. You must have means to communicate."

"Thank you, Madame Lunel," said Erwan.

The tavern looked like any in Braiz, broad and squat, but they were guided not to the main building but a smaller one adjacent. They dispersed to different rooms. The hearth burned steadily as Solenn changed into the supplied pantsuit of Braizian blue.

Someone knocked on the door. She opened it to find Lunel standing there. She held out to her a new pouch, a lighter tan and smaller than what she'd possessed before. "You'll find a packet of papers inside," Lunel said. "My apologies that it's not closer to what you already have."

Solenn promptly opened the pouch to pull out a thick stack of yellow-hued paper, bound together at one corner by a leather thong. Several pencils were loose within the pouch.

Thank you so very much, Lunel. What's the queen's condition?

Lunel glanced over her shoulder. Erwan stood behind her in the hallway. "I know little. I did hear that in Nont, she argued to stay and fight, but you convinced her to return here. We are grateful for your insistence." After Solenn ducked her head and smiled in acknowledgment, Lunel continued. "Would you like food now, Ambassador?"

Water, please. As much as she would like to eat, that would take too long. The battle was still ongoing. *Has Queen Abonde stated anything about my intentions here?*

"Not that I have heard."

Solenn had to warn them, lest kin flood the room in her defense. *I'm going to confer with the Gods. Unless we call for help, please don't interfere.*

Lunel's dark eyes were thoughtful as she nodded. "Understood. Blessings upon you as you engage in difficult diplomacy. Captain Corre, have you any needs at the moment?"

Erwan entered the room, shaking his head. "I have the feeling that we will be as brief as possible here. Thank you." Lunel bowed and exited. Erwan stopped near the fire. "When we passed through Arcady earlier, we were blindfolded all the while, and Ada's mouth was befouled. My imagination didn't do this place and these beings justice. Or your capabilities." Love and fear shone in his smile. "When I saw you fall into the bay—I feared—it was such a long drop . . ."

She quivered at the memory. *I survived with Selland's help, and my own.* She hesitated. She knew Erwan better than she knew most anyone, but how would he accept the news that he was descended from a God?

"What do you mean?" Erwan asked.

Her hand trembled as she wrote. *We're of Selland's line.*

He had leaned forward to better read her text, but straightened as he shook his head. "What? No. Selland is too grand, too mighty. My family cannot possibly be—we are *ordinary.*"

Am I, really? She looked at him with an arched eyebrow.

He laughed, the pitch higher than usual. "I take your point, Solenn. I found it much easier to accept that Ada was of Gyst's lineage. There was always something extraordinary about her—and you as well. I suppose that makes more sense now. You are a child descended from two Gods."

She nodded. *The absence of my tongue didn't change my . . . divinity, it only removed my Chef senses and Gyst's means of control.*

"I see." He paused in thought. "I don't understand our reason for coming here, beyond escorting Abonde into treatment. Is it somehow easier to speak with the Gods in Arcady? And if Hester could do so, was making the stone head necessary?"

The other Gods can visit Arcady, but Hester's powers are more limited everywhere. Hester, are you there?

Solenn showed the paper to the fire. Nothing happened. That couldn't be right. Even in the human world, Hester could suppress flames.

"Hester?" she voiced aloud. "Can you hear me?" She leaned forward, fear clenching her heart. As hobbled as Hester was, she *must* still have some ability to communicate in Arcady. She must. Gyst had certainly done so with ease.

"Hester?" Solenn repeated, leaning dangerously close to the fire. She sensed Erwan a step behind her. "Give me some sign that you hear me, please."

The blaze wobbled as it might if someone had opened and closed a door across the room, but no doors had moved, nor had Solenn and Erwan. With a question in her eyes, Solenn glanced back at Erwan. His lips were pursed.

"I know not," he said. "That was such a subtle thing."

Subtle. Feeble. Perhaps even the product of a desperate imagination. But she knew that Hester definitely had some presence here in Arcady; Abonde and Aveyron had acknowledged that much and been concerned about increasing the God's power. Solenn took a deep breath, drawing on her faith, and again queried Hester for a sign.

The flames dipped once more. Solenn shot a look at Erwan as he released a long exhalation. "I saw it as well," he said.

"Can you read my writing?" Solenn asked the blaze. Nothing. Perhaps Hester was unable to see here, but at least they had established that she could hear. "Should we use high flames for yes, low for no?"

The fire made a tiny flare, as if a sheet of paper had been thrust into the hearth. The flicker could've been missed in a blink.

Tears smarted Solenn's eyes. Hester's voice had been so bold and unceasing, and now it'd been reduced to *this*. Had Hester made herself weaker here when she created the schism between worlds, or was this a defense mechanism erected by the kin? Solenn supposed the reason didn't matter right now; they had to work within these new constraints regardless.

"Can you read my writing?" she asked anew. The flames dipped. So Hester *was* essentially blind in Arcady. Solenn couldn't help but slump in frustration. She was grateful that Hester could still understand her speech—for the time being—but Erwan's furrowed brow and focus indicated that he was having more trouble doing so as her throat strained to produce sounds. They all needed to be able to communicate. She wrote to Erwan, *Can you read my words aloud?*

"Of course," he murmured. That would have to do. They couldn't waste more time.

Can you still gauge how the war is progressing in Nont?

The fire flared again in its small, fierce way.

Was Lord Whitney the commander with dragon wings?

No hesitation. The fire flared.

Solenn sucked in a breath. *Is he alive?*

Again, the flames spurted.

She thought on what the soldiers had said about the commander crashing into the sea. *Has he returned to his flagship?*

Another lash of heat.

Is he hurt?

The flames stayed still.

Does that mean you don't know?

They rose again.

"If I understand what you're implying, you intend to . . . what, send assassins after a man who has proved incredibly challenging to kill?" Erwan asked, to which she nodded. "Our sources in Albion have reported that Verdania has made multiple attempts to kill Lord Whitney over the years. And you know very well why they have failed."

Yes. Lord Whitney likely had among the best epicurea larders in the world, and unlike passionate hobbyists like the late Marquis Dubray, he had the Gods-blessed skill to enhance everything himself. He'd also sense if any approaching killers were using epicurea—or if they *were* epicurea. She had to imagine that the kin of Albion had sought his life as well.

We need to strike him today, when he least expects a personal assault. Carrying her writing implements, Solenn walked to face the darkest corner of the room.

Does Lord Whitney bear wounds that could cause greater infection, Most August Gyst? She showed the paper to the darkness.

The shadows shifted as a misty shape of a human figure formed. Solenn knew she hadn't imagined it, as Erwan promptly took a protective pose before her, a hand to his hilt.

"*Ah, ever the noble chevalier. As good as you are with that blade, Erwan Corre, I would prove difficult to strike.*"

Solenn glanced at Erwan as he sucked in a breath. He had apparently heard Gyst.

Solenn wrote quickly. *Gyst is not flesh. His form is made of mold and other things too small to see unless they are massed together.*

Erwan acknowledged the words with a brisk nod but remained on guard. A symbolic act, and she loved him for it.

Is Lord Whitney injured? she repeated.

"*I don't know, is he?*" Gyst's raspy voice sounded amused. The first time they'd spoken in Arcady, he'd feigned weakness to gain control of her. She knew to be wary of his antics now. "*I do know that Adamantine Garland is injured, and by rusted metal, no less. Such a misfortune.*"

"You're threatening her," Erwan said. Incredibly, even he could hear Gyst speak while in this realm.

"*War is dangerous.*" Gyst shrugged.

These dangers are why people turn to the Gods for solace and aid.

"*Is that what you're doing, Solenn? Expecting me to help you after how you treated me—how you disrespected me?*" His voice hardened like the crackle of dense ice. "*You think that I will handle the hardest tasks on your behalf?*"

Solenn shook her head, weary. Gyst would always make a martyr of himself. *I am asking, without expectation.*

Gyst seemed to loom taller, straighter. He was reshaping himself to appear more intimidating. "*Good. Then you won't be terribly disappointed when I say no. You wanted control of your life, Solenn. Congratulations. You have it.*"

And then Gyst was gone.

She blinked, and then she quietly laughed. He hadn't been wrong. Turning to him had indeed been audacious on her part.

Erwan sighed. "From everything I've recently learned of him, he wouldn't have been trustworthy, even if he had agreed to help. You'd ask him for blue cheese, and the mold would be a dangerous one." He removed his hat to run a hand through his long hair. "I am worried about what he said of Ada, though—which was likely his intent."

Solenn agreed.

An authoritative knock shuddered through the door. Erwan moved to answer, then bowed at the sight of Queen Abonde. She looked no better than before, but now, an adult, human-size tree-person acted as her support. Branches and what seemed to be sentient vines had snared the queen in a secure vise. Her feet hovered above the floor as she was brought into the room. Abonde's stare focused on the corner where Gyst had briefly been.

"How went your meeting with the God of Unknowns, Ambassador?" Exhaustion carried through her words. Solenn was glad she hadn't thought to rely on Abonde to mediate with the krakens; she was in no condition to do so.

He's a stinkard.

Abonde managed a light laugh, but ceased as she winced. The tree-being had no recognizable face but seemed to twitch in reaction to the queen's discomfort. "I assume you already spoke with Hester, best as you could."

"August Hester can offer only minimal engagement through the flames," said Erwan.

Abonde's eyes widened in surprise. "Truly?"

She's not weakened here?

"Hester *is* weaker than the other Gods, of course, but she's still part of our world, much to our dismay in recent centuries." Abonde looked thoughtful. "There were many fires in Nont as we left. If much of her focus is there, on restraining them . . ."

Solenn felt a surge of relief, especially as the hearth again leaped upward in a blatant gesture of affirmation. Good. She'd much rather Hester's modest strength aided Nont.

Abonde continued, "What of the other Gods?"

I will address them now.

Solenn appealed to Lait and Melissa in turn. Neither manifested within the room. Solenn wasn't sure how they could've directly aided at the moment, anyway.

That leaves Selland. Let's go closer to the water to confer with

She ceased writing midsentence as a sudden sea wind within the room stole away her breath and almost flattened Hester's fire. Erwan cried out, flinging an arm against Solenn. As much as they both loved Selland, she realized, he was right to guard her, as this was no mere wind. It was Selland in force, and this current of air was imbued with a mood—a warning—to not move. Even Queen Abonde in her tree could only stare wide eyed.

Solenn comprehended her own foolishness. Of course Selland could come within this building with ease. *All* of Arcady was accessible to him. Gyst had materialized in the middle of a meadow before; she'd gone to the shadows of the room out of human habit. Hester was the only God who required a specific venue.

"Selland." Erwan's voice was dim against the roar. The wooden walls around them rattled.

"Most August God of Salt." Abonde's words were dimmer yet.

As for Solenn, she fought against the pressure to raise her hand past Erwan's arm. She pinched the air in greeting, as if she could seize the salt so fragrant to her nostrils.

The room turned black and utterly still, a deeper nothingness than she'd experienced as she sank in the ocean. "Greetings?" she called, her voice echoing strangely.

A blink later, the world existed again in the familiar gray tones of a Braizian day. Solenn was lower to the ground, Erwan standing above her. A younger Erwan, his fully black hair in a thick wave upon his shoulders. This wasn't like the memory flashes of home that Hester had evoked; she was actively reliving the past.

Solenn was a child, she realized. She was short, perhaps around seven of age. She knew with certainty that she was in the past because of her tongue—oh, by the Gods, she had a tongue! She felt it pressed against the gap of her missing top front teeth. The nub of a new tooth was teasing through the gum. This felt more real than any dream, because it *was* real.

"But I want to stay out!" Petulance rang in young Solenn's tone. The shock of that voice—of witnessing herself but not being in control—brought a flash of panic. This was like Gyst, when he—no, no, this wasn't like Gyst at all. Selland preserved memories, as he did food within his salt. This younger Solenn still had her full autonomy. Solenn wouldn't want to control her other self—that would be wrong.

"You can't always get what you want." Erwan smiled down at this younger Solenn, amusement in his gaze.

The scene faded, but Erwan's words echoed. *You can't always get what you want.*

Selland had no voice by which to speak. He was using her own memories to communicate.

He had intuited that she'd wanted him to intercede with krakens on her behalf. He was denying such aid.

"Why?" she asked the darkness. The word, rounded by her tongue-less pronunciation, echoed as if she were in a cave. A salt cave, perhaps, like the famed ones in Grand Diot. If there were any walls around her, they were distant.

Color bloomed around her again. She recognized the particular pale granite of the palace in Nont. She stood in the same private audience hall where she had recently argued with her grandmother and father, but in this memory, only her mother was with her. Mamm wore a deep-blue dress, her skirt swirling as she faced Solenn.

"Perhaps it will be easier if you meet him without such high expectations," Mamm said, sympathy in her brown eyes.

The room faded away with her voice. Solenn placed that moment—this had happened during the prolonged marriage negotiations on behalf of herself and Prince Rupert. She'd pleaded to write a letter directly to him so that she might know him better before their nuptials were finalized. She had so desperately hoped that he shared her love of horses.

"My expectations for my meeting with you were too high," she said to the darkness. "I understand." She did, with a deepening sense of shame. Gyst, she had queried with no expectation of success—but the opposite had been true with Selland. She hadn't planned to address him last among the Gods simply because she thought to speak with him at the seaside—she'd taken for granted that he'd endorse her effort.

An instant later, Solenn was sitting at her familiar desk in Malo. The glass window was open to admit the breath of the sea. The breeze carried a musty waft of distant rain. "I can do the work. I *want* to do the work," she said with articulated stubbornness.

Her arms leaned on the desk. Around her balled fists were stacks of papers and books—logs and testimonies from the fire of Nont. Oh! This was a memory from scarcely a year ago. This would've been about a week after the conflagration. She had requested to take on the important role of representing civilians who had lost everything in the fire. Other young nobles had passed through Malo and expressed satisfaction that their families had offered money toward those in need. That wasn't enough for Solenn. She needed to *act*.

Truly, she'd had no idea of the onerous task she was getting herself into.

Tad sat in the leather and wood chair before her, his cocked hat in his hands. "I'm not doubting you, Solenn, but I also want you to know that it's fine to ask for help from me, Erwan, your mother, anyone. We may not be able to provide it, but perhaps we can still direct you the right way. In the end, however, this responsibility is yours." His smile for her radiated fondness and pride.

Solenn took in his direct gaze with a pang. Maybe, eventually, he would be able to look at her like that again—not as someone damaged or now a stranger, but as simply his daughter.

"Thank you," said this slightly younger Solenn, with equal measures of relief and satisfaction. The simple motions of her tongue, the very weight of the flexing muscle, made Solenn-the-witness ache to cry.

The scene faded, leaving her in the stillness of the dark.

Selland was reminding her that she could engage with the krakens herself—but also that it was fine that she had asked for his assistance.

"You're right. I presumed," she said. "I'm sorry. I never even considered that I could address the krakens myself today."

She had taken for granted she couldn't or wouldn't succeed, just as she had taken for granted that Selland would support her because he had repeatedly done so. This, even though she knew Aveyron had been unharmed when he'd mediated before. This, even though she had recognized her own inner spark of divinity today.

How very human of her.

"Thank you for directing me the right way," she said. The sharp fragrance of salt flared in her nose again, and then she was back in the tavern room in Arcady, no longer in a memory but in the present. She gasped in relief.

Erwan leaned into her vision. His black hair included white strands, creases lining his eyes. "Solenn?" He tentatively reached toward her, relief drenching his features as he was able to touch her sleeve. She cocked her head, brow furrowed. "You were within a shell of thin salt for a matter of minutes. I could barely see you through the distortion of the crystals. It all . . . dissolved in an instant. Are you well?"

She nodded, though she experienced renewed grief as she felt the vacancy in her mouth.

"Ambassador Solenn," said Abonde. "Selland conferred with you?" At her nod, Abonde's pale face showed awe. "An old tale says that he lost the ability to articulate words when his voice became the ocean's roar. You were able to understand him?"

Solenn had never heard such a story before. She realized that she still held her tablet and pencil, and so she wrote with a shaky hand. *I think so. He spoke with me through my own memories.* She paused as she realized what that meant. Selland had delved into her most private thoughts in a way that even Gyst had not, but she wasn't left with a sense of violation. After all, Selland had been there as a witness all along. *He encouraged me to try to communicate with the krakens on my own.*

"What is especially trying about this communication?" Erwan asked, his brow furrowed to create lines in his forehead. Solenn was strangely aware of how old he looked now after seeing him younger only minutes before.

"Krakens do not vocalize speech," said Abonde. "Through the touch of a tentacle, they can communicate with other species using pictures in the mind." She looked outright limp amid the branches. The brief wind of Selland's arrival seemed to have sapped more energy from her.

"Thank you, Queen Abonde," Erwan murmured. "Now I think I understand. This type of conversation—Solenn, it reminds you of Gyst?"

She nodded with a renewed sense of chagrin. *I was going to ask Selland to mediate on my behalf. He knew. He corrected me.*

She'd felt hesitant and guilty when she allowed Aveyron to act on her behalf before—and yet now, she'd been ready to pass along the hardship to not only Selland but the krakens. They were already risking their lives and limbs in battle—and here she was, for the moment, safe and secure in Arcady. She would've stayed on the shore when she asked them to seek out Lord Whitney too. She'd already almost died today, yes, but the battle wasn't done.

Erwan motioned gratitude to the God of Salt. "And so Selland preserved you."

She looked at Erwan. He read the new conviction in her face and responded with a bow. "You have my sword, and my love. Whatever you need of me, ask."

That rattled her anew. Blinking back tears, she wrote to Abonde. *We must leave. I'll ask Lunel for help to reach Land's End.*

"It's not far, by Arcady's distances," said Queen Abonde, haggard amid her branches. "Blessings upon you, Ambassador."

Solenn put away her table book, terrified yet resolute. Today, somehow, someway, she and her companions would end Lord Whitney and his war.

CHAPTER
THIRTY-FIVE

ADA

Steel knives, so prized for their excellence, are humbled by simple fruit. Not only will lemon juice eat at the blade but a terrible flavor will carry to the food. A silver knife, therefore, is an essential item in a Chef's kit.

—Excerpt from *Manual for Tour Chefs*

Ada hurried through the château. Hester had said the closer she was to those she helped, the less power she expended. Ada was all about efficiency. She dodged frantic people carrying blankets, weapons, children. Two bleeding musketeers stood in a corridor, cleaning their muskets. Hester was strangely quiet.

Are you sensing something more? Ada asked her.

Yes, treasured Solenn confers with me. Muted as I am, I speak to her through the flicker of flames.

Solenn! Where is she? Is she well?

She's across the veil, yes, in the land of magic. And Erwan is with her, ever her guardian. Ada gasped aloud. Erwan was back in Arcady? *Solenn looks well. I must repeat, she is quite well, but by the words uttered by other fires, Hester knows that Solenn fell from Queen Abonde into the ocean.*

Ada stopped, leaning on a wall. Despite the burbling warmth of Hester within her body, her veins seemed to suddenly run cold. *How far did she—no, I don't want to know. Nothing seems broken?* Selland must have intervened. She pinched her fingers, love and urgency in the motion.

Hester stayed quiet for a moment. *Nothing is obviously broken, no. Chef Ada, step into a side room with no one else present, and do so with haste.*

Despite their need to rush, Hester's renewed hard tone made Ada take her quite seriously. She found a linens room with laden shelves and shut the door behind her. The space was a narrow ten feet, the only light from a high, small leaded glass window.

What is it, Hester? How quickly they'd become familiar.

Your festering leg wound. Gyst, my miserable brother, he speaks with Solenn and Erwan. He crowed to them of your injury. When did you last check beneath your bandages?

Not in hours. Erwan drained and rebandaged it before we took the shortcut through Arcady. Right now it doesn't—

Remember Mallory Valmont, dear Ada, remember him. You perceived how good he felt after ingesting my powder, did you not? He was otherwise near death, yes, mere breaths from that particular veil. Check your wound.

Part of Ada wanted to argue with the order; she had never favored obedience to authorities, and a God was no different. Even so, she remembered Mallory's status all too well. He'd been delusional in the thrall of godly power. That meant that she shouldn't trust her own judgment either.

Ada wedged the tip of her knife beneath the wrapping and cut it through, revealing a leg swollen with pus, the wound blackening on both sides. She prodded the swelling with a fingertip. She felt pressure rather than pain.

Is your powder keeping me *alive?* Ada asked. She already understood that she was tolerating an enhanced dose of Hester's statue that would've been fatal to anyone else, even Mallory Valmont.

Hester was quiet a moment. *No, no, you are not near that veil as he was.*

Meaning that point could come yet. Gyst has set me up to lose my leg or die, or perhaps both in sequence. Even though she'd worried about this possibility earlier, the threat felt more real now that a God was expressing concern for her life.

Better for Gyst to physically strike her rather than Solenn, but Solenn was still the true target. Gyst would love to make Solenn a spectator of Ada's decline, and neither of the women could reveal the truth of their relationship.

Dear Ada, do you remember when Mallory Valmont channeled fire through his direct touch? When he drew upon my celestial glory?

I would hardly forget how he wanted to cook me between his very hands.

You can cauterize the wound. Yes. You have that power yourself now, through my incomparable divinity.

Ada couldn't speak for a moment, overwhelmed by horror. *But a burn carries the risk of infection as well, and this wound goes all the way through my calf muscle. Would cauterization do enough?*

Hester knows not. Her tone was frank and frustrated.

I can't worry about this right now. Ada grabbed a clean sheet and used her knife to start a cut, then shredded it into strips with her hands. *We need to combat the Graecian fire, normal fires, and maybe a few Albionish for good measure. My slow, agonizing death by infection or lockjaw or however else Gyst is attacking me isn't our highest priority at the moment.* With practiced hands, she wrapped her leg again and pulled down her trouser leg to cover it.

Hooves echoed in the corridor, dull and heavy. Wait—a horse was in the building? The steps lacked the metallic clang of horseshoes. People were yelling and speaking in high voices as the horses came closer.

Ada didn't perceive anything, nor would she. Camargas radiated magic only when in their human forms.

She opened the wooden door to confront two angry white and gray stallions. Both Brillat and Aveyron regarded her with flattened ears and bared teeth. They'd sensed Hester's use, and had every reason to react with alarm.

Ada held up her hands in a gesture of surrender. "I can explain," she said quietly, "but not here." People were gathering in the hallway, including several soldiers with pikes. No one with sense would strike a Camarga, especially in light of their recent association with Solenn, but during a battle, sense could be as absent as fresh strawberries in winter.

Ada was flanked by Brillat and Aveyron as she walked to the courtyard. With quiet urgency, she described her reasons for channeling Hester's power—and most importantly, that she had the God's express permission.

By their flattened ears, she knew she had yet to convince them, especially Brillat, who bared his long teeth more than once.

"She has yet to try to dominate me," Ada murmured. "I began this brazen idea with desperation, still holding some doubts about her change for the better. I now believe her shift to be genuine. We need to get close to the Graecian fires to suppress them. We could use your help as well." Brillat and Aveyron shared a look, ears moving, as they communicated in the way of horses. She had a hunch that Aveyron argued on her behalf, for which she was grateful. "I *was* going to stop in the stable with the hope of finding you both there. My alliance with Hester wasn't something I was going to hide from you. I'm very aware of your heightened senses."

Brillat released a snort that seemed much like the guffaw he made as a man.

"I'm not sure what else I can say to convince you," Ada said, frustrated by their hesitance and the delay.

Tell Brillat this, said Hester. Ada then repeated what the God said aloud. "Hester wants me to say that, though she is a mighty God, she has been slow to learn. Only now does she understand the degradation that comes of being epicurea. That it means being alive, loved, and blessed, and then masticated, digested, and rendered into feces." Ada paused. "I'm going to paraphrase somewhat, as her speech tends toward flowery. Hester says she didn't intend to be subject to her own curse, but that she now realizes it was for the best. She's learned from this experience, and many others recently, largely thanks to Solenn." Ada hesitated a moment, processing what Hester spoke. "She says that Gods are regarded as the highest beings, but she doesn't believe that herself anymore. The Gods are truly a mix of human and kin. That's their strength, and their vulnerability."

She was left awed. Hester's words made sense.

The two horses shared a look. The smoke in the courtyard, carrying the acrid hint of dragon oil, made clear that they couldn't continue to dither. Brillat sighed and used his head to gesture to his back.

Ada propelled herself aboard. "Ride for the nearest Graecian fire."

He cantered downslope as fast as he dared among streets clouded by smoke. Aveyron followed. People thronged the streets, battling normal fires and ready to fight any Albionish invaders. They were ready to defend their city. Their home. Their fierce love buoyed Hester's presence, feeding her. Drawing out the power instilled by a single oatcake.

A bright sense of home imbued the burning building at which they stopped, a bold contrast to the innate, repulsive feel of the fire itself. Ada wondered if that deep awareness of destruction arose from her familial bond with Gyst. The two-story, half-timbered structure consisted of wattle and daub, the roof thatched. The fire had already leveled much of the block and continued to burn in the ruins. A few soot-blackened people stood with buckets in hands, staring helplessly. One stooped woman near Grand-mère's age was frantically using a shovel to dump dirt from the unpaved street over a low fire that crept across the ground. It had no immediate fuel; it needed none.

Ada dismounted. The God had been quiet, but Ada had an integral awareness that Hester had been assessing the surrounding conflagrations.

Hester finally spoke up in her mind. *Focus, Chef Ada, as you would when perceiving food. Together we will work to accomplish what must be done, yes.*

She did, immediately reaffirming that the dragon oil was the carrier of flames. It was viscous. Sticky. If its burning flow met human flesh, it wouldn't slow until it reached bone, and even then it'd do its utmost to *cook*.

Through Hester, she understood that aspect better than ever before.

Ada extended a hand and caused the creeping oil to balk. "Bury the fire! Stop its flow!" she said through gritted teeth. The onlookers ceased gawking and dug in with shovels, boards, even a cook pan. More people emerged to join the effort. The progress of the fire was stopped, but nothing could be done to save the tall building alight. Now, at least, it was more isolated.

"Aveyron, can you find the best path to the next-closest fire?" Ada asked.

He bolted away to return minutes later, rearing and jerking his head in a clear plea to be followed. Ada mounted Brillat.

"Hey! Should we follow you?" called a man with a pitchfork.

Ada hesitated a second, then nodded. "Yes, if you're mobile and able, but we also need people to deploy through the city and spread word to not use water on any Graecian fire, but to bury it or force its flow into dead-end trenches."

"Graecian fire!" several people cried out.

"Albion used *Graecian fire* on us?" exclaimed a high voice.

"It uses dragon oil," she said over her shoulder. "As horrified as you are, imagine how the dragon queen feels, to know the bodies of her dead family are being used in this way." Horror and anger painted every face.

"Bah. Epicurea." The old woman with the shovel spit into the dirt. "Never once needed it in my life. Never will."

Mutters agreed with her. Some people took off to spread word about how best to fight the fire, while others jogged after Brillat as Aveyron guided them along the twisted, sloped streets.

The next Graecian fire had set alight a granite wall that supported one of the city's tiers. At first she wondered why Aveyron had brought her to this fire rather than one that engulfed buildings, but then she noticed fiery chunks of stone were beginning to rain downward as the bricks crumbled under intense heat. She could see at least five fires on lower tiers that had likely been started by this one.

Ada, Hester, and the townsfolk worked in cooperation to oppress the flames, then moved to the next blaze, then the next. As that scene came under full control, she noticed Brillat and Aveyron dancing in agitation to get her attention.

Yes, yes. Hester's voice sounded strained. *Onward we must go. The Albionish in the city are encouraging the Graecian flames to spread, oh, they are doing so with great effect. The Grand Pentad—*

Of course. That landmark would be their foremost target. There was no greater symbol of Braizian resiliency against disaster.

"Are we going to the Grand Pentad?" Ada confirmed with Aveyron as she mounted Brillat. Aveyron had been scouting the area for the worst fires. Soot had turned his white-gray coat the deeper shade of a Camarga foal. He nodded as he half reared, lunging to guide them through the smoke-choked streets.

The spires of the Grand Pentad loomed below, the approaching flames visible like high, living walls.

Ada felt Hester's anger. The God held an intense love of old pentads—that had been evident in her rage over the destruction of the ancient temple she'd built in Lutecia—but this place was special now. This was where she'd recently come *alive.*

She wasn't the only being to hold the Grand Pentad in high affection. By its ambient glow, it was like a home to many. Perhaps even to Solenn. This would be the ceremonial pentad for the royal family, after all; she'd know it well.

As Brillat slowed, Ada pulled an oatcake from her coat and began to eat. Her tongue, her very brain, tingled.

"We're going to save this place," Ada said aloud for Hester, Brillat, and Aveyron. Her tone showed no doubt. She had none.

She felt good. Powerful. Confident.

Like a God.

CHAPTER
THIRTY-SIX

SOLENN

Bread is made of grain, wine from grapes, and cheese from milk. As divergent as these items are, each relies on unknowns to develop, and they do so in different ways dependent upon the environment. The complexities are truly beyond comprehension. One marvels at how the Gods do what they do.

—Excerpt from *Manual for Tour Chefs*

With the aid of Lunel and another Camarga, Solenn and Erwan soon arrived at Land's End. She'd spent the full ride praying krakens would be there and willing to help; she would take nothing for granted now. The Camargas stayed back as she and Erwan continued to the cliff. The midday was blustery, few clouds adrift in a startlingly blue sky.

"Land's End looks exactly as it does on our side," Erwan said in a loud voice to be heard over the wind and the crash of water upon rocks. "Solenn, if I can be of help in any way, please, try to let me know."

There'd be no writing in this weather, but they'd find a way. She nodded, taking careful strides from boulder to boulder.

A peer over the cliff confirmed that tentacles writhed in the waters below. Perhaps Selland had still helped in one additional way—or perhaps last time, they'd truly come because *she* called them, and now they had returned. In any case, she released a deep sigh of relief—until a tentacle extended upward.

Solenn took a step back, her heart hammering. Erwan's hand glanced her back, subtle but present. That's right—she wasn't alone. She needed to do this. Krakens weren't like Gyst. Aveyron was well after speaking with them. Krakens weren't like Gyst. They weren't.

"Solenn, are you sure?" Erwan asked.

She nodded. She didn't want to. She *needed* to. Not only for Braiz, but for herself. She needed to prove she could do this.

Then a tentacle was before her, a stubby, dripping tip pressing to her forehead. She knew a moment of vertigo, like when she crossed the veil.

Gladness. A feeling of joy, as if she were being hugged. She hadn't expected that, though Aveyron had described krakens as friendly.

Even with her fear, she felt the need to reciprocate the feeling. *I hope you're not hurting much in the ongoing battle?* she thought at them, to receive blankness in response. Aveyron was right. Words weren't going to work. She had to use pictures *and* emotions. She projected worry, the sound and shudder of cannonade, flinches of pain.

A sense of understanding and sympathy flared in her mind. Pain, yes—she knew it in brief prickles. But also—full bellies, the satisfaction of a good hunt. Fortunately this was not accompanied by memories of flavor.

Now, how to get her query across to them? She pictured the three-decker flagship that had brought Lord Whitney to Braiz for marital negotiations, in the deep water of the bay.

Acknowledgment—yes, this was a ship! But also confusion. Her intent wasn't coming across. Muddled concepts flowed through her—ships came from different places, and that made them good or bad—krakens came from different places, and that made them family or foe.

She pictured the ship again, emphasizing its extra flags and gilt, to another flare of confusion.

Finally, she understood. They didn't comprehend each ship as a distinct entity. Krakens themselves were too interconnected by touch; they assumed the same of ships and everyone else. Why, that was probably why Aveyron had been readily accepted when he stepped into her role. They thought he was a piece of a whole that also included Solenn.

She mulled for a moment, then envisioned Queen Abonde, selkies, Camargas, other kin they might know by sight or association, and then the full sensory load she had experienced after her tongue awoke. The flavors, the tingles, the magic. She followed this with a question.

Positivity flowed toward her. Yes, krakens recognized epicurea by its radiant magic. She followed this up by asking if they sensed it more on the bad ships—the ones that made them hurt. Yes, yes, yes. This connection had been made even clearer to them in recent days. She recognized the Braizian ships they showed her, rainbow-shrouded as they were through krakens' unique vision, and how their goodness had been reasserted by the absence of epicurea.

"Solenn?" Erwan's voice seemed to come from the other side of a tunnel.

"I'm fine." The words sounded strange and garbled to her ears, as if she were distant.

She pictured the field of battle as she last saw it from above, but tried to shift her perspective to sea level. She placed Lord Whitney's flagship there, and showed tentacles gripping the ship. She earned excitement as her reply—but no sense of recognition related to their previous conversation.

If they couldn't consistently identify the ship she sought and what to do . . . could they tell apart *people* by sight?

Solenn showed them humans—herself as seen in a mirror, Aveyron, Erwan, Mamm, many others—and krakens reciprocated by sharing their vision of people. She realized that distinct facial features meant nothing, nor did clothes or variations of hair. A kraken's eye was the size of her torso. Its idea of detail was far different from hers.

This was already taking too long. She could no more expect krakens to understand these minutiae than krakens could expect her to eat sailors whole. She suddenly realized that not only had her initial hope for Selland's aid been presumptuous, it'd been impossible; the God would've had to change the very nature of krakens for them to do as she would have bid. He was right to refuse her.

Solenn would need to escort krakens to the flagship. If they made it that far, there was then the issue of Lord Whitney. Krakens couldn't identify him by sight, and they might not be able to reach him at all within the interior. How was she to make certain Lord Whitney didn't escape? The epicurea at his disposal gave him ready means of egress.

She needed to bring the fight specifically to him—but fighting wasn't her strength.

She willed her distant-feeling lips to move. "Erwan?"

She sensed his face drawing close to hers. "Yes?"

Tears tried to escape her eyes and only dried at the corners. If she asked him to go with her, there really was no question. He'd go, without hesitation, even if it meant his death. Even if it meant that he never had the full reunion with Ada they both deserved.

"Yes, what is it?" he repeated.

She reflexively gestured to Selland for comfort. The tingle of his presence came as a reply. "Will you go with me to the ship?" She took care to pronounce each word so that even if he didn't understand her, he could read her lips.

His hand squeezed hers. "Yes. I'll go with you. But how?"

That was the next dilemma.

To the krakens, she depicted herself and Erwan together and indicated that they needed to somehow reach the bad ship, and she was surprised when one kraken had an immediate idea for a conveyance: a giant shell. They apparently had many such shells in their submarine shrine. When she expressed the human need for fresh air, she found ready understanding; after all, they knew how humans could die in the water by various means. The shell would be large and contain plentiful air for the journey through the water, and be sealed by a tentacle that also stayed in contact with her all the while.

When Solenn expressed regret that krakens were being harmed in this battle and that more danger awaited, their reaction was nonchalant. Life meant death. Suffering was not ideal, was best avoided, but it happened. Even more, they comprehended that the Albionish were great killers of their kind. Sacrifice today meant many lives saved.

That was true of her and Erwan's roles as well.

CHAPTER
THIRTY-SEVEN

ADA

You will often find cheese makers and pig farmers as neighbors and business partners, as the incredible amounts of whey created by cheese making are used to feed pigs, making them plump and healthy. Reduce your own waste in such a way. Efficiency is most assuredly a divine trait.

—Excerpt from *Book for Cooks to Excel as Do Chefs*

Ada approached August Chef Gurvan. Though she was aware that he'd been at the Malo beach to attend the dead sailors, she hadn't seen him up close. Here, she knew him by his ornate robes of office and the way in which he labored to create a firebreak outside the Grand Pentad. His reputation for compassion and hard work had been known in Verdania even twenty years ago. Ada would've been ready to like the man even before Hester spoke of him with deep love.

His reaction to Ada was, quite understandably, not as kind.

"You!" He marched upon her, a shovel held ready to swat her down like a fly. His pale face was splotched black as if he'd been working with coal. "Who are you? What matter of sac—"

"I'm Adamantine Garland, formerly Adamantine Garland Corre, also formerly an empathetic Chef conscripted by Verdania, now a rogue of some sixteen years." Ada felt incredibly chipper, courtesy of her recent oatcake. "I act with Hester's blessing, and not hers alone." She motioned to the Camargas not far behind her. "Hester's told me that you are in Aveyron's confidence."

Only at the sight of the cooperative Camargas did his expression soften, the shovel lowering. "This is . . . wrong, and yet . . ."

"I don't disagree. I'm the Chef-lieutenant who apprehended Mallory Valmont seventeen years ago. Rupic is the foulest of curses. What I do now is out of desperation."

"I see."

This was a figurative statement on his part, as the low, terrible smoke made it hard to see more than fifteen feet. The immediate areas north and east were aflame. It was a mercy the city had already burned on the other sides, or the conflagration would've been too much for Hester's direct intervention.

The Albionish focused a great deal of oil here, an oil foul even to my accustomed senses. They wanted this place to burn, perhaps more than even the château, and oh yes, they called upon Hester to bless them in this mission. They succeeded in gaining her attention amid chaos, the errant fools. Even though Ada had just eaten an oatcake, Hester's voice sounded diminutive as she sought to dampen the flames.

She needed more power, as did Ada. Though the taste of the last oatcake lingered in her mouth, she pulled out her third. She had a plan.

"August Chef, Hester's working to hold back this blaze, but she needs more support. Can someone brave the bell tower to ring the sequence for Hestersday? If everyone in the city focuses on Hester at once—"

"She'll be fed through intent. This is in keeping with what Itron Solenn did with the stone head. Chef! Chef! Come here!" Gurvan yelled to one of his subordinates.

Thank the Gods that Ada didn't need to stand around and argue with the man. There was no time. Gurvan's face reflected a kind of sick fascination as he watched the God's power increase in her body as she chewed.

Gunfire rang out to the north, near the fire. Everyone crouched down, people yelling. In the smoke, it was impossible to see who was firing at what. These were the kinds of battlefield conditions where a comrade would kill a comrade and not know the truth for hours, if ever.

These were the conditions under which Ada would've expected to be anxious, sweating, frozen in terror.

I'm calm. Calculated. Like my old self.

Living without pain was seductive. Dangerous. It was amazing, really, how quickly this good feeling felt normal, even as Ada still experienced faint twinges from her infected leg. Hester couldn't undo that damage. She instead created stasis and distraction, but that was an incredible thing. Ada had needed a prolonged time to work up the nerve to make her oatcakes, but now that it was done, it would be easy to indulge again and again, telling herself each time would be the last, that she just needed the brief help to get through a public ceremony, a dinner, to do something she truly wanted to do in public without shaking and sweating all the while.

By the Five, she could end up like her father. She'd seen him some dozen times in her childhood before he died. Only once had he been sober.

Hester, after today, I can't use your powder again. I know you can't withhold fire from burning or stop the effects of your powder, but impede me however you can. Please.

Chef Ada, I understand, I do. I will aid however I may. Hester sounded shaken. *How strange to hear a human make a request with such willpower.*

I can do so readily now. I feel good. When I'm crying in need, begging for your balm, contriving to find your statue again and stuff your powder in my face as Mallory Valmont did—that will be more difficult. For me, for you, for everyone around me.

You speak from experience that burns.

Yes. I've lived enough to know that it's wise to fear myself sometimes. She crawled closer to Gurvan in time to hear the other Chef speak.

"Yes, yes, I'll ring Hestersday's bells." He was a hirsute man with smoke-reddened eyes. "I recognized Hester's presence yesterday. I'll be honored to call more people to her worship." He slunk up the steps to the pentad.

More gunfire punched the air nearby. Ada narrowed her eyes, trying to see. At her query, Hester extended energy to ascertain who was firing weaponry. *Albionish. Three of them right near the fire, very near. Almost directly ahead of you, mother of Solenn. Their musket balls fly toward the firefighters.*

Ada perceived more in the same wave of power. *They ate fire salamander, and therefore are using the blaze for cover,* she said to Hester, then spoke aloud. "Brillat! Aveyron!" Her words projected in a strange way against the crackle and din. The Camargas trotted closer. "I need to go closer to the fire. Stay here, out of Albionish range." Brillat tossed his head, making it clear that he thought she was daft. Ada wasn't going to argue on that point.

"Hester protect you," Gurvan said with such reverence that Ada felt strengthened through his faith.

She advanced on the fire at a crouch. Several firefighters had taken shelter behind the pile of dirt they'd been using to bury and barricade the flames. They beckoned to Ada, urging her to join them. She shook her head. She paused behind an abandoned wagon to load two pistols, one ready in her hand.

She couldn't see the Albionish yet, but even through the potency of the fire, she could read the epicurea in their bodies. Beast. Fire salamander. Vandrossa eagle. By the Five, they'd eaten an entire *meal* laden with epicurea—and by the vibrancy, it had been ingested right after they landed. That kind of heady dose would be debilitating or even fatal later on in the digestion process, if they lived that long.

The bells began to ring. Each God had a distinct five-tone sequence, and Hester's was associated with the end of a workday, of a holiday to rest. It was a call for time together with family. For gratitude.

An Albionish soldier edged forward, a silhouette against the fire. Ada surged forward, pulling the trigger. The shot caught the surprised soldier, still bundled up thickly for flight, square in the head. They flopped backward heavily just as Ada came into sight of two more soldiers. They raised their muskets as Ada dropped her empty turn-off pistol and switched to the second. She fired. She hit the lead soldier in the chest, causing them to fall forward atop their dead companion.

The third soldier retreated, heat wavering around them. Ada drew her rapier. She didn't fancy running that close to an inferno, but if there was ever a chance for her to use fire, it'd be—

No, Ada, said Hester.

The fire surged as if encouraged by a mighty breath of air. The flames seemed to snatch up the soldier as if in a large hand. They had no chance to scream. Ada knew they were dead by the prompt cessation of their digestion.

Cinders rained down on Ada. She grabbed her dropped gun as she backed away, swatting sparks from her hair. *Hester, you—*

Hester knows when to cease exercising her great strength. There was a dramatic pause. *I released my hold on the blaze. They set that fire, yes, and they now know the consequences of that act.* Hester said this with no anger, no regret.

Ada retreated behind the wagon again. The firefighters were still behind their shelter. The approaching Graecian fire was so intense, there was little more the Nontians could do at this point. She could feel Hester slowing the blaze's progression again, but onward it came.

If the burning building fell in the direction it leaned, it'd land in the street before the Grand Pentad—which was slightly downslope.

The pentad would catch fire next.

Ada pulled out another oatcake.

Hester's sense of alarm flared within her body, along with increasing power. *Ada, Ada, this is tremendous divine energy, so much of me—a hundred times beyond what Mallory Valmont—*

Oh, and she felt that as she chewed and swallowed, oh, she felt that. Her entire body vibrated with energy, her full form made into a conduit, not just her tongue. She *knew* the fire in all its destructive glory. She *knew* the profound sense of home encompassing the kitchen-temple.

Ada remembered how Mallory had unwittingly blasted air in a way that left her unconscious and addled for an extended period. Therefore, she knew that she could similarly control the course of the conflagration.

Heat and bound energy caused sweat to roll down her jawline. An arm extended outward, she shoved with an unseen force. The engulfed building groaned and fell backward with a violent crunch and clatter. Her attention turned to the firefighters.

"Create a wall of dirt and stone! Hold back the fire!" she yelled, her voice projected as if she used white fluff.

The ruins still burned with ferocity, but now in a roughly seven-foot-high jagged jumble, not as a multistory torch. The Graecian fire would still be pulled downward by gravity, but the firefighters had more space and time with which to hold it back. They scrambled to work.

The bells continued to toll. Ada felt the song like a massive heartbeat. People were heeding the call. They were praying. Casting offerings into the hearths, into the burning ruins of their homes.

Ada took in their hopes and prayers and gratitude like water into a dry rag. Hester was using the energy. She was still holding back the fire here, battling other fires around Nont, on the Braizian ships that defended the bay. But Ada was the narrow point of a funnel, flooded.

Even as she drowned, she felt *good.* Deliriously, exquisitely *good.*

Her soul seemed to compress beneath the weight of Hester's divinity. When Ada began to walk, she had the eerie, detached realization that she wasn't controlling her body.

Hester was.

No, no. Ada would not endure what Solenn had. She would not—could she even carve off her own tongue? She wasn't simply a woman with Chef abilities. She *wanted* to be a Chef, even if she never wielded epicurea again. She could still cook and enjoy what she cooked.

She was walking into the Grand Pentad. The bells continued to ring. The chambers of the Gods were vacant, but—hooves echoed behind her. She was being followed. She turned.

"Brillat Silvacane, elder ambassador of the Coterie." The voice that came from Ada's lips was hers, yet not. A white stallion stood before her, ears flattened. A member of the kin. One of Hester's old enemies. *"Chef Adamantine has taken in much power, too much. Hester's great statue was of a size to handle such an inundation as if it were drops in a bucket. Ada cannot."*

What? Hester was only controlling Ada's body . . . to request help?

Brillat's swiveled ears showed his own surprise. He neighed. Aveyron trotted up behind him, Gurvan only steps behind. In a blink, a reedy, naked young man crouched where the smaller of the horses had been.

"August Hester, if Madame Adamantine focuses, she will be able to expel more power, will she not?" Aveyron asked.

"Focus, ah, focus is difficult for her now, a dilemma I well understand. She's a dreamy presence within herself. This power, if it continues to build—" The voice cracked.

"She could be untethered from her own body," said Brillat, pushing himself to stand upright.

"What to do, what to do—the hearth fire!" Gurvan rushed ahead into Hester's chamber. "That'll provide a more direct conduit to your full self, will it not? If she focuses on fueling that, the power could then flow into your larger self."

But it'd be better for the energy to help the people of Braiz. If the power coursed along a longer route, less would reach the destination—it'd evaporate, like water during transit. Ada wanted to expel energy to those in immediate need, but the prayers were like little flying bugs swirling over her head, and she was too slow and heavy to catch them.

"That may work, yes," said Hester through Ada. At Gurvan's incredulous expression, she laughed. *"Gods are mysteries in many ways, even to themselves, dear August Chef. Such is true even of my brother Gyst."*

"Madame." Aveyron took Ada by the hand and pulled her after Gurvan. "Focus on the hearth fire, and as you become more grounded, *then* focus on the needs in Nont. You have the blood of Gyst in you. You inherently understand unknowns that many cannot. Utilize that skill."

"The blood of . . . Gyst?" Gurvan muttered, then shook his head.

Yes. We can do this, Ada, Hester said within her mind.

How? Thousands upon thousands of people were in need right now, pleading for the safety of their homes, their sailors and soldiers, their children. Offerings. Pleas. Ada floated between voices, fires, screams.

Someone was telling her to focus on the large hearth ahead of her, but she barely saw it, barely felt it. But that was fine. She wasn't hurting. Why, she felt almost nothing at all.

"—Solenn and Erwan."

Wait. Solenn and Erwan. Someone had mentioned Solenn and Erwan. Aveyron. Yes, Aveyron was speaking.

"Solenn and Erwan are out there, and you know their deepest prayer is to come home, and to be safe and together."

Yes. Focus on Solenn, Erwan, and your grandmother. Those you love, those that mean home to you more than any single place. Hester seemed to know that those names had snagged Ada's attention like nothing else.

Grand-mère was by the kitchen hearth in Malo. Ada saw her from flames that illuminated the concern in her leathered face, the intensity in her hazel eyes.

"Ah, you've come to visit me, Most August Hester," said Grand-mère, "but you keep on going. You have more important things to do right now than to focus on an old woman like me. Shoo." She whisked her hand toward the hearth, as if she could shun a God so easily.

Ada had to laugh. That action was so perfectly like her grandmother. And she was right, as she often was in her coherent moments.

Ada needed coherency herself. She pushed power toward the hearth. Solenn and Erwan were out there somewhere. They weren't near a fire now or appealing to Hester and home, but as soon as they did, she'd know. She'd be there to answer their prayers.

CHAPTER
THIRTY-EIGHT

SOLENN

Epicurea exists for the use of Chefs—the Gods have enabled us to recognize and employ it, after all, and we are not to discard such a blessing. However, with this gift comes responsibility. If we kill all unicorns, how are we to produce more? If awake oaks are leveled, from where are the acorns and other ingredients to come? We must exercise temperance, or we offend the Gods all the more through our avarice.

—Excerpt from *Manual for Tour Chefs*

With its height in consideration, the swirled, conical shell was as large as the rooms of some buildings. The tip of a kraken's tentacle plugged the cave-like hole at the base, staying in constant contact with Solenn's body as it cushioned her front. She had Erwan braced behind her. The shell's interior was slick, but the wall angled upward at his back, keeping them from sliding too much. The kraken, through its connection with Solenn, knew the humans needed to stay fairly stable, as they were fragile things.

Solenn and Erwan said little. Intense nausea was something of a conversation dampener, and sharing visions with the kraken required focus. Every so often, Erwan and the kraken couldn't help but touch as well. He gasped in shock each time, after several such moments remarking, "We in Braiz have long had the idea that krakens are the fierce warriors of the sea. That is true, I think, but no one would've ever guessed at the sheer happiness they also exude. Each touch is like embracing an old friend."

The kraken crested the waves, giving her a rainbow-arrayed, brief view of a three-decker ship. It then dived down again, lurching the shell even as Solenn gave the kraken an affirmative. Ahead sailed the Albionish premier ship *Blessing of the Five*. Through the kraken, she could sense the intensity and incredible variety of the epicurea aboard. To krakens, it throbbed like a heartbeat without vessel or body. None of the other vessels carried such a trove. Here, with the ship in sight, the kraken understood what she had tried to communicate from atop the cliff.

She showed the kraken where to strike and how. Lord Whitney wasn't escaping this time.

The swish-roar of water outside the shell shifted, their transportation lurching upward. Solenn clutched at Erwan's hand on her waist as she swallowed down her gorge. The shell jostled. She knew other tentacles were prying and hammering at the hull, and the time would soon come when the shell was used to—

A screech escaped her as the shell became a bludgeon, striking a hull already weakened by dexterous tentacles. The tentacle against Solenn tried to cushion her from the violent smack, but nevertheless, she and Erwan were flung back and forth. An agonized gasp escaped Erwan, but still he tried to shield her back, his own body crunching into the shell wall. Her face suffocated against the slick cushion of the tentacle for a matter of seconds. Again, *bang*. Again. She and Erwan clung to each other, dizzied, bruised. A magnificent crunch and crack of wood caused a shudder throughout the shell.

The tentacle slid away from Solenn. She would've flopped forward but for Erwan's tenacious grip upon her. The tentacle unplugged from the shell's hole with a juicy popping sound. There was a brief view of blue sky, and then the shell pushed forward, spinning around, disorienting her yet again. She shook her head to regain her senses. They were inside the ship, the view ahead of dark cabinets with ornate marquetry. They could only be within what was termed the poop—the quarters of a ship's captain or other high-ranking officials. Deep voices yelled in Albionish. Erwan propelled himself forward on his hands, seat, and feet and, upon standing, extended his left hand to balance against the shell as he drew his rapier.

How he managed to regain equilibrium so quickly, she didn't know, but she scrambled after him, staggering. The colors of the world seemed drab after seeing through a kraken's eyes. As Solenn stood, the ship heaved. She and Erwan rocked against each other as they appraised their surroundings.

Yes, this most certainly was the poop with its heavy drapes and gold-fringed upholstery, Albionish flags incorporated on everything from the rugs to the cabinet inlay. Behind them, almost the entire wall had become a gaping hole edged by jagged wood. The massive shell took up perhaps a third of the chamber, a pudgy purple tentacle still curved behind it. The kraken was bracing the entire ship, ready to carry them away once their job was done—that was the kraken's idea during transit, for which she was grateful.

Sounds boomed from the decks above—gunfire, screaming, the chaos of battle. The sailors would be fighting back against the krakens' assault with everything they had. Several were attacking this ship and its companions.

"You're unharmed from our peculiar transit?" asked Erwan, appraising her. He looked especially pale for someone of white skin, but then, her brown skin was also likely blanched. To her relief, her dizziness and nausea were quickly dissipating. Perhaps that was part of Selland's legacy—she'd never been one to get seasick.

The ornately filigreed door to the room burst open to reveal a figure Solenn had met only once before. Lord Whitney was quite average of face, with a beak-like nose and eyebrows that drew together a touch too close, but he made up for any normalcy through his outlandish dress. He wore a white wig that consisted of tiers of curls cascading to his gold epaulet-adorned shoulders, which were covered in a double-breasted red velvet jacket heavy with gold thread and shiny walnut-size buttons. Behind him were sailors, musket barrels visible. He took in his intruders, his eyes widening.

"Priñsez Solenn ar Braiz?" She was surprised that he addressed them in Braizian, but then, he'd expressed fluency before. "And this is . . . your captain?" He read Erwan's rank by his distinct cassock. He clearly hadn't retained Erwan's name in his memory, had they been introduced at all.

"Lord Whitney of Albion," Erwan said, his rapier ready. "I, Captain Erwan Corre, represent Braiz in a matter of honor. You stand accused of grievous crimes: that you masterminded the fire that laid waste to Nont this past year and that you conspired to assassinate Prince Rupert of Verdania and place the blame on Princess Solenn. Your crimes beyond that are myriad, but on those two I will place emphasis. If you retain any dignity within your soul, accept my challenge to duel and settle accounts, here and now."

Whitney smiled beneath a broad, flared mustache dyed an unnatural white. "Captain Corre. Ah yes. You are of the princess's contingent to Verdania." The ship heaved again, but he kept his footing even as he waved the sailors behind him to stay put. "Do you have evidence of these crimes to lay forth at this time?" A rejoinder of this nature was part of duel etiquette. Few combatants would actually present proof at this point.

"I have my blade and you have yours." Erwan tilted his head toward a section of wall that was a miniature armory. Several glistening rifles and pistols were mounted there, some by their ornamentation more trophies than functional weapons. The row of rapiers, however, looked serviceable to even Solenn's amateur eye.

"Indeed." Lord Whitney turned and spoke Albionish to the figures in the hall, then shut the door behind him. There was some honor to him after all. He walked to his armory. "You catch me at a disadvantage. The battle of the day has left me battered and bruised." Such a statement of weakness was also part of the setup when a combatant was surprised by their challenge. Whitney did walk with stiffness to his gait, but that could be a feint. "Princess Solenn would have some awareness of the events of the day, as we had a brief encounter earlier."

She wouldn't have been recognizable when she rode Abonde earlier that day, bundled up as she had been—but yesterday she'd worn fewer clothes, and could indeed have been observed, her identity reported to Whitney. That, or spies within the city had relayed news of her alliance with Queen Abonde.

"So you were indeed the commander who engaged my dragon-ally in combat, Lord Whitney." She focused to project the syllables as much as she could. His eyes widened with what could only be described as surprise and pity.

"I was, Princess." He selected a blade, testing its weight. "How fares your dragon? Gyst could make that blow of my lance fatal, but it would certainly be crippling for now."

"The dragon is not mine."

"Mmm, yes. I suppose your horse isn't yours either." He thought he was being clever but looked perplexed when she laughed. The ship rocked, followed by more yells and racket from above.

"Shall we begin?" Erwan asked, saluting Lord Whitney.

"We shall."

The ship quivered again, but the duel began nevertheless, Whitney lunging as if to test Erwan. He reposted. Again, Whitney attacked. While his movements retained jerkiness, he also moved *fast*.

"Epicurea!" Solenn shouted, pointing at him.

"But of course." Lord Whitney didn't cease his strikes. His tone was casual, whereas Erwan's breaths were already labored. "I'm still digesting my meal from prior to battle." That meant he still had dragon epicurea in his system. On Queen Abonde's behalf, Solenn's rage boiled. "I am engaged in singular combat in accordance with Lucanian standards. If a combatant enters a bout drunk or under other effects—well, that is what it is, hmm? It would've been cheating had I ingested something *after* the challenge." Whitney's grin was toothy, feral, confident in his righteousness and certain victory—of Albion's overall victory.

"This is true," Erwan said.

"Whereas you, Captain, seem to have entered combat in an injured state. You favor your side."

To illustrate, Lord Whitney lunged, tapping Erwan's ribs. Had he desired to do so, Solenn realized in horror, he could've plunged in his entire blade. "Right there," he said, smiling beneath his mustache. "Broken ribs, unless I miss my guess?"

What? Erwan had acted fine earlier, but—oh. The injury must have happened as he was flung backward within the shell. He'd taken the blows to cushion her.

"That is my conjecture as well, Lord Whitney." Erwan tried to sound as nonchalant as his opponent, and failed.

"Do you yield?" asked Lord Whitney, all but battering Erwan with a series of strikes. It was all Erwan could do to parry and maintain his ground. Solenn felt utterly useless, standing there with balled fists.

"Never," panted Erwan. "Neither will Braiz."

"A pity. Braiz's usefulness is in its ports. As a country, you have minimal exports. Your farming is for mere subsistence. You don't even offer much in the way of unique epicurea. You lot will be as contumacious as the Caldians, I'm sure." He sighed, wearied by the very idea.

"I see no insult in that comparison," said Erwan.

"You should," quipped Lord Whitney, thrusting his blade into Erwan's right forearm. Erwan retreated, fingers spasming on his hilt, but he didn't lose hold of his rapier.

Solenn hadn't expected the battle to be easy if they made it this far, but neither had she anticipated *this*.

A juicy-sounding spurt caused her to glance over at the tentacle. Two harpoons had lodged in it, right where it bent over the side of the ship. The distal tip of the tentacle quivered like set gelatin but kept a steadying hold upon the shell.

"Braiz isn't a doormat for you to wipe your boots upon as you continue into Verdania," said Erwan.

Solenn turned to see Erwan thrust his blade into Lord Whitney's torso, into the very vicinity in which Erwan was also injured. The man gasped as the sword withdrew, but continued his offense. If anything, his smile broadened. The dragon epicurea could be bolstering him at this moment, but more likely, he'd also eaten something like beast meat, which reduced awareness of pain during battle. He could lose fingers—a hand—and fight on as if he'd been scratched.

More juicy thuds rang out behind her. Albionish on the deck above were flinging any available sharp projectile into the tentacle. It quickly began to resemble a large Lucanian porcupine, adorned with spears, swords, more harpoons, even wooden poles. The other tentacles cradling the ship were likely under similar assault. Marines and sailors employed guns as well, the wounds like large black freckles. The ship heaved back and forth, the rhythm uneven. Solenn balanced herself against the wall of cabinets, suddenly noticing that the ornate marquetry contained more than the Albionish flag, but inlaid unicorns, selkies, even dragons.

She no longer had a Gods-touched tongue, but she knew what to expect as she opened the double doors.

Epicurea. Shallow wooden drawers full of the stuff, each niche labeled in neat pen. She was reminded of Marquis Dubray's pantry and how it had sickeningly overwhelmed her senses. Her reaction now was of zealous determination.

Solenn yanked out one drawer, then another, hurriedly stacking them in her arms. Each drawer was some five inches across and ten inches deep, loaded with bags and boxes or, in some cases, epicurea exposed to air. She rushed across the floor as fast as she dared with the ship's uneven movements. Nearing the edge, she flung the whole armful into the sea. She leaned on the tentacle to check with the kraken. The slick surface was drying.

The kraken hurt. Here, there, everywhere, but there was compassion in what it shared, as none of the actual pain flowed through to her. The kraken held no regret, no anger, not even sadness. The kraken was content. The statement of pain was just that, an observation. Even more, it expressed joy that she was there—that she was fighting the Bad Man who had caused so many krakens to die. Through the kraken, she recognized its dawning awareness of the epicurea inside Lord Whitney. The tentacle perceived his magic like heat, like the warmth of the sun.

Solenn sent the kraken a surge of gratitude and sympathy, calling upon Selland's blessing, then scrambled back across the room. She collapsed onto one knee as the ship bounced. Both Erwan and Whitney fell as well, though the men also quickly rebounded. Erwan's upper arms had been grazed multiple times, the cloth pierced, revealing red. Whitney was toying with him, just as Gyst and Hester had played with each other in their own battle, drawing it out in their sheer enjoyment of human movement and danger.

With savage delight, she ripped out more drawers.

"Princess Solenn, whatever are you doing?" By Whitney's peevish tone, he knew exactly what she was doing. He probably enjoyed goading her to speak.

She didn't deem him worthy of a response.

Cannons fired from the decks above. The ship rocked. Solenn flung another armful of epicurea into the water, but slipped as she turned away. Her heart thudded as her soles braced on the low boards of the hull, the hole in the wall beginning mere inches above. She pulled herself away by her hands just as the ship listed toward the water. Screams rang out from the upper deck. She glanced back in horror as a sailor landed on the tentacle, straddling it long enough to give Solenn a look of shock, and then he fell backward with a screech.

She smelled fire.

She scrambled back toward the cabinets. One more trip, and that side would be done. Two more to go.

"Princess," said Lord Whitney, "you cannot do that—those are my—"

She could read little Albionish, but she knew enough to experience intense satisfaction as she pulled out stores labeled for different parts of dragons.

"Those ingredients are incredibly rare, you cannot—argh!" Whitney had been distracted. Erwan had scored a hit.

"It is not your place to offer the princess counsel," said Erwan as more cannon and gunfire roared from the decks above.

A horrendous slurping sound caused her to turn. The pudgy curve of the tentacle dropped away from the ship—the tip had been severed. The end remained still for a long moment, poised against the shell, until the ship listed, hard. The five feet of tentacle flopped away, the shell scraping against planks and rugs to fall back through the hole.

Screams and cries rang out from all around, but Solenn remained speechless in horror as she clung to the gap-filled cabinet fixed into the wall.

She and Erwan had lost their safest transit away. A kraken could fetch it again—given time, given its own health—but as smoke billowed over the side and began to pour in through the gaps around the entry doors, she understood their dire position.

Even so, she had a job to do.

Without the shell and tentacle closing much of the hole in the hull, Solenn didn't dare advance too near the edge. One little lurch and she'd go over too. Therefore, she dropped to the floor and began to fling each individual drawer toward the hole, thinking of Abonde, wishing that she could know that her kin's remains wouldn't see further abuse. Some of the drawers sailed out to the water, but most crashed to the floor. Powders, leaves, dried meats, and other bits and pieces of kin scattered across a partially shredded ornate rug.

Like the krakens, Solenn experienced a sense of resolution and peace. She'd made the choice to come here and knew it was the right one—she only wished that Erwan wouldn't suffer for it as well.

She'd flung the last drawer away as the ship again tilted toward the hole, this time at a more sudden, severe angle. A squeak of alarm escaped her as she slid halfway across the floor. Her thin fingernails gripped at a gap between the planks. Nearby, the duel came to an immediate stop as both men grasped the nearest wall to hold on. Erwan had clung to the brace that had held Whitney's sword, while Whitney had grabbed one of his cabinet doors, and held on even as it swung back and forth. Books and artifacts crashed to the floor, pages sprawled. He yelled something undoubtedly profane in Albionish. The doors of the empty epicurea cabinets clattered like wooden wings.

Reminded of his profound loss, he glared at Solenn. "You meddlesome—" Judging by the condition of the ship, all she'd done was speed up the disposal of his epicurea, but she didn't mind the blame. She was proud of her actions, and showed him as much through a wide grin.

Solenn gripped a higher plank, then another, inching her way closer to the wall. More smoke seeped in around the door and rolled over her, making it hard to breathe.

"Meddlesome in the best of ways," retorted Erwan.

The cannons had stopped. There was another lurch downward, the ship's angle unchanging. Solenn felt the tingle of Selland's presence, as did Erwan, by the way he offered the sea a salute with his rapier. She knew there'd be no relying on Selland to nudge them to shore, not from this far out. Their bodies might eventually make it, but not their souls.

Erwan released his hold on the wall and assumed a fighting stance again, his legs wider than normal by necessity. "Whitney!" he called in challenge.

"Are you really . . . ?" Lord Whitney sounded awed but laughed. "Why not? Best to go out fighting, eh?" He coughed amid the smoke.

Solenn made it to the wall, where she gripped a lower inner shelf vacated by a drawer. Mere feet away, Whitney released the tall cabinet door to face Erwan just as the ship listed a touch more. Erwan immediately grappled the wall, but Lord Whitney slid a short distance while still standing, whereupon he found epicurean debris underfoot.

What it was exactly, Solenn could only guess—awake oak flour, perhaps? The leather bag had burst open, scattering a fine pale powder across the planks. Whitney fell to his hands and knees, clutching the gaps as Solenn had. His beautiful rapier scraped the floor and bounced out the hole.

"I'm Lord Chef. I will not die in such an ignoble fashion." He panted with exertion as he inched his way back up the incline. "This battle will resume, even if by bare hands!"

A tentacle flared up beyond the hole—an intact tentacle. A kraken had remained at the ship, Solenn realized. The limb plunged inside the gap, finding Lord Whitney conveniently near the edge. The purple length wrapped around him, plucking him from the floor as a courtier might an hors d'oeuvre from a tray.

"What?" Lord Whitney said with a yelp as he pivoted around in the kraken's grasp. His shocked gaze met Solenn's as he was pulled out of the ship—and *squeezed.*

Blood gushed outward. A small, distinct *snap* carried over the din of battle. Whitney's upper body drooped, limp as a rag doll. His hat fell from his tipped head and spiraled downward like a heavy leaf. She continued to gape in both relief and horror as the tentacle uncoiled. Two halves of the man's body plummeted toward the water.

"I don't suppose epicurea will help him recover from *that*," Erwan said with a wheezy laugh.

"The kraken knew him by the epicurea in his body," Solenn said with effort. "They knew he needed to die."

"And so he did. Gyst take him." That was a statement of unusual callousness from Erwan, but Solenn couldn't disagree with the sentiment.

Gyst would be certain to enjoy revealing Whitney's life secrets to him. Solenn supposed she'd have made a lousy God of Unknowns. She didn't savor such drama and intrigue.

The ship leveled considerably even as it again eased downward. Erwan sheathed his rapier. "Solenn, our predicament doesn't bode well. I don't suppose a kraken could gently carry us to shore."

She shook her head. A kraken couldn't swim like that, and certainly not through battle lines. The shell would be needed to carry them away, and surely it had drifted deep below by now.

"So be it. We've helped Braiz and the Coterie. That's what matters most." His wistfulness pained her. He should have had a chance to reunite with Ada, to build the life that they'd both yearned for, for so long.

Solenn had no tongue to connect her directly to the Gods, but she carried her own divinity. Concentrating on that certainty within herself, she prayed. If there was a way to escape here alive, together—if they could find a way home—

Home. The stink of burning wood and fire filled her nose. Hester was watching Nont more closely than anywhere else in the world. She would recognize this ship on fire in the bay.

"Hester." Solenn put all her soul into the invocation. "Hester, we need you. We need to get home alive." The God of Hearth and Home would understand her words, however garbled they sounded to Solenn's own ears.

Most every fire was a pathway home.

She'd heard the saying from Lyria and Gurvan. Each had a different interpretation, but what if the phrase was a literal one—or could become literal now, through empowerment and faith?

She could make it genuine through her own inherent power and the aid of a God she now considered a friend. As with things such as cheese and bread, the Gods did their best work when they did so in cooperation.

"Hester," she whispered. "Hear me. Guide us through your fire. Protect our flesh, as you recently protected Aveyron's. Please. Help us. Save us."

She couldn't sense Hester's presence anymore, but she didn't need to. She had faith.

"Erwan. We need to walk into the fire."

He blinked, and she couldn't be certain whether it was because he didn't understand her or because he couldn't believe her words. "What?"

"Hester. We must trust in Hester. She's empowered right now. She's watching Braiz."

"That's still asking much of a God."

"It is, but I'm not delegating. We'll do it together. We can get us home." She knew it could be done, because she now accepted there were not Five but Six Gods. She was minor compared to the others, undoubtedly, but still of enough might that Gyst had desired to wield her potential while keeping her ignorant.

She extended her hand. Erwan considered her for a moment, then nodded as he grabbed hold. His touch around her fingers was familiar from her earliest memories. Calloused, tender. Ready to bandage her when she'd fallen from a horse, eager to press a beloved Sellandsday sea biscuit flecked with gray salt into her palm.

These were her father's hands.

They edged toward the smoking double doors. Erwan tapped a door handle, grimacing. "It's burning hot."

"Are you hurt?"

He checked his fingers. "No, but I should be." He nodded, suddenly understanding. Hester had already graced them with resistant skin. "When I open the door, the air will feed the fire."

She nodded. "I love you."

"And I, you. Solenn. My daughter."

Smoke and emotion brought tears to her eyes as he opened the door. The inferno embraced them as, against all wisdom, they stepped forward.

Heat engulfed Solenn. A very human part of her braced for a terrible death with her teeth gritted and heart pounding, but she didn't stop. They would survive this walk. They would make it home. To Braiz. With its cloudy skies and brisk winds and Maiwenn greeting her with a huff of breath. Solenn would live to hug Mamm again. She'd talk about birds with Mamm-gozh. She'd see Erwan and Ada finally maintain a family together, as they had long craved.

Warmth surged against Solenn's skin, evoking discomfort rather than pain. She choked on a breath, blinking to see through the smoke. Figures moved on the other side of the flames.

"Solenn! Solenn!" Aveyron's familiar voice rang above the roaring crackle. Clutching Erwan's hands, she took two more steps, emerging into the Grand Pentad. They'd passed through Hester's very hearth.

Hands slapped at her smoldering clothes. She blinked several times to clear her eyes and to make out August Chef Gurvan and Brillat patting her down. The latter was naked, as was Aveyron, but that was of passing curiosity after all that had just happened. Aveyron was putting out a small fire on Erwan's cassock—but his chest was smoking. Solenn lunged to smother the flame, only for pain to sting at the very center of her palm. Her skin was resistant no more.

"Water! We should get water for their throats and any burns—" began Gurvan.

"I'll get it!" Aveyron sprinted away.

"You're home." Solenn didn't notice Ada until she spoke. She sat cross-legged against a pillar that faced the mighty hearth. Her clothes were gray and black, her face a sooty smear that made her grin all the bolder. Everything about her posture spoke of slumped exhaustion.

"Oh, Ada." Erwan crouched down before her, pushing a stray strand of black hair from her forehead. "Whatever have you gotten up to?"

"You'll scold me. Rightfully." Her head lolled as if she were drunk as she met Solenn's gaze. "I heard your prayer. We opened the door through the flames."

"*We* opened the door?" Erwan turned to Brillat. "What's she done?"

"She used some of the empowered statue powder as an ingredient, then amplified it as a Chef. She and Hester worked in cooperation to save Nont from the fires—Hester never dominated her." This, Brillat hastily said to Solenn, as she couldn't contain her horror. "Not in a cruel way, at least. When Hester did control her, it was to get help from us."

"They saved much of the city," Gurvan said softly.

Aveyron pressed a carafe of water into Solenn's hands. She yearned to tip back her head for a big gulp, but instead took a controlled sip before passing it to Erwan.

"There are still fires burning, of course," Aveyron said. "According to Hester, Graecian fire can continue to burn for weeks, even buried. The important thing is for its progress to be curtailed. That work is underway."

"What of the Albionish fleet?" Erwan asked.

"We don't know," Gurvan murmured. "Our attention has rested on Nont and on Chef Garland's plight. Forgive me." He motioned to Selland.

"At least their flagship is a loss. Perhaps that'll break their resolve, if it still holds." Erwan also pinched his fingers.

Brillat's gaze narrowed. "You know that ship was lost?"

"That's where we were," Solenn said.

As she reached for her new table book to write the words as well, Erwan spoke up. "Krakens delivered us to the *Blessing of the Five*, at great sacrifice."

Solenn thought again of how the tentacle had been severed, and shuddered.

"You were that far away?" Ada mused, her head lolling again.

"How much of August Hester is still within you?" asked Erwan.

"Her voice is fading in here." She pointed at her own head to make herself clear. "I've already offered the rest of the empowered oatcakes into the flames. Before Hester's divine power is fully gone, though, we need to discuss what's coming next."

Solenn smiled. Nont would be rebuilt again. It was a stubborn city, a barnacle upon Braiz. She loved it so.

"Verdania is still positioning to attack Braiz. We cannot forget that," Erwan said.

Ada's head wobbled as she smiled. "That. Yes. I was referring to something else, and doing a poor job of it. I have an immediate personal matter that I need help with. Hester told me that Gyst threatened you in regards to my leg wound?"

Erwan went very still. "Yes?"

Solenn's gaze went to Ada's legs. One trousered calf was thicker than the other. "How bad is it?" she slowly asked.

"It's bad," Brillat answered for Adamantine. "I can smell it through the stink of smoke." That said much, as the odor completely dominated Solenn's senses.

"I couldn't feel the injury when in the full thrall of Hester's power." By Ada's evident strain, she did now. "Hester says she can assist in cauterizing the wound to eradicate the worst of the unknowns, but it . . . won't be pleasant. Nor does it come with any guarantees of success."

Erwan released a long exhalation. "What does these days? Let's do this forthwith."

Ada squeezed his hand. "I'm glad you're here. It'll be nice when our intimate moments don't involve wound care."

Solenn averted her eyes, smiling. She wasn't self-conscious about their subject of discussion, but she did feel like she was eavesdropping on a private moment.

High-pitched bells began to peal from the Grand Pentad tower— and from other pentads in the city. They were Melissa's bells, the sweetest of sounds. They could mean only one thing.

"The ships must be retreating," Gurvan said, upholding five fingers to hail the divine intervention. "Blessed be the Five."

"Blessed be us all," Solenn said, pressing splayed fingers against her heart. She breathed in a sudden waft of sea air that seemed to briefly clear the stink of smoke from her nose, and smiled. She was home.

CHAPTER
THIRTY-NINE

ADA

To make sugar cakes, combine a pound of fine flour, half a pound of sugar, half a pound of butter, and enough eggs to wet it through. Mix well and place within a large tin to bake until golden and soft. Taste a slice, and you'll know you and your household are blessed by the Gods, even with your tongue untouched.

—Excerpt from *Book for Cooks to Excel as Do Chefs*

Ada sat upon Lunel in her Camarga mare form, the pair overlooking a marshy green valley. Her calf ached, as it often did these days, having lost some muscle, the flesh still slow to heal. Riding, at least, was more comfortable than walking, which now required a walking stick.

Brillat, in his dapper human form, was mounted alongside her. Below her on the sloped road was Erwan on another Camarga. He wore formal musketeer regalia, his skirt long over breeches. He cut a fine figure, even from behind.

Farther down was Prince Morvan on another Camarga. The use of the magicked white horses for transportation was necessary because Queen Abonde, in her full dragon form, sat upon her haunches on the grassy hillside, taking a vanguard position. A week after the Battle of Nont, Abonde was still unable to fly, but the thousands of Verdanian soldiers cresting the far ridge didn't know that. Upon sight of her, their movement stopped.

Prince Morvan held a white flag upon a pole, his intentions clear. He was ready to address King Caristo's continued ludicrous demands that Princess Solenn be returned to face justice in Lutecia.

Solenn shifted in her position atop Abonde's back, a hand shielding her eyes against the sun. At this distance, Ada couldn't make out what Solenn was saying, but that was why Aveyron was in human form beneath Abonde's right wing. "Solenn is wondering how far they'll advance," he repeated for the benefit of her advisers.

"That *is* the question," Brillat mused. He, Ada, and Erwan had placed bets as to how far Verdania would progress upon seeing Abonde.

Erwan thought they'd at least parley.

Brillat surmised that Verdania would continue their advance into the valley. According to kin reconnaissance, Verdania had deployed five thousand soldiers in this force, with more amassing near Lutecia now that the Blessed revolt had been crushed. Merle Archambeau's tennis-playing days were over. Verdania's missive of the previous day had declared that the head of the king's cousin now adorned a pike at the city gates. This was stated as a threat to Braiz if they continued to be mulish, as if the dead musketeers delivered to Nont days before hadn't already proved what their southern neighbor meant by "justice."

Ada, as an army veteran herself, predicted a different result to the day: that Verdania would simply turn around and leave. Though there were only some five hundred Braizian soldiers assembled behind them, Braiz had a dragon.

The Coterie had also dogged the Verdanians throughout their march. Days ago, leaflets had been dropped among their ranks, advising them to cast their epicurea into fires or they'd soon suffer. The Verdanians had been provided a day's grace before targeted attacks upon epicurea holders began during the night. These assaults—a few deaths, multiple individuals mauled—almost exclusively affected officers but had left the entire body unnerved and demoralized.

A distant horn blew. Ada knew that signal well—the soldiers had been ordered to advance. No one came forward. Nearby flags rippled in the wind, harnesses and gear jingling as the Braizians and their allies watched in breathless silence. The wind brought the smell of musty greenery from the valley below. Wildflowers gleamed in bright red, purple, and yellow from amid the verdant green. Ada fervently wanted them to continue to grow, for them to not be trampled beneath hooves and claws as a battle began.

The horn blew again, a pleading note. After a long moment of wavering, the soldiers backtracked, their lines breaking.

Verdania was in retreat without a shot fired. The wildflowers could continue to bloom.

"You win," Brillat ruefully said to Ada.

"I can't say that I mind," said Erwan, smiling as his horse turned. Of course he wouldn't. The winner got to choose the kind of cake that Ada would make upon their return to Malo. Ada's favorite sugar cake, four simple ingredients baked to perfection, also happened to be one of Erwan's, one he hadn't had in a great many years. The fine quality of Braizian butter would make the cake all the better.

The partaking of the cake, however, might be a few weeks away yet. Tonight they'd return to a nearby camp, where they'd continue to stay as they made certain that Verdania was indeed in retreat. She wouldn't be surprised if they were here again in another week or two to stare down another assembly, perhaps repeating the experience several times until Caristo either realized the effort was in vain or their forces actually initiated combat. By that point, Braiz would be in a better place to engage in a land conflict.

Queen Abonde would also be able to fly soon. That would change the battlefield dynamics in an interesting way.

The continued involvement of the Gods was another undeniable factor. Hester's newly formed avatar was currently within the hearth in Gurvan's private quarters. Close enough to take in the energy of the many people coming to the Grand Pentad to express grief and gratitude, but private enough to keep her new stone form safe as she was imbued with life. Ada looked forward to speaking with the God face-to-face soon.

Solenn shifted in her seat to smile back at them. She said something to Aveyron, who laughed before he repeated her words. "Solenn says she cannot wait to return to Malo and enjoy your cake, Madame Adamantine."

Ada shifted to ease the pressure on her leg, her fingers twitching with the need to bake. She wanted to be in Malo right now, gathering her ingredients. Her grandmother would be there, ensuring the sweetness was just right and choosing the beverage to accompany the repast. Erwan would likely act as he had years ago, checking on the progress and swiping a spoonful of batter when he thought she wasn't looking. Brillat and Erwan had no experience at all with the cakes favored in the north—oh, Ada had many delights to share.

Soon, soon, they'd be gathered near a fire, laughing, chatting, eating cake, eating more cake. Cozily warm as rain pattered upon the shutters and the seeping wind delivered hints of the nearby sea.

Blessed to be together, at home. At long last.

ACKNOWLEDGMENTS

My foremost gratitude is for my agent, Rebecca Strauss, who has supported me through ups and some considerable downs for over a decade now. Thanks for encouraging me to "get to the dead bodies faster."

My friends at Codex are a tremendous daily support. Particular thanks to Rebecca Roland and Cécile Cristofari for reading an early draft on a very tight deadline. Rachael K. Jones helped me with foundational work on how Solenn might live and communicate without a tongue; any errors or inaccuracies that developed from there are entirely my own.

A special shout-out to Tracy at Tracy Dempsey Originals in Tempe, Arizona, for not only making available wondrous cheeses and baked goods, but for restocking a natural muscadet wine that I asked after for my book research.

The team at 47North has been wonderful—thank you, everyone! Major thanks for my editor, Adrienne Procaccini, and my developmental editor, Clarence A. Haynes. You've challenged me and sometimes rightly chastised me, and these books are all the better for it.

Last but not least, my family. I love my husband, Jason, more than I love cheese, and he knows that's a statement of considerable magnitude. My son, Nicholas—you are awesome, my dude. My cats, Luke and Finn—thanks for inspiring some magic with your ubiquitous hair.

ABOUT THE AUTHOR

Beth Cato is the Nebula Award–nominated author of the Clockwork Dagger series, the Blood of Earth trilogy, and the Chefs of the Five Gods series. Her short stories and poetry can be found in hundreds of publications, including *Fantasy Magazine, Escape Pod, Uncanny Magazine,* and the *Magazine of Fantasy & Science Fiction.* Beth hails from Hanford, California, but currently writes and bakes cookies in a state of confusion that she shares with her husband, son, and two feline overlords. For more information, visit www.bethcato.com.